Sarah Mallory was born in the West Country and now ~~live~~ n the beautiful Yorkshire moors. She has been ~~writing f~~ or more than three decades—mainly historical ~~romanc~~ es set in the Georgian and Regency period. She ~~has won~~ on several awards for her writing, including the ~~Roma~~ ntic Novelists' Association RoNA Rose Award in ~~2012~~ (for *The Dangerous Lord Darrington*) and 2013 ~~(for B~~ eneath the Major's Scars).

Regency Rogues

Regency Rogues:

Rakes' Redemption

SARAH MALLORY

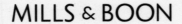
MILLS & BOON

First Published in Great Britain 2019
By Mills & Boon, an imprint of HarperCollins*Publishers*
1 London Bridge Street, London, SE1 9GF

REGENCY ROGUES: RAKES' REDEMPTION
© 2019 Harlequin Books S.A.

Return of the Runaway© 2016 Sarah Mallory
The Outcast's Redemption© 2016 Sarah Mallory

ISBN: 978-0-263-27679-4

0919

RETURN OF
THE RUNAWAY

To Marianne –
from the proudest mum in the world.

Chapter One

Verdun, France—September 1803

The young lady in the room at the top of the house on the Rue Égalité was looking uncharacteristically sober in her dark-blue linen riding habit. Even the white shirt she wore beneath the close-fitting jacket bore only a modest frill around the neck. She had further added to the sobriety by sewing black ribbons to her straw bonnet and throwing a black lace shawl around her shoulders. Now she sat before the looking glass and regarded her reflection with a critical eye.

"'Lady Cassandra Witney is headstrong and impetuous,'" she stated, recalling a recent description of herself. Her critic had also described her as beautiful, but Cassie disregarded that. She propped her chin on her hand and gave a tiny huff of dissatisfaction. 'The problem with being headstrong and impetuous,' she told her image, 'is that it leads one to make mistakes. Marrying Gerald was most definitely a mistake.'

She turned and surveyed the little room. Accompanying Gerald to Verdun had been a mistake, too, but when the Treaty of Amiens had come to an end in May she had not been able to bring herself to abandon him and go home to England. That would have been to admit defeat and her spirit rebelled at that. Eloping with Gerald had been her choice, freely made, and she could almost hear Grandmama, the Dowager Marchioness of Hune, saying, 'You have made your bed, my girl, now you must lie in it.'

And lie in it she had, for more than a year, even though she had known after a few months of marriage that Gerald was not the kind, loving man she had first thought him.

A knock at the door interrupted her reverie. After a word with the servant she picked up her portmanteau and followed him down the stairs. A light travelling chaise was waiting at the door with Merimon, the courier she had hired, standing beside it. He was a small, sharp-faced individual and now he looked down his long narrow nose at the bag in her hand.

'C'est tout?'

'It is all I wish to take.'

Cassandra answered him in his own language, looking him in the eye. As the bag was strapped on to the chaise she reflected sadly that it was little enough to show for more than a year of married life. Merimon opened the door of the chaise and continued to address her in coarse French.

'Milady will enter, if you please, and I will accompany you on foot. My horse is waiting at the Porte St Paul.'

Cassie looked up. The September sun was already low in the sky.

'Surely it would have been better to set off at first light,' she observed.

Merimon looked pained.

'I explained it all to you, milady. I could not obtain a carriage any sooner. And this road, there is no shelter and the days can be very hot for the horses. This way we shall drive through the night, you will sleep and when you awake, *voilà*, we shall be in Reims.'

'I cannot sleep in *here*.' Cassie could not help it, she sniffed. How different it had been, travelling to France with Gerald. She had been so in love then, and so hopeful. Everything had been a delicious adventure. She pushed away the memories. There was no point in dwelling on the past. 'Very well, let us get on, then. The sooner this night is over the better.'

It was not far to the eastern gate, where Cassie knew her passport would be carefully checked. Verdun still maintained most of its medieval fortifications, along with an imposing citadel. It was one of the reasons the town had been chosen to hold the British tourists trapped in France when war was declared: the defences made it very difficult for enemies to get in, but it also made it impossible for the British to get out.

When they reached the city gate she gave her papers to Merimon, who presented them to the guard. The French officer studied them for a long moment before brushing past the courier and approaching the chaise. Cassie let down the window.

'You are leaving us, *madame*?'

'Yes. I came to Verdun with my husband when he was detained. He died a week since. There is no longer any reason for me to remain.' She added, with a touch of hauteur, 'The First Consul Bonaparte decreed that only English men of fighting age should be detained.'

The man inclined his head. 'As you say. And where do you go?'

'Rouen,' said Merimon, stepping up. 'We travel via Reims and Beauvais and hope to find passage on a ship from Rouen to Le Havre, from whence milady can sail to England.'

Cassie waited, tense and anxious while the *gendarme* stared at her. After what seemed like hours he cast a searching look inside the chaise, as if to assure himself that no prisoner was hiding on the floor. Finally he was satisfied. He stood back and handed the papers to Merimon before ordering the postilion to drive on. The courier loped ahead to where a small urchin was holding the reins of a long-tailed bay and as the chaise rattled through the gates he scrambled into the saddle and took up his position beside it.

Cassie stripped off her gloves, then removed her bonnet and rubbed her temples. Perhaps now she was leaving Verdun the dull ache in her head would ease. It had been a tense few days since Gerald's death, his so-called friends circling like vultures waiting to strike at the first sign of weakness. Well, that was behind her now. She was going home. Darkness was falling. Cassie settled back into one corner as the carriage rolled and bumped along the uneven road. She found herself hoping the roads in England were as good as she remembered, that she might not suffer this tooth-rattling buffeting for the whole of the journey.

The chaise began to slow suddenly and Cassie sat up. For some time they had been travelling through woodland with tall trees lining the road and making it as black as pitch inside the carriage. Now, however, pale moonlight illuminated the window and Cassie could see that they were in some sort of clearing. The ground was littered with tree stumps and lopped branches, as if the trees had only recently been felled and carried away. She leaned forward and looked out of the window, expecting to see the lights of an inn, but there was nothing, just the pewter-coloured landscape with the shadow of the woods like a black wall in every direction.

The carriage came to a halt. Merimon dismounted, tied his horse to a wheel and came up to open the door.

'Step out, milady. We take you no further.'

Cassie protested furiously as he grabbed her wrist and hauled her out of the carriage.

'How dare you treat me thus,' she raged at him. 'Your contract is to take me to Le Havre. You will not get the rest of your money if you do not do so.'

His coarse laugh sent a chill running through her.

'No? Since you have no friends in Le Havre, and no banker, you must be carrying your money with you. Is that not the truth?'

The chill turned to icy fear.

'Nonsense,' she said stoutly. 'I would not be so foolish as to—'

Another horrid laugh cut through her protests.

'But certainly you would. Give me your purse now and perhaps we will not hurt you quite so much.'

Cassie glanced behind her to see that the postilion had dismounted and hobbled his horses. He was now walking slowly towards her. If only she had not left her bonnet in the chaise she might have made use of the two very serviceable hatpins that were secured in it. As it was she had only her wits and her own meagre strength to rely on. She took a step away from Merimon who made no move to stop her. Why should he, when the postilion was blocking her retreat?

'I shall be missed,' she said. 'I have told friends I shall write to them from Rouen.'

'A week at least before they begin to worry, if they ever do.' Merimon gestured dismissively. 'No one cares what happens to you, apart from your husband, and he is dead. I cannot believe the English *détenus* will be in a hurry to tear themselves away from their pleasures.'

No, thought Cassandra, neither could she believe it. Gerald had ensured that all her friends there had been his cronies, selfish, greedy persons who only professed affection if it was to their advantage. She was alone here, she was going to have to fight and it was unlikely that she would win. Cassie tensed as Merimon drew a long knife from his belt. He gave her an evil grin.

'Well, milady, do we get your money before or after we have taken our pleasure?'

'Never, I should think.'

The sound of the deep, amused drawl had them all turning towards the carriage.

A stranger was untying the reins of Merimon's horse. The man was a little over average height, bare-headed, bearded and dressed in ragged homespun, but there was nothing of the peasant about his bearing. He carried himself like a soldier and his voice was that of one used to command.

'You will move away from the lady now, if you know what's good for you.'

'We have no quarrel with you, citizen,' called Merimon. 'Be on your way.'

'Oh, I do not think so.'

The stranger was walking towards them, leading the bay. With his untidy hair and thick beard his face was but little more than a dark shape in the moonlight, but Cassie saw the gleam of white as he grinned. For a long moment there was silence, tense and expectant, then everything exploded into action. With a howl of rage Merimon hurled himself at the stranger and at the same time Cassie saw the postilion bearing down upon her.

That was fortunate, she thought. Merimon was the bigger of the two and he had a knife. With the postilion she had a chance. Cassie tensed as he approached, his arms outstretched. His ugly, triumphant grin told her he thought she was petrified, but just as he launched himself forward she acted. In one smooth, fluid movement she stepped aside, turning, bending and scooping up a branch about the length and thickness of her own arm. Without a pause she gripped the branch with both hands and carried it with all her force against the back of the postilion's knees. He dropped to the ground with a howl.

'Nicely done, *mademoiselle*.' The stranger trotted up, mounted on the bay. He held out his hand to her. 'Well?' he said. 'Do you want to come with me, or would you prefer to take your chances here with these *scélérats*?'

Villains indeed, thought Cassie, quickly glancing about her. Merimon was on his knees, groggily shaking his head, and the postilion was already staggering to his feet. Swiftly she ran across to the stranger. She grasped his outstretched hand, placed one foot on his boot and allowed him to pull her up before him. He lifted her easily and settled her across his thighs before urging the horse to a canter.

Cassie had no fear of falling, the stranger's strong

arms held her firmly before him. The choice, since she was sitting sideways, was to turn into the man or away and Cassie opted for the latter, twisting her body to look ahead. The black shawl had snagged on one arm of her riding habit and now it fluttered like a pennant over her shoulder. It must have flown into the rider's face because without a word he pulled it free, tossing it aside as they pounded away into the darkness of the trees. Cassie turned her head to watch it drift slowly to the ground behind them. Her only symbol of grieving for her husband, for her marriage. It was gone. She faced forward again, looking ahead into the darkness. Into the unknown future.

Chapter Two

They rode through the woods with only the thudding beat of the cantering horse to break the silence. Cassie made no attempt to speak. It was difficult to see through the gloom and she wanted her companion to concentrate his efforts on guiding them safely between the trees. Only when he slowed the horse to a walk did she break the silence.

'Do you know where we are going?'

She immediately berated herself for asking the question in English, but he answered her with only the faintest trace of an accent.

'At present I have no idea,' came the cheerful reply. 'Once we are clear of the trees and I can see the sky I shall be able to tell you.' He added, when she shifted before him, 'Would you like to get down? We should rest this nag for a while.'

He brought the horse to a stand and eased Cassie to the ground. It was only then she realised her legs would not hold her and grabbed the saddle for support.

The man jumped down beside her.

'Come, let us walk a little and your limbs will soon be restored.'

He put his arm around her shoulders and pulled her close. His clothes were rough and smelled of dirt and sweat, but Cassie was in no position yet to walk unaided so she allowed him to support her. His strength was comforting, but he puzzled her. His manner and his voice belonged to an educated man, yet he had the ragged appearance of a fugitive.

She said cautiously, 'I have not thanked you for coming to my rescue. What were you doing there?'

'I needed a horse.'

His calm answer surprised her into a laugh.

'That raises even more questions, *monsieur*.'

She thought he might fob her off, but he answered quite frankly.

'I was being pursued and ran into the woods for cover. I saw the horse tethered to the carriage wheel with no one to guard him, since your companions were too busy threatening you. I was very grateful for that and thought it would be churlish to ride off and leave you to your fate.'

'It would indeed.'

Cassie kept her voice calm, but she was beginning to wonder if she had jumped from the frying pan to the fire.

She made a slight move to free herself and immediately he released her. Reassured, she continued to keep pace with him, the horse clip-clopping behind them while the moon sailed overhead in the clear, ink-blue sky.

'So you *are* a fugitive,' she said, with some satisfaction. 'I thought as much.'

'And you are not afraid of me?'

Cassie's head went up.

'I am afraid of no one.' She realised how foolish her swift retort would sound, considering her current situation, and she added slowly, 'Not afraid. Cautious. As one should be of a stranger.'

'True, but we can remedy that.' He stopped and sketched a bow. 'I am Raoul Doulevant, at your service.'

He expected a reply and after a moment she said, 'I am Lady Cassandra Witney.'

'And you are English, which is why we are conversing in this barbaric tongue.'

'Then let us talk in French,' she replied, nettled.

'As you wish.' He caught her left hand. Neither of them was wearing gloves and his thumb rubbed across the plain gold band on her third finger.

'Ah. I addressed you as *mademoiselle* when we first met. My apologies, *madame*.'

She was shocked that his touch should feel so intimate and she drew her hand away. 'We should get on.'

When she began to walk again he fell into step beside her.

'Where is your husband?'

Cassie hesitated for a heartbeat's pause before she replied.

'At Verdun.'

'He is a *détenu*?'

Again she hesitated, not wanting to admit she was a widow. That she was alone and unprotected.

'Yes. That scoundrel you knocked down was the courier I hired to escort me back to England.'

'A bad choice, clearly.'

She felt the hot tears prickling at the back of her eyes and blinked them away. This was no time for self-pity.

'And what of you?' she asked him, anxious to avoid more questions concerning her situation. 'Who is pursuing you?'

'Officers of the law. They think I am a deserter.'

'They *think* it? And is it not so?'

'No. I was discharged honourably from the navy six months ago.'

She said, a hint of censure in her voice, 'In the present circumstances, with the country at war, I would have thought any true Frenchman would wish to remain in the service of his country, *monsieur*.'

'Any true Frenchman might,' he retorted. 'But I am from Brussels. I grew up in the Southern Netherlands, under Austrian rule.'

'And yet your French is excellent.'

'My family came originally from a town near the French border and moved to Brussels when I was a babe, so I grew up learning the language. Then I moved to Paris and later joined the French Navy, so you see, for years I have spoken nothing else.'

The lady made no reply and Raoul asked himself bitterly why he put himself out to explain. What difference would it make to her? She was English and everyone knew they thought themselves superior to the rest of Europe. It was the very worst of bad fortune that he should have saddled himself with an English aristo!

'The horse is rested now,' he said shortly. 'I think we can ride again.'

He mounted and reached down for her, pulling her up before him. He tried not to think how small and feminine she was, how the faint trace of perfume reminded him of balmy summer days. She settled herself on the horse, her dark curls tickling his chin. When the horse stumbled in the dark she clutched at his sleeve and instinctively he wrapped one arm around her waist.

She gasped and said haughtily, 'Thank you, you do not need to hold me so tightly. I am in no danger of falling now.'

His jaw clenched. If she thought he had designs upon her she was much mistaken. Silently he released her and put both hands back on the reins, but it was impossible not to be aware of her for she was practically sitting on his lap. He thought ruefully that he would have enjoyed the situation, if she had been anything other than an Englishwoman.

They travelled on, alternatively walking and riding, but maintaining an awkward silence. Raoul concentrated on guiding their mount through the near darkness of the woods. At length he noticed that the trees were thinning and they emerged on to a wide track that stretched like a grey ribbon in the starry darkness. They dismounted and Raoul stared up at the sky. The moon had gone and the stars were dimming in the first light of dawn.

'Do you know where we are now?' she asked him.

'We have been travelling north.'

'The wrong direction.'

'That depends upon where one wishes to go, *madame*.'

Cassie bit her lip. She was in a foreign land, enemy country. This man had saved her from an immediate danger, but there was no reason why he should do more for her. Indeed, the alacrity with which he had released her when the horse had missed its step suggested he had no wish to help her further. Yet she needed help. Her encounter with Merimon had shown her that.

She asked politely, 'What is *your* destination, *monsieur*?'

'Brussels.'

'I want to get to England. Do you think it might be easier from there?' She added, trying not to sound anxious, 'I gave my passport to the courier.'

'Then you have no papers.'

'No.'

Suddenly she felt very vulnerable, alone in the middle of France with a stranger. A fugitive and she had only his word that he was not a villain. His next words sent a chill of fear through her blood.

'Do you have any money?'

Even in the gloom Raoul saw the look of apprehension flicker across the lady's face and it incensed him.

He said coldly, 'I am no thief, *madame*, I do not intend to steal from you.'

She came back at him with all the arrogance he had come to expect from the English, head up, eyes flashing.

'How do I know that? You stole the horse, after all.'

His lip curled, but it occurred to him that she had no other defence so he reined in an angry response. Instead he growled, 'Remember, *madame*, I could have left you to your fate with those two villains.'

'That is very true,' she acknowledged. 'I am obliged to you and I beg your pardon.' She drew in a long breath, 'And, yes, I do have a little money.'

Her stiff apology doused his anger immediately. He smiled.

'Then you have the advantage of me, *madame*, for I have not a sou.'

'Oh, I see. Let me give you something for rescuing me—'

He recoiled instantly.

'That is not necessary,' he said quickly. 'After all, I have this fine horse, do I not?'

'Yes, of course. He will carry you to Brussels, I am sure.' She paused. 'Is it far from here?'

He shrugged. 'Depending on just where we are, three or four days' travel, I would think. *You* would do better if you head for Reims, it is much closer and you will be able to buy your passage from there to the coast.'

'Thank you.' He watched her look at the sky, then up and down the track. 'So, Reims would be that way?'

She pointed in a southerly direction, trying to sound matter of fact, as if she was well accustomed to setting off alone, in the dark, along a little-used road through an alien land, but Raoul heard the note of anxiety in her voice.

She is not your concern.

'Yes,' he replied. 'If you keep to this track I have no doubt it will bring you to the Reims road. The sun will be coming up soon, you will have no difficulty finding your way.'

'Then I will bid you *adieu*, Monsieur Doulevant,' she said quietly. 'I thank you for your assistance and I hope you reach Brussels safely.'

She gave a little curtsy, suddenly looking so lost and woebegone that every protective instinct he had rose to the fore.

'Wait!'

Don't do this, man. You owe her nothing.

Raoul ignored the warning voice in his head.

'I will take you as far as Reims.'

The flash of relief he saw in her face was quickly replaced with suspicion.

'How do I know you will not strangle me for my money?'

He ground his teeth.

'If I strangle you, milady, it will be for your sharp tongue!'

Strangely, his words seemed to reassure her. She gave an imperious little nod.

'I accept your escort, sir, and I thank you.'

'It is my pleasure,' he replied with equal insincerity. 'Come, we will ride.'

As she allowed herself to be pulled once more on to the horse Cassie was relieved that she was not obliged to make the long walk alone. Her escort explained that they must not overtax their mount and they made slow progress. The road was deserted and they saw no one except a swineherd who was happy to sell Cassie his food sack in exchange for a handful of coins. The bag contained only wine and bread, but it was enough for two and at noon they rested in the shade of a tree to eat.

Cassie was hot and thirsty and when he handed her the flask she took a long draught. The wine was very rough and she felt its effects immediately.

Her companion broke off a piece of bread and held it out to her.

'So you left your husband in Verdun?'

'Yes.' Cassie was tempted to tell him her husband was dead, but she remembered Merimon's taunt and decided it was safer to infer she had a husband to protect her honour, even if he was many miles away. 'Yes, he is at Verdun.'

She took the bread and nibbled at it as he surveyed her with his dark eyes.

'I am surprised he allowed you to travel alone. You are very young to be married.'

Cassie straightened.

'I am old enough!'

One dark brow went up.

'How old?' he asked her. 'You do not look more than eighteen.'

'I am nearly one-and-twenty and have been married a full year.'

'*Vraiment?* Tsk, what were your parents about to allow such a thing?'

'My parents died when I was a child.'

'Even worse, then, for your guardian to approve it.'

Cassie thought of Grandmama.

'She did not approve. We eloped.'

Cassie wondered why she had told him that. She was not proud of how she had behaved and the fact that it had all gone wrong just showed how foolish she had been. Falling in love had been a disaster and it was not a mistake she intended to make again. Glancing up at that moment, she thought she detected disapproval in those dark eyes. Well, let him disapprove. She cared not for his opinion, or for any man's. She scrambled to her feet and shook the crumbs from her skirts.

'Shall we continue?'

With a shrug he packed away the rest of the wine and bread and soon they were on their way again. Cassie maintained what she hoped was a dignified silence, but she was very much afraid Raoul Doulevant would

think it more of a childish sulk. However, it could not
be helped. She could not justify herself to him without
explaining everything and that she would not do to a
total stranger.

The sun was sinking when they met a farmer and his
wife approaching them in a cumbersome wagon. Cassie
listened while her escort conducted a brief conversation. The farmer confirmed that they were indeed on the
road to Reims, but it was at least another full day's ride.

'You are welcome to come back with us,' offered
the farmer's wife. 'It is an hour or so back the way you
have come, but we can give you and your lady a meal
and a bed for the night.'

Cassie froze. The idea of food was enticing, but
these people clearly thought that she and this unkempt
stranger were, were...

'Thank you, but, no, we had best press on.'

Raoul Doulevant answered for them both and exchanged a few more friendly words with the farmer
before they parted. Cassie felt the hot flush of embarrassment on her cheek and it was all she could do to
respond to their cheerful farewell with a nod of ac-
knowledgement.

'It is fortunate I refused their hospitality,' he remarked, misinterpreting her silence. 'A farmer's hovel
would not suit your ladyship.'

'You are mistaken,' she retorted. 'A bed and a good
meal would be very welcome, since I suspect the alternative will be a night spent out of doors. But you were
very right to refuse. I would like to get to Reims with
all haste.'

'Certainly. We cannot get there too soon for my liking!'

'Good. Let us ride through the night, then,' Cassie suggested, rattled.

They rode and walked by turns until the last of the daylight faded away. Cassie was fighting to stay awake, but nothing would make her admit it. She was the daughter of a marquess, granddaughter of an Arrandale and it was beneath her to show weakness of any sort.

Thick clouds rolled in from the west, obscuring the sky and plunging the world into almost complete darkness. When the bay stumbled for the third time she heard Raoul Doulevant curse softly under his breath.

'This is sheer foolishness, *monsieur*,' she told him. 'We should stop until the cloud lifts.'

'That would delay our journey; I was hoping to make a few more miles yet.'

'If the horse breaks a leg that will delay us even more,' Cassie pointed out.

When he did not reply she admitted, albeit reluctantly, that she would like to rest. Immediately he drew the horse to a halt and helped Cassie to dismount. Without ceremony he took her arm and guided her and the horse from the near darkness of the road into the blackness of the trees.

'Stay here, *madame*, while I see to the horse.'

Cassie slumped down against the base of a tree. Stay here, he had said. Did he think she would run away? She had no idea where she was, or which way she should go. She recalled how she had complained that she could not sleep in the carriage. What luxury that seemed now, compared to her present predicament. Not only must she sleep out of doors, but in the company of a stranger. The fact that they had introduced themselves made no difference; she knew nothing of this man.

She listened to the rustle of leaves as Raoul Doulevant secured the horse before coming to sit down beside her. She felt his presence rather than saw him and his silence unnerved her. She tried to recall what he had told her of himself.

'So you are a sailor, *monsieur*?'

'I was ship's surgeon on the *Prométhée* for six years.'

'Really?'

She could not keep the surprise from her voice and he gave a short laugh.

'My clothes tell the different story, no? I was obliged to…er…acquire these to escape detection.'

'If you were being pursued, then clearly that did not work.'

'No. There is one, Valerin, who is very determined to catch me.'

'He holds a grudge against you, perhaps?'

'I stopped him from forcing himself upon my sister. I should have killed him, instead of leaving him alive to denounce me.'

Cassie shivered. The words were quietly spoken, but there was no mistaking the menace in them.

'Where is your sister now?'

'I sent her to Brussels. We still have friends there. She is safe.'

'No doubt she is anxious for you to join her.'

'Perhaps. Her last letter said she had met an old friend, a wealthy merchant who is now a widower. I think they will make a match of it. Who knows, they may already be married. She is a widow and does not need to wait for my blessing.'

It was the most he had said to her all day and his tone was perfectly polite so she pushed aside her animosity.

'All the same, *monsieur*, it is good of you to delay your journey for me.'

When he did not reply she wondered if he was regretting his decision.

'Try to sleep,' he said at last. 'I will wake you if the light improves enough to move on.'

'Will you not sleep, too?'

The black shape shifted, as if he had drawn up his knees and was hugging them.

'No.'

Cassie was too exhausted to wonder at his stamina or to fight off her low spirits. Eloping with Gerald Witney had been shocking enough, but she was very much afraid that her friends and family would be even more shocked if they could see her now, alone under the stars with a strange man. She sighed as she curled up on the ground. There was nothing to be done and she was quite desperate for sleep, so she made herself as comfortable as she could and closed her eyes.

Raoul sank his chin on his knees and gazed at the unremitting darkness. The track was well-nigh invisible now. They had been right to stop, he acknowledged, but he wished it had not been necessary. The sooner he was relieved of this woman's presence the better. He travelled best alone, he did not want the responsibility of a foreign female, especially an arrogant Englishwoman. She could find her own way from Reims. After all, Bonaparte had no quarrel with women, she could hire a carriage to take her to the coast. Raoul closed his mind to the fact that she had been duped once by an unscrupulous courier. He had problems enough of his own to think of. He glanced up, although the darkness was so complete it was impossible to see where the trees ended and the sky began. There was no sign that the cloud would lift any time soon, so eventually he laid himself down on the ground, knowing he would be wise to rest.

Dawn broke, but not a glimmer of sun disturbed the uniform grey of the sky. Raoul put his hand on Lady Cassandra's shoulder to rouse her. He could feel the bones, fine and delicate as a bird beneath his hand. But she was not that delicate. He remembered how she had brought her attacker down with the tree branch. He could not deny this aristo had spirit.

He shook her gently. 'We must be moving.'

She stirred, smiling as if in the grip of some pleasant dream, and he thought suddenly that she really was very pretty, with her clear skin and a heart-shaped face framed by hair the colour of polished mahogany. Her straight little nose drew his eye to the soft curves of her lips and he was just wondering how it would feel to kiss her when she woke up and looked at him.

It was the first time he had looked into her eyes. They were a clear violet-blue, set beneath curving dark brows and fringed with thick, long lashes. He watched the violet darken to near black with fear and alarm when she saw him. He removed his hand from her shoulder, but the guarded look remained as she sat up. When she stretched he could not help but notice how the buttons of her jacket strained across her breast.

Raoul shifted his gaze, only to note that her skirts had ridden up a little to expose the dainty feet in their boots of half-jean. Something stirred within him, unbidden, unwelcome. He jumped up and strode off to fetch the horse. This was no time for lustful thoughts, especially for an English aristo.

Cassie scrambled to her feet and shook out her skirts before putting a hand to her hair, pushing the pins in as best she could without the aid of a mirror. She must look almost as dishevelled as her companion, but it could not be helped. He brought the horse alongside and held out his hand to her. As he pulled her up before him she marvelled again at his strength, at how secure she felt sitting up before him. She could not deny there was some comfort in being pressed close to that unwashed but decidedly male body. There was power in every line of him, in the muscular thighs beneath her and the strong arms that held her firmly in place. When she leaned against him, his chest was reassuringly solid at her back. Gerald had never made her feel this safe. Immediately she felt a wave of guilt for the thought and it was mixed with alarm. Raoul Doulevant was, after all, a stranger.

It was not cold, but the lack of wind allowed the mist to linger and the low cloud seemed to press on the treetops as they rode through the silent morning. Cassie's stomach rumbled, reminding her that she had not eaten since yesterday.

'There's a village ahead,' said Raoul presently. 'We should find a tavern there.' He drew the horse to a halt. 'It might be best if you give me a few coins before we get there. It would not do for you to be waving a fat purse before these people.'

'I do not have a fat purse,' she objected. Cautiously she reached into her skirts to the pocket and drew out a small stockinette purse. She counted out some coins and handed them to Raoul, who put them in his own pocket.

'Thank you. Now, when we get there, you had best let me take care of everything. You speak French charmingly, milady, but your accent would give you away.'

Cassie kept her lips firmly pressed together. He intended no compliment, she was sure of that. She contented herself with an angry look, but his smile and the glint of amusement in his eyes only made her more furious. If they had not been riding into the village at that moment she would have given him a sharp set-down for teasing her so.

The village boasted a sizable inn. When they had dismounted Raoul handed the reins to the waiting ostler and escorted Cassie into the dark interior. It took a few moments for Cassie's eyes to adjust to the gloom, then she saw that the room was set out with benches and tables, but was mercifully empty of customers. A pot-bellied tapster approached them, wiping his hands on a greasy apron. Raoul ordered wine and food and their host invited them to sit down.

'Been travelling long?' asked the tapster as he banged a jug of wine on the table before them. Raoul grunted.

'Takin' my sister home,' he said. 'She's been serving as maid to one of the English ladies in Verdun.'

'Ah.' The tapster sniffed. 'Damned English have taken over the town, I hear.'

Raoul poured a glass of wine and held it out for Cassie, his eyes warning her to keep silent.

'Aye,' he said cheerfully. 'But they are generous masters, only look at the smart habit my sister now possesses! And their English gold is filling French coffers, so who are we to complain?'

'You are right there, my friend.' The tapster cackled, revealing a mouth full of broken and blackened teeth. He slapped Raoul on the shoulder and wandered off to fetch their food.

Cassie could hardly contain her indignation as she listened to this interchange.

'Sister?' she hissed in a furious undertone, as soon as they were alone. 'How can that man think we are related?'

His grin only increased her fury.

'Very easily,' he said. 'Have you looked at yourself recently, milady? Your gown is crumpled and your hair is a tangle. I am almost ashamed to own you.'

'At least I do not look like a bear!' she threw at him.

Cassandra regretted the unladylike outburst immediately. She chewed her lip, knowing she would have to apologise.

'I beg your pardon,' she said at last and through clenched teeth. 'I should be grateful for your escort.'

'You should indeed,' he growled. 'You need not fear, *madame*. As soon as we reach Reims I shall relieve you of my boorish presence.'

He broke off as the tapster appeared and put down two plates in front of them.

'There, *monsieur*. A hearty meal for you both. None of your roast beef here.'

Raoul gave a bark of laughter. 'No, we leave such barbarities to the enemy.'

Grinning, the tapster waddled away.

'Is that how you think of me?' muttered Cassie. 'As your enemy?'

'I have told you, I am not French.'

'But you served in their navy.'

He met her gaze, his eyes hard and unsmiling.

'I have no reason to think well of the English. Let us say no more of it.'

'But—'

'Eat your food, *madame*, before I put you across my knee and thrash you like a spoiled brat.'

Cassie looked away, unsettled and convinced he might well carry out his threat.

The food was grey and unappetising, some sort of stew that had probably been in the pot for days, but it was hot and tasted better than it looked. Cassie knew she must eat to keep up her strength, but she was not sorry when they were finished and could be on their way.

Raoul Doulevant's good humour returned once they were mounted. He tossed a coin to the ostler and set off out of the village at a steady walk.

'The tapster says Reims is about a day's ride from here,' he told Cassie. 'We might even make it before nightfall.'

'I am only sorry he did not know where we could buy or hire another horse,' she remarked, still smarting from their earlier exchange.

'You do not like travelling in my arms, milady?'

'No, I do not.'

'You could always walk.'

'If you were a gentleman *you* would walk.'

She felt his laugh rumble against her back.

'Clearly I am no gentleman, then.'

Incensed, she turned towards him, intending to say something cutting, but when she looked into those dark eyes her breath caught in her throat. He was teasing her again. Laughter gleamed in his eyes and her traitorous body was responding. She was tingling with excitement in a way she remembered from those early days following her come-out, when she had been carefree and had flirted outrageously with many a handsome gentleman. Now she wanted to laugh back at Raoul, to tease him in return. Even worse, she found herself wondering what it would be like if he kissed her. The thought frightened her. In her present situation she dare not risk becoming too friendly with this stranger. Quickly she turned away again.

Raoul closed his eyes and exhaled a long, slow breath, thankful that the lady was now staring fixedly ahead, her little nose in the air as she tried to ignore him. What was he about, teasing her in such a way? There was something about the lady that brought out the rake in him and made him want to flirt with her, even though he knew it would be much more sensible to keep his distance. He had no time for women, other than the most casual liaisons, and instinct told him that involvement with Lady Cassandra Witney would be anything but casual.

He glanced at the lady as she rode before him. His arms were on either side, holding her firm while his hands gripped the reins. The bay was a sturdy animal and did not object to the extra weight and Raoul had to admit it was not excessive. She was petite, slender as a reed. He was almost afraid to hold her too close in case he crushed her. She was trying hard not to touch him, but sometimes the movement of the horse sent her back against him and those dark curls would tangle with his beard and he would catch a faint, elusive scent of summer flowers. Confound it, he was enjoying himself! He could not deny that having her sitting up before him made the journey much more pleasurable.

It soon became clear that the tapster's estimate of the journey time was very optimistic. With only the long-tailed bay to ride progress was slow and in the hot September sun Raoul was reluctant to push the horse to more than a walking pace. He was glad when their road took them through dense woodland; that at least provided some welcome shade. The lady before him said very little. Perhaps she was still cross with him for teasing her, but he did not mind her reticence, for he was not fond of inconsequential chattering.

Raoul judged they had only an hour or so of daylight left and was beginning to consider where they would spend the night when the horse's ears pricked. Raoul heard it, too, the jingling sounds of harness and male voices from around the bend ahead of them. Lots of voices. Quickly he dragged on the reins and urged the horse into the shelter of the trees.

Their sudden departure from the road shook his companion out of her reverie. She asked him what was happening and he answered her briefly.

'It may be nothing, but I think there may be soldiers ahead of us.'

* * *

Cassie's heart thudded with anxiety as they pushed deeper between the trees. It was bad enough that she had no papers to prove her identity, but she was also travelling with a fugitive. She could imagine all too well what would happen if they were caught. The ground had been rising since they left the road, but now it began to climb steeply and they stopped to dismount. In silence they moved deeper into the woods until they were out of sight of the road and the raucous voices had faded to a faint, occasional shout.

'Stay here,' muttered Raoul, tethering the horse. 'I will go back and see what they are about.'

'I shall come with you.'

'You will be safer here.'

'Oh, no.' She caught his sleeve. 'You are not leaving me alone.'

He frowned and looked as if he was about to argue, then he changed his mind.

'Very well. Come with me, but quietly.'

He took her hand and led her back through the bushes, following the sound of the voices. At last he stopped, pulling Cassie closer and binding her to him as they peered through the thick foliage. She could see splashes of colour through the trees, mainly blue, but touches of red and the glint of sunlight on metal. The air was redolent with woodsmoke.

'They are making camp for the night,' breathed Raoul.

'What shall we do? Can we circle around them and back to the road?'

He shook his head. 'We have no idea how many of them there are. They may be the first of several units, or there may be stragglers. We must give them a very wide berth. We need to move deeper into the woods, too, in case they come foraging for firewood.'

It was at that inopportune moment, with French soldiers dangerously close, that Cassie discovered she did not wish to go anywhere. Raoul still had his arm about her waist and despite his rough and dirty clothes her body was happy to lean into him. She was disturbingly aware of that powerful figure, tense and ready to act. Growing up, she had always been impatient of convention and had craved excitement and danger. Instinct told her this man was both exciting and dangerous. A heady combination, she thought as he led her away. And one she would be wise to keep at bay.

They retrieved the horse and set off into the woods. Raoul was no longer holding her and Cassie had to fight down the temptation to grab his hand. She was perfectly capable of walking unaided and she told herself it was useful to have both hands free to draw her skirts away from encroaching twigs and branches. It was impossible to ride, the trees were too thick and their low branches were barely above the saddle. They walked for what seemed like hours. Cassie was bone-weary but stubborn pride kept her silent. As the sun went down it grew much colder and the thought of spending another night in the open was quite daunting.

It was almost dark when they saw before them a small house in a clearing. An old woman appeared at the door and Cassie stopped, knowing the deep shadows of the trees would hide them. She almost gasped with shock and surprise when Raoul put his arm about her waist and walked her forward into the clearing.

'Come along, *madame*, let us see if we can find a

little charity here.' He raised his voice: 'Good evening to you, Mother. Could you spare a little supper for two weary travellers? We were taking a short cut and lost our way.'

The old woman looked at them with incurious eyes until he jingled the coins in his pocket. She jerked her head, as if inviting them in.

'I have salt herring I can fry for you and a little bread.'

'That would suit us very well, Mother, thank you.'

They followed her into the cottage. Raoul's arm was still about Cassie and he was smiling, but she knew he was alert, ready to fight if danger threatened. A single oil lamp burned inside and by its fragile light Cassie could see the house was very small, a single square room with an earth floor and a straw mattress in one corner. Cassie guessed the old woman lived here alone. A sluggish fire smoked in the hearth, but it was suffi-cient to warm the small space and Cassie sank down on to a rickety bench placed against one wall. The old woman gestured to Raoul to sit down with Cassie while she prepared their meal.

Cassie was exhausted. Raoul's shoulder was so temptingly close and she leaned her head against it, watching through half-closed eyes as the woman poked the fire into life and added more wood. Soon the pun-gent smell of the fish filled the room. Cassie's eyes began to smart and she closed them, but then it was too much trouble to open them again and she dozed until Raoul gave her a little nudge.

'Wake up now. You must eat something.'

Sleepily Cassie sat up to find a small table had been pushed in front of them and it was set now with plates and horn cups. They dined on salt herring and bread, but when the old woman offered them some of her white brandy Raoul refused, politely but firmly.

'Would it be so very bad?' Cassie murmured when their hostess went off to fetch them some water.

'Very likely,' he replied, 'but even if it is drinkable, to take it with the herring would give you a raging thirst.'

She accepted this without comment. She did not like the fish very much, but the bread was fresh and Cassie made a good meal. When it was finished the old woman cleared everything away. Raoul took a few coins out of his pocket and held them out.

'Thank you, Mother, for your hospitality. There is double this if you will let us sleep on your floor tonight.'

The old crone's eyes gleamed. 'Double it again and I'll let ye have the paillasse.'

Cassie glanced from the woman to the bed in the corner and could barely suppress a shudder at the thought of what might be crawling amongst the straw. To her relief Raoul did not hesitate to decline her offer.

'We would not take your cot, Mother, nor your covers. We shall be comfortable enough before the fire.'

She shrugged and took the coins from his palm.

'As you please.'

The old woman banked up the fire and cleared a space before it, even going so far as to find a threadbare rug to put on the ground. Raoul went outside to attend to the horse and the old woman gave Cassie a toothless smile.

'You've got yourself a good man there, *madame*.'

'What? Oh—oh, yes.' Cassie nodded. She was too tired to try and explain that they were not married.

* * *

When Raoul returned the old woman blew out the lamp and retired to her bed with her flask of brandy, leaving her guests to fend for themselves before the fire. There was no privacy and they both lay down fully dressed on the old rug. Raoul stretched out on his back and linked his hands behind his head.

'Do not fret,' he murmured. 'I shall not touch you.'

Cassie did not deign to reply to his teasing tone. She curled up on her side with her back to Raoul. She was nearest the fire and glad of the heat from the dying embers, but she could not relax. She was far too on edge, aware of Raoul's body so close to her own. He was so big, and rough and…*male*. Gerald had been more of a gamester than a sportsman. He had been fastidious about his dress and she had never seen him with more than a slight shadow of stubble on his face. That is what she had loved about him; he had always looked like the perfect gentleman. She stirred, uncomfortable with the thought that he had not always acted like a gentleman.

Not that it mattered now, Gerald was dead and she would have to make her own way in the world. Sleepily she wondered why she had not told Raoul she was a widow. After all, it could make no difference to him, since as far as he was aware her husband was still in Verdun. But some deep, unfathomable instinct told her Raoul Doulevant was an honourable man. Now her hands came together and she fingered the plain wedding band. It was little enough protection, but it was all she had.

Cassie lay still, tense and alert until she heard Raoul snoring gently. The old woman had told them it was a full day's walk from here to Reims, so by tomorrow they would be in the city and she could be rid of her ragged companion. She closed her eyes. The sooner dawn came the better.

Cassie stirred. She was still lying on her side, facing the fire which had died down to a faint glow, and the room was in almost total darkness. She reached down to make sure the skirts of her riding habit were tucked around her feet, but she could feel the chill of the night air through the sleeves of her jacket. She tried rubbing her arms, but that did not help much. She sighed.

'What is the matter?' Raoul's voice was no more than a sleepy whisper in the darkness.

'I am cold.'

He shifted closer, curving his body around hers and putting his arm over her. The effect was startling. Heat spread quickly through her body and with it a sizzling excitement. It did not matter that Raoul was dressed in rough homespun clothes, or that his ragged beard tickled her neck, her pulse leapt erratically as he curled himself about her.

'Is that better?'

Cassie swallowed. She could not reply, her throat had dried, her breasts strained against the confines of her jacket. She was wrapped in the arms of a man, a stranger. Even worse, she wanted him to kiss and caress her. Heavens she should move away, immediately! But somehow she could not make her body obey, and the idea of lying cold and alone for the remainder of the night was not at all appealing. It was confusing, to feel so secure, yet so vulnerable, all at the same time.

Raoul's arm tightened, pulling them closer together. So close she could feel his breath on her cheek, feel his body close against hers. She should protest, she should object strongly to being held in this way, but she was so warm now, so comfortable. The initial burning excitement had settled into a sense of wellbeing. She had never felt so safe before, or so warm. She felt a smile spreading out from her very core.

'Oh, yes,' she murmured sleepily. 'Oh, yes, that is much better.'

Raoul lay very still, listening to Cassie's gentle, regular breathing. It was taking all his willpower not to nuzzle closer and nibble the delightful shell-like ear, to keep his hands from seeking out the swell of her breasts. He uttered up a fervent prayer of thanks that the thick folds of her skirts prevented her knowing just how aroused he was to have her lying with him in this way.

He had been too long without a woman. How else could he explain the heat that shot through him whenever they touched? Even when she looked at him he was aware of a connection, as if they had known each other for ever. Fanciful rubbish, he told himself. She was a spoiled English aristo and he despised such women. By heaven, at eight-and-twenty he was too old to fall for a pair of violet-blue eyes, no matter how much they sparkled. And there was no doubt that Lady Cassandra's eyes sparkled quite exceptionally, so much so they haunted his dreams, as did the delightful curves of her body. Even now he wanted to explore those curves, to run his fingers over the dipping valley of her waist, the rounded swell of her hips and the equally enchanting breasts that he judged would fit perfectly into his hands.

He closed his eyes. This was nothing short of torture, to keep still while he was wrapped around this woman. He turned his mind to consider how he must look to her, with his dirty clothes and unkempt hair. She must think him a rogue, a vagabond. He was not fit to clean her boots.

And yet here she was, sleeping in his arms.

Chapter Three

~~~

They quit the cottage soon after dawn and followed the narrow track through the woods that the old woman told them would bring them to the highway a few miles to the west of Reims. They rode and walked by turns as the sun moved higher in the clear blue sky, but although Cassandra was cheerful enough her companion was taciturn, even surly, and after travelling a few miles in silence she taxed him with it. They were walking side by side at that point and Cassie decided it would be easier to ask the question now, rather than when they were on horseback. For some inexplicable reason when she was sitting within the circle of his arms it was difficult to think clearly.

She said now, 'You have scarce said a dozen civil words to me since we set out, *monsieur*. Have I offended you in some way?'

'If you must know I did not sleep well.'

'Oh.' Something in his tone sent the blood rushing to her cheeks as Cassie realised that she might have been the cause. She had woken at dawn to find they were still curled up together but even more intimately, his cheek resting against her hair and one of those strong, capable hands cradling her breast. It was such a snug fit she thought they might have been made for one another. A preposterous idea, but at the time it had made her want to smile. Now it only made her blush. He had still been sleeping when she had slipped out of his unconscious embrace and she had said nothing about it, hoping he would not remember, but perhaps he had been more aware of how they had slept together than she had first thought.

Cassie closed her eyes as embarrassment and remorse swept over her like a wave. If eloping with Gerald had dented her reputation, what had happened to her since leaving Verdun was like to smash it completely.

Raoul Doulevant cleared his throat.

'How long have you been in France, milady?'

He was trying to give her thoughts a different turn and she responded gratefully.

'Just over a year. Gerald and I travelled to Paris last summer, shortly after we were married. The Treaty of Amiens had opened the borders and we joined the fashionable throng. Then, in May this year, the Peace ended.'

'Ah, yes.' He nodded. 'Bonaparte issued instructions that every Englishman between the ages of sixteen and sixty should be detained.'

'Yes.'

Cassie fell silent, unwilling to admit that she had already been regretting her hasty marriage. She had stayed and supported her husband, even though he had given her little thanks for it after the first anxious weeks of his detention.

'But now you return to England without him. I had heard the English in Verdun lived very comfortably.'

'Only if they have money. Our funds were running very low.'

'Ah. So now your husband's fortune has gone you have abandoned him.'

'No!' She bit her lip. She should correct him, tell him it was her money they had lived on, that she was now a widow, but the words stuck in her throat. Pride would not let her admit how wrong she had been, how foolish. Instead she said haughtily, 'You have no right to judge me.'

'Why, because I am not your equal, *my lady*?'

'You are impertinent, *monsieur*. I had expected better manners from a doctor.'

'But I have told you I am not a doctor. I am a surgeon.'

'But clearly not a gentleman!'

A heavy silence followed her words, but she would not take them back. An angry frown descended upon Raoul's countenance, but he did not speak. Cassie kept pace with him, head high, but his refusal to respond flayed her nerves. She tried telling herself that it was better if they did not talk, that it was safer to keep a distance, yet she found the silence unbearable and after a while she threw a question at him.

'If you are no deserter, why are you being pursued?'

'That need not concern you.'

Cassie knew his retort was no more than she deserved, after what she had said to him. Her temper had subsided as quickly as it was roused; she knew it was wise to keep a distance from this man, but that did not mean they had to be at odds.

She tried to make amends by saying contritely, 'I beg your pardon if my words offended you, *monsieur*, but you must admit, your appearance, your situation… We shall have a miserable journey if we do not discuss *something.*'

There, she had apologised, but when he said nothing she glanced at his angry countenance and thought ruefully that his pride was equal to hers. They were not suited as travelling companions. Cassie walked on beside him, resigned to the silence, but presently the strained atmosphere between them changed. The black cloud lifted from his brow and he began to speak.

'A year ago—about the time that you came to France—I quit the navy and went to Paris to live with my sister Margot. She and her husband had taken me in when I had gone there ten years before to study at the Hôtel-Dieu under the great French surgeon, Desault. Margot was widowed three years ago, so by moving into her house I thought I could support her. Unfortunately last winter she caught the eye of a minor official in Paris, one Valerin. Margo did not welcome his attentions and I told him so. He did not like it.'

'You were rather rough with him, perhaps,' she observed sagely.

'Yes. I came home one night and found him trying to force himself upon Margot. I threw him out of the house and broke his nose into the bargain. That was my mistake. Life became difficult, we were suspected of being enemies of the state, the house was raided several times. It became so bad that a couple of months ago I sent Margot to Brussels. I planned to follow her, once I had wound up my affairs in Paris, but Valerin was too quick for me. He accused me of being a deserter.

When I looked for my papers they had gone, taken during one of the house raids, I suppose, and when I applied to the prefect to see the record of my discharge the files were missing.'

'And could no one vouch for you?'

He shrugged. 'My old captain, possibly, but he is at sea. A response from him could take months. I thought it best to leave Paris. And just in time. I was still making my preparations when Valerin came with papers for my arrest and I was forced to flee with nothing. He was so intent upon my capture that he sent word to the Paris gates, which is why you find me dressed *en paysan* and, as you put it, looking like a bear.'

Cassie bit her lip.

'I should not have said that of you. I am in no position to preach to you now, *monsieur.*' She wrinkled her nose. 'I have never been so dirty. What I would give for clean linen!'

'I fear that will have to wait until we reach Reims, *madame.*'

They kept to the woodland paths and avoided the main highways. It made the journey longer, but Raoul was anxious to avoid meeting anyone who might ask for their papers. Their only food was some fruit, wine and bread they purchased from a woodsman's cottage and at noon they stopped on a ridge, sitting on a fallen tree to eat their frugal meal.

'Is that Reims ahead of us?' asked Cassie, pointing to the roofs and spires in the distance.

'It is. We shall be there before dark, milady.' He sensed her anxiety and added, 'I shall see you safe to a priest, or a nunnery, *madame*, before I leave you.'

'Thank you.' She sighed. 'Travelling alone is very perilous for a lady.'

She was trying to make light of it, but he was not deceived. She was frightened, as well she should be. It was no good to tell himself she was not his responsibility, Raoul's conscience told him otherwise. He made an attempt to stifle it, saying harshly, 'You should have thought of that before you left your husband.'

He glanced down at her and saw that she was close to tears. The urge to take her in his arms was so great that he clenched his fists and pressed them into his thighs. He searched for something to say.

'Why did you elope with him?'

One dainty hand fluttered.

'He was handsome and charming, and he swept me off my feet. Grandmama, who is my guardian, said I was too young, but I thought I knew better. When Gerald suggested we should elope I thought it would be a great adventure. I do not expect you to understand, but life in Bath was very…tame. Oh, there were parties and balls and lots of friends, but it was not enough. I wanted excitement. Gerald offered me that.'

'No doubt being in an enemy country and detained at Verdun has given you a surfeit of excitement.'

She frowned a little, considering.

'One would have thought so, but do you know, it was not so very different from Bath. There are so many English people there and they are determined to carry on very much as they always do. There are parties and assemblies, race meetings and gambling dens, everyone finding silly or frivolous entertainments to fill the time. In truth it is a very a foolish way to live. To be perfectly honest, I was *bored*.'

Raoul watched her. She had clearly forgotten to whom she was talking, there was no reserve as the words poured forth and when she turned her head and smiled up at him, completely natural and unaffected, it shook him to the core. He had the very disturbing sensation of his whole world tilting. The ground beneath him turned to quicksand and it threatened to consume him. It was not that she was trying to attract him, quite the opposite. Her look was trusting and friendly, and it cut through his defences like a sword through paper.

He dragged his eyes away. He needed to repair his defences, to put up the barriers again.

Cassie sucked in a ragged breath, unsure what had just happened to her. In telling Raoul about her elopement she had opened her soul to him in a way she had never done with anyone before. Even when she had thought herself hopelessly in love with Gerald she had never felt such a connection as she did with this dark stranger. It frightened her.

He rose, saying gruffly, 'We should go, we still have several hours travelling to reach Reims.'

Cassie nodded and followed him towards the horse. His voice was perfectly composed. He had not commented, displayed no emotion at what she had told him. No doubt he thought her an idle, frivolous woman, worthy only of contempt. When he sprang into the saddle and put his hand out to her she glanced up at his face, an anxious frown creasing her brow.

'No doubt you think me a silly creature. Contemptible.'

The black eyes gave nothing away.

'What I think of you is unimportant,' he said shortly. 'Come, let us press on.'

* * *

The afternoon grew warmer as they made their way towards Reims and the bay's walking pace slowed to an amble. The city was lost to sight as they descended into a wooded valley where the air was warm and filled with the trill of birdsong. It was enchanting, reminding Cassie of hot summer days in England, but much as she wanted to share her thoughts with her companion she held back, knowing she must keep a proper distance. She had already told him far too much and feared she had earned his disapproval. Her spirit flared in momentary rebellion. Well, let him disapprove, it did not matter to her in the least.

When at last they dismounted she was thankful that the rough path was wide enough to walk with the horse between them. There must be no accidental brushing of the hands and heaven forbid that he should be gentleman enough to offer her his arm, for she would have to refuse and that might give rise to offence. How difficult it was to maintain propriety in this wilderness! The heat in the valley was oppressive and the sun beat down upon her bare head. She sighed, regretting the loss of her bonnet.

'Are you tired, milady?'

'No, merely hot and a little uncomfortable.' She unfastened the neck button of her shirt. Even that was an indiscretion, she knew, but a very minor one, considering her situation.

'Would you like to rest in the shade for a while?'

'Thank you, but I would prefer to keep going and reach Reims. Perhaps there we can find some clean clothes.' She could not help adding, 'For both of us.'

His breath hissed out. 'Does my dirty raiment offend you, milady?'

'No more than my own,' she replied honestly. 'We are both in need of a good bath. I suppose it cannot be helped when one is travelling.'

He came to a halt.

'An answer may be at hand,' he said. 'Listen.'

'What is it? I cannot—'

But he was already pushing his way through the thick bushes. Cassie followed and soon heard the sound of rushing water. It grew louder, but they had gone some way from the path before they reached the source of the noise. Cassie gave a little gasp of pure pleasure.

They were on the edge of a natural pool. It was fed by a stream tumbling down the steep cliff on the far side and the midday sun glinted on the falling water, turning the spray into a glistening rainbow.

'Oh, how beautiful!'

'Not only beautiful, milady, but convenient. We can bathe here.'

'What? Oh, no, I mean—'

Cassie broke off, but her blushes only deepened when Raoul gave her a scornful look.

'You have warm air and clean water here, *madame*, I cannot conjure an army of servants for you, too. I am going to make the most of what nature has given us. I suggest you do, too.'

He tethered the horse and began to strip off his clothes, throwing his shirt into the pool to wash it. Cassie knelt on the bank and dipped her hands into the water. It was crystal clear and deliciously cool against her skin. From the corner of her eye she saw that Raoul had now discarded all his clothes. She looked away quickly, but not before she had noted the lean athletic body. How wrong she had been to describe him as a bear, she thought distractedly. There was only a shadowing of hair on his limbs with a thicker covering on his chest, like a shield that tapered down towards...

Oh, heavens! She must not even think of that.

She heard the splash as he dived into the pool and only then did she risk looking up again. Raoul was a strong swimmer, sending diamond droplets flying up as he surged through the water and away from her. For a moment she envied him his freedom before berating herself as a ninny. He had said she should make use of what he had termed nature's gift and she would. The pool was large enough to keep out of each other's way. There were several large bushes at the edge of the water and she moved behind one of them to divest herself of her riding habit. She shook out the jacket and the full skirts and draped them over the bush where they could air in the sunshine, then she followed Raoul's example and tossed her shirt into the water. Once she had removed her corset she did the same with her shift, then she knelt at the side of the pool and washed the fine garments as best she could before wringing them out and hanging them over another convenient shrub. The sun was so high and strong she thought they would both be quite dry by the time she had bathed herself.

The pool was shallower in the secluded spot she had chosen and the cold on her hot skin made her gasp as she stepped in. Cautiously she walked away from the bank until the water was just over waist deep and she lowered herself until only her head was above the surface. Now her body was submerged she felt more comfortable. She moved into slightly deeper water and closed her eyes, feeling the heat of the sun on her face. Her body felt weightless, rocking with the gentle movement of the water, cleansing, relaxing.

'There, do you not feel better?'

Cassie gave a little scream. Raoul was only feet away from her, his wet hair plastered to his head and his eyes gleaming with laughter.

'G-go away, if you please,' Cassie ordered him, praying the sun glinting on the surface of the water would prevent him from seeing her naked body. 'Pray, go and wash your clothes, sir, and let me be private.'

'I came to tell you I have been standing beneath the waterfall,' he said, ignoring her request. 'It is refreshing, I think you will like it.'

'No, thank you.'

'Why not? I will stay here, if you wish to be alone.'

'I want to be alone *here*,' she said, trying to keep her voice calm. The amusement in his eyes deepened and she glared at him. 'Go away. I wish to dress. Now.'

'But your linen cannot be dry yet.'

'That is my concern, not yours.'

'It is not far to swim across to the waterfall. You would feel better for the exercise.'

'Most definitely I should not.'

His eyes narrowed. 'You cannot swim.' When she did not reply he reached out to her. 'Let me teach you.'

'No!' The word came out as a squeak. 'You c-cannot teach me.'

'It is very easy.'

She shook her head, backing away a little, towards the bank, but having to crouch down in the shallower water.

There was a splash as he pushed himself upright.

'Look, it is not so very deep, you could walk across, if you wished.'

Cassie was looking. Her eyes were fixed on those broad shoulders and that muscled chest glistening in the sunlight. Thankfully the rest of his body was still submerged.

'Come.' He held his hand out to her. 'I want you to stand beneath the waterfall and tell me if it is not the most invigorating sensation you have ever experienced.'

It was madness. She should dress immediately, but a glance at the bank showed her that her shirt and her shift were still too damp to wear. She could sit here in the shallows while the sun baked the skin on her face to the colour of a biscuit or she could go with Raoul into the shade beneath the waterfall.

No, it was not to be contemplated, but already her hand was going out to his and she was edging out of the shallows. As the water came up over her shoulders she felt its power rocking her off her feet. Raoul's grip tightened.

'Do not worry,' he said. 'I will hold you.'

It surprised Cassie just how safe she felt with her hand held so firmly in his warm grasp.

'Did you learn to swim in the navy?' she asked in an effort not to think about his naked body, just an arm's reach away from her own.

'No. My father taught me.'

'I would imagine it is a useful accomplishment for a ship's surgeon.'

'It is not difficult, you should try it. Even dogs can swim.'

'I am not a dog, *monsieur*!'

'No, I can see that.'

Cassie set her lips firmly together and suppressed an angry retort. If it wasn't for the fact that they had reached the middle of the pool and the water was so deep that she was forced to stand on tiptoe, she might have moved away, but she needed his support. She maintained a stern silence and kept him at arm's length as they moved forward. Cassie was also leaning away from her partner and she was reminded of seeing Grandmama performing a stately minuet. The thought made her want to giggle and she wondered what the marchioness would think if she could see her grand-daughter now, naked as a babe and in the company of a strange man.

Raoul was guiding her to one side of the waterfall, where there was a gap between the sheer cliff and the falling water. Soon she began to feel the spray on her face, a fine mist that cooled her heated skin, but she did not have much chance to enjoy it, for an incautious step found nothing but water beneath her foot and she plunged beneath the surface. Panic engulfed Cassie before Raoul's strong arms caught her up.

'It's all right, you are safe now, I have you.'

She grabbed his shoulders, coughing, and as he pulled her close her legs came up and wrapped them-selves about his waist.

'My apologies, milady,' he muttered, his voice un-steady. 'I had not noticed that the pool floor was so un-even here. I will carry you the rest of the way.'

She clung on, no longer concerned that they were naked, all that mattered was that she was safe in his arms. Her face was hidden against his neck, the salty taste of his skin was on her mouth. Whenever she breathed in she was aware of the faint musky scent of him. The sound of rushing water was loud and constant, but she could also hear Raoul's ragged breathing and felt his heart hammering against her breast as he moved slowly, step by step, through the water. At last he stopped.

'You can stand down now, *madame*. It is not so deep. Trust me.'

Trust him? She had no choice. It had been sheer madness to come so far from the bank, to put herself at the mercy of a man she did not know. She swallowed. How could she claim not to know Raoul Doulevant, when their naked bodies had been entwined so intimately? Even now his hands were moving to her waist, supporting her, giving her confidence. Keeping her head buried against him, Cassie unwrapped her legs from his body. Gingerly she reached down to find firm, smooth rock beneath her feet. She stepped away from Raoul, but could not bring herself to release his hand as she gazed around. It was much darker here and she looked up to see that they were standing behind a curtain of water that cast a greenish hue over everything. Without the sun to warm her, Cassie realised that the parts of her body above the water were tensed against the cold. She glanced down, noting with relief that her hair was hanging down and concealing her breasts, then thought wryly that it was a little late for modesty, when moments ago she had been clinging like ivy to her companion. She glanced towards him and gave a little laugh of surprise.

'Your skin looks green!'

Raoul glanced at her.

'And you look like a mermaid.'

'Oh? You have seen one of those mythical creatures, I suppose.'

He grinned. 'Hundreds.'

She was laughing up at him. Raoul was inordinately pleased that she shared his delight in this place and it was the most natural thing in the world to lean a little closer and kiss her. He felt a tremor run through her, felt her body yield a little before she regained control and backed away from him, eyes wide and dark. She released his hand, clearly preferring to run the risk of drowning rather than touch him.

'We, we should go back now, *monsieur.*'

She would not meet his eyes and Raoul silently cursed himself. What was he about, consorting with this woman? He could not resist flirting with her, but she was not for him. Yet his body told him differently, it had known it from the first time he had pulled her into his arms and ridden away with her. Now it remembered every step he had taken with her in his arms, every moment of her warm flesh pressed against his, arousing him and sending the hot blood pounding through his veins and making him dizzy. Enough of such madness. He did not want her naked body in his arms again, she was too tempting. The instant and powerful arousal when she had flung her legs about him had almost toppled them both beneath the water. Yet she had felt as fragile as a bird when he held her close, her heart beating erratically against his chest, rousing in him a protectiveness that he really did not wish to feel for any Englishwoman. He must get them both back to the far bank without further embarrassing the lady. He set his jaw. That would not be easy when her naked form was so temptingly close. The apprehension in her face told him that she, too, was wondering how they would get back.

He turned away from her.

'Put your hands on my shoulders and let your body float up behind you. If you relax you will find it easier.'

Obediently she placed her hands on his shoulders. Briefly he covered her fingers with his own.

'Hold tight now.'

Cassie was gripping as tightly as she could, feeling the knotted muscle moving beneath her hands as he used his arms to help pull them through the water. Her body was still vibrating from his kiss, her blood felt hot and she wondered what would have happened if they had not been standing up to their shoulders in the cold water. She thought it might then have been much more difficult to pull away from him, to remember the dangers of her situation. Even now she was not safe; she could not make it back across the pool without his help. She knew she must keep her body away from that broad back and not pull herself close and allow her breasts to rest against him, which was what some wild and wanton part of her wanted to do. She kept her body straight, pushing her legs up towards the surface of the water and keeping her eyes fixed on the tendrils of dark hair curling at the nape of Raoul's neck. At first it took all her energy to concentrate, but gradually she managed to relax a little and discovered it required less effort. She was floating out behind him and where her back broke the surface she could feel the heat of the sun on her skin. Her grip on Raoul's strong shoulders eased, she tried a few tentative kicks with her legs and heard a chuckle.

'A few more trips across the pool and I think you might be swimming, milady.'

Quite unaccountably, his words pleased her, but she managed not to give herself away when she responded. 'No, I thank you.' They had almost reached the bank and her feet sank to the pool's floor. 'I can manage from here. If you will leave me I will dress myself.'

'Are you sure you would not like me to help you with your corset?'

She gritted her teeth. Really, he was quite infuriating.

'I will manage,' she told him. 'Pray, go and dress yourself, *monsieur*. Over there, out of my sight.'

Grinning, Raoul swam away. Milady was back, as haughty and commanding as ever, but when he had climbed out of the water and was pulling on his shirt he heard a faint but unmistakable sound coming from the other side of those concealing bushes. Lady Cassandra was singing.

When at last she emerged from the bushes she was fully dressed and she had removed the pins from her hair, letting the thick, dark tresses spread around her shoulders while they dried. She looked better, he thought. Less tired and her eyes were brighter. She looked beautiful. A sudden, exultant trill of birdsong filled the air, like a fanfare for the lady.

Scowling, Raoul turned away and busied himself checking the girth on the saddle. This was no time for such fanciful ideas. Resolutely he kept his eyes from her until he was mounted on the horse.

'Well, *madame*, shall we continue?'

He put out his hand. She sprang nimbly up, but from the way she held herself, tense and stiff before him, he knew that she, too, was trying to avoid touching him more than necessary.

* * *

Raoul pushed the bay to a canter and they covered the rest of the journey to Reims in good time. The sun was low in the sky when they reached the main highway and dismounted for a final time to rest the horse before they rode into the city. They had hardly spoken since leaving the pool, both caught up in their own thoughts, but as he waited for her to pin up her hair again he noted the frown creasing her brow.

'What is in your mind, *madame*?'

'How far is it from Reims to Le Havre?'

He shrugged. 'Three days, perhaps, to Rouen, then another two to Le Havre. Or you may be in luck and find a ship in Rouen that will take you to the coast. You might even find one to take you all the way to England.'

'But France is at war with England, will that not make it more difficult?'

Raoul shrugged. 'Difficult, but not impossible, if you have money.'

Le Havre could be bustling with troops. Dangerous enough for him, but a pretty young woman, travelling alone, would have to be very careful. He glanced at her. She had finished pinning up her hair, but even so she looked remarkably youthful. An unscrupulous man might take advantage of her. He might steal her money, thought Raoul. Or worse. He remembered when he had first seen her, about to be attacked by the courier and his accomplice. She had been prepared to fight, but without his help she might not escape so lightly next time.

'If you will help me to reach the coast and find a ship to take me home, I will pay you.'

The words came out in a rush and she fell silent

after, keeping her eyes fixed on the distant horizon as if afraid to look at him.

Why not? Raoul asked himself. *Because she is English and an aristocrat. Everything you despise. Everything you have cause to hate.*

He glanced at the lady, noticed how tightly her hands were clasped together as she waited for his answer. She was also a woman and for all her bravado she was vulnerable and alone and it was not in his nature to turn his back on a defenceless creature.

He would prefer to travel to Brussels, but he had to admit that without money to pay his way any journey would be difficult. And once they reached a port he might well be able to find a ship to take him north along the coast.

'How much?'

She shook her head.

'I cannot say. I will pay for a carriage from Reims and our lodgings on the way and after that I need to find a ship to carry me home. I do not know how much all that will cost. However, if you will trust me, I will give you whatever I can spare, once I have booked my passage to England.'

Well, whichever way he went there was danger, but Raoul could not deny that the going would be easier if he had money.

'Very well,' he said. 'I will help you.'

She smiled, visibly relieved.

'Good.' She put out her hand. 'In England our tradesmen shake hands on a bargain. We will do the same, if you please.'

His brows went up, but after a brief hesitation he

took her hand. Once they had shaken solemnly he did not let go, but carried her hand to his lips.

'Now I consider our bargain sealed, milady.'

He might have been holding a wild bird, the way her fingers fluttered within his grasp. Desire reared up again and he wanted to pull her into his arms. A shadow of alarm crossed her face. Had she read his mind? Perhaps she, too, was recalling that moment in the pool when she had wrapped herself about him, their warm bodies melding together in the cold water. Had she felt that tug of attraction?

'Yes, very well.' She pulled her hand free and turned away from him, saying briskly, 'If we are going to travel together, then the first thing is to find you a decent set of clothes, and a razor. You are a disgrace. I cannot have my servant dressed in rags.'

His lip curled. There was his answer. That was what she thought of him.

'So, *madame*, I am to be your servant?'

The look she gave him would have frozen the sun.

'Of course. I am the daughter of a marquess and—'

He broke in angrily. 'I do not acknowledge that your *birth* gives you superiority over me.'

Cassie had been about to confess that it would not be easy for her to imitate the behaviour of a servant. She had intended it to be self-deprecating, but his retort sent all such thoughts flying and she responded with icy hauteur.

'I shall be *paying* you for your services, *monsieur*, since I have money and you do not.'

She was immediately ashamed of her response. It was ill bred, but his bitter interruption, the assumption that she was so full of conceit as to think herself superior, had angered her. Yet that in itself was wrong. What was it about this man that put her usual sunny nature to flight so easily? She was still pondering the problem when he jumped to his feet.

'Well, now we have settled our roles in this little charade we should be on our way.'

He held out his hand to her, his face unsmiling, his eyes black and cold. As he pulled her to her feet Cassie bit back the urge to say something conciliatory.

This is how it should be. You do not want to become too close to this man.

He would help her reach England, she would pay him. It was a business arrangement, nothing more.

When they reached the city gates the road was so crowded and bustling with traders and carriages they were able to slip through without being questioned. The savoury aroma of food emanating from a busy tavern tempted them to stop and dine.

'What do we do now?' asked Cassie, when they had finished their meal and were once more on the street, Raoul leading their tired horse. 'My preference is to find a respectable inn, like the one ahead of us, but...' she paused and, recalling their recent altercation, she chose her next words carefully '...I fear our appearance would cause comment.'

Raoul rubbed his chin. 'Yours may be explained by an accident to the carriage, but I agree my clothes are not suitable for a manservant. I have a plan, but I will need money, milady.'

Her eyes narrowed. 'What do you intend?'

'You will go ahead of me, tell them your servant follows. I will find new clothes and join you in an hour.'

Cassie dug a handful of coins from her purse and gave them to him, then she watched him walk away. There was a tiny *frisson* of anxiety at the thought that he might not return.

'Well if he does not come back there is nothing I can do about it,' she told herself as she turned her own steps towards the inn.

Despite her own dishevelled appearance Cassie's assured manner and generous advance payment secured rooms without difficulty. She requested a jug of hot water and set about repairing the ravages to her hair and her dress. She was only partly successful, but once she had washed her face and hands and re-dressed her hair she felt much more presentable. A servant came in to light the candles and Cassie realised with a start that darkness was falling outside now. Where was Raoul?

She sat down on a chair and folded her hands in her lap, willing herself to be calm. If he had taken the money and gone on his way she could hardly blame him, but she could not help feeling a little betrayed and also very slightly frightened at the thought of being alone.

Her ears caught the thud of quick steps on the stairs and she rose, looking expectantly towards the door, only to stare open-mouthed as a stranger entered the room.

Gone was the rough beard and shaggy, unkempt hair. Gone, too, were the ragged clothes. In fact, the only things about Raoul Doulevant that she recognised were his dark eyes, alight with laughter.

He was, she realised with a shock, devastatingly handsome. His black hair had been cut and brushed back from his brow. His cheeks, free of the heavy black beard, were lean and smooth above the firm jaw. His lips were so finely sculpted that Cassie felt a sensuous shiver run through her just looking at them. He stood tall and straight in a coat of dark-blue wool that stretched over powerful shoulders. The white linen at his throat and wrists accentuated the deep tan of his skin, while his long legs were encased in buckskins and top boots that showed his athletic limbs to advantage. To complete the ensemble he held a pair of tan gloves and a tall hat in hands. He flourished a deep bow and Cassie swallowed, unable to take her eyes off him. The laughter in his eyes deepened.

'Well, milady, do I have your approval?'

'Very much so.' Her voice was nothing more than a croak and she coughed, hoping to clear whatever was blocking her throat. 'Where did you find such elegant clothes in this little town?'

He grinned. 'There are ways.'

It was all he would say and she did not press him. On closer inspection it was seen that the coat and breeches were not new and although the boots were highly polished they bore signs of wear. However, Raoul Doulevant presented the picture of a very respectable gentleman and Cassie glanced ruefully at her own clothes.

'I fear the servant is now more grand than the mistress.'

'That *is* a concern,' agreed Raoul, coming further into the room. 'When I arrived the landlord took me for your husband.'

'Oh, heavens.' She put a hand to her cheek, distracted by memories of standing with him beneath the waterfall. Suddenly her mind was filled with wild thoughts of what it might be like to be married to such a man. She closed her eyes for a moment. It would be disastrous. She had rushed into a marriage once and had suffered the consequences. Falling out of love had been almost too painful to bear. She would not go through that again.

'Our host appears to be in some confusion over our name, too,' Raoul continued, unaware of her agitation. 'I told him we are Madame and Monsieur Duval.' Her eyes flew open as he continued. 'I believe, upon reflection, that it would be best if we travel as man and wife.' He put up his hand to silence her protest. 'I considered saying we were brother and sister, but although your French is enchanting, milady, you do not speak it like a native.'

'No, but—'

'And it would be impossible to pass you off as my servant, you are far too arrogant.'

'I am not arrogant!'

He continued as if she had not spoken.

'No, it must be as man and wife. It is settled.'

Cassie took a long and indignant breath, preparing to make a withering retort but he caught her eye and said with quiet deliberation, 'You asked for my help, milady.'

There was steel in his voice and she knew it would be dangerous to cross him. She doubted he had ever intended to travel as her servant. Well, she had a choice—she could dispense with his escort, and thus break the bargain they had struck, or she could go along with his plan. The infuriating thing was she could not think of a better one.

'Man and wife in name only,' she told him imperiously.

'Even after the...er...intimacies we shared in that shady pool?'

The laughter was back in his eyes, although his voice was perfectly serious. Cassie fought down her temper. He was teasing her, he *enjoyed* teasing her.

'We shared nothing but being in the same water,' was her crushing reply. 'It was a mistake and will not be repeated.'

'No, milady.'

'It should be easy enough to keep a safe distance between us. It is not as if we are in love, after all.'

'Indeed not.'

'And in my opinion,' she continued airily, 'love is an emotion that is best left to poets and artists. Its importance in real life is grossly exaggerated.'

'Truly? You believe that?'

He folded his arms and regarded her with amusement. Really, she thought angrily, he was much more at home in these new clothes. He was so assured. So arrogant!

Even as she fumed with indignation he said, grinning, 'Explain yourself, milady, if you please.'

Very well, she would tell him. Cassie had had plenty of time to ponder on this over the past year. She waved her hand.

'What passes for love is mere lust on the man's part. It makes him profess feelings he does not truly feel and engenders a false affection that can never last.' He was still grinning at her. Cassie said bluntly, 'Let us say that the man is led by what is in his breeches, not his heart. And for the woman, why, it is nothing more than a foolish infatuation that fades quickly once she becomes better acquainted with her swain. Marital bliss and heavenly unions are not to be had by mere mortals. I am right,' she insisted, when he had the audacity to laugh at her. 'I have been—am married, after all. I know what goes on between a man and a woman. It is not as special as the poets would have us believe.'

'If you think that, milady, it occurs to me that your husband is not an expert lover.'

Her brows rose. 'And you are, perhaps?'

'I have had no complaints.'

She met his dark, laughing eyes and for one panic-stricken moment she feared he meant to offer a demonstration of his prowess. She said hastily, 'This is a most improper discussion. Let us say no more about it.'

'Very well. But I fear my next news will not please you. Our host sends a thousand pardons to milady, but the servant's room is not available.' He patted his pocket. 'He has refunded your payment for it.'

Cassie's eyes narrowed and, as if reading her mind Raoul put up his hands.

'This is no plan of mine, I assure you. The prefect has bespoke the room for a visitor and the landlord dare not refuse him. We must think ourselves fortunate he did not throw us out on the streets.'

Cassie was in no mood to consider anything but the fact that she must now share a room with this insufferable man. She dragged two of the blankets from the bed and handed them to him.

'Then *you* will sleep on the floor!'

With that she threw a couple of pillows on to the chair, climbed up on the bed and pulled the curtains shut around her.

Cassie sat in the dark, straining her ears for every sound from the room. She was half-afraid Raoul might tear open the curtains and demand to share the bed. She remained fully dressed and tense, listening to him moving about the room, and it was not until she heard the steady sound of his breathing that she finally struggled out of her riding habit and slipped beneath the covers.

Raoul scowled at the blankets in his hand. By the saints, how would he make himself comfortable with these? But honesty compelled him to admit it was no more than he deserved. It was his teasing that had angered her, but for the life of him he could not help it. He had seen the flash in her eyes when he walked in. It had been a look of admiration, nay, attraction, and it had set his pulse racing. He had been determined to treat her as an employer, to convey the landlord's news dispassionately and then they might have discussed the sleeping arrangements like two sensible adults. Instead he had given in to the temptation to bring that sparkle back to her eyes. He grinned at the memory. Even now part of him could not regret it, she looked magnificent when she was roused, a mixture of arrogance and innocence that was irresistible. With a sigh be began to spread the blankets on the floor. And these was his deserts. Well, he would make the most of it. He had slept in worse places.

Cassie had no idea of the time when she woke, until she peeped out through the curtains to find the sun streaming into the bedchamber. Cautiously she pushed back the hangings. The room was empty, the blankets and pillows on the floor showing her where Raoul had slept, but there was no sign of the man himself. Cassie slipped off the bed and dressed quickly, but a strange emptiness filled her as she wondered if Raoul had left for good. Perhaps, when he had realised she would not succumb to his advances he had decided to go his own way. The thought was strangely depressing and she could not prevent hope leaping in her breast when she heard someone outside the door, nor could she stop her smile of relief when Raoul strode into the room, a couple of large packages beneath one arm and a rather battered bandbox dangling from his hand. His brows rose when he saw her.

'I hardly expected such a warm welcome, milady.'

'I thought you had gone,' she confessed.

'And break our bargain? I am not such a rogue.' He handed her the parcels. 'I had a little money left from yesterday, plus the reimbursement from the landlord, and I decided to see if I could find something suitable to augment your wardrobe. There is also a trunk following; to travel without baggage is to invite curiosity, is it not?'

She barely acknowledged his last words, for she was busy opening the first of the packages. It contained a selection of items for Cassie's comfort including a brush and comb and a new chemise. The second was a round gown of yellow muslin with a matching shawl.

'Oh,' she said, holding up the gown. 'Th-thank you.'

'I had to guess your size, but it is fastened by tapes and should fit you. And there is this.' He put the bandbox on the table and lifted out a straw bonnet. 'The fine weather looks set to continue and I thought this might be suitable.'

'Oh,' she said again. 'I—thank you. I am very grateful.'

'I cannot have my wife dressed in rags. My wife

in name only,' he added quickly. 'Although after last night we must make sure we demand a truckle bed for the maid.'

'But we do not have a maid.'

'We shall say she is following on and then complain that she has not turned up. At least then I shall have a cot to sleep in.'

'You seem to have thought of everything, *monsieur*.'

'I spent a damned uncomfortable night considering the matter,' he retorted. 'Now, *madame*, shall we go downstairs and break our fast?'

Chapter Four

The lure of a fresh gown was too tempting to resist.
Cassandra begged Raoul to wait for her downstairs and
twenty minutes later she joined him in the dining room
dressed in her new yellow muslin. She saw his eyes
widen with appreciation and was woman enough to
feel pleased about it. They were alone in the room at
that moment and as Raoul held the chair for her Cassie
murmured her thanks again.

'The gown fits very well, *monsieur*, and the maid has
promised to have my riding habit brushed and packed
by the time we are ready to leave.'

'Good.' He took his seat opposite and cast an apprais-
ing eye over her. 'The woman in the shop was correct,
that colour is perfect for you.'

Cassie looked up, intrigued. 'How then did you describe me to her?'

'A petite brunette with the most unusual violet eyes.'

'Oh.' Cassie blushed. 'Th-thank you, *monsieur*.'

Raoul berated himself silently. She thought he was
complimenting her, but it had not been his intention. It

was true he thought her beautiful, but he did not wish
her to know that. Confound it, he did not want to admit
the fact to himself. He gave his attention to his breakfast. He had told the truth, nothing more.

While she was busy pouring herself a cup of coffee
he took another quick glance. There was no denying
it, she *was* beautiful. The lemon gown enhanced her
creamy skin and set off the dusky curls that she had
brushed until they shone. She had pinned up her hair,
accentuating the slender column of her throat and her
bare shoulders that rose from the low-cut corsage. His
pulse leapt and he quickly returned his gaze to his plate.
Strange how the sight should affect him. After all, he
had seen her shoulders before, and more, when she had
been bathing in the lake. But something was different.
He looked up again. Yes, there was a thin gold chain
around her neck from which was suspended an oval
locket set with a single ruby. But it was not the jewel
that held his attention, it was the fact that the ornament
rested low on her neck, directing the eye to the shadowed valley of her breasts.

'You are staring at me, *monsieur*. Is something
wrong?'

Raoul cleared his throat.

'I have not seen that trinket before.'

'The locket?' She put one hand up to her breast.
'Until today I have worn it beneath my riding shirt.
It is the last of my jewellery. I sold the rest to pay for
my journey.'

'It holds special memories for you, perhaps.'

Her hand closed over it.

'A portrait of my husband.'

'Ah. I understand.'

* * *

Cassie did not reply, but gave her attention to finishing her breakfast. It was better that he thought she loved her husband. She was now sure enough of his character to know he would not wish to seduce another man's wife.

They left Reims looking every inch a respectable couple. The trunk was packed and strapped on to the hired chaise, Cassie made herself comfortable inside, and Raoul rode as escort on the long-tailed bay. Their journey continued without incident. Cassie had given Raoul sufficient funds to pay for their board and lodgings, they were civil to one another when they stopped to dine on the road, and Raoul made no demur about sleeping in a dressing room at the wayside inn that provided their lodgings for the night. Their fear of discovery receded, too, for whereas the soldiers at the bridges and *gendarmes* at the town gates might question a pair of ragged travellers, a wealthy gentleman and his wife roused no suspicions and they were waved through without question. However, she agreed with Raoul that they should take a more circuitous route and avoid the main highway, which was constantly busy with soldiers. Their journey was going well. Raoul was very different from Merimon, her first, rascally escort, and she knew she was fortunate that he was such an honourable man.

Cassie wondered why, then, she should feel so discontented. Her eyes moved to the window and to the figure of Raoul, mounted upon the long tailed bay. She wanted him. She wanted him to hold her, to make love to her.

Shocking. Reprehensible. Frightening. She had already admitted to herself that eloping had been a mistake. How much more of a mistake to allow herself to develop a *tendre* for a man like Raoul Doulevant? A man whom she would not see again once she returned to England. Besides, it was nothing more than lust, she knew that. They were constantly at odds with one another and had he not told her himself he had no cause to like the English? Reluctantly she shifted her gaze away from him. No, much better to keep her distance, it would be madness to allow the undoubted attraction between them to take hold. If only she could forget what had happened in the lake, forget his kiss, the way it felt to have her naked body pressed close to his, the heat that had flowed between them despite the cool water.

She gave herself a little shake. The strong yearning she felt was because she was lonely. The last few months with Gerald had been very unhappy. She had no close friends in Verdun and loyalty had kept her from confiding her problems to anyone. Once she was back in England, living with Grandmama, taking up her old life again, she would be able to put from her mind her time in France. She smoothed out the skirts of her yellow muslin and tried to smother the quiet voice that told her Raoul Doulevant would not be easy to forget.

It was some time past noon and they were passing over a particularly uneven section of road when there was a sudden splintering crash and the carriage shuddered to a halt, lurching drunkenly into the ditch. Cassie was thrown from her seat and was lying dazed against the side of the carriage that now appeared to be the floor when the door above her opened. She heard Raoul's voice, sharp with concern.

'Are you hurt?'

Cassie moved cautiously.

'I do not think so.'

He reached down to her. She grasped his hand and he lifted her out of the chaise and on to the ground. She found she was shaking and clung to Raoul for a moment until her legs would once more support her.

'What happened?' she asked him.

'One of the wheels is broken,' said Raoul, adding bitterly, 'It is no surprise when you look at the state of the road. We should be thankful the windows did not shatter.'

'Ah, well, you see, now the aristos are gone there's no one to pay for the upkeep.'

They looked around to find a burly individual standing behind them. The man jerked a thumb over his shoulder.

'The great house back there. When the family was in residence they paid handsomely to maintain this road in good condition for all their fine friends. Since they've gone...' he shrugged '...no one around here cares to repair it for others to use.'

'Who are you?' Raoul asked him. 'Do you live at the chateau?'

'No, but I farm the land hereabouts and live in the grounds with my wife. Looking after the place, you might say.'

Cassie glanced through the trees towards the large house in the distance. The once-grand building looked decidedly sorry for itself, windows broken and shutters hanging off.

'Then you are not looking after it very well,' said Raoul, giving voice to Cassie's thoughts.

'Ah, good *monsieur*, I am but a humble farmer. The damage occurred when the family left.' He spat on the ground. 'They are either dead or fled abroad and I have neither the money nor authority to repair it. I merely keep an eye on it, so to speak.'

'Enough,' said Raoul. 'It is not our concern. We need to get this chaise repaired, and quickly.'

The man lifted his cap and scratched his head.

'The nearest wheelwright is back the way you came.'

'I was afraid of that,' Raoul muttered. 'Even if we were riding we would be hard pressed to get back there by nightfall. Is there an inn nearby and perhaps a chaise that we might hire?'

The man spread his hands and shrugged. '*Monsieur*, I am desolated, but I have only a tumbril. The nearest inn is back in the town.' He brightened. 'But all is not lost. I can provide you with shelter for the night.'

Cassie looked to Raoul, but he had gone to help the postilion free the horses from the overturned chaise. Only when they were securely tethered to a tree did he return. The postilion was beside him and it was clear they had been considering the situation.

'I think the best thing is for the post boy to take my horse and ride back to the town,' said Raoul. 'Tomorrow he can bring a new wheel and help to repair the chaise. In the meantime we need to stable the carriage horses.'

'Well, the stables were burned out some years ago, but you can put them in the barn,' replied the farmer genially. 'And in the morning I have a team of oxen that we might use to pull the carriage out of the ditch. For a price, of course.'

'Yes, well, we will come to that once the postilion has returned.'

Raoul issued a few brief instructions and the post boy scrambled up on to the bay. Cassie watched him trot away and turned back to where Raoul and the farmer were discussing the next problem.

'We require a room for the night. You say you can accommodate us, how much will you charge?'

'Ah, *monsieur*, my own house is small and my wife's aged mother is bedridden, so I have no bedchamber I can offer for you. But do not despair, you and your lady are welcome to sleep in the barn.'

'The barn!' exclaimed Cassie.

'But, yes, *madame*. It is a very good barn. The roof is sound and there is plenty of room for you and the horses. The animals keep it warm and there is plenty of clean straw.'

An indignant protest rose to Cassie's lips, but Raoul put a warning hand on her shoulder.

'Let us get the horses into shelter first,' he said. 'Then we will discuss our accommodation.'

Silently Cassie accompanied the two men as they led the horses off the road and through the gap in the hedge into the remains of the chateau's formal gardens. The wide gravelled paths were so overgrown with weeds they were difficult to discern from the flowerbeds, and what had once been parterres and manicured lawns were now grazed by cattle. As they approached the house itself she could see it was in a very sorry state, the stucco was peeling, tiles had shifted on the roof and weeds flourished on the surrounding terrace. Cassie could not help exclaiming at the sight.

'How sad to see such a fine house in ruins.'

'There are many such places in France now, *madame*.' The farmer grinned at her. 'But it is empty and you are free to sleep there, if it's more to your taste than my barn over there.'

The farmer indicated a collection of large buildings set back and to one side of the main house. Cassie guessed they had once been outhouses and servants' quarters. What looked like the stable block was no more than a burned-out shell, but the other buildings and a small house beside it were now the farmer's domain. He led the way to one of the large barns. The sweet smell of straw was overlaid with the stronger tang of cattle. Cassie quickly pulled out her handkerchief and held it over her nose. It did not surprise her that the carriage horses objected to being led inside, but with a little persuasion and encouragement from Raoul they were eventually stabled securely at one end of the great building, as far away as possible from the farmer's oxen.

'You see,' declared their host, looking about him proudly, 'there is plenty of room. So where would you like to sleep, here or in yonder palace?'

Cassie sent Raoul a beseeching look and prayed he would understand her.

Raoul grinned. 'We'll bed down in the chateau, my friend.' He winked and gave the farmer's arm a playful punch. 'My wife has always considered herself a fine lady.'

The man shrugged. 'It will cost you the same.' He added, as Raoul counted out the money on to his palm, 'You'll find it pretty bare, *monsieur*, but 'tis weatherproof, mostly. I'll bring your dinner in an hour, as well as candles and clean straw for your bed.'

Raoul added an extra coin. 'Can you have our trunk brought in, too? I would not want it left at the roadside overnight.'

'With pleasure, *monsieur*. My boy shall help me with it as soon as I've told the wife to prepare dinner for you.'

The farmer went off, gazing with satisfaction at the money in his hand.

'We might perhaps have argued for a lower price,' observed Raoul, 'but I suspect the fellow will serve us well in the hope of earning himself a little extra before we leave here tomorrow.' He turned to Cassie. 'Shall we go and inspect our quarters?'

He held out his arm and she placed her fingers on his sleeve.

'I am relieved that I do not have to sleep with the animals,' she confessed.

'I could see that the idea did not appeal. However, I doubt the chateau will be much better. I expect everything of value has been removed.'

'We shall see.'

Her optimistic tone cheered him. He had expected an angry demand that they should go on to find an inn and was fully prepared to ask her just how she thought they were to get there with no saddle horse. There was also the trunk to be considered; having purchased it he did not think she would wish to leave it behind. But instead of being discontented the lady appeared sanguine, even eager to explore the chateau. They went up the steps to the terrace and carefully pulled open one of the long windows. The glass had shattered and it scrunched beneath their feet as they stepped into a large, high-ceilinged salon. A few pieces of broken furniture were strewn over the marble floor, the decorative plasterwork of the fireplace was smashed and there were signs in one corner that someone had tried to set light to the building. He heard Cassie sigh.

'Oh, this is so sad, to think of the family driven out of their home.'

'It was no more than they deserved, if they oppressed those dependent upon them.'

'But you do not know that they did,' she reasoned. 'In England we heard many tales of innocent families being forced to flee for their lives.'

'What else would you expect them to say? They would hardly admit that they lived in luxury while people were starving.'

'No doubt you believe it was right to send so many men and women to the guillotine, merely because of their birth.'

'Of course not. But I do *not* believe a man's birth gives him the right to rule others. Aristocrats like yourself are brought up to believe you belong to a superior race and the English are the very worst!'

Cassie smiled. 'You will not expect me to agree with you on *that*, *monsieur*.' She looked around her once again. 'But while I admit there are good and bad people in the world, I cannot believe that all France's great families were bad landlords. Some will have fled because there was no reasoning with a powerful mob.'

'But before that the king and his court were too powerful, and would not listen to reason,' Raoul argued.

'Perhaps.' She walked to the centre of the room and turned around slowly, looking about her. 'I grew up in rooms very like this. A large, cold mansion, far too big to be comfortable. I much prefer Grandmama's house in Royal Crescent. That is in Bath,' she explained.

'I have heard of it,' he said. 'It has the hot baths, does it not?'

'Yes. Many elderly and sick people go there to take the waters.' Her eyes twinkled. 'And many wealthy people who *think* they are sick enjoy living there, too, and pay high prices for dubious treatments. The doctors of Bath have grown fat giving out pills and placebos to the rich and privileged. It is not as fashionable as it once was, but it is still very pleasant with its concerts, and balls and the theatre, and all one's friends in such close proximity. I lived there very happily with Grandmama until...'

'Until you met your husband?'

'Yes. I have not seen Bath for nearly eighteen months.'

'You must have had the very great love to elope with this man,' he said. 'To give up your family and friends, everything you knew.'

He saw a shadow flicker across her eyes before she turned away from him.

'Yes.'

Cassie hurried across the room, giving Raoul no time to question her further. A very great love? It had been a very great foolishness. She had ignored Grandmama's warnings and thrown her cap over the windmill. She had been in love with Gerald then. Or at least, she had thought herself in love, but the last few months had brought her nothing but pain and disillusion. She had learned that love could not make one happy, it was merely a device used by men to delude poor, foolish females. She had witnessed it often enough in Verdun, especially amongst Gerald's friends. A gentleman would profess himself hopelessly in love, then as soon as he had seduced the object of his affection the passion would fade and he would move on to another lover. A salutary lesson and one she would never forget.

Pushing aside the unwelcome thoughts, Cassie grasped the handles of the double doors and threw them wide, drawing in a sharp breath at the sight of the once-magnificent ballroom before her. 'Oh, how wonderful it must have been to dance in a room such as this!'

She wandered into the cavernous space. The walls were pale primrose with huge blocks of darker yellow where large paintings had once hung. Between the windows were gilded mirror frames, the glass shattered and glittering on the floor. At each end of the room four Italian-marble pillars rose up and supported a ceiling that was decorated with a glorious scene of cherubs playing hide-and-seek amongst white clouds.

'Oh, how I loved to dance,' she murmured wistfully. 'Grandmama took me to so many assemblies in Bath and it is one of the things I have missed most since my marriage. Gerald never took me to balls.'

A wave of unhappiness washed over her, so suddenly that it took her by surprise. She pressed her clasped hands to her chest and was obliged to bite her lip to hold back a sob. It had been a shock to discover so recently that her husband had escorted plenty of other ladies to balls in Verdun. She was a fool to let it upset her now. Gerald could never resist a pretty woman. In the end that had been his downfall.

Raoul watched as sadness clouded her face and suddenly he was overwhelmed with the need to drive the unhappiness from her eyes. He stepped closer, saying recklessly,

'Then let us dance now.'

She frowned at him. 'I beg your pardon?'

'I say we should dance.'

She laughed as he plucked the shawl from her shoulders and tossed it aside.

'But we have no music, *monsieur.*'

'I will sing for us.' He took her hand. 'What shall it be, the Allemande?'

He started to hum a lively tune and bowed. Cassie looked a little bemused, but she followed his lead, singing along quietly as she twisted beneath his arm and stretched up to let him turn beneath hers. By the time they performed the rosette, holding both hands and twirling at the same time, she was giggling too much to sing. Raoul persevered, leading her through the dance steps again. He felt inordinately pleased that he had put that troubled look to flight and as they skipped and stepped and twirled about his imagination took flight.

They were no longer dancing in a derelict house, but in a glittering ballroom with the most accomplished musicians playing for them. The music soared in his head and he imagined them both dressed in their finery. He could almost feel the shirt of finest linen against his skin, the starched folds of the neckcloth with a single diamond nestling at his throat. And instead of that poor yellow muslin, Cassie was wearing a ball gown of silk with diamonds glittering against her skin, although nothing could outshine the glow of her eyes as she looked up at him. When they performed the final rosette and ended, hands locked, she was laughing up at

Raoul in a way that made his heart leap into his throat, stopping his breath.

Time stopped, too, as their eyes met. Raoul had felt this same connection between them before, but this time it was stronger, like a thread drawing them together. He watched the laughter die from those violet-blue eyes, replaced by a softer, warmer look that melted his heart and set his pulse racing even faster. His heart was pounding so hard that he felt light-headed and quite unsteady. His grip on her hands tightened. Those cherry-red lips were only inches away, inviting his kiss.

Cassie's heart was beating so heavily that it was difficult to breathe. Raoul was standing before her, holding her hands, filling her senses. He was all she could see, his ragged breathing the only sound she heard. She was swathed in his powerful presence and it felt wonderful.

Kiss me.

She read it in his eyes. An order, a plea that went straight to her heart and filled her soul. She clung to his hands, trembling. She desperately wanted to close the gap between them and step into his arms, but above the excitement and exhilaration that filled her an alarm bell clamoured, faint but insistent. She knew there would be no going back if she gave in now. Raoul would take her, consume her, and she would be lost. It was a perilous situation; she was a widow, alone in an enemy country.

Strange, that this foolish, impromptu dance had so quickly driven all her troubles from her mind, but now that alarm bell could not be ignored. It was not just the physical perils that threatened her. She had thought Gerald had broken her heart, but now some instinct told her that if she gave herself to Raoul the parting would be much, much worse. That thought frightened her more than all the rest and made her fight for control.

She dragged up a laugh. 'Well, that has surprised me.'

Clearly not a gentleman!

Those scornful words echoed in Raoul's brain, reminding him of the gulf between them. He dropped her hands and moved away, allowing his indignation to turn into anger. It was necessary, if he was to combat this attraction that could only end in disaster. He should be pleased she was in no danger of falling in love with him. He had no room for a woman in his life and he would not want her broken heart on his conscience.

'Yes, you considered me a savage, did you not?' he threw at her. 'Because I have not lived in your exalted circles. Whatever you might think of me, *madame*, my birth is respectable even if I was not born into the nobility. We moved amongst the first families of Brussels. My father was a doctor, a gentleman. It was *I* who let him down; I was determined to become a surgeon, despite the fact that many still regard them as mere tradesmen.' He turned his finger, stabbing angrily into the air. '*That* is where the future lies, in a man's skill and knowledge, not in his birth. But you and your kind do not recognise that yet. My father never recognised it, either. He was disappointed; he had such high hopes of me.'

Cassie saw the fire in his eyes and heard the bitterness behind his harsh words, but she knew his anger was not directed at her. He had misunderstood her, but in his present mood it would be useless to try and explain so she made no attempt to correct him.

She said carefully, 'Parents are always ambitious for their children. At least, I believe that is the case. My own parents died when I was very young, but Grandmama always wanted the best for me. It must have grieved her most dreadfully when I eloped.' She touched his arm, saying gently, 'There must still be a little time before the farmer will bring our dinner. Shall we continue to explore?'

Raoul shrugged.

'Why not?' he said lightly. He scooped her shawl from the floor and laid it around her shoulders. She noted how carefully he avoided actually touching her. 'Lead on, *madame*.'

The magical moment was broken, shattered like the ornate mirrors and tall windows. She felt the chill of disappointment and tried hard to be thankful that she had not weakened. A momentary lapse now would cost her dear.

The chateau had been stripped bare and they did not linger on the upper floors. Cassie pulled her shawl a little closer around her as the shadows lengthened and the chill of evening set in. She had been a child when the revolution in France had begun, only ten years old when King Louis had been murdered. It had been the talk of English drawing rooms and inevitably the news had reached the schoolroom, too. She had listened to the stories, but only now, standing in this sad shell of a house, did she have any conception of the hate and fear that must have been rife in France. She could only be thankful that such a bloody revolution had not occurred in England.

'It grows dark,' said Raoul. 'We should go down and look out for our host.'

Cassie readily agreed. The stairs were in semi-darkness and when Raoul reached for her hand she did not pull away. She told herself it was merely a precaution, lest she trip in the dim light, but there was no mistaking the comfort she gained from his warm grasp. They heard the farmer's deep voice bellowing from somewhere in the lower regions of the house and as they reached the hall he emerged from the basement stairs.

'So there you are,' he greeted them. 'We've put your dinner in the kitchen and my boy is lighting a fire there now. You'll find 'tis the most comfortable room, the windows are intact and there's a table, too.'

They followed him down to the servants' quarters and through a maze of dark corridors until they reached the kitchen. It was a large chamber, but a cheerful fire burned in the huge fireplace and numerous candles had been placed about the room to provide light. A plump woman with a spotless apron tied over her cambric gown was setting out their dinner on the scrubbed wooden table and the farmer introduced her as his wife. She looked up and fixed her sharp black eyes upon Raoul and Cassie. It was a blatantly curious stare and not a little scornful. Cassie's head lifted and haughty words rose to her lips, but she fought them down. She had no wish to antagonise the woman, so she smiled and tried to speak pleasantly.

'It is very good of you to let us stay here tonight.'

The woman relaxed slightly.

'*Eh bien*, your money's good and I suppose you will prefer this to sharing a bedchamber with the animals. The boy'll be over with a couple of sacks of straw later and he'll collect the dishes, too.' She pointed to a small door in the corner of the room. 'There's a water pump in the scullery. It still works, if you need it.'

'Thank you.'

The woman moved towards the door.

'We will leave you, then.' She gave a reluctant curtsy and followed her husband out into the dusk.

'We should eat.' Raoul indicated the bench.

They sat together and Cassie was relieved that there would be no awkward glances across the table. In fact, there was no need to look at him at all. They were facing the fireplace, where the fire crackled merrily and they could eat their meal in companionable silence. But it was *not* companionable, it pressed around her, pricking at her conscience and making her uneasy. At last she was unable to bear it any longer and had to speak, however inane her conversation.

'This is where they would have cooked the food,' she said at last, keeping her eyes on the dancing flames.

'Yes.' Raoul reached across to pick up the wine flask and poured more into their glasses. 'The turning-spit mechanism and all the cooking irons have been plundered. No doubt they have found a home elsewhere, or been melted down and turned into farm tools.'

Cassie picked up her wine glass and turned it this way and that, so that the crystal glinted and sparkled in the candlelight.

'These are very fine, perhaps the owners of this house used to drink from them.'

'And now they are being used by their tenants,' remarked Raoul coolly. 'It is merely a redistribution of wealth.'

Her chin went up a little and she turned to regard him. 'Something you heartily approve.'

Raoul met her eyes steadily. 'I have never approved of violence, Lady Cassandra. It is my calling to save lives, not take them.'

She turned her gaze back to the fireplace, knowing she did not wish to fight him tonight.

'So they cooked on an open fire. How old-fashioned,' she murmured, thinking of the closed range in Grandmama's house in Bath.

'There might well have been a dozen or more servants in here,' Raoul replied. 'Slaving to provide meals for their masters.'

'Not necessarily slaving,' Cassie demurred. 'In Bath my grandmother was at pains to provide the very best equipment for her cook. She said he is a positive tyrant.'

'Yet she has the power to dismiss him on a whim.'

Cassie shook her head, smiling a little. 'You are wrong, sir. The man is very aware of his own worth and paid well for his skills, I assure you. He also is the one with the power to hire or dismiss his staff as he wishes.' Her smile grew. 'And before you berate me again for the inequality of English society, I would tell you, *monsieur*, that the cook is a Frenchman.'

He grinned, acknowledging the hit.

'Very well, I will admit that it is in most men's nature to be a tyrant if they are not checked.' He turned slightly and raised his glass to her. 'A truce, Lady Cassandra?'

She returned his salute. 'A truce, Monsieur Doulevant.'

They returned their attention to the food, but the atmosphere had changed. Cassie no longer felt at odds with her companion and she was a great deal happier.

A basket of logs had been placed near the fireplace, but the size of the hearth was such that it was soon emptied and by the time the farmer's boy brought over their bedding and carried away the empty dishes the room was growing chilly.

'We should get some sleep,' said Raoul. 'We will have another busy day tomorrow.'

There were two sacks of straw. Raoul placed one on either side of the kitchen table and handed Cassie one of the two blankets that had been provided.

'Your bed awaits, my lady.'

She tried to make herself comfortable, but the sack was not well filled and the straw flattened quickly beneath her. She could not help a sigh that sounded very loud in the quiet, echoing kitchen.

'Is it not luxurious enough for you, my lady?'

Tiredness made her irritable and she snapped back.

'This is not what I expected when I left Verdun.'

'I am surprised your husband agreed to your travelling alone.'

'He did not agree. He's—'

She bit off the words.

'He what?' Raoul asked suspiciously. 'He does not know?'

'That is true.'

It was not exactly a lie. Cassie knew it would sink her even further in his estimation, yet she was unwilling to admit she was a widow. She clung to the belief that there was some small protection in having a husband.

'But of course. You told me yourself that you grew bored at Verdun. *Tiens*, I feel even more sympathy for your spouse, *madame*. You have quite literally abandoned him, have you not?'

The darkness was filled with his disapproval. It cut her and she responded by saying sharply, 'That is not your concern.'

'No indeed. *Mon Dieu*, but you are a heartless woman!'

'You know nothing about me!'

Tell him, Cassie. Explain how you remained with your husband, endured the pain and humiliation of knowing he only wanted your fortune.

Pride kept her silent. Better Raoul should think her heartless than a fool. She turned on her side and pulled the thin blanket a little closer around her. 'Oh, how I pray there will be a ship in Rouen that will carry me all the way to England,' she muttered angrily. 'The sooner we can say goodbye to one another the better.'

He gave a bark of bitter laughter.

'Amen to that, my lady!'

Chapter Five

It took the best part of the morning to repair the chaise. Discussions with the farmer elicited the information that their meandering route, chosen to minimise the chances of encountering soldiers on the road or passing an army garrison, meant that they were a good half-day's drive away from Rouen and he doubted they would reach the city before nightfall, but Cassie was as anxious as Raoul to press on and echoed his refusal to remain another night.

She climbed into the chaise and watched Raoul scramble up on to the long-tailed bay. She was thankful he was not in the carriage with her, she did not enjoy travelling in the company of one who disapproved of her so blatantly. He saw her as a rich and spoiled lady who had run away from her marriage when the novelty had begun to pall. It would be useless to explain, because she knew that men saw these things differently. A wife was a mere chattel, was she not?

Cassie looked up as the chaise slowed. The road was winding its way between dilapidated cottages at the edge of a village. Through the window she watched

Raoul exchange a few words with the postilion before bringing his horse alongside the carriage. Cassie let down the glass.

'This is Flagey, it is very small and the post boy tells me there is a much better inn about an hour from here where we may change horses and dine,' he informed her. 'If we do not tarry he thinks we may still make Rouen tonight.'

'Very well, let us push on. I—' Cassie broke off as a loud rumble, like thunder, filled the air. It shook the ground and the carriage jolted as the horses sidled nervously. 'What on earth was that?'

Raoul was already looking towards the cluster of buildings ahead of them. Above the roofs a cloud of dust was rising, grey as smoke. The bay threw up its head as the church bell began to toll.

'An accident of some sort,' he said, kicking his horse on. Cantering around the bend, he saw that a large building had collapsed on the far side of the village square. People were already congregating at the scene. Some of the women were wailing, a few holding crying babies, but most were helping the men to drag away the stones and rubble.

Raoul threw the horse's reins to a woman with a babe in her arms and immediately ran forward to help, casting his jacket aside as he went.

'How many men are in there?' he demanded as he joined the rescuers.

One of the men stopped to drag a grimy sleeve across his brow.

'Eight, ten, perhaps more. 'Tis the tithe barn. They were working to secure the roof before the winter when the timbers collapsed.'

Raoul joined the group, scrabbling at the wreckage. The dust was still rising from the debris, making everyone cough. It was clear that the roof had collapsed inwards, bringing down parts of the old walls. Muffled shouts and screams could be heard, so there were survivors, but Raoul knew they must reach them and quickly.

The first man they pulled out had a broken arm, but the next was badly crushed and groaning pitifully. An old woman standing beside Raoul crossed herself before trying to drag away another rotted timber. There would be more crushed bodies, more broken limbs.

'You will need a doctor. Or better still, a surgeon.'

'Dr Bonnaire is ten miles away, *monsieur.*' The old woman took a moment to straighten up, pressing her hand to her back. She nodded to a group of young men working frantically to pull away more stones. 'Jean can go, he is the fastest runner.'

'Take the horse.'

Raoul heard Cassandra's voice and turned to see her leading the bay forward.

She said again, 'Take the horse. It will be much quicker to ride.'

'Then let me go,' said an older man, stepping up. 'I can handle a horse and Jean's strength would be better used getting those poor fellows out.'

'Good idea,' agreed Raoul.

He watched the man mount up and gallop away, calculating how long it would take the doctor to get there.

'What can I do?' asked Cassandra.

'Where is the carriage?'

'I have told the post boy to drive to the *auberge* at the far end of the village. What may I do to help you?'

He regarded her as she stood before him. She was too petite to be of help moving the rubble; her hands were unused to any type of work at all. He was also afraid that they would be bringing bodies out soon and he did not want her to witness the carnage. He looked towards a group of women and children crying noisily as they watched the proceedings.

'Get them away,' he muttered. 'They are doing no good here.'

'Of course.'

She nodded and Raoul went back to the laborious process of dragging away the rubble stone by stone.

As word of the disaster spread more people turned up to help with the rescue. Raoul left them to finish digging out the survivors while he attended those they had already pulled out of the building. He had not wanted to reveal that he was a medical man, but there was no sign of the doctor and these people needed his help.

After sluicing himself down at the village pump he went to the nearest house, where the injured men had been taken. There were four so far: a quick glance showed him that the man who had been severely crushed would not survive. There was nothing he could do for the fellow so he left him to the care of the local priest while he set the broken arm and patched up the others as best he could. Thankfully they were not seriously hurt, but others were being carried in, each one bringing with him the damp, dusty smell of the collapsed building. He had no instruments and his equipment was limited to the bandages piled on a table, but there was hot water in a kettle hanging over the fire and a large flask of white brandy to ease the suffering of the injured men.

* * *

It was growing dark and Raoul was working alone in the little room when he heard the thud of horses and the sudden commotion outside the door. The doctor, at last. He looked up, his relief tempered by surprise when he saw a fresh-faced young man enter the room.

'You are Dr Bonnaire?'

'Yes. And you are?'

'Duval. My wife and I were passing through here when the accident happened.'

'It was good of you to stay and help.' Dr Bonnaire looked about him. 'Are all the men recovered, did everyone survive?'

'Everyone is accounted for now, nine men in all. Two are dead, four had only slight injuries. I patched them up and sent them home. These three are the most seriously injured.' He nodded to a man sitting by the fire. 'I have set his arm, but he has also had a blow to the head and is not yet able to stand.' He walked over to the two men lying on makeshift beds. 'These two are the worst. They were both trapped by their legs.'

As Bonnaire knelt beside the first of the men Raoul heard a soft voice behind him.

'I thought you would need more light.' Cassandra came in, followed by three of the village women, each one of them carrying lamps and candlesticks. 'We collected these from the other houses.'

The doctor shot to his feet. 'How thoughtful of you, Madame…?'

'Duval,' she said quietly.

'Ah…' he glanced towards Raoul '…your wife, sir. *Enchanté, madame.*'

Raoul saw the faint flush on Cassie's cheek and knew

she was not happy with the subterfuge, but it was necessary.

'Aye, Madame Duval and her husband arrived most providentially,' put in one of the other women.

'Madame Deschamps owns the *auberge* at the far end of the village,' explained Cassie. Her eyes flickered over Raoul and away again. 'She and her husband have offered us a room for the night.'

'Well, 'tis too late for you to be travelling on now and 'tis the least we can do, for all your trouble.'

'You are very kind,' murmured Raoul.

'Nay, 'tis you and *madame* that have been kind, *monsieur*, helping us as you have done.'

Madame Deschamps appeared to be in no hurry to leave, but once the other women had gone Cassie touched her arm and murmured that they must not keep the good doctor from his work. She cast a last, shy glance at Raoul and ushered the landlady from the room. Bonnaire stood gazing at the door and Raoul prompted him gently.

'Well, Doctor, would you like to examine your patients?'

'What? Oh, yes. Yes.'

It did not take long. Raoul had already stripped the men of their clothing and cleaned their lacerated bodies. The doctor gently drew back the thin blanket from each of the men and gazed at their lower limbs.

'Legs crushed beyond repair,' he observed.

'Yes.' Raoul nodded. 'Both men will require amputation at the knee.'

The young doctor blenched. He placed his case upon the table, saying quietly, 'I thought that might be the situation and brought my tools.'

He lifted out a canvas roll and opened it out on the table to display an impressive array of instruments, very much like the ones Raoul had lost when he had fled from Paris, only these looked dull and blunt from lack of use.

Raoul frowned. 'Have you ever performed an amputation, Doctor?'

Bonnaire swallowed and shook his head.

'I saw one once, in Paris, but I could not afford to finish my training. These tools belonged to my uncle. He was an army surgeon.'

Raoul closed his eyes, his initial relief at finding a medical man on hand rapidly draining away. He sighed.

'Then you had best let me deal with this.'

'You? You are a surgeon, Monsieur Duval?'

'Yes. And I have performed dozens of these operations.'

The relief in the young man's face was only too apparent. A sudden draught made the candles flicker as the door opened and the priest came in.

'Ah, Dr Bonnaire, they said you had arrived. Thanks be! A sad business, this. Will the Lord take any more souls this night, think you?'

'I hope not, Monsieur le Curé,' was the doctor's fervent response.

'Good, good. I came to tell you that you are not to worry about your fee, Doctor. If these poor people have not the means there is silverware in the church that can be sold. You shall not go unrewarded for this night's work.'

The young doctor bowed.

'Thank you, but if anyone is to be paid, it should be this man.' He glanced at Raoul. 'He is the more experienced surgeon and is going to perform the operations necessary to save these two men.'

'Is that so indeed?' declared the priest, his brows rising in surprise.

'It is,' said Raoul, grimly inspecting the instruments spread out before him. 'But to do so I will require these to be sharpened.'

'But of course, *monsieur*! Give me the ones you need and I shall see it is done without delay.'

'And get someone to take this fellow home,' added Raoul, nodding at the man dozing in the chair by the fire.

'I will do so, sir, I will do so.' The priest gathered up the instruments and bustled away, leaving Bonnaire to fix Raoul with a solemn gaze.

'Thank you, *monsieur*, and I meant what I said about payment.'

'I do not want the church's silverware, but you should take it, Bonnaire, and when this night is done you should use it to go back to Paris and finish your training.'

They set to work, preparing the room and arranging all the lamps and candles to provide the best light around the sturdy table that would be used to carry out the operations. The situation was not ideal, but Raoul had worked in worse conditions during his time at sea. A woman crept in timidly and helped the injured man out of the room just as the priest returned with the sharpened instruments.

'Thank you.' Bonnaire took the honed tools and handed them to Raoul. 'Perhaps, *mon père*, you could send someone to attend to the lights and the fire while we work.'

'But of course. I will ask Madame Duval to step in.'

'No.' Raoul frowned. 'She is not used to such work.'

The priest stopped and looked at him in surprise.

'Really, *monsieur*? If you say so. Madame Deschamps, of course, is a woman most resourceful, but she is very busy at the *auberge*.'

'Well, there must be someone else who can come in,' said Raoul irritably.

The priest spread his hands.

'These are simple people, *monsieur*, uneducated. They are easily frightened and I fear they would be sorely distressed by the sight of their neighbours in such a situation as this.'

'But my wife…'

Raoul's words trailed off. What could he say, that his wife was a lady? That she was too cosseted and spoiled to be of any use here?

'Madame Duval has shown herself to be most resourceful in this tragedy,' the priest continued. 'The villagers turned to her in their grief and she did not fail them. While they could only weep and wail she arranged who should go to the fields to fetch the mothers and wives of those who were working in the barn. She helped to feed the children and put them to bed and it was *madame* who organised the women to prepare this house for you, to boil the water and tear up the clean sheets for bandages. Even now she is helping to cook supper at the *auberge* for those who are grieving too much to feed themselves or their families.'

'Practical as well as beautiful,' remarked Bonnaire. 'You are to be congratulated on having such a partner, Monsieur Duval.'

Raoul's jaw clenched hard as he tried to ignore the

doctor's remark. He did not want to be congratulated, did not want to think how fortunate a man would be to have a wife like Lady Cassandra.

He shrugged and capitulated.

'Very well, let her come in.'

They had tarried long enough and he had work to do.

They lifted the first man on to the table. He and his fellow patient had been given enough brandy to make them drowsy and Raoul worked quickly. He was aware of Cassandra moving silently around the room, building up the fire to keep the water hot, trimming the wicks on the lights and even helping Bonnaire to hold down the patient when necessary. He glanced up at one critical point, fearing she might faint at the gruesome nature of the business, but although she was pale she appeared perfectly composed and obeyed his commands as steadily as the young doctor.

Midnight was long past before the operations were complete and the patients could be left to recover. Raoul felt utterly drained and when Bonnaire offered to sit with them through the night he did not argue. He shrugged on his coat and escorted Cassie to the *auberge*, where the landlady was waiting up to serve them supper.

Cassie was bone-weary and after all she had seen that evening she had no appetite, but she had eaten very little all day and she sat down opposite Raoul at the table while Madame Deschamps set two full plates before them.

The hot food warmed her and she began to feel better. She reached for her wine glass and looked up to see Raoul watching her.

'I am sorry we have had to delay our journey, milady.'

'I am not.' She continued, a note of wonder in her voice, 'Truly, I do not regret being here. It has been a difficult day and a sad one, too, but I am pleased I could be of help.'

She took a sip of wine while she considered all that had happened. Raoul had thrown himself into assisting the villagers and she had done the same. The people had been shocked and frightened, unable to think for themselves. They had needed someone to take charge and it had felt like the most natural thing in the world for her to step in, deciding what needed to be done and setting villagers to work. They had not questioned her, instead as the day wore on they had looked to her even more for guidance. She glanced shyly at Raoul.

'For the first time in my life I think I have done something truly useful.'

Silently he raised his glass to her and, smiling, she gave her attention to her food. They finished their meal in silence and she sat back, watching as Raoul wiped a piece of bread around his plate. He was looking a little less grey and drawn than when they had come in, but she knew how tirelessly he had worked all day.

She said suddenly, 'You must be exhausted.'

He pushed away his empty plate.

'It has been a long day, certainly, and I cannot wait to get to my bed.' He drained his wine. 'Well, *madame*, shall we retire?'

Cassie had given little thought to the sleeping arrangements until the landlady showed them upstairs to what was clearly the best bedroom. A large canopied bed filled the centre of the room, its curtains pulled back to display the plump, inviting mattress. It was then that Cassie's tiredness fled, replaced by a strong sense of unease. She stopped just inside the door and did not move, even when the landlady left them.

'Ah. There is no truckle bed,' she muttered. 'I forgot to mention it.'

'Then we must share this one.' Raoul unbuttoned his coat and waistcoat and threw them over a chair.

'No!' Cassie was scandalised. To sleep in the open was one thing—even to curl up together on the floor before the fire had not felt this dangerous, after all the old woman had been sleeping in the same room and providing some sort of chaperonage. But to share a bed, to have that strong, lithe body only inches away— 'Out of the question,' she said firmly.

Raoul yawned. 'You need not fear for your virtue, milady, but if you think I will sleep on the floor tonight you are much mistaken.'

She eyed him suspiciously. If her own fatigue could vanish so quickly, she was sure his would, too. She remembered waking on the cottage floor to find his hand cradling her breast. The thought made her grow hot, but not with embarrassment. She began to recognise her own yearning for a man's touch. She watched in growing alarm as he sat down to pull off his boots.

She said quickly, 'I know how men use soft words and pretty gestures to seduce a woman, but I am not so easily caught, *monsieur*.'

'Confound it, woman, I am not using any soft words,' he snapped, but Cassie was so on edge she paid no heed.

'I know 'tis all a sham,' she continued, in an attempt

to quell the flicker of desire that was uncurling inside her. 'A man must have his way and the result for the woman is always disappointing.'

'Disappointing, milady?'

With a growl he rose from the chair and came purposefully towards her. It took all Cassie's willpower not to back away from him. She tensed as he put out his hand and took her chin between his thumb and forefinger.

'Mayhap you have only had English lovers so far.'

She pulled her chin from his grasp. Her heart was hammering and panic was not far away, because she knew she was ready to fall into his arms at any moment. She started to gabble, trying to convince herself that such an action would be foolish in the extreme.

'Lovers? The word is too easily used, *monsieur*. Love rarely comes into it, in my experience. The coupling that ensues is for the man to enjoy and the woman to endure.'

His eyes narrowed and for one fearful moment she thought he might see that as a challenge, but after a brief hesitation he turned away.

'You might be the famous Pompadour herself and I could not make love to you tonight. I am too tired to argue the point with you now, *madame*. Sleep where you will, but I am going to bed.'

To Cassie's dismay he threw himself on to the covers. He could not sleep there! She must reason with him, persuade him to move.

'I am glad you will not try to woo me with soft words,' she told him. 'It will not work with me. Let me remind you I have had a husband.'

'But not a very good one,' he muttered, putting his hands behind his head and closing his eyes.

'Gerald was a very accomplished lover,' she told him indignantly.

She turned away to place her folded shawl on the trunk. Would he notice she had used the past tense? Suddenly she did not want to lie any more and she exhaled, like a soft sigh.

'At least, he had any number of mistresses and he *told* me they were all satisfied with his performance. I confess I never found it very enjoyable, even when I thought I was wildly in love with him.' She clasped her hands together and stared down at the shawl, as if gaining courage from its cheerful, sunny colours. 'But perhaps it is wrong of me to say that, now he is no longer alive. You see, *monsieur*, I did not abandon my husband. I remained at Verdun, at his side, and would be there still, if he had not been killed. I made up my mind that I would not leave him, even though the provocation was very great indeed.'

There. She closed her eyes, feeling a sense of relief that she had at last confessed it. She was a widow and her husband had been unfaithful. Let him sneer at her if he wished.

A gentle snore was the only answer. Cassie turned to see that Raoul was fast asleep. Even a rough shake on the shoulder failed to rouse him. How dare he fall asleep while she was pouring out her heart! She looked at the sleeping figure. At least he was not taking up the whole bed. She blew out most of the candles and sat down on the edge of the bed, her indignation dying away as she regarded him. She reached out and gently brushed a stray lock of dark hair from his brow. He had worked tirelessly today, using all his strength and his skill to help the villagers. He deserved his rest.

* * *

Raoul surfaced from a deep sleep and lay still, eyes closed. He felt supremely comfortable, a soft mattress beneath him and a feather pillow under his head. He was still wearing his shirt and breeches but someone had put a blanket over him.

Someone.

Lady Cassandra.

He turned his head, expecting to see her dark curls spread over the pillow next to his, instead he found himself staring at a wall of white.

'What the—?' He sat up, frowning at the line of bolsters and pillows that stretched down the middle of the bed. On the far side of this downy barrier was Cassandra, wrapped snugly in a coverlet. He felt a momentary disappointment when he saw that her hair had been tamed into a thick plait.

She stirred, disturbed by his movements.

'It is called bundling,' she said sleepily.

'I beg your pardon?'

She yawned. 'The feather barricade between us. It is a device that I understand is often used in village courtships in England, so a man and woman could spend time together and find out if they truly liked each other without…committing themselves.'

'I do not think it would prove much of a deterrent, if the couple were willing.'

She was awake now and eyeing him warily.

'Well, in this case one of the couple was *not* willing,' she told him, throwing back her cover and slipping off the bed.

He saw she was still wearing her stays on top of a

chemise that stopped some way above her very shapely ankles.

'I would consider that contraption of whalebone and strong linen to be a more effective deterrent than a few bolsters, milady.'

'If you were a gentleman you would not be looking at me.' She added scornfully, 'But what else should I expect from a foreigner?'

Raoul picked up one of the bolsters and put it behind him, so he could lean back and watch Cassandra as she walked across to the washstand. He was well rested now and fully appreciative of the picture she presented.

'So it is only foreigners who look at pretty women? *Mon Dieu*, Englishmen are not only dull, they must have ice in their veins.'

She turned, clutching the towel before her.

'Of course they do not. They——' She stamped her foot. 'Ooh, you delight in teasing me!'

He grinned. 'I cannot resist, you bite so easily. By the way, how did you sleep in that corset? It must have been very uncomfortable.'

'I loosened the laces, naturally. And before you say anything more I do *not* need your help to tighten them again!'

He laughed and climbed out of bed.

'No, of course not, milady. I shall tease you no more. We must break our fast and move on. What is the time?' He looked out of the window. '*Tiens*, it must be noon at least.'

'It was almost dawn before we went to bed,' said Cassie. 'I asked Madame Deschamps not to disturb us.'

She felt her cheeks burn as she remembered the land-lady's knowing wink when she heard the request. When she had eloped she had been subjected to many such looks and rude jibes, too, but *then* she had thought herself too much in love to care about such things. How she was ever to explain these past few days she did not know. She could only hope that when she returned to England the details of this journey would remain a secret.

Raoul turned from the window.

'I had best go and see the patients. I hope Dr Bonnaire would have called me, if he needed my help in the night.' He grabbed his clothes and dressed quickly. 'We are still a good half-day's travel from Rouen. We will need to leave soon if we are to get there tonight.'

'Naturally we must stay here, *monsieur*, if you are needed.'

He looked a little surprised at her words and nodded as he picked up his hat. 'I will go now to see how the men are doing.'

With that he was gone. Cassie finished dressing in silence, pushing aside the fleeting regret that Raoul had said he would stop teasing her.

Raoul spent an hour in the house that had become a makeshift hospital and when he returned to the *auberge* Cassandra was waiting for him at the door. His mood brightened when he saw her, pretty as a picture in her yellow gown, her dark curls brushed and pinned in a shining disorder about her head.

'Madame Deschamps insisted on cooking for us,' she greeted him. 'I have packed everything, and the carriage and your horse are ready to depart as soon we have broken our fast.'

At that moment the landlady herself came bustling

out, insisting that they must not leave Flagey until they had eaten a good meal.

'I have bread and eggs and ham waiting for you, *monsieur*, and you will have the room to yourselves, you will not be disturbed.'

There was no point in arguing, so Raoul followed Cassie and their landlady into the little dining room.

'How did you find your patients?' asked Cassie as they settled down to their meal.

'The two men we operated on are awake and recovering. It will be slow, but I have hopes that with a little ingenuity they will be able to get around again. Most do and consider themselves fortunate they have only lost a leg and not their life. Bonnaire is happy to look after them now. And I called in on the fellow with the broken arm. His head has cleared, I think he will make a full recovery.'

'They must all be thankful you were here to help them.'

'They were. That is why it has taken me so long to get back. Everyone in Flagey wanted to speak to me.' He grinned. 'I cannot tell you the number of gifts I have had to decline, but I did not think you would wish to have a basket of eggs or a plucked chicken in the chaise with you, although I was tempted by the flitch of bacon.'

Cassie laughed.

'These poor people have little enough of their own. It is very generous of them to offer to share it with you. They are clearly very grateful for what you have done.'

'This is not just for me, milady, your efforts too were much appreciated.'

Cassie blushed. 'Truly?'

'Yes, truly.'

Raoul had received nothing but praise this morning for his 'good lady'. They had told him how she had supported everyone, organising them, comforting those in grief and cajoling the mothers into looking after their little ones. A saint, one man had called her. Raoul looked at her now, remembering how she had helped him during the operations, quietly and calmly doing as she was bid without question. He had expected that she would crumble at the sight of the crushed limbs, that she might cry, or swoon and need to be escorted away, but she had faced everything with a calm determination that surprised him.

And yet had he not seen signs of her resourcefulness even before they reached Flagey? There had been no tears, no tantrums during their time together. She had matched him step for step without complaint. His respect for her was growing.

Cassie was clearly pleased at his praise and he had to fight the urge to smile back at her. He dragged his eyes back to his plate. Heaven defend him from actually *liking* this woman! He scraped together the last of the ham and eggs.

But she would make a good wife.

Some demon on Raoul's shoulder whispered the words into his ear, but he closed his mind to them. He was not the marrying sort. He lived for his work. Surgery was his first love and a man could not have two mistresses.

'Our lack of a servant has not gone unnoticed, however.' He told her, sitting back in his chair. 'I have already set it about that you are so demanding no maid will stay with us.'

As he expected, she bristled at that. Her smile disappeared.

'Me, demanding?'

'Why, yes. They have experienced your managing ways for themselves. To their benefit in this instance, of course, and once I had explained that you were English they were not at all surprised when I told them you were extremely domineering.'

'*Domineering?*'

'I also said you were a scold.'

'You did not!'

'I did. A positive virago.'

She sat up very straight.

'You are insulting sir.'

'But truthful, milady. You have all the arrogance of your race. And your class.'

'Oh, you—you—' Her knife clattered on to her empty plate. She pushed back her chair and jumped up. 'I shall wait for you in the chaise!'

Raoul laughed as she stalked out. Best to keep her outraged. That way she was much less likely to end up in his arms.

Darkness had fallen by the time they reached Rouen. They found a small inn near the cathedral and Cassie stood silently beside Raoul while he enquired of the landlord if they had rooms. She waited anxiously, wondering if they would be questioned or asked for their papers but their host showed little curiosity about his guests, merely took their money and summoned a serving maid to show them upstairs.

Cassandra had been icily polite to Raoul on the few occasions they were obliged to speak during the journey and when they sat down to a late dinner in their private rooms she was determined to maintain her frosty manner. Her companion seemed unconcerned and applied himself to his food with gusto, while Cassie only picked at her own meal. Her lack of appetite drew an anxious look from the maid when she came to clear the table and Cassie was obliged to assure her that she found no fault with the inn's fare. Her smile faded once the servant had quit the room and she allowed her thoughts to return to the matter that had been worrying her all day. She could not forget what Raoul had said of her. It was very dispiriting and surely it could not be true.

'You are not hungry?'

Raoul's question cut through her reverie. She shook her head, feeling tears very close.

'Is something wrong, milady?'

'Did you mean it, when you said I was arrogant?'

'Aha, so that still rankles, does it?'

'Disdain for others is not a trait I admire,' she said quietly, keeping her eyes lowered. 'If the villagers thought me conceited yesterday, then I am sorry for it.'

She heard him sigh.

'No, no, they saw nothing but goodness in you. I said what I did this morning because...'

'Yes?' Cassie looked up hopefully.

Perhaps he had not meant it, perhaps he had been teasing and she had been too quick to take offence. He held her gaze for a moment and she was heartened by the sudden warmth in his eyes, but then it was gone. He looked away and she was left wondering if she had seen it at all.

'Because we needed a convincing reason for not having a servant with us,' he finished with a slight, contemptuous shrug. 'Your arrogance comes from your breeding, milady, it is hardly your fault.'

His words hit her like cold water. She had been selfish, yes, and thoughtless in eloping without any concern for the effect upon her grandmother, left alone to face the quizzes of Bath, but she had thought herself truly in love and Gerald had convinced her that they had no choice but to run away, or be parted for ever. Perhaps she had appeared arrogant towards Raoul, but only to keep him at a distance. She found him so dangerously attractive, but after what she had experienced with Gerald she had no intention of complicating her life by falling for the charms of another man. Ever.

Raoul watched Cassandra's countenance, saw the changing emotions writ clear upon her face. He had intended to make her angry, but his taunts had wounded her, she had not shrugged them off as he had expected. The hurt in her eyes tugged at his conscience, but it also affected him inside, like a giant hand squeezing his heart.

Bah. He was growing soft. The woman was an English aristo. She would take what she needed from him and then cast him aside without a second thought. She did not need his sympathy. He pushed back his chair and rose.

'It is late and we should sleep,' he said. 'As soon as it is light I will go to the docks and see if there is any ship there to take us to Le Havre. Who knows, I might even find a captain who is willing to take you all the way to England.'

'Yes, that would be the ideal solution and would suit us both,' she agreed.

Her tone was subdued and Raoul guessed she would be pleased to see the back of him.

Well, milady, the feeling is mutual!

'At least we have the benefit of two rooms here,' he remarked. 'If you will allow me to remove a pillow and blanket from the bed I will not bother you again tonight.'

She nodded her assent and he picked up one of the branched candles and went into the bedchamber. The large canopied bed looked very comfortable. Raoul found himself imagining Cassandra lying there between the sheets, her glossy hair spread over the pillows and those dark-violet eyes fixed upon him, inviting him to join her. It was a tempting picture and the devil on his shoulder whispered that a few soft words would bring the lady into his arms. There was no denying the attraction, he had seen it in her eyes, felt it in her response when he had kissed her. There was passion in her, he would swear to it, just waiting to be awoken.

Why not? In a few more days she will be safely back in England and you will be free of her. What have you got to lose?

'My honour,' muttered Raoul savagely. 'I will not demean myself to lie with my sworn enemy.'

Enemy? The word sounded false even as he uttered it. She might be a lady, and an Englishwoman at that, but over the past few days he had come to know her, to see the strength and resourcefulness in her character. The uncomfortable truth was that he was afraid. He could not give himself totally to any one woman and Lady Cassandra Witney was not the sort to settle for anything less. Brave and resourceful she might be, but she was born to command. To take, not give.

And what have you to give her, save perhaps a few nights' pleasure and that would demean you both.

Quickly he pulled the coverlet from the bed, grabbed a couple of pillows and returned to the sitting room.

'I have left the candles burning in there for you, milady,' he said, dropping the bedding on the floor. 'I will bid you goodnight.'

'Yes, thank you.'

When she did not move he turned. She was holding out her purse to him.

'You will need money tomorrow, if you find a suitable ship for us. For me. I do not know how much it will be, so it is best that you take this. I have kept back a few livres in case I need it, but you are attending to all the travel arrangements.' She looked up fleetingly. 'I am not so arrogant that I do not trust you, Monsieur Doulevant.'

Raoul took the purse, feeling its weight in his hand. She was giving him *all* her money? When he did not speak she gave a tiny curtsy and hurried away.

'Cassandra, wait—'

But it was too late; the door was already firmly closed between them.

Cassie undressed quickly and slipped into bed. She had done it. She had handed over her purse to Raoul, put herself wholly in his power. Perhaps that would show him she was not the proud, disdainful woman he thought her. It should not matter, but it did. She was a little frightened at how important it was that he did not think badly of her. She turned over, nestling her cheek against one hand. She had known Raoul Doulevant for little more than a week and yet she... Cassie shied away from admitting even to herself what she thought of the man. It had taken her months to fall in love with Gerald Witney and look how quickly she had recovered from that grand passion. Clearly her feelings were not to be trusted.

In the morning Cassandra's sunny spirits were restored. They had reached the Seine. From her window she could look over the roofs and see the masts of the ships on the quayside. With luck they would find a vessel to carry them to the coast. The inn was very quiet, so she guessed it was still early, but she scrambled out of bed and into her riding habit ready for the day ahead. She emerged from her bedroom to find Raoul already dressed. She responded to his cheerful greeting with a smile.

'Are you going out immediately, sir?'

'I have not yet broken my fast, so we may do so together, if you wish.' He picked up the bedding piled neatly on a chair. 'We had best put this out of sight before I ask the maid to bring up the tray.'

It was only a matter of minutes before they were sitting at the table with a plate of ham and fresh bread rolls before them. Cassie poured coffee and they fell into conversation like old friends. On this sunny morning it was easy to forget the harsh words of yesterday. And the fact that they were both fugitives, fleeing the country.

'How do you think you will go on today?' she asked when they had finished their meal.

'I have every hope of finding a ship, but it may take some time,' Raoul warned her. 'I shall have to be careful when I make my enquiries. Rouen is a busy port, there will be plenty of ships going to the coast, but not all of them will be prepared to take passengers without papers.'

He picked up his hat and she accompanied him to the door.

'Raoul, you will take care?' Impulsively Cassie put her hand on his arm. 'I would not have you put yourself at risk for me.'

He paused and gazed down at her, but she could not read the look in his dark eyes.

'I shall take care, milady.' He lifted her hand from his sleeve and pressed a kiss into the palm. 'Bolt the door and wait here for me. I shall be back as soon as I can.'

He went out, closing the door behind him and Cassie listened to his firm step as he went quickly down the stairs. She cradled the hand that he had kissed, rubbing her thumb over the palm for a moment before she turned and ran to the window. Their room overlooked the street and she saw him emerge from the inn. There was a pleasurable flutter of excitement in her chest as she watched his tall figure striding away. Excitement, but not fear; she had given Raoul nearly all her money, but she knew enough of the man now to know he would not cheat her. She trusted him. Smiling, Cassie turned from the window and looked about the room, wondering how best to amuse herself until Raoul returned.

The day dragged on and with no clock or pocket watch Cassandra had no idea of the time except from the length of the shadows in the street below. She reminded herself that it might take Raoul all day to find a suitable ship, but the shadows were lengthening before at last she heard a heavy footstep on the landing and she flew across the room to unbolt the door.

'Raoul, I was beginning to—'

Her smiling words ended abruptly. It was not Raoul at the door but a tall, pallid stranger in a black coat. At his shoulder was the weasel-faced Merimon, her rascally courier.

Merimon put up his hand and pointed an accusing finger at Cassie.

'That's her,' he declared. 'That's the woman who ran off with your deserter.'

Chapter Six

Cassandra stared at the men in horrified silence. Two uniformed *gendarmes* stood behind Merimon and the man in the black coat. Another look at the stranger showed her that his sallow face was badly marred by the crookedness of his nose. A memory stirred. Something Raoul had said, but for the moment it eluded her.

Gesturing to her to stand aside, they all marched into the room and the officers began to search it.

'What do you think you are doing?' she demanded angrily.

The black-coated stranger bowed. 'I am Auguste Valerin and I am here to arrest the deserter Raoul Doulevant.'

Cassie remembered now; Raoul had broken the man's nose. If that disfigurement was the result it was no wonder Valerin wanted revenge. She must go carefully.

'I have never heard of him,' she said with a dismissive shrug. 'I am staying here with my husband, Monsieur Duval.'

'But I heard you call him Raoul.'

'What of it?'

Cassie spoke calmly, but Valerin's sneering smile filled her with unease.

'A coincidence, perhaps, that your husband and the deserter should share the same name. It is also a coincidence that travellers coming into Rouen yesterday brought with them tales of a doctor helping to save the lives of peasants in a village not a day's ride from here. It is said he could set broken bones and even remove a crushed leg. Such skill is a rarity and news of it was bound to spread.'

The *gendarmes* emerged from the bedchamber.

'There is no one here, sir,' declared one of them.

'Stand guard on the landing,' ordered Valerin. 'Keep out of sight, ready to apprehend the deserter when he returns. I will question Madame Duval.'

'She is no more Madame Duval than I am,' put in Merimon.

'No,' Cassie admitted. 'You would know that, since you stole my papers.' She turned to Valerin. 'My name is Lady Cassandra Witney and I hired this man as a courier to escort me from Verdun to the coast. He and his accomplice stole my passport and would have murdered me if I had not escaped.'

Merimon threw an aggrieved glance at Valerin, his hands spread wide.

'What cause would I have to do that, *monsieur*? I am an honest man, why else would I have come to you with information about Doulevant?'

'For the reward,' Valerin snapped. 'Tell me your story again and we will see what Madame Witney has to say.'

Cassie drew herself up and said in her haughtiest

tone, 'As the daughter of a marquess it is customary to address me as Lady Cassandra.'

She saw a slight wariness enter Valerin's eyes, but he replied coldly.

'We do not recognise such titles in France now, *madame*. And from what you have said, you do not have any papers to prove who you are, do you?'

'There are many people in Verdun who will vouch for me.'

'Possibly, but that is not my concern. Where is Doulevant?'

'I have no idea who you mean.'

'Do not lie to me, *madame*. The landlord described the man staying here with you, the man calling himself Duval. I am satisfied he and Doulevant are the same person. Now where is he?'

Cassie ignored the last question. She was thinking quickly and knew she must play a convincing part.

'La, so he is not Raoul Duval?' she said, opening her eyes wide at Valerin. 'That would explain a great deal.'

'Just tell me where he is, if you please.'

'But I do not know,' Cassie insisted. She decided it would be best to stick as close to the truth as possible. 'You are very right, I am not Madame Duval. The man calling himself by that name rescued me from this villain.' She pointed at Merimon. 'I was grateful and hired Duval to escort me to the coast. We were travelling as man and wife because there is no money to spare for servants and it seemed safer that way.' She clasped her hands together and assumed an anxious look. 'When we arrived here, he asked for my purse, that he might book me a passage on a ship for England. I have not seen him since. I think perhaps he has abandoned me.'

'You seem to be singularly unfortunate in your choice of escorts, *madame*.'

She returned Valerin's glare with a steady look of her own.

'France seems singularly full of rogues, *monsieur*.'

He walked slowly to a chair and sat down, a deliberate insult while she was still standing. 'True, and I expect one of them to return here sooner or later.'

Cassie's blood ran cold. She could think of no way to warn Raoul and could only hope that he would see the *gendarmes* waiting on the stairs before they spotted him.

'You may wait if you wish,' she said with studied indifference. 'I told you, he has gone and taken my money with him. He will not be back.'

'We shall see,' purred Valerin. He looked round when the courier cursed impatiently. 'We need waste no more of your time, Monsieur Merimon. You may leave.'

'Not until I have had my reward.'

'The reward was for information leading to the apprehension of one Raoul Doulevant. So far I have not seen him.'

'But I told you, she is his accomplice.'

Cassie replied to that bitterly. 'I was *forced* into his company when you attacked me!'

Merimon was inclined to argue the point, but Valerin put up his hand. 'Enough. We know where we can find you, citizen. Good day to you.'

'But I have received nothing for all my trouble,' Merimon whined. He turned his sharp little eyes to Cassie. 'She still owes me for my services.'

'I owe you nothing. I gave you half your fee when

we set out from Verdun, the agreement was that you would get the other half when we reached Le Havre.'

'It was not I who ran off.' He turned to Valerin again. 'Believe me, sir, she is Doulevant's whore.'

'How dare you!' Cassie raged.

'You are in league with him.'

'He rescued me from your attack, that is all. And I have told you, I have no money.'

'None?' snapped Valerin. Cassie's slight hesitation was enough. He said coldly, 'Will you give me your purse, or shall I call in the *gendarmes* to search you?'

She did not doubt he would carry out his threat. She pulled the remaining coins from her pocket and displayed them on her palm.

'You see, nine, ten livres, nothing more.'

Valerin scraped the coins from her hand. He held them out to Merimon.

'Take these, it will pay your passage back to Verdun.'

Merimon looked as if he would argue, but at last he took the coins and went grudgingly from the room.

'But that is all I have,' Cassie protested.

'If you are indeed in league with Doulevant you will find yourself in prison soon enough and will have no need of money.'

'And when you discover I am telling the truth, that I am innocent?'

Valerin's glance was sceptical.

'*If* you are innocent, *madame*, I shall personally escort you to the mayor and you may throw yourself upon his mercy.'

'Thank you,' she said coldly. 'I will ask him to write to my grandmother, the Marchioness of Hune. She will send funds for my passage home. Your First Consul himself has decreed that the wives of the English *déte-nus* are free to leave.'

'Providing they have not shown themselves to be enemies of France,' said Valerin, adding sharply, 'Do not go near the window, *madame*. I would not have you warn your lover.'

'He is not my lover.'

'No?' Valerin got up and came closer. 'Then he is a fool.'

Before she could guess his intention he put his hand around her neck and dragged her close to kiss her. Cassie struggled against him and when he finally let her go she brought her hand up to his cheek with such force that it left her palm stinging. His eyes narrowed.

'A mistake, *madame*, to strike a government officer.' Holding her prisoner with one hand he drew a length of cord from his pocket and bound her wrists together. 'There,' he regarded her with an unpleasant smile. 'That should stop you scratching my eyes out while I show you—'

The door crashed open and one of the *gendarmes* burst in.

'Sir, we have him! The pot-boy says the deserter is in the taproom.'

Cassie's heart was hammering hard. Relief that she had been spared a loathsome groping was replaced by fear for Raoul. She saw the leap of triumph in Valerin's eyes.

'Very well,' he barked, 'arrest him. I will follow you.' He turned back to Cassie. 'What shall I do with you while I make my arrest?'

He glanced around the room, his eyes alighting on a stout peg sticking out high in the wall behind the door. He picked her up. Cassie kicked wildly but it was useless. He lifted her hands and hooked the cord over the peg. She was suspended, facing the wall, with the cord biting painfully into her wrists and her toes barely reaching the floor.

'Perfect. That should keep you safe until I return.' His hand squeezed her bottom through the thick folds of her skirts and Cassie shivered. She knew it was a promise of what he had in store for her.

Valerin went out, Cassie heard him clattering down the stairs, then there was silence. In addition to worries for her own safety Cassandra felt the chill of dread clutching at her insides. Had they caught Raoul? Had they hurt him? She tried to concentrate on her own predicament. Her toes just touched the ground, barely enough to relieve the pull on her wrists and stop the thin cord from biting deeper into the flesh. The wooden peg was angled upwards and strain as she might she could not reach high enough to lift her bound wrists free of it. The light was fading, soon it would be dark. In despair Cassie rested her forehead against the wall. Valerin would return for her and there was nothing she could do about it.

Her ears caught the faint sounds outside the door and she quickly blinked away her tears. This was no time for self-pity; she needed all her wits about her if she was to get through this. She heard the door open and close again. He was in the room. She turned her head, but the scathing remark on her lips died when she saw Raoul standing behind her.

Relief flooded through Cassie. She wanted to cry

but would not give in to a weakness she despised and instead she took refuge in anger.

'Well, do not stand there like an idiot, get me down!'

Raoul had not known what to expect when he entered the room. His imagination had rioted and his blood had gone cold as he considered what Valerin might have done to Cassie. To find her apparently unhurt was a relief and it increased tenfold when she addressed him in her usual haughty manner. He could not stop himself from grinning, although the effect was like pouring oil on hot coals. Her eyes positively flamed with wrath.

'Get me down, this instant!'

He put his hands on her waist and lifted her so she could unhook herself from the peg. He lowered her gently to the ground and she turned, her arms still raised. Despite their perilous situation he could not resist the temptation to slide his hands up quickly from her tiny waist and pull her bound wrists over his head. He held her arms against his shoulders.

'Shall I steal a kiss, as my reward for rescuing you?'

His pulse raced even faster when he recognised the gleam of excitement that mixed with the anger in her eyes, a gleam that told him she was not averse to kissing him. It was gone in an instant, but he knew he had not been mistaken and it both thrilled and alarmed him; he could no more stop flirting with her than a moth could ignore a flame.

She shook her head at him. 'This is no time for funning, Raoul! We must go, quickly.'

Reluctantly Raoul released her.

'You are right,' he said, untying her wrists. 'I have bought us a little time, but not much.'

'How—?'

He put a finger to her lips.

'No time to explain now. Come.'

'Not so fast.'

At the words Raoul whipped about to find Valerin standing in the doorway. He pushed Cassie behind him, putting his body between her and the deadly pistol Valerin was holding. The sneering smile on that thin face made Raoul's blood boil, but he knew he must not lose his head.

'She said you had gone, but I knew you would not abandon your whore.'

'She is a lady, Valerin, as you would know if you had any intelligence.'

'Indeed? If that is so what is she doing here, with you?' His lip curled. 'Do you think any *lady* would look to you for protection? Why, you are not even a Frenchman.'

'And that is where I have the advantage of you,' Raoul drawled insolently.

The sallow face flushed with anger and hatred.

'You are nothing but a damned deserter. The scum of the earth! I find you here, dressed like a gentleman— aping your betters, Doulevant! Men such as you should be whipped at the cart's tail.'

Raoul knew Valerin was goading him. He did not need Cassandra's warning hand on his arm to tell him Valerin was trying to make him attack, so that he would have an excuse to shoot. He must act and quickly. The hubbub of noise and confusion from below drifted in through the open door. At any moment Valerin's lackeys might return and then all would be lost.

He smiled and shifted his gaze to look over the man's shoulder.

'You would be wise to give me the pistol, Valerin. I have an accomplice behind you.'

'Do you think I am fool enough to believe that?'

Raoul's smile turned into a full grin.

'You are a fool if you do not. Any moment now you will feel my friend's pistol against your ribs.'

Raoul saw Valerin's certainty waver. There was a lull in the noise below that made the sudden creak of boards on the landing sound like a pistol shot. Valerin look around.

It was enough. Raoul launched himself at his opponent, one hand reaching for the pistol, the other connecting with the man's jaw in a sickening thud. Valerin fell back, catching his head on the doorpost and collapsing, unconscious, in the doorway.

Cassie had not realised she had stopped breathing, but now she dragged in air with a gasp and felt her heart begin to thud heavily as relief surged through her. On the landing stood the pot-boy, grinning.

'Good work, master,' he told Raoul. 'I saw him slip away and guessed he'd rumbled our plan.'

'Well, here's a little extra for your trouble.' Raoul tucked Valerin's pistol into his belt and tossed the boy a coin. 'Now we must be gone. Milady?'

He reached for Cassie's hand, but she shook her head. She pointed at Valerin.

'Pull him into the room first, then we can lock the door. It will slow up his men when they come looking for him, or for us.'

With the pot-boy's help it was done in a trice. The

lad pocketed the key and pointed to a door further along the landing.

'That room's empty and the window will bring you out on the back alley. I'll go down and see if I can make 'em think you've gone out into the street.'

With that the lad dashed back down the stairs to the taproom, from where sounds of an altercation could still be heard. Raoul took Cassie's hand and they slipped into the empty bedchamber. He immediately went to the window and threw up the sash.

'Your skirts will make it more difficult,' he said to Cassie, who had followed him, 'but I think you will manage.'

The window looked out over a deserted yard and the sloping roof of an outhouse abutted the wall only feet beneath the sill. It was dark now, but there was the faint glimmer of a rising moon to light their way. Raoul jumped down into the yard and turned to help Cassie but she was already on the ground and shaking out her skirts, as if escaping from bedroom windows was an everyday occurrence for her. Together they crept out of the yard and into the alley.

Cassie glanced quickly right and left. The alley was deserted, but where it joined the street she could see people running towards the inn, eager to see what was going on. Raoul grabbed her hand and pulled her in the opposite direction, where they soon found themselves in a labyrinthine mesh of alleys and narrow streets that led down to the quay. He pulled her hand on to his arm.

'We must go slowly, we do not want to attract attention.'

Cassie nodded, forcing her body to a walk while every instinct screamed at her to run. Her eyes darted back and forth and her spine tingled with fear. She had a strong conviction that they were being watched and it was as much as she could do not to look around. She took a deep steadying breath, trying to match Raoul's apparent insouciance. He walked easily, head up, as if he had not a care in the world and she must do the same. They were an innocent couple, making their way to the quay.

She said quietly, 'You could have escaped easily, if you had not come back for me.'

Raoul heard the humble note in her voice, but there was something else: wonder and a touch of disbelief. He tried and failed not to feel aggrieved.

'Did you think I would leave you, *madame*? We made a bargain.'

'We did indeed, but you risked your life to save me. I am very grateful.'

He was tempted to say he did not want her gratitude, that he was a gentleman and always kept his word. That he would have done the same for anyone, but he knew it was not true. He recalled the chilling fear that had gripped his heart when he realised Valerin would find Cassandra alone. A shudder ran through him as he thought again what might have happened to her. But she was safe and he must not waste time dwelling on what might have been. He forced himself to speak lightly.

'It was the greatest good fortune that I saw Valerin and his fools entering the inn as I was returning from the quay.'

'But they said you were in the taproom!'

'It was a man of similar build and dress. I met him in the street and persuaded him to go in and buy himself a drink. A few coins to the pot-boy did the rest. I am only thankful the lad had the wit to follow Valerin up the stairs.'

'That could have been very dangerous for him.'

'It *could*, although I'd seen Valerin cuff the lad even before he entered the inn, so I knew there'd be no love lost there. But enough of that, we have evaded capture and without much hurt, except to your wrists. And your dignity,' he ended with a laugh in his voice, remembering her outrage.

'Both of which will recover,' she told him, unmoved. 'That scoundrel Merimon was with him. He was hoping for a reward for your capture.'

'He will be disappointed, then. I suppose Valerin must have come upon him after we had made our escape from the forest.'

'That is what I think, too. But, Raoul, news has already reached here from Flagey, of how you helped the men caught under the collapsed barn. Valerin knew of it, that is why he was so certain you were here.'

'*Diable!* So soon? *Tiens*, if Bonnaire had known how to wield the knife I would not have needed to show my hand.'

Cassandra clutched his arm. 'You must not regret what you did for those poor people. I do not.'

'Truly?' He felt his heart lift a little. 'Even though it has put you in danger?'

She waved one tiny hand.

'Life is full of danger, Raoul. One must do what is right and helping the villagers was right.'

Raoul walked on, his head spinning at her words. She saw these things as he did. How had he ever thought her arrogant? Spirited, yes, headstrong and wilful, perhaps, but when he thought of the way she had worked with him to help the villagers and her bravery today, when Valerin had threatened her with heaven knows what, his heart was almost bursting with…

With what, respect? Admiration?

Her soft voice brought his wandering mind back to the present.

'Where do we go now? Did you find a ship to take us out of Rouen?'

They were approaching a tavern and he stopped, realising that hunger was affecting his ability to think logically.

'Let us go in here. I have not eaten anything since we broke our fast together this morning.'

'Nor I.'

'Then we shall dine in here and I can tell you of my success. Or lack of it.'

The tavern was gloomy, but that was to their advantage. He looked about and chose a small table in one shadowy corner where they could talk undisturbed. Raoul sat on the bench facing the entrance, keeping one eye on everyone who came in. He had deliberately chosen a table near the back door, where they could make their escape if necessary. A serving wench had brought them wine and bread and gone off to the kitchens to order their food.

'So you had no luck with finding a ship to take me home,' Cassie prompted him, once they were alone.

'I found one vessel that was going as far as Le Havre.' He stopped when a rough-looking fellow stumbled against their table. Raoul grabbed at his cup as the man muttered an apology and lurched off, falling on to a chair at the next table and impatiently calling for wine.

Raoul frowned. 'We should go.'

Cassie put a hand on his arm. 'No,' she whispered, keeping her eyes lowered. 'If we leave without eating that would cause comment.'

She was right. Raoul rested his elbows on the table and appeared to study his wine, but from the corner of his eye he watched as the landlord brought a bottle and cup to the fellow, who drank greedily. With a gusty sigh of satisfaction he dragged his grimy sleeve across his bearded mouth and looked about him. Catching sight of Cassandra, he grinned in a bleary fashion before settling back in his chair and closing his eyes. Within moments he was snoring.

Cassie held out her cup for Raoul to refill it.

'You see,' she murmured. 'The man is drunk, he will not trouble us.'

'And here is our dinner,' said Raoul loudly. 'And in good time, too, thank you, landlord.'

'So,' she said when they were alone again. 'You have booked our passage to Le Havre?'

He shook his head. 'I think it would be safer to go north by road to Dieppe. It would be easier for you to sail from there since it is closer to England and the crossing would be much quicker. I would wager an illicit trade still goes on between the two countries.'

'Do you mean smugglers?'

'Yes.'

She considered the matter. 'If they will take me to England, then I care not what they are. Very well, if you think that would be best, Raoul, we will go to Dieppe.'

If you think that would be best, Raoul...

The trustful look in her eyes unsettled him and he shifted uncomfortably in his seat. He had not suggested they go to Dieppe because it was best for Lady Cassandra. He would have to tell her the truth.

'There is another reason I want to go there.' He pushed his empty plate away. 'I learned today that the *Prométhée* is currently at Dieppe.'

He watched her tear off a little piece of bread and wipe it across her plate.

'That is the ship where you were surgeon?'

Raoul nodded, but his eyes were following that dainty morsel as she popped it into her mouth and licked her fingers. It was so neatly done, but the sight of her lips closing over one little finger tip was too fascinating for him to look away.

'The *Prométhée*, Raoul,' she prompted him gently. 'That was your ship?'

'What?' Raoul blinked, cursed himself for a fool and gathered his wits as best he could. 'Oh—yes, it was my ship. Captain Belfort will vouch for me, give me copies of my discharge papers and make everything *en règle*, I am sure.'

'Then of course we must go to Dieppe.'

She spoke with such cool certainty that Raoul's conscience pricked him still further.

'There is no need for you to undertake the journey. I could book your passage to Le Havre from here. The captain I spoke with today was a decent fellow. I would trust him to keep to his word and look after you.' He paused. 'I know we struck a bargain, we agreed that I would find you a ship to take you to England, but in truth, milady, the captain would be far better placed to do that, once you reach Le Havre. I will give you back what is left of your money and you can arrange matters directly with him.'

There, he had said it. He had told her the truth. If the lady had a particle of sense she would take her purse and quit his company as quickly as possible.

'And what of you, do you plan to go on to Dieppe alone?'

'Once I have discharged my duty to you, yes.'

She sipped at her wine.

'From what you have told me of Valerin, he will have men on the quay here, looking out for us.'

'True, but that is a small problem. I could distract them while you slip aboard.'

'And put yourself in more danger?' She shook her head. 'I would prefer we took our chances together.'

'It will be dangerous to come with me to Dieppe. Valerin is no fool and he will have alerted the guards at the gates. You would be safer to embark upon a ship here in Rouen. You could be in England in a couple of days.'

A party of men pushed in through the door and made their way noisily to a table in the far corner. Raoul leaned forward as if to shield Cassie from view and once they had settled down he eased back, only to discover she had moved closer.

'I would rather stay with you. I have placed my trust in men before and been deceived.'

'Ah, you mean that scoundrel courier.'

'Not just Merimon.' Her eyes slid away from his. 'We have a saying in England, *monsieur*,' she said stiffly. 'We say 'tis better the devil you know. If I have a choice, I would rather take my chances with you than trust another stranger.'

'You think me a devil, milady?'

'All men are devils,' she retorted. 'But perhaps you are less of one than most.'

'*Merci, madame*, a concession indeed.'

She ignored that. 'Besides, Valerin will think it most likely that we will try to leave Rouen by ship, will he not?'

'That is my opinion.'

'Then we shall go by road and confound him. I am wearing my riding habit. Can you obtain a lady's mount for me?' She turned to him, a faint, shy smile lighting her eyes. 'I would rather not share a horse this time.'

'I think that can be arranged.'

He felt a smile tugging at his own lips. Her courage enchanted him. He wanted to pull her close and plant a kiss upon those cherry-red lips. To smell her, taste her...

He knew she had read his thoughts. Even in the dim light of the tavern he saw a flash of recognition in the violet depths of her eyes. She moved slightly away from him.

'Now, let us think how we are to get out of Rouen. Doubtless there will be sentries at the gate.'

Her cold tone sobered him, reminded him that they came from different worlds. A mutual attraction was not enough to bridge the differences between them.

'I met several fellows at the quay today who I am sure would help us,' he replied. 'Have you finished your meal? Then let us make a start.'

Chapter Seven

By dawn they were galloping north from Rouen. In the grey, misty half-light it seemed to Cassie that all the world was asleep, save her and Raoul. She was tired, for the night had been spent in preparation. She had accompanied Raoul as he held stealthy meetings with shadowy figures. She was at his side, silent and watchful while he made all the arrangements. She heard the soft chink of coins at times and guessed that their purse was now considerably lighter. It had been an anxious time, for Cassie could not shake off the feeling that they were being followed. She often glanced behind as they made their way through the darkened streets and peeped back as they slipped through doorways. She saw no one, yet her unease persisted.

Once away from Rouen they avoided the main highways and rode along little-used tracks through the wooded countryside. Raoul had told her they would rest during the day and travel mainly at night to avoid detection and Cassie hoped she would not fall asleep and tumble out of the saddle as they pressed on northwards.

* * *

A blanket of cloud obscured the sun, but she guessed it was nearing noon when at last they made their first stop. The little-used road had led them deep within ancient woodland and Cassie followed Raoul as he turned off the track and pushed his horse through the thick undergrowth. The trees grew tall and close and the autumn gales had not yet arrived to strip the leaves from the canopy. As they moved away from the path they entered deeper into a murky half-light.

'We can rest here,' Raoul declared at last, dismounting and tethering his horse.

'Are we safe from pursuit?' She glanced back, peering anxiously between the trees. 'Are you sure we are not being followed?'

'I have seen no one and heard nothing,' he told her. 'We are far enough from the road now to escape detection, but we should not risk lighting a fire.'

'No, I would rather we did not. The cloaks you purchased will keep us warm.'

She considered jumping down before Raoul came over to help her, but her body was too weary for such independence. When he reached up for her Cassie slid down into his arms and when he held her for a moment she did not resist, but gave in to the temptation to rest her head against the broad wall of his chest.

'You are exhausted,' he said gently.

She summoned up a smile as she pushed away from him.

'I shall feel better for a little bread and wine.'

He handed her the saddlebag.

'Go and sit down. Rest and I will join you as soon as I have seen to the horses.'

Cassie unstrapped her cloak from the saddle and sought out a smooth piece of ground. The earth beneath the trees was soft and loamy. She wrapped herself in the voluminous folds of the cloak and sat down to wait for Raoul. When at last he settled beside her he began to take various packets of food from the bag. She took a small piece of bread and drank from the flask of wine that Raoul held out to her.

He said, when she handed back the flask, 'There is sausage, too. It is very good.'

'Thank you, I am too tired to eat more.'

'It will give you strength.' He cut off a slice with his knife and held it to her lips. 'Try it.'

The savoury smell was indeed enticing and she opened her mouth, gently taking the meat from him. Her lips touched his fingers, like a lover's kiss, and she felt the heat flowing up through her body. It set her cheeks on fire and her eyes flew to his face. What she read there made her heart pound. Quickly she looked away.

'Yes, you are right, it is very good. I am not usually fond of such meats, but perhaps the long ride has sharpened my appetite.' She was aware she was gabbling to cover her confusion.

He was cutting another slice for her and she put out her hand to take it from him. She could not risk another intimate touch. When Raoul offered her the flask again she shook her head. She watched him put back his head to drink, noting the powerful lines of his throat. There was a shadow of dark stubble on his lean cheeks and she thought by the evening it would be quite thick again, the beginnings of another bushy beard such as he had worn when they had first met. How long ago that seemed. How far they had travelled since he had first taken her up before him and carried her away. Her ragged, bearded rescuer.

Cassie fell into a reverie, contemplating whether she preferred him clean shaven or hirsute. She had told him once he looked like a bear, but that was untrue. He had never looked anything other than a man. Strong, resolute, reliable.

Honourable.

'We should rest now, milady.'

Raoul was packing away the remains of their scant meal and she watched him in silence, wanting to thank him for all he had done for her, yet not knowing how to begin. Instead, without a word she pulled her cloak tighter around her and lay down. She fell asleep almost immediately, but following the deep repose of exhaustion came the memories. She was back in Verdun, trying to keep up appearances and eke out the little money they had left. She knew if she wrote to Grandmama the marchioness would find a way to send her more funds, but she did not tell Gerald that. She had realised soon after they had reached Paris that Gerald was an inveterate gambler. Even before they were detained and moved to Verdun their funds were running low, but Gerald would not economise, he was certain that the next evening the cards or the dice would prove lucky and they could repair their fortunes at a stroke.

She stirred restlessly, reliving the strained silences and heated arguments. When their disagreements became more bitter Gerald took to going out without her. He accused Cassie of not liking his friends and she could not deny it, she did not trust them. She was afraid to let him go out alone, but it was impossible to go with him. She rarely saw him sober, and as the weeks went on his taunts took an unpleasant turn, wheedling, cajoling, pleading, bullying, until she grew to dread his return to their lodgings...

'Cassandra. Cassie, wake up.'

The memories receded, angry voices were replaced by birdsong and the smells and sounds of the woods filled her waking senses. Her cheeks were wet with tears and she sat up quickly, alarmed. She never cried.

'I beg your pardon,' she muttered. 'Did I disturb you?'

'No, I was awake.' Raoul's hand had been warm on her shoulder, but now he drew it away and immediately she missed the comfort of his touch. He said, 'Your dreams were not happy, I think.'

She did not reply. She could not bring herself to describe them, shamed by the failure of her marriage.

Raoul was still sitting beside her, but his cloak was already folded neatly, ready to strap on to his saddle.

'Is it time to go?' she asked.

'Soon. You may rest more first if you wish.'

Cassie shuddered, her dreams still too vivid, too fresh.

'No.' She jumped up and shook out her skirts, saying resolutely, 'I would much rather we went on.'

Raoul threw Cassandra into the saddle and mounted his own horse. He would have liked to ask what her dream was about, but she was clearly not ready to share it. He had been awake when she had become restless, muttering incoherently, growing more distressed. More than once he had heard her crying out, 'Gerald, no!' Gerald was the name of her husband. Was he a cruel man, perhaps? A wife beater? Cassandra did not have the appearance of an abused wife, but just the thought of it angered him. Perhaps he had been too hasty in thinking she had abandoned her husband.

What did it matter? He asked himself the question as they made their way through the woods, weaving between the trees until they reached the road again. If it had been a bad marriage, then she was well out of it, but it could make no difference to him. He shifted uncomfortably in his saddle. That was not true; it would be easier for him to leave her if she was a selfish aristo, as he had first thought. Now he would remember her as a brave, noble creature and he would always regret what might have been, in another time, another place. He gave himself a little shake. No. Even if she had not been another man's wife there was no future for them. He had dedicated his life to medicine, there was no room for anything other than a casual liaison and he could not imagine Cassandra would ever agree to that. Raoul glanced across at her, noting the proud tilt to her head. She was a lady, so let her return to England, to her life of ease and comfort. It was what she knew, where she would be happy. And he would be happy for her. Another night and they would be at Dieppe. Then, with a little luck, she would be off his hands.

They made slow progress through the night as the clouds thickened to obscure the moon. Whenever they came to a river Raoul avoided the bridges with their sentries and searched for a ford where they could cross. It lengthened their journey, but the country was at war and especially near the coast the guards were on the alert. Without papers they could not afford to be stopped and questioned. By dawn a steady drizzle was falling,

soaking into their cloaks and chilling the air. He saw a
huddle of farm buildings ahead of them and struck off
into the trees to wait and watch. Experience had taught
him to be cautious; such buildings could be full of soldiers. The farm looked deserted save for a few hens
pecking in the doorway of an old outhouse. He saw
an old woman hobble outside to fetch water from the
well. They had dismounted and Raoul glanced at Cassie,
who was resting against a tree. Her face was grey and
drawn in the dim light. She was shivering, too, and he
made up his mind. He gathered the horses' reins, put
one arm about Cassandra and walked purposefully towards the farmstead.

The farmhouse door was shut firm and only Raoul's
repeated knocking brought any sign of life. A small
casement window opened and the old woman looked
out.

'Good day to you,' Raoul called cheerfully. 'My wife
and I would be grateful if you would allow us to warm
ourselves by your fire for a while.'

'No, no, I am too busy. Go away.'

Raoul pulled out a handful of coins and shook them.

'I can pay you.'

The old woman hesitated.

'You can shelter in the barn, yonder,' she said at
last. 'You and your horses. I'll not have strangers in
the house.'

'You are wise, *madame*, in these uncertain times.
And could you spare us a little food? I would gladly
catch one of those hens and wring its neck for you.'

Agreement was soon reached. Raoul took Cassie
and the horses to the old wooden barn before going

off to find a plump bird for the pot. When he returned he found the horses had been unsaddled and Cassandra was busy rubbing them down with sweet-smelling straw. He frowned.

'You should not be doing that.'

'Why not?' She turned, smiling. 'It was the least I could do, since you were catching our dinner. Besides, the exertion has warmed me and I feel better for that.'

He grabbed a handful of straw and began to help her.

'So, we dine on chicken today?' she asked him.

'Yes, but not until this evening. We are to fetch it from the window when we hear the bell ring.' He nodded to the sack he had brought in with him. 'She has sent over wine and some sort of cake to keep our hunger at bay for a few more hours.'

Cassie finished rubbing down her horse and threw down the straw, yawning. 'That is very good of her, but I think sleep is what I need first.'

She shook out their cloaks and threw them over a low wooden partition to dry off.

'And I.' Raoul scrambled up into the loft and pushed down a pile of hay for the horses to eat before collecting up some empty sacks and placing them over the straw piled in the far corner of the barn. 'I hope this will be soft enough for you, milady.'

She chuckled. 'I am growing used to such deprivation.'

'Hopefully it will not be for much longer.'

'No. I hope soon to be back in England.' She fell silent and he saw she was looking a little wistful. The pensive frown vanished when she realised he was watching her and she smiled.

'To be honest I am so tired I do not think I would notice if my bed was made of stone,' she admitted.

She made herself comfortable on the sacks and Raoul thought suddenly how much he would like to see her lying naked on the very finest feather bed. He turned away quickly. She had told him her husband was an accomplished lover, so he must have often seen her like that. Lucky man.

'Are you not going to sleep, too?'

Her question only flayed his raw desire. Sleep was the last thing on his mind. He dared not look at her.

'No, not yet. I will eat something first.'

He picked up the food bag and moved away, sitting down on the sacks of turnips piled against one wall. His appetite had quite disappeared and he only made a pretence of looking in the bag until Cassie's soft, steady breathing told him she was asleep. He found another empty sack and placed it on the straw, as far away from Cassie as possible. He was dog tired, but it was some time before his blood had cooled sufficiently for him to sleep.

Cassie opened her eyes. She had slept soundly, dreamlessly and was aware of a feeling of well-being. She stretched luxuriously. The straw beneath her was very comfortable and the patter of rain on the roof made her thankful they were not sleeping out of doors again. She reached out one hand, expecting to feel Raoul's solid body beside her and when it was not there she panicked, sitting up and looking about her wildly.

'Is anything wrong, milady?'

He was stretched out on the far side of the piled

straw, lying on his back with his hands behind his head, watching her.

She answered him without thinking. 'I thought I had lost you.'

He sat up, saying shortly, 'I gave you my word I would see you safe aboard a ship for England.'

That had not been her concern, but it would be too difficult to explain so she did not try. Instead she rose and tried unsuccessfully to brush tiny wisps of straw from her skirts.

'I am thankful we found shelter here today,' she said. 'Even if it is only a barn.'

'The old woman thawed considerably once I handed over the bird for her to prepare,' said Raoul. 'She told me her son has been conscripted into the army and she has to manage here alone now, except for the occasional visits from her brother.'

'Poor thing, no wonder she is wary of us. But I do not mind staying in this barn. At least we are warm and we are protected from the rain.' She paused. 'What did you tell her, about us?'

'I did not need to say much at all. The old mother has a fertile imagination.'

'Oh?'

He grinned. 'I let her think we were man and wife, that is all. She guessed we had been on a pilgrimage to Rouen and I did not correct her.'

Cassie nodded. 'The French government may well have tried to abolish religion, but I am sure many people still cling to their beliefs, especially in remote areas such as this.'

'And marriage here still means a lifelong commitment, milady.'

The words were out before Raoul could stop them. Cassie looked up, her eyes flying to his face. He read the hurt there, but could not apologise. If she thought his words were aimed at her, then he could not deny it. He knew he should not blame her for the desire she roused in him, but he could and did blame her for abandoning her lawful husband. She looked away. He knew she was aware of his disapproval, but when she spoke her voice was calm enough, although he heard the note of reserve.

'Perhaps, *monsieur*, we should try a little of the food our hostess has supplied?'

The wine was rough, but palatable enough and it helped Cassandra to swallow the cake, which was dry and stale. She knew Raoul thought her contemptible for leaving her husband. She thought with a quick flash of annoyance that if he had not fallen asleep in Flagey he would know the truth. She had to admit she was reluctant to confess it all again. She did not want to tell Raoul she had lied to him in the first place. Understandable, perhaps, since he had been a stranger then and she had been wary of trusting him.

He was still a stranger, she reminded herself. They had known each other such a short time, so why did she feel that she had known him all her life? It was strangely comfortable, sitting in the dim barn with horses snuffling in the far corner. She glanced up at Raoul under her lashes. She trusted him with her life, so surely she should trust him with her secrets.

'Raoul,' she began tentatively, 'what I told you, about my husband—'

She got no further. Raoul put up his hand to silence

her. He was listening intently and Cassie heard it, too, the bright jingle of harnesses and beating tattoo of many of hoofs. Riders were approaching. Raoul ran to the wall of the barn. The planks had weathered and the gaps were large enough to look out.

'Soldiers.' He turned and came back to her. 'Quickly, up into the hayloft, out of sight.'

Cassie gathered her skirts in one hand and scrambled up the ladder. Raoul threw their cloaks and food bag into the hayloft and followed her, drawing the ladder up after him. Outside she could hear the soldiers' voices. Quietly, Cassie moved to the side of the barn and peered through a crack. The yard was filled with horses and the men were gathered about the well, filling their water canteens while the rain dripped from their hats. Two of the officers were standing at the farmhouse door, talking to the old woman. Cassie held her breath, expecting at any moment that they would turn towards the barn.

Raoul had crawled across beside her and he, too, was peering out through the gap. Cassie's heart almost stopped when one of the men moved away from the troop and headed for the barn. Instinctively she reached for Raoul's hand and gripped it as they watched the soldier approach. The man did not head for the door, but stopped to relieve himself against the wall just below them. Raoul put his arm around Cassie's shoulder and pulled her away from the wall. She looked at him, one hand across her mouth to stifle the giggle that was welling up. He frowned and shook his head, but his eyes were alight with laughter. Their amusement died, however, when they heard more footsteps approaching the barn. Cassie held her breath. Raoul was tense and alert beside her. She knew he had the pistol he had taken from Valerin, but what use would that be against a dozen or so soldiers?

A sudden crackle of musket fire from the woods changed everything. Shouts went up, the soldiers were running back to their horses and moments later the whole troop had clattered away from the farm. A few more shots were heard, at a greater distance, and the thunder of hoofs died away, followed by almost complete silence. Cassie rolled on to her back, eyes closed and grinning with relief at their narrow escape. She heard Raoul's ragged laugh.

'You, milady, are a baggage. How could you give way to amusement at such a time?'

When she opened her eyes he was propped on one elbow, looking down at her.

'I did not give way,' she protested, still smiling broadly. 'I was as quiet as a mouse…'

Her words trailed away into silence as she held his gaze and recognised the hot glow in his dark eyes. She fancied that there were devils dancing there, but strangely the thought did not frighten her. Raoul cupped her face with his free hand, his thumb stroking the skin of her cheek. His touch left a burning trail in its wake and made the breath catch in her throat. She tilted her chin, running her tongue over her lips. She was inviting him to kiss her and he needed no second bidding.

Raoul captured her mouth, his heart jumping as he tasted her sweetness. It was every bit as delightful as he remembered. The bolt of desire that had shot through him as she lay laughing up at him drove itself deeper, sending the hot blood pumping through his veins and putting to flight all rational thought. His fingers slid from her cheek and down to the soft swell of her breast. She did not recoil, instead her body tensed and pushed against his hand. He deepened his kiss, allowing his tongue to tease and explore her mouth while he unbuttoned her jacket and the shirt beneath. Her arms wound around his neck, fingers driving through his hair as she gave him back kiss for kiss. She stilled, he heard the moan deep in her throat when his hand slipped beneath the stays and lifted one breast free, rubbing his thumb across the stiffened peak.

Cassie threw back her head, but pushed her body closer to Raoul, measuring her length against his as he trailed kisses down her neck, his fingers working their way beneath the hard linen of her stays to free her breasts. He cupped one in his hand, his thumb circling wickedly while his lips and his tongue played with the other. Her body ached with the sheer pleasure of his touch; he was wreaking havoc with her senses and turning her very bones to water. She cradled his head in her hands, aware of the silkiness of his hair between her fingers as he continued to caress her. When she felt his teeth tug oh so gently at one aching nub she could not suppress a soft, animal cry, a mixture of longing and delight.

She arched against him, excitement spiralling through her when she felt his body pressed against her. He was hard and aroused, she was aware of it, even through the folds of her skirts. She wanted to feel his skin against hers, to have him assuage the ache that was spreading through her body, taking control. When he raised his head she was bereft, but only for a moment, until his mouth found hers once more and she could return his kiss with a fervour that she had not known she possessed.

He slid one hand down over her hips, pulling aside the skirts and petticoats. His fingers smoothed over the fine silk of her stocking, moving up past the garter and on to the skin of her thigh. She trembled at his touch and her heart leapt and hammered with anticipation. All considerations of propriety, of caution, counted for nought. She wanted him inside her with a desperation that shocked her, but she had never felt so sure of anything in her life. Her hands scrabbled at his breeches until he pushed aside her fumbling fingers and unfastened the fall flap himself.

Cassie wrapped her arms around his neck again as he continued to kiss her. She slipped one leg around him, wanting him to satisfy the hunger that was consuming her. His fingers were stroking her thigh, moving closer to her heated core. She was almost crying out with her need, her head ringing.

Through the mist of her excitement Cassie realised that the ringing was not inside her head. It was coming from somewhere outside the barn. Raoul had stopped kissing her, his body was poised above her, but he had grown very still.

'Ah.'

Slowly, painfully Raoul fought for control as the insistent clamour of the hand bell forced itself into his consciousness. Could anything have been worse timed to prevent him sating his desires? Or better timed to stop him from taking another man's wife. As a boy he had seen how *Maman* had suffered at his father's neglect. How much more painful would it have been if he had actually committed adultery? Raoul had vowed then he would never succumb to the charms of a married woman and he had kept that vow. Until now.

He eased himself away from the warm, yielding body beneath him and sat up, turning his back on Cassandra. He dared not look at her lest his control should snap. He knew it was still as fragile as fine glass.

'A most judicious interruption, I think.' He spoke lightly, his tone completely at odds with the fire that was raging through him like a fever.

'Raoul.'

He heard the uncertainty as Cassie murmured his name and he closed his eyes, breathing deeply. He was fighting with everything he had not to turn back and finish what they had started. When she touched his arm he shook her off, saying harshly, 'I know you English think nothing of infidelity, milady, but in my world such betrayal is wrong. I could not forgive myself if I came between a man and his wife. I have seen the pain such an act can inflict.' He began to fasten his clothes, keeping his back to her lest he should look into her eyes. Even now he knew he might weaken. 'If I am not mistaken our hostess is calling us and not a moment too soon. Straighten your clothes, milady, while I go and fetch our dinner.'

Cassie watched as Raoul dropped the ladder back in place and quickly descended without sparing her another glance. Hot tears burned her eyelids and she blinked them away, determined that she would not cry. She crossed her arms over her stomach. She should be thankful for Raoul's restraint. A coupling here, with a man she would most likely never see again was sheer madness, but at this very moment, with her body still burning up with desire, it was hard not to regret the clamouring hand bell that had put an end to that madness.

She sat up and felt a slight tug on her neck as the locket she wore beneath her riding habit dropped back into place. She put up one hand to clasp the cool metal, her fingers tracing the outline of the large ruby fixed in the cover while she thought of the picture inside. Her husband. A handsome, smiling face that hid a weak and selfish nature. So different from Raoul. She felt dizzy, her body still thrumming from Raoul's touch, but she must forget how right it felt to be in his arms, how his kiss had thrilled her. How much it had hurt when he rejected her.

He still thinks you are a married woman, that you were about to commit adultery.

She must tell him the truth, then perhaps he would not hold her in such contempt. And then what would happen? She would give herself to him in the heat of passion, only to discover once again that she had mistaken her feelings. Or even worse, that his were transitory. She shivered. How could they be anything else, upon such a short acquaintance? Slowly she fastened the buttons of her shirt and jacket.

No, better to let him think ill of you, since you do not have the strength of will to withstand the attraction.

But as she carefully descended the ladder Cassie knew she would tell him the truth. Whatever the dangers, she could not bear to have him thinking badly of her.

* * *

Raoul returned a few moments later carrying a large tray laden with plates and dishes.

'Dinner is served, milady.'

He was smiling, his voice perfectly friendly, but his eyes were shuttered, and Cassie felt as if a barrier had come down between them. His demeanour was that of a stranger and she was too raw, too uncertain to confide in him now.

They consumed their meal sitting apart, like two strangers, and as soon as they had finished Raoul collected up the dishes and took them back to the farmhouse.

'We will set off again when it is dark,' he said when he returned. 'The rain has stopped and the sky is clearing, we should have the moon to light our way. I believe if we press on we will reach Dieppe by morning, but it will be a long ride, so we had best try to get some sleep.'

Without another word he threw himself down on his makeshift bed of straw and sacks and turned his back on her. Cassie swallowed a sigh and lay down on the sacks she had used earlier. They were lying at the far sides of the pile of straw so even if she threw out an arm she could not touch him, but the distance between them could not be measured now in feet and inches. It was imperative that she explain to him that she was not the selfish, adulterous wife he thought her, but not now. Now they both needed to rest before the long ride to Dieppe.

Their final journey started well enough. A light breeze blew small clouds across the sky, but rarely obscured the sliver of moon that hung above them. However as they rode north the air became heavier, the cloud thickened and thunder rumbled ominously in the distance. They followed a track through a narrow, wooded gorge with bare rock rising up like high black walls on either side. Cassie shivered and looked around nervously. As she did so a flash of lightning made the world as light as day and she screamed.

'Raoul, there is someone back there, in the trees!'

Immediately Raoul stopped and turned his horse, staring hard into the darkness. They both listened intently, but there was nothing, other than the keening wind that was rustling the leaves.

'Perhaps I imagined it,' she muttered.

'Perhaps, or it could have been an animal,' said Raoul. 'If there was anyone there they have gone now.' More thunder rumbled, accompanied by bright, searing flashes. 'Come along. I think we would do well to find shelter.'

The storm clouds were gathering rapidly, there was very little moonlight left and when Raoul spotted the black mouth of a cave just ahead he turned his horse from the path and made his way towards it.

They were just in time. Even as they approached the cave the first, fat drops of rain began to fall. They dismounted and led the horses towards the shadowy aperture. The cave turned out to be little more than a rocky overhang, but it was deep enough to provide shelter for them and the horses. They had barely reached it when the rain turned to a heavy, drenching downpour. The animals snorted nervously as a clap of thunder rent the air and rumbled around the skies. Apart from the occasional flicker of lightning it was very dark and everything was reduced to shades of black.

Cassie peered out into the gloom. 'Do you think there is anyone out there?'

'I doubt it. Valerin would not hesitate to move in if he had us in his sights.'

Cassie nodded. She tried to remember just what she had seen, but it had been so fleeting, a mere shadow moving quickly between the trees. It was nerves, she told herself. She was growing fanciful. She found a small ledge at the back of the shallow cave to rest upon while Raoul paced restlessly up and down, little more than a black shadow moving against the darkness.

'Will you not sit down?' she asked him. 'There is enough space here for two.'

'Thank you, no. I am glad to stretch my legs.'

'You would rather not be near me.' She stated it baldly, trying not to sound wistful.

'That is true.'

She clasped her hands tightly and screwed up her courage. It was time to speak.

'Raoul, I have to tell you, I…I lied to you. When we first met. I *was* married, yes, but I am a widow now. My husband died at Verdun and it was only then that I decided to return to England.'

He had stopped pacing, but she could not see his face. She fancied he had his back to her, looking out into the night. She would have to listen carefully to his reply and judge his reaction by his tone.

'Ah.'

There was nothing to be learned from that brief response. She felt rather than saw him turn.

'Why do you tell me this now?'

'Because I do not want you to think badly of me. Or to blame yourself for...for what nearly happened in the barn.'

He said politely, 'I am grateful, milady.'

A flicker of lightning showed him standing before her, his face impassive. As the darkness returned he was moving again, muttering that he would just check the horses were securely tethered. Moments later he was back, a black presence, almost invisible in the darkness.

'These storms rarely last too long,' he said. 'We shall be able to resume our journey again soon.'

She frowned. Was that all? He had no other comment to make about her confession? She strained her eyes against the blackness.

'It is not just that you thought me a married woman, is it? There is something more. Is it my birth that makes you dislike me?'

'I do not...dislike you.'

'No.' She sighed. 'At times I have thought we might even be friends, but at others...'

'You are English. You are my enemy.'

'But you told me yourself you are from Brussels, that is not part of France.'

'True, but I wanted it to be, at one time. I was full of revolutionary zeal when I joined the French Navy to fight the English.'

'And you left it because you have no faith in the Consulate or in Bonaparte.'

'That does not mean I no longer hate the English.'

'Hate is a strong word, Raoul. What happened to make you so bitter?'

He cursed angrily.

'Damn your arrogance! You are paying me to escort

you to Dieppe, nothing more. It does not give you the right to pry into my life.'

She reeled in dismay at his outburst and quickly begged pardon.

'I did not mean to pry, I…' She hesitated. What should she say; that she cared about him? She knew he did not want that. She murmured again, 'I beg your pardon.'

Silence. When Raoul did speak it was to say merely, 'The rain has stopped. We may continue our journey.'

The conversation was at an end and Cassie almost screamed with frustration. Raoul said he did not dislike her, yet he hated her race. She wanted to know why, but the moment was lost and he would not tell her now. She stood up and looked about her. She had been so intent on their conversation she had not noticed that the thunder had moved away and the downpour had ceased. The clouds were breaking up, too, and the crescent moon had once more made an appearance.

Raoul threw Cassandra up into the saddle before scrambling on to his own horse. He had never been more thankful to be moving. He had no wish to explain himself to this infuriating woman. How dare she ask it of him? He owed her nothing. She was no more than an arrogant, self-seeking aristocrat. How did he know she was a widow, how could he be sure she was not merely saying that to placate him, now he had told her he disapproved of adultery?

Even as the angry thoughts drove through his brain he remembered the night they had met, the black lace shawl fluttering in his face. He had discarded it then without a second thought. Perhaps it was true, she was a widow, but why should she not admit it from the start? Did she think a man would be deterred from seducing her by the thought of an outraged husband seeking vengeance? That might be so, but it did not alter the fact that she was by birth a detested aristocrat, a proud, selfish creature.

No. Raoul could not pretend he truly believed that. Cassie had made no complaint during their long journey although the hardships had been great for a gently bred lady. And he could not forget how she had wanted to help when they came upon the collapsed barn. She could have taken a room at the *auberge* and remained there safe and comfortable, instead she had worked tirelessly.

He glanced over his shoulder at the upright little figure riding behind him. When he had told her his reasons for going to Dieppe she had not hesitated. They could have parted at Rouen, she might well have been on her way to England by now, instead she chose to ride with him. Why should she do that? His mind shied away from the answer that presented itself.

A grey dawn was lightening the eastern sky when Raoul next looked back at Cassie. Through the gloom he could see unhappiness clouding her face. *He* had done that, he had turned on her, accused her of prurient curiosity when all she wanted was to understand.

He slowed his horse and waited for her to come alongside.

'I told you my father was a doctor,' he began, not wasting time with preliminaries. 'He was well respected in Brussels and amongst his patients were several grand English families. They had titles and money, even though most had fled from England to escape their creditors. They were also arrogant and demanding, none more so than a certain English countess. It was "Oh, Doctor, I have the headache…" and "Doctor, I am in pain…" This countess would think nothing of sending a servant to fetch my father in the middle of the night for the mildest of ailments. He was at her beck and call at all hours. He never complained, never delayed a visit or refused to go. She dazzled him, I think, even more so than the other English nobles. He was in awe of her title and her grand ways. So much so that he neglected his other patients and his family.' Raoul's jaw clenched as the memories flooded back. 'He did not even notice that his own wife was in failing health. In fact, I believe he deliberately avoided it, since to tend his wife would have given him less time to spend with the English milords. *Maman* sickened and died. I was just thirteen at the time, my sister was even younger. We did what we could to nurse her, but we could not save her. From what I have learned since I believe that if the growth had been diagnosed, if an operation had been carried out early enough, she might have lived, but my father would not even acknowledge that she was ill.

'Is it any wonder that I grew up with a burning resentment against the aristos with their money and selfish demands? And especially I hated the English. France was in the grip of its revolution then and I understood why the old regime had to go. I thought then that change was good, whatever the cost. I was young and idealistic, I thought Europe would be a better place under this new, fairer French government. I also believed that it would be a good thing to bring England under French rule, to destroy the aristocracy that bled its people dry. Older, wiser friends in Brussels tried to counsel caution, but

I would not listen and my father showed no interest at all in my views. I did not understand then that he was crippled with guilt and regret. After *Maman's* death he threw himself even more into his work. His patients and his duty always came before any consideration for his family. We were left to fend for ourselves.'

'And yet you, too, wanted to study medicine?'

'Being a surgeon is not a choice for me, milady. It is what I am.'

'I know that,' she said quietly. 'I have seen you at work.'

Having started to explain, he could not stop now. 'Only when he was dying did my father admit that he had failed us, especially he had failed my mother. He blamed his calling, he had never wanted to be anything other than a doctor, it was his life, an all-consuming passion.'

She interrupted him. 'Forgive me, but your father believed his *calling* prevented him from seeing that your mother was ill? How can that be?'

'It was only a part of it. He confessed that being physician to the rich and privileged in Brussels had turned his head, especially the attentions of the English countess.' He added bitterly, 'He was so busy pandering to her imagined illnesses that he ignored the symptoms of illness that *Maman* displayed. He was always more interested in his patients than his family and that was his final piece of advice to me. He would have preferred me to be a doctor, but if I was determined to be a surgeon, then so be it, but he told me that medical men—physicians, doctors—should never marry. They live for their work, to the exclusion of all else. There can be no compromise.'

'What if they should fall in love?'

He had asked himself this question many times and the answer came easily.

'They must not. They may take lovers, yes, but there should never be any serious attachment.' He glanced towards her. 'You should appreciate such sentiments, milady, since you believe love to be overprized in your society.'

'I do,' she agreed, putting up her chin. 'There is much to be said for your view. I fell head over heels in love with Gerald and eloped with him, thinking the world well lost, but it did not last. Such a heady passion never could. Although *my* affection lasted considerably longer than my husband's,' she ended bitterly.

'How did he die?' asked Raoul.

'A duel.' She paused, her brows drawing together slightly as she frowned. 'A duel over another man's wife. I told you my husband would never take me to a ball. I would not play his games, you see. I did not wish to flirt with other men and I objected to his attentions to other women. So, I was left at home. He told me he was meeting friends, going to gambling hells, and I chose to believe that. In fact, he was escorting other ladies to balls and assemblies. Any number of them. One husband took exception and called him out.'

'I am very sorry.'

'Do not be. He had spent all our money on gambling and women. If he had lived he would have continued until we were deep in debt. His morals, too, were not what I first thought them. He was sinking into depravity and...' she swallowed '...and he was close to taking me with him.'

'Those dreams,' said Raoul. 'I heard you call out for him to stop. Did—was he—?'

He saw her shudder.

'A husband is entitled to his rights,' she said.

Raoul was silent. So he was wrong, she had not abandoned her husband. Or at least so she said. Could he believe her? The answer was already in his heart. He knew this woman now as if she was a part of him.

'Raoul.' Her voice broke into his thoughts. She was sitting straighter in the saddle, staring at the road ahead. 'There are some men on the road in front of us.'

Raoul heard the urgency in her voice, but he had already spotted the men and unease was prickling his skin. There were four of them approaching and at a point where the terrain would make it difficult to evade them.

'Stay behind me,' he muttered. 'If there is trouble you must turn and ride away, do you understand?'

It was light enough now for Raoul to see that the men were in ragged uniforms and two of them held short, heavy sticks in their hands. Deserters, perhaps, rogues certainly. They were in a line across the road, blocking the way.

'Good day to you,' he hailed them cheerfully. 'I hope you mean to move aside and allow two weary travellers to pass.'

One of the men, presumably the leader, stepped forward to answer him.

'With pleasure, my friend, once you have given us your purse and your horses.'

'I think not.'

The fellow slapped the club menacingly against his empty palm. 'Hand them over freely, *monsieur*, and you and your woman may walk on unharmed. Resist and I will smash your horse's knees and then we will kill you. And the woman, too, after we have taken our pleasure.'

Raoul pulled out the pistol. He would have to make good use of his one shot and pray he could give Cassie time to escape. He decided he would rather face them on foot, so he quickly slipped out of the saddle and took a few steps towards the leader, who bared his teeth in an ugly grin.

'One bullet against four men? The odds are not in your favour, *monsieur*.'

It was the truth and Raoul knew it, but he must give Cassie a chance to get clear. He was bracing himself for a tough fight when a voice spoke behind him.

'Then let us make the odds a little fairer, shall we?'

A tall black-bearded figure in riding dress emerged from the bushes at the roadside, a pistol in each hand and a serviceable-looking sword at his side.

'You see there are three pistols now,' the stranger continued. 'And I warn you that I am an excellent shot.'

He stepped up beside Raoul, but even as he did so the four ragged assailants were backing away and a moment later they were crashing away through the bushes.

Cassie had watched the whole from a distance, her chest constricted with fear, but now the immediate danger had passed she jumped down, collecting up the reins of the loose horse and walking towards Raoul and the tall stranger.

'We are very grateful for your assistance, *monsieur*,' she said, smiling up at the man and holding out her hand. 'Your arrival was most opportune.'

He bowed over her fingers. 'Do I have the pleasure of addressing Lady Cassandra Witney?'

Cassie stared up at him, surprised.

'Why, yes,' she said. 'How do you know my name?'

'I am your cousin, Wolfgang Arrandale.'

Chapter Eight

'Wolfgang!' Cassie exclaimed. 'But how—? What—?'

Raoul cut short her stammering questions with a wave of one hand.

'I suggest we move away from here. Those rogues might well return.'

'I agree,' said Wolfgang. 'My horse is hidden in the trees. I will collect him and we will ride on. There is an inn about half a mile ahead, we can talk there.'

He walked off, leaving Cassie to stare after him.

'Let me help you to mount.'

Raoul's words took a few moments to penetrate her bemused state, but at last she allowed him to throw her up into the saddle.

'So he claims to be your cousin,' said Raoul. 'Do you recognise him?'

'No, of course not. He fled England nearly ten years ago.'

'Fled?'

'Yes. He was accused of killing his wife and stealing her jewels.'

'And did he?'

A tiny crease furrowed Cassie's brow.

'I do not know,' she said slowly. 'Why would he run away, if he is innocent?'

Raoul was tempted to remind her that he was doing just that, but at that moment the man calling himself Wolfgang Arrandale trotted up on a glossy black hunter and instead Raoul turned to appraise horse and rider.

'I'd wager that beast is no hired hack.'

'No.' The man leaned forward to pat the glossy neck. 'Satan is my own. We have been through many adventures together.'

Cassie brought her mare alongside the black.

'Is that how you live, Cousin, as a soldier of fortune?'

Cousin. Raoul's brows rose a little. So she had decided to accept that he was who he claimed to be.

Arrandale gave a little shrug and said indifferently, 'Something like that. Shall we go?'

Raoul scrambled up into his saddle and trotted after the others. There was no doubt that Arrandale's intervention was timely, for the situation had been looking decidedly ugly, but Raoul could not help wishing it had been a chance stranger who had come to their aid. He might then have accepted their thanks and gone on his way. The fact that the fellow was Cassie's cousin could not be coincidence. If he *was* Wolfgang Arrandale. After all they only had his word for it.

He watched Cassie turn her head to look up at her companion and felt something twist in his gut. Something suspiciously like jealousy. He dragged his eyes away and glowered at his horse's ears.

'Do not be ridiculous,' he muttered savagely to the hapless animal. 'If the fellow is her cousin and he has come looking for her, then your job is done. He can take care of her'.

But as they clattered into the cobbled yard of the inn Raoul realised with a jolt that he did not wish to consign Lady Cassandra to anyone's care.

'So, Cousin, what are you doing here?'

Cassandra could hardly wait until the landlord had left them at their table before she put the question.

'I have been following you.'

'So I was not imagining it.' She threw a triumphant glance at Raoul. 'I thought I saw something in the woods last night.'

'Yes, it was careless of me to get so close.'

'But why was it necessary for you to hide?' demanded Raoul. 'Why did you not declare yourself and ride with us?'

Wolfgang spread his hands. 'I could have been wrong. It wasn't until I looked my cousin in the eye just now that I was sure.'

Raoul nodded. Despite Arrandale's full beard it was possible to see a strong similarity between him and Lady Cassandra. Both had an abundance of curling dark hair and thick, dark lashes fringing those unusually coloured eyes. In Wolfgang's case his eyes were more blue than violet, but the likeness was sufficient to convince Raoul that they were related.

'Well I am very glad you decided to follow us,' said Cassie, smiling at her cousin in a way that made Raoul grit his teeth. 'You saved us from those horrid men.'

'I also saved your skin at the farm.'

'Ah,' said Raoul, remembering the musket shots that

had sounded so opportunely. 'Was it you who drew off the soldiers?'

Those eyes, so like Cassie's, turned to look at him.

'It was the least I could do, for a fellow fugitive.'

'But how did you find us?' Cassie demanded. 'And why were you even looking for me?'

'Lady Hune.'

'Grandmama's letters reached you? I did not think they would. No one has had any word from you for years. To be truthful I thought you were dead.'

'My great-aunt—your grandmother—is very persistent. I believe she wrote many letters in the hope that at least one of them would reach me. She numbers amongst her acquaintances several members of the French aristocracy who survived the Terror and now live...er...outside the law. When I first came to France Lady Hune asked them to look out for me. Let us say I am returning the favour.'

Cassie frowned. 'But that does not explain how you found us, or what Grandmama expects you to do.'

'She wants me to spirit you back to England, of course.'

'*Could* you do that?' asked Raoul.

'Quite possibly. I went to Verdun with the intention of getting my cousin and her husband out of France, but I learned there that Witney was dead and his widow had left for England.' He looked at Cassie. 'I had only missed you by a matter of days and thought there might be a chance to catch up with you, so I went to Rouen. There was no trace of a Lady Cassandra Witney ever having arrived there. However, I did learn of an English milady and her husband staying in the town, so I thought I might take a look, in case you had got yourself into some sort of scrape.'

Cassie straightened in her chair and said indignantly, 'Why should you think I was in a scrape?'

'Because you are an Arrandale, Cousin. We have a talent for getting into trouble.'

Raoul laughed at that.

'Very true!' He saw the angry fire sparkling in Cassie's eyes and continued, before she could retort, 'But never mind that, now. You followed us from Rouen?'

'Yes. I arrived at the inn soon after the law officers. The tapster told me some government man from Paris was there to arrest a deserter and his English lover. The serving maid's description was enough to convince me the lady might well be my cousin. With so many *gendarmes* milling around the inn I thought it would be safer if I did not tarry so I retired to the street corner, keeping an eye on the place and trying to decide what to do. Then a commotion broke out. From my vantage point I think I was the only one to see a couple running away through the alley at the back of the inn. I followed you from there.'

Cassie remembered her unease as they had walked through the narrow streets.

'But I do not understand. Why did we not see you?'

'I had...*acquired* the clothes of a common seaman. It seemed more fitting, since we were so close to the quay.'

'The snoring sailor,' remarked Raoul, grinning.

'The very same.' Arrandale straightened in his chair and fixed Raoul with a piercing gaze. He said with a touch of hauteur that reminded Raoul strongly of Lady

Cassandra, 'But I have not yet discovered why *you* are escorting my cousin, *monsieur.*'

'Oh, it is all quite simple,' Cassie rushed in to explain. 'The courier I hired to take me to Rouen was a villain and Raoul rescued me.'

Her cousin did not look to be impressed. He kept his eyes upon Raoul.

'Word in Rouen was that you are one Raoul Doulevant, a deserter from the navy.'

'It is no such thing,' said Cassie indignantly. 'That horrid man Valerin destroyed Raoul's records and put out a false report about him.'

Wolf sat back in his chair. 'Really?'

'You do not believe me,' she exclaimed. 'It is true, Cousin, I assure you. Raoul is an honourable man.'

Without thinking she had put her hand over Raoul's, where it rested on the table, and he was obliged to quell the sudden soaring elation he felt at the gesture.

'Your cousin is rightly concerned for you,' he said, reluctantly withdrawing his hand. 'Rest assured, *monsieur*, we travel as man and wife in name only. Funds are low and milady has no maid to accompany her.'

'I can see that,' growled Arrandale. 'The question is, Doulevant, what is your plan?'

'To find a ship to carry milady to England from Dieppe.'

Arrandale nodded. 'The town is crawling with soldiers, but it should be possible. I have friends there who can help us.'

'You will come to England with me?' Cassie asked hopefully.

'Alas, I cannot return to England. You forget, Cousin, there is a price on my head. I am wanted for the murder of my wife.' He added bitterly, 'Even worse in the eyes of the English, I am accused of stealing a diamond necklace belonging to her family.'

'But if you are innocent—'

'Who would believe me? Even my own father thought I was guilty. He shipped me out of the country before I could be arrested. It is better that I remain in France. There is nothing for me in England now.'

'There is Arrandale,' said Cassie. 'And your daughter.'

He looked up at that. 'I have a daughter?'

'Yes, a little girl called Florence. Surely you knew that?'

He shook his head. 'I thought the child had died with her mother.' He was silent for a moment. 'I moved around a great deal when I first came to France and in truth I did not wish to keep in touch with my family. I was angry that they should believe the worst without giving me a chance to defend myself. I saw only the report in an English newspaper that there was a reward for my capture. Where is Florence now?'

'She lives with Lord Davenport's family.'

'Then she is better off without me.'

'But—'

'No, Cassandra. I cannot accompany you to England. It is impossible. You will have to make do with Doulevant's escort.'

'No, no, you misunderstand,' said Raoul quickly. 'It was never my intention to go to England. My service to milady ends once she is safely aboard ship.'

Cassie was still smarting from the way Raoul had pulled his hand away from hers and his last words stung her even more. She should not care, after all it would not be long now before they parted for ever, but she was surprised how much it hurt to discover that he would be very relieved once she was off his hands. Wolfgang was speaking and she tried to concentrate upon his words.

'You would send her alone? What do you think will happen once she reaches England?'

Cassie braced herself to hear Raoul say he neither knew nor cared. His reply was a tiny crumb of comfort.

'I have been thinking about that. Is there a way we can send ahead to this Lady Hune? Then she could send someone to meet Lady Cassandra.'

'That is possible, I suppose. It would mean delaying until we could get a message to the marchioness. Her letters to me were from London, but she may be back in Bath by now.'

'No, she is in Essex,' put in Cassandra. 'At Chantreys. The last letter I have from her says she will be staying at Lord Davenport's house there until December at least, to look after the earl's wards while he and his new wife are on honeymoon.'

Wolfgang looked up in surprise. 'James has married again?'

'Did you not know? James and his wife were drowned last winter. His brother Alex is now the earl.'

'Alex!' Wolfgang exclaimed. 'I did not think he was the marrying kind, he was always a wild one, but I suppose he must think about the succession.' He cast another searching look at Cassie. 'And Alex is now my daughter's guardian?'

'Yes, I believe so and also to James's daughter, Margaret. They are of a similar age.'

Her cousin frowned, as if digesting all he had heard, then he gave a shrug.

'Essex is closer than Bath, so in the event it works out better for us. I will send word to Lady Hune as soon as I have organised your passage and we know where on the coast you will be coming ashore, Cousin.'

'You seem to have forgotten the war,' put in Raoul. 'It may not be so easy to arrange all this.'

For the first time since they met Cassie saw her cousin smile.

'It is easy enough if you know the right people. I lived in this area for a few years when I first came to France and I still have friends along this coast. However, it may take a few days to arrange everything. In the meantime you would be best staying in Dieppe, I think. Strangers would attract less attention there than in any of the smaller ports along this coast.'

'That will suit me very well,' agreed Raoul. 'I have business in Dieppe.'

'Then it is settled.' Wolfgang drained his tankard and set it down on the table. 'We should press on, there will be much to do once we reach the town.' He leaned closer. 'One more thing, I am known here as Georges Lagrasse, a citizen of Toulouse. I think it will be best if I claim acquaintance with Doulevant rather than you, Cassandra. Your French is good, but you are clearly a foreigner.'

'Just what I told her, *monsieur*,' remarked Raoul, draining his own cup. 'We are in agreement on one thing, at least.'

Cassie, offended by this display of male solidarity, swept out of the tavern before them.

* * *

By the time they reached Dieppe it was past noon and beginning to rain again. Wolfgang gave them directions to an inn.

'It is clean and comfortable and I know the landlord, he is to be trusted. He is accustomed to travellers and is unlikely to ask you for your papers. If anyone *should* enquire, Cassandra, it would be best to say you are Irish. The recent bombardment of the town has made the people here less friendly towards the English.'

'Let us hope it is not necessary to say anything,' put in Cassie. 'I would rather we did not attract any more attention than necessary.'

'I agree,' said Wolfgang. 'Very well, get you to the inn. I shall be in contact once I have secured for you a safe passage to England.'

'You are not coming with us?' she asked him.

'No. I have friends here who will give me a bed and help me find you a ship.'

Cassie was tempted to ask him about his friends, but decided it would be wiser not to know. From her conversations with her cousin during their journey she guessed that he lived a precarious existence in France, so now she merely wished him good luck and followed Raoul to the inn.

For Cassie it had become a familiar charade. She hung, exhausted, on Raoul's arm while he gave a false name and told the landlord they required accommodation with a separate bedchamber for their maid, who was following with the luggage. The recent storm accounted for their dishevelled appearance and they were shown upstairs to a comfortable suite overlooking the street. Their accommodation comprised a small ante-room which opened on to the main bedchamber and a truckle bed was prepared in the dressing room beyond. Cassie made no demur when Raoul ordered dinner to be served in their rooms. She was too tired to eat in public, knowing she would have to be on her guard against any slip of the tongue. Now all she had to resist was the growing attraction she felt for Raoul Doulevant.

'I am going out again,' he said as soon as they were alone. 'There is an hour or so before dinner and I must see if the *Prométhée* is in the harbour. I may be too late; she may already have sailed elsewhere.'

'Of course,' she replied. 'I wish you luck, Raoul.'

With a nod he went out and she moved restlessly about the apartment, making herself familiar with the rooms. She could not forget the last time Raoul had left her alone at an inn and she took time to look for possible routes of escape. But it was not fear of Valerin finding them that disturbed her most, it was Raoul's cool manner. It had become very marked since they had met her cousin and if Cassie didn't know better she would have thought he was jealous. But that was ridiculous, of course, and it was also quite ridiculous that she should *care*.

Cassie sighed and clasped her hands together. If only there was no war, no social divisions. If only they could meet and talk as equals. If only...

She found she was obliged to blink back a tear. Angrily she stalked back into the anteroom. There was no point in wishing for the impossible. She could not deny her birth; she was the daughter of a marquess and her ancestors could be traced back to the Conqueror. She was going back to England, to the world she knew and understood. She thrust aside the shadow of loneliness that clouded her vision of the future. It was quite possible that Grandmama would find her a husband, a kind, generous man who would care for her and whom she would grow to love. It would be a safe, comfortable existence in a world she knew. It was where she belonged. Raoul could never be happy there, even if he had wanted to join her. And that was the point, wasn't it? He did not want her in his life. This new coolness was most likely a sign of relief that their time together was almost over.

'Which just goes to show that he is far more sensible than you,' she lectured herself. 'You have already made one *mésalliance*, but Gerald was at least English and a gentleman. To marry outside your sphere would be an even greater folly and not to be countenanced.'

Cassie made herself comfortable in a chair by the table and settled down to wait. She must concentrate now on the future. She would return to Grandmama's care, Raoul would go to Brussels and take up his life again as a surgeon. Perhaps, one day when this wretched war was over they might meet again, as friends. For the present she could only hope that he would find his captain and obtain the papers he needed to prove he was no deserter.

Raoul returned just as the serving maid brought in their dinner, and Cassie was obliged to hold her questions until they were alone.

'The *Prométhée* was not there,' he informed her at last. 'She was due here two weeks since, but the English were attacking the town and she narrowly escaped capture. She is expected to be back in port here tomorrow. I am hopeful I shall be able to see Captain Belfort then.'

'I am glad you have not missed him.' She pushed a piece of chicken about her plate. 'Once you have your papers you will be free to go where you will, Raoul. I think you should do so, Dieppe is not safe for you. You do not need to stay here for my sake.'

'We are agreed, I shall not leave until you are safe on board a ship for England.'

Safe? Cassie's spirit quailed, but she could not let Raoul see how much she had come to rely upon his protection.

She said brightly. 'How long do you think it will take my cousin to secure a passage for me?'

'A day, two perhaps. *If* it is true that he is familiar with the town and the people, then he stands a better chance of striking a deal than I.'

'But you do not trust him?'

'I know nothing of the man, save that he is a fugitive, like myself.'

'I believe he is innocent,' said Cassie quietly. 'Like yourself.'

Raoul poured the rest of the wine into their glasses and sat back, staring moodily into the fire. There was no doubting Arrandale had proved himself useful, but he could not like the man. He wished Cassie disliked him, too, and immediately berated himself for such ignoble thoughts. By heaven, anyone would think he was jealous! A ridiculous idea. He shifted on his chair. Why, then, was it like a pinprick in his flesh every time she directed a smile towards her cousin, why the sudden burning anger whenever they conversed together?

His gaze moved to Cassandra. She was concentrating on cutting an apple into small pieces. The candlelight glinted on her dark curls and gave her skin a golden glow. He watched her take a piece of apple, holding it daintily between her fingers as she nibbled at it with her even, white teeth. She was a lady, from the tips of her toes to the top of those glossy curls. She was made for a life of ease and luxury, with servants at her beck and call. It was not her fault if she was bred to be no more than a selfish, arrogant ornament.

He had a sudden, vivid memory of her felling the postilion when he came to attack her. Another of her working beside him when he was operating on those unfortunate men in Flagey. He had known grown men to faint at the sights she had witnessed that night. Dr Bonnaire had been impressed. She had displayed no signs of arrogance then. True, she had taken charge of the village, organising the food, settling the children, comforting the grieving, but no one had complained. They had not called her arrogant. They had described her as a saint…

He pushed his chair back, saying roughly, 'I am going downstairs, I may be able to glean some news of how the war is going.'

'Oh, may I come with you?'

'No. I am going to the taproom. It is not a place for ladies.' He hesitated, then pulled the purse from his pocket. 'Perhaps it is time we divided up our remaining funds.'

'I need only enough to get me to England,' she said as he counted out the coins.

'We agreed we would share any surplus, did we not?' He held out the purse. 'There. It should be sufficient to pay for your passage to England, unless the captain is a rogue.'

'Thank you. And I still have my locket, I can sell that, if I am desperate.' She managed a smile. 'Let us hope Wolfgang can strike a good bargain.'

Raoul felt the now-familiar pain like a knife in his gut when she mentioned her cousin. He could only reply with a curt little nod before he left the room.

Cassie sat very still and watched the door close behind him. Only when she was alone did her shoulders slump. She could not ignore the fact now. They were no longer friends.

The serving maid came in to clear the table and Cassie moved away into the bedchamber, pretending to tidy her hair in the looking glass and avoiding the servant's scrutiny. It was very dispiriting to know that Raoul did not want her with him. They had gone together to make the arrangements to leave Rouen, she had remained cloaked and silent while he had negotiated with dubious characters in dimly lit taverns and shadowed alleys, but she had been there, at his side. Now, it seemed, he did not want her company and she must keep to her room. It went very much against her nature to remain idle, but she had little choice. For the moment she must allow Raoul and her cousin to make the necessary preparations for her repatriation.

When the maid had carried away all the empty dishes Cassie wandered back into the room. The long journey was beginning to take its toll, she felt very weary, but it was more than that. She pulled one of the dining chairs towards the fire and sat down, hoping the flames would dispel the chill of unhappiness that had crept into her soul. She should be happy. In another day or two she would be back in England, amongst her own people and she would be able to forget all about her disastrous marriage. She could forget about France. About Raoul.

The taproom was crowded and noisy, and most of the talk was on whether the English warships would return. The last bombardment had set fire to the town in three places and while the damage had been minimal the townsfolk were nervous that more attacks might follow. Raoul fell into conversation with a group of merchants who were in Dieppe to await the arrival of their ships, if they ever came. They bemoaned the English blockade of the ports, but none of them doubted for one moment that France would be victorious. After all, was not Bonaparte even now planning to invade England? Then the country would be annexed and brought under French rule, as had happened to the Southern Netherlands and so many other territories.

Raoul bit his tongue when they talked about his homeland. Growing up in the shadow of the revolution, he had been as keen as any that the people should be victorious, that the old tyranny should be ended and replaced with a just and fair system of government by the people, but that had not happened. He wondered what it would be like returning to Brussels, living under French rule. Not so bad, he told himself. As long as he was allowed to get on with his work he did not care. But to practise his trade he needed his papers and that meant finding Captain Belfort. He continued to talk to the merchants, asking them about the harbour and what ships were coming in, but they knew very little. He would have to make the trip to the quayside in the morning, not only to see if the *Prométhée* had docked, but also to try and ascertain if anyone would be willing to take Cassandra to England. She had pinned her faith on her cousin finding her a berth, but it would do no harm to have a second plan, should Arrandale fail.

Raoul spent a couple of hours in the taproom. Even after he had learned all he could he tarried there, fighting the urge to go back to Cassandra. Knowing they must soon part for ever, he wanted to spend every moment with her, to memorise her face, her smile, the sound of her laughter. He called for more wine. As if all those things were not already burned into his heart.

Eventually he made his way back upstairs. A good night's rest and an early start were needed now. With luck Cassie was already asleep with the curtains drawn tightly around the bed. He entered almost silently. Candles still burned on the mantelshelf and at first he thought she had left them to light his way. Then he saw her hunched on her chair, her hands over her face and her shoulders shaking as she cried quietly.

'*Tiens*, what is this!'

He crossed the room in a couple of strides, but Cassie had already jumped up and turned her back on him. She wiped her fingers across her cheeks.

'I did not hear you come in.'

He reached out, but his hand stopped just inches from her.

He said gently, 'What is it, *chérie*, why are you weeping?'

'I am *not* weeping. I abhor such weakness.'

She would have walked away, but he put his hands on her shoulders.

'Of course you do.' He turned her towards him and pulled her closer. 'You are far too sensible for such a thing.'

Her resistance was half-hearted. When he would not let go she leaned against him, burying her face in his coat.

'I am t-tired, that is all.'

Her voice caught on a sob and his arms slid around, binding her to him. He rested his cheek on her hair and closed his eyes. They had been travelling for days and yet still there clung about her a faint summer fragrance. The subtle, elusive quality of it undermined his resolve to keep her at a distance. He raised his head and put two fingers beneath her chin.

'Cassandra, *chérie*—'

She called up every ounce of willpower to push herself out of his arms, reminding herself that the pain would be even worse if she allowed herself to succumb to this man's attraction, even for a moment.

'I do not want you to k-kiss me,' she lied, taking a few steps away from him and averting her face. 'I have told you I have no time for that, or your soft words. They bring nothing but pain.' Yes, that was better. She must remember that all men were deceivers. Had she not had proof enough of that in Verdun? She added, 'I know now that there is no joy to be found in any man's arms.'

'Ah, my dear, if we had time I would show you that is not true. But soon you will be back in England.'

'Yes.' She wrapped her arms around herself. Scant comfort after being held in Raoul's embrace, but the greater the joy now, the greater the pain to follow, so it would have to suffice. Now and for ever. 'And you, I hope, will have your captain's testimonial and be free to return to your home.'

There was silence, as if they were both considering the future. It was as much as Raoul could do not to let out the howl of anguish that filled his soul. He watched Cassandra put her hands by her sides and straighten her shoulders, as though she was mustering all her strength. She picked up one of the branched candlesticks from the mantelpiece and held it out to him. 'You will need this to light you to bed. Goodnight, *monsieur.*'

Raoul did not move. She stood before him, head high, every inch a haughty aristo, but the hand holding the candles was not quite steady. Perhaps it was the wavering flames that made the air shimmer around them, but he could feel the tension, too, so great it was almost visible, yet even so he was aware that their whole future was balanced on a knife's edge. One false move, one unwise word and he would knock the candles aside and drag her into his arms.

He would kiss her until she succumbed to the passion he knew she possessed. It was simmering just beneath the surface. The temptation was almost overpowering. He wanted to hold her again, to taste her, to have her body soft and yielding beneath his. Just once. But the consequences of that would be too great. *He* might walk away afterwards and immerse himself in his work, but what if he were to send Cassie back to England carrying his child?

Slowly and with infinite care he reached out and took the candlestick, making sure their fingers did not touch.

'Goodnight, milady.'

Just uttering those two words had been agony. Raoul

turned and walked out of the room, every step an effort, his body stiff and burning with desire.

'Good morning, *monsieur.*'

Cassie greeted Raoul with cheerful politeness, determined that he should not guess the miserable night she had spent tossing and turning in her bed. Her dreams had been troubled by memories of her husband's infidelity. Even his death had been a betrayal, a duel fought over another woman, and Cassie awoke several times in the night, feeling wounded and defenceless, afraid to trust anyone. The dawn had brought resolution and she had fixed her mind on her return to England. Raoul Doulevant must be kept at a distance. He was a paid escort, nothing more, and must be treated as such.

While they breakfasted on hot, fresh bread washed down by scalding coffee they discussed their plans for the day. Raoul told her his first task was to ascertain if the *Prométhée* had docked.

'I think I shall do a little shopping,' she responded, keeping her tone light, as if she was discussing a trip to Bond Street. 'I would like to find a bonnet and veil.'

'You could ask the landlady to direct you,' Raoul suggested. 'I have already given them to understand that your maid and the rascally postilion have absconded with our baggage coach, so she would not be surprised at the question.'

Cassandra's errand was soon complete. She made her way to the shop recommended by the landlady, where the milliner commiserated with her upon the loss of her bags and was only too happy for her to make use of the mirror to fix the neat little bonnet over her dusky curls and arrange the veil. She also purchased a new reticule to complete the outfit. Thus attired, Cassie sallied forth and spent a pleasant hour or two browsing the shops and market stalls. Her purse was growing woefully thin. There was barely enough in it now to pay her way on the long journey home. However, when she came upon a stall selling a miscellany of goods she stopped. The stallholder hailed her with bluff good humour.

'Ah, *madame*, with what can I tempt you this bright morning? A pretty looking glass for your wall, or this fine bracket clock from the Netherlands? Or perhaps this sable-lined cloak, fit for a duchess. Everything was acquired honestly, *madame*,' he assured her, grinning. 'These days there are many who are only too glad to part with their possessions. After all, what good are such things if one cannot afford to eat?'

Cassie pointed to the large, leather-covered box that had caught her eye. 'That case—'

'This one? Why, 'tis is an old surgeon's set, *madame*. You see, it still contains the tools of his trade. It is a little worn, but it would make a fine addition to your baggage. As a dressing case, perhaps.' He added quickly, sensing a sale. 'I could remove the instruments—'

'No, no it is for a medical man.' She stared at the case. 'Where did you get it?'

'Where? It was amongst the goods sold by a bankrupt to pay his debts, *madame*.'

'And how much do you want for it?'

A sly look came into the man's eyes.

'Ah, now, here's the thing,' he said. 'I thought perhaps I might take it to the hospital in Rouen. There are many doctors and surgeons there who would pay me a good price for such a set...'

Cassie unfastened the chain about her neck.

'I will trade you the case and its contents for this chain and locket.' She held it out to him. 'It is solid gold and that is a real ruby embedded in the locket. It will fetch you a very good price.'

The man studied the locket, weighed it in his hand before shaking his head.

'Nay, *madame*, the surgeon's set is worth twice what this would fetch.'

Cassie was not accustomed to bargaining, but she had a stubborn streak and she was determined to put up a fight for the leather case. She held out her hand.

'I doubt that, but it is your choice,' she said indifferently. 'I will keep my trinket, then, if you would prefer a long and dusty ride to Rouen—'

As Cassie reached for the locket the stallholder closed his fingers over it.

'As you say, it is a long way to Rouen, whereas this pretty bauble I could sell much more easily.' He gave a gusty sigh. 'It is a great bargain for you, *madame*, and I shall most likely make a loss on this deal at the end of the day. But I will let you have the case in exchange for your locket and chain.'

It was done. Cassandra reached out to close the lid upon the gruesome-looking instruments and to lift the case off the stall while the stallholder was busy inspecting his new possession. He prised open the locket.

'A moment, *madame*. Who is this handsome gentleman portrayed inside?'

'My husband,' she said quietly. 'He is dead.'

'Ah, a thousand regrets! You are desolated to part with his likeness, no? But it need not be,' he said, holding the locket closer to his eyes. 'It is painted on ivory and it is a little loose…' She watched him take out a small knife and ease the miniature from its mount. 'There, *madame*, you may have your husband back again. It shows you that I have a great heart, have I not?'

'Thank you.' Cassie slipped the little painting into her reticule. It was the last thing she had bought with her pin money before she and Gerald ran off together. It would remind her that she had thought herself in love with him and had been mistaken. Perhaps it would also help her avoid making the same mistake again.

In the privacy of the inn she inspected her purchase. The corners of the leather case were worn, but the instruments, although dull, looked to be in good condition and similar to the ones she had seen Raoul use at Flagey. Would he appreciate the gesture, or would he think her foolish? After all, what did she know of his profession? These instruments might be of poor quality. Not only would he think her foolish, he might be offended. The sound of his now-familiar step on the stair made her heart race. She would soon know.

Chapter Nine

When Raoul entered the room to find Cassie was waiting for him his spirits rose and the day seemed a little brighter. He noted immediately the new bonnet and the heavy veil which she had put back so that the black lace fell like a mantle over her shoulders. He thought how well she looked, a faint flush on her cheeks and a shy, tentative smile trembling on her lips.

'How was your morning?' she asked him, by way of greeting.

He stripped off his gloves and threw them on to a chair.

'There is news. The *Prométhée* was coming into the harbour even as I reached the quay. I did not wait. Captain Belfort will be busy for hours yet so I will go back later, after we have dined.' The delay was frustrating, but he had waited so long that he could be patient a little longer. He smiled at her. 'You have your hat and veil, I see. Very fetching.'

'I bought something else,' she said, waving towards the table. 'Something for you.'

For the first time Raoul saw the battered case upon the dining table.

'You bought this for me?'

He walked to the table while Cassie rushed to explain.

'I saw it in the market and thought you might be able to use it, since you left all your own instruments in Paris. I have no idea if these are the right tools for you, or if indeed they are any good, but I thought, I hoped they might suffice until you could find yourself a new set...'

Her words trailed off but Raoul barely noticed, he was too engrossed in assessing the familiar instruments. The contents were almost complete. No drugs or opiates, of course, that was too much to expect, but everything else was there: a few dressings and bandages, various types of knives and forceps, a bullet probe, even an amputation saw. The finish was dulled, but Raoul could see that they were all made from the finest cast steel.

'The stallholder assured me they were legally acquired. He said they were from the sale of a bankrupt's effects.'

'Indeed?' Raoul murmured. 'One man's misfortune is another's gain, then.' He looked at her, frowning. 'But this must have cost you something. Have you spent your passage money?'

'No, of course not.'

'Then how did you pay for it?' When she did not reply immediately his imagination rioted as he considered what possible folly she might have committed. He said brusquely, 'The truth, milady, if you please.'

'I exchanged my locket for it.'

Raoul regarded her in silence as more wild thoughts chased around in his head. She had little enough money for her journey, so why had she sold her last item of jewellery to buy this for him?

'But it contained the picture of your husband.'

'The stallholder prised that out. I have it safe. Not that I really want it,' she said quickly. 'I thought I might send it to Gerald's family when I get back to England.' When he said nothing she gave a tiny shrug, 'I saw the case and thought you might be able to use it. However, if it is not what you require, I shall not be offended. Perhaps we could sell it back.'

He reached for her hand and carried it to his lips.

'No need for that, milady. I have never received a better gift. Thank you, a thousand times.'

Her fingers trembled and the blush deepened on her cheek.

'I thought perhaps it might help you to remember me,' she murmured.

I could never forget you.

Raoul heard the words in his head, but he dare not say them aloud. To do so would be to admit his weakness. He knew he should have left her at Rouen, insisted she take a ship from there, but somehow, he found it impossible to let her go. There was always some reason to keep her with him, just another day.

The long dark lashes had swept down so that he could not see her eyes, but she made no move to free herself from his grasp and he could not bring himself to release her. Silence settled around them and with each moment that passed the peace of it drained away. The air became charged with anticipation, as if an electrical storm was imminent. They were locked in a silent tableau, their bodies inching closer. Gently Raoul ran his free hand down her cheek.

'Cassie, look at me.'

He saw the nervous movement of her throat before she slowly raised her head and lifted her eyes to his. They were huge and dark with only a narrow ring of violet around the black centres and as Raoul stared into the liquid depths he thought that he was drowning. He saw himself mirrored in those luminous eyes and he had a sudden, wild idea that he had found his soulmate.

A knock at the door shattered the moment. They jumped apart as the door opened and a serving maid entered.

'A letter for *madame*,' said the maid. She handed over the letter then waited, wiping her nose on her sleeve. Cassie turned the note over and over in her hands. She was dazed and unable to concentrate. She felt like someone dragged suddenly from a deep sleep.

Raoul threw the girl a coin. 'You may go.'

At last Cassie broke the seal and read the note while the servant clumped noisily back down the stairs.

'It is from Wolfgang,' she said at last. 'He says the arrangements are in hand. He is going to join us here for dinner.'

'That is promising.' Raoul glanced towards the window. 'Judging by the sun's shadow there is still an hour or so until dinner, are you tired or would you like to stroll out with me? A little air might do us both good.'

'Yes, thank you, I would like that.'

Cassie carefully pulled the veil over her face and preceded him out of the room. She was still confused by the look she had seen in Raoul's eyes. What would he have said, if they had not been interrupted? Her heart skittered and she decided she would rather not know the answer. Therefore to walk out, where there would be much to see and discuss, would be infinitely preferable to sitting indoors together.

The town was bustling and it was easy for them to mingle amongst the crowds, enjoying the autumn sunshine. They talked very little, but they were comfortable together again and Cassie was glad of it.

'I am sorry the market stalls are empty now,' she said, when at last they turned to make their way back to the inn. 'I would have liked to show you where I purchased the case. I—'

Raoul put his hand over her fingers where they rested on his sleeve and gave them a squeeze. She was silent immediately. A large group of uniformed riders was approaching.

'Keep walking,' Raoul told her quietly.

Obediently Cassie accompanied him along the street, but she peered out through her thick veil as the riders trotted past them towards the town centre. At their head was a figure she had seen only once before, but would never forget. Valerin.

'Has he come for you?' she murmured.

'It is most likely. He will know that the *Prométhée* is in port and has guessed that I would try to see the captain.'

They walked on unhurriedly, but the last few yards to the inn seemed to go on for ever and it was all Cassie could do not to glance back over her shoulder. When they reached the inn the landlord was looking out for them and told them somewhat severely that dinner was ready and their guest had already arrived.

'I have taken the liberty of setting a table for you in

a private room,' their host informed them. 'Monsieur Lagrasse is waiting for you there.'

'Yes, very good,' said Raoul. 'Tell him we will be with him once we have washed the dust of the streets from our hands.' He followed Cassie up the stairs. 'I am very glad we chose to stay here under a different name, it will take Valerin a little longer to find us out. I hope, by the time he does, you will be safely on your way to England.'

It was an added worry, but Cassie tried not to let it show as she made her way into the private parlour. She waited impatiently for the servants to set out their dinner and leave the room and as the door closed behind them she asked Wolfgang for his news. He responded in a bluff, cheerful voice.

'I am very well, I thank you, and business is good.' He gave his head a little shake and said much more quietly, 'It is best not to take chances, even when we are alone. Someone may be listening on the other side of the panelling.' He beckoned to them to lean closer. 'We will meet at the church of St Valery at midnight tomorrow. It is barely five miles from here and there will be a boat standing off the coast, ready to sail for England. The captain is an old friend of mine. I did him a service some years ago and he is pleased now to be able to repay it.'

'I take it we should not ask what trade this ship is engaged in?' murmured Raoul.

Wolfgang shot him a quick grin. 'No, you should not.'

Cassie said eagerly, 'And he will take me to England?'

'Yes. He has agreed to put you ashore near New-haven. I have already sent word ahead, informing Lady Hune and asking her to send a carriage to meet you there.'

Cassie was doubtful. Her fingers plucked nervously at the tablecloth.

'Do you really think she will do so?' she asked. 'After all the grief I have caused her?'

Wolfgang reached out and squeezed her hand.

'The marchioness was never one to turn her back on an Arrandale in trouble and you are her granddaughter. She loves you.'

'Yes, yes, of course.'

Cassie blinked back her tears and quickly drew her hand away as the door opened. When the servant came in with more dishes she forced herself to chatter about inconsequential things.

Raoul pushed his food about his plate, his appetite gone. It should not matter to him that Cassie and her cousin were getting on so well, but it did. He had to admit that Lady Cassandra had confounded his ideas about the English aristocracy. He had tried to tell himself she was spoiled and selfish, he had tried to hate her, but he could not. The only thing he could hold against her was her race and even that seemed less important now.

'And what of you, Doulevant, how goes your search for your sea captain?'

Arrandale's voice broke into Raoul's reverie and he realised they were alone again.

'I go to see him tonight,' he said shortly.

'No!' Cassie's knife clattered to her plate. 'You must

not go near the *Prométhée* while Valerin is in Dieppe.'
Without giving Raoul time to reply she turned to her
cousin. 'The officer who accused Raoul of being a deserter rode into the town with a party of police officers
this afternoon. He is bent on revenge and I am sure he
will not allow Raoul to see Captain Belfort.'

'Revenge?' Raoul found himself subjected to an enquiring stare from Arrandale. 'What did you do to him,
monsieur?'

'I stopped him forcing his unwanted attentions upon
my sister.'

'Ah, I see. Well, Cassie is right. If he believes you
are here he will surely prevent you meeting up with
the captain.'

Raoul shrugged. 'He may try.'

'You must not go,' said Cassie firmly. 'His men will
be looking out for you. At least leave it for a day or so.
Valerin may begin to doubt you are here and relax his
guard. Raoul, *please*, do not go.'

The pleading look in her eyes confirmed what he had
seen there earlier, before the servant had interrupted
them. She cared for him. He tried to be grateful for that
interruption, to pretend the moment had no significance
but he could not ignore what his heart was telling him.
Yet there could be no future for them. Could there? The
first tiny spark of hope flickered, but he quickly crushed
it. Their lives were too different. He could never enter
her world and he certainly could not allow her to sacrifice her life to stay with him. Even if he became the
most successful surgeon in Brussels he could not ask
her to give up everything she had known to become
his wife. To risk being neglected, like *Maman*. No, his

work was his life. There was no room for anything else. He shook his head.

'I cannot wait. The *Prométhée* is only in port to re-victual, then she will be off to sea again and I may not get another chance.'

'It is madness,' said Cassie. 'Valerin will have made sure every *douanier* and police officer in Dieppe has your description, they will stop you as soon as you go near the ship. You had as well walk into a lion's den.'

'She is right,' Arrandale agreed. 'If this Valerin is determined to destroy you he will not hesitate to shoot you on the least pretext.'

'That is a risk I must take. I need my papers if I am to practise my profession.'

'There is one way.' Arrandale was regarding him over the rim of his wineglass. 'Let me go for you.'

'Impossible,' said Raoul immediately. He did not want to be any more beholden to this man. 'I rely upon you to get Lady Cassandra safely out of the country.'

'I shall be back in time to take care of that.' Arrandale gave a careless shrug. 'And if not I will make sure you know all the arrangements before I leave here tonight.' He grinned. 'Trust me, Doulevant, I will see your captain and be back here before dawn with those papers for you.'

'But how?' asked Cassie. 'Is it not equally dangerous for you, Cousin?'

'Not at all. No one could mistake a longshanks like me for Doulevant. And as you have seen, I can look far less respectable when I try! I shall become a common sailor. Believe me, I can do this. I have spent the past ten years passing myself off as someone I am not. Once more will be no problem.'

Raoul did not want to accept, but every one of his arguments was refuted and in the end he gave in. Arrandale drained his glass and sat back in his chair, grinning.

'Very well, then. You had best tell me all I need to know to convince this Captain Belfort to trust me.'

There was no possibility of sleep. Cassie sat with Raoul before the glowing embers of the fire while the night drifted slowly towards morning. After Wolfgang had left they had played at cards until midnight, but when Raoul suggested she should go to bed Cassie refused.

'*You* will not do so,' she told him. 'You cannot expect me to sleep while my cousin is risking his life.'

Raoul growled at that and looked angry, but Cassie was adamant. She would share his night-time vigil and although she did not say so it was not only Wolfgang's plight that concerned her. She prayed that her cousin would secure the documents Raoul needed to prove his innocence.

It was some time shortly before dawn and Cassie was dozing in her chair when she was awoken by a faint scratching at the door. Raoul opened it carefully and the landlord slipped into the room.

'*Monsieur—madame*—your *friend* is below. He is waiting for you in the stables, I cannot allow him into the inn at this time of the night. If the servants should see him and talk, we would all be undone. Come, *monsieur*, I will take you down to him.'

Cassie tried to contain her anxiety. Wolfgang had said they could trust the landlord, but she was unsure.

By the way Raoul hesitated she knew that he, too, was suspicious, but after a moment he nodded.

'Very well.'

As he moved towards the door she flew across the room to catch his arm. Her cousin might be in trouble, but she could not bear to think of Raoul walking into a trap.

'Raoul!' He looked down at her and all the words she wanted to say caught in her throat. At last she managed just two. 'Be careful.'

He nodded silently, squeezed her hand and was gone. She closed the door and stood with her ear pressed against the wood, listening to the two men's stealthy footsteps fading into silence. An agonising wait ensued. She walked the floor, imagining the worst, and when Raoul returned to the room only minutes later she threw herself at him. His arms tightened around her for an instant before he gently held her away from him.

'What is this, milady? I thought you had no nerves.'

'I beg your pardon.' She moved away, trying to sound calm. 'I thought there might be trouble. You have seen Wolfgang?'

'Yes, and he has given me a packet of papers from Captain Belfort. The good captain was able to furnish him with a copy of my discharge as well as writing a testimonial for me. He is also sending copies to Paris, with a letter of explanation. Valerin cannot touch me now.'

'And Wolfgang is safe?' She saw immediately that something was wrong and pressed him for a reply.

'There was some shooting as he left the quay and one bullet found its mark,' said Raoul, adding quickly,

'Arrandale told me it is only a scratch and he managed to get away quite easily. No one followed him here and he is gone now to prepare for tomorrow—no, tonight.'

Cassie closed her eyes for a moment, uttering up a silent prayer of thanks. 'And you have your papers.'

'Yes.' He patted the pocket of his coat. 'Your cousin told me Belfort was only too happy to oblige. It appears Valerin had already called and the captain did not take to him at all. He has sworn he will reveal nothing of my meeting with him.'

'That is good. And Wolfgang's injury, you are sure it is not serious?'

'He would not let me look at it, but assured me it was nothing.'

She nodded, relieved. He was standing temptingly close and she wanted nothing more than to walk back into the comfort of his arms, but it would not do. She turned away from him.

'So,' she said. 'You have your papers and by morning I will be on my way home. Our adventure is nearly over.'

'Yes.'

Her fingers were locked together, pressed against her stomach.

'I shall go back to England and you will join your sister in Brussels.'

'Yes, I will. And I have every hope that I shall be able to take up my profession again.'

Something was in her throat and she closed her eyes, praying the tears would not fall.

'I wish you success, *monsieur*. I am sure you will save many lives, even though I may never know of it. I doubt we shall ever meet again.'

* * *

Her words hung in the silence. Raoul wanted to go to her, to take her in his arms and kiss away the unhappiness he heard in her voice, but it must not be. The gap between himself and Lady Cassandra could not be measured in the arm's length that now separated them. She was a lady, daughter of a marquess, no mate for a common surgeon. Even if by some miracle he did not break her heart with his neglect she would be ostracised from the world she knew and over time she would grow to resent that and with resentment would come heartbreak. He must draw on every argument to keep from crossing that boundary and doing something he knew full well they would both regret.

'No,' he said quietly. 'It is unlikely we shall meet again. My country is part of France now, so we are at war. You are my enemy.' With that he picked up a bedroom candle and left her.

Cassie stared at the closed door, his final words echoing round and round in her head. Was this how they were to part, as enemies? She pressed her hands to her temples. It was barely two weeks since she had left Verdun, two weeks since Raoul had galloped away with her. Madness to think that in such a short time she could learn to know a man, but as she paced the floor she felt such a certainty that she knew Raoul Doulevant as well as she knew herself. He was no enemy.

With no servant to help her Cassie had become adept at undressing and she slipped into her nightgown, her thoughts revolving around the future. Raoul had his papers now. It was almost dawn. At midnight she would begin the final leg of her journey back to England and he would go north. All they would have of one another would be memories. She climbed into bed and blew out her candle. Memories. Her hands slid low across her body, trying to cover the aching, yearning void she felt there. She wanted one more memory to take with her.

The little dressing room was chilly. Raoul quickly threw off his clothes and slipped between the sheets. Even as he blew out the candle he knew sleep would not come easily. But he must rest. Once he had seen Cassie safely on her way to England, he would begin the long journey north, to Brussels. He was known there, he still had friends in the city and he doubted Valerin would follow him that far, and even if he did, he could now prove he was no deserter.

He could hear Cassie moving about in the main bed-chamber. His blood heated at the very thought of her. He could not help but remember how it felt to hold her in his arms, to kiss her. He stirred restlessly. Just a few more hours to endure the torment of having her so near. He rolled on to his side, just in time to see the thin strip of light beneath the adjoining door disappear. Good. She would sleep now and so would he.

He closed his eyes, only for them to fly wide again a moment later at the sound of the door opening. Cassie was standing in the doorway, her white nightgown pale and wraithlike in the near darkness.

'I could not sleep,' she whispered.

Confound it, she was coming closer and his body was reacting violently.

'You have not tried hard enough,' he growled. 'Go back to your bed, milady.'

'I do not want us to be enemies, Raoul.'

In silence he watched her throw off her nightgown and slide down beside him on the low truckle bed. Her skin was cool as silk against his heated body and he could not resist taking her in his arms. She sighed and he felt her breath soft against his cheek.

'I want you to make love to me, Raoul,' she whispered. 'Show me you are not my enemy.'

He should send her away, but she was pressed against him and it was impossible to deny his arousal.

'Cassie, you should leave, while you can.'

'I do not want to leave you. This may be our last night together and already it is almost over. I want to remember it for ever.' She was nuzzling his neck and the last shreds of his resolve melted into the darkness.

'This is madness,' he muttered, even as he covered her face with kisses and breathed in the sweet, flowery perfume of her hair. 'You should not be here.'

'Love me, Raoul, just once, before we part for ever. I will ask nothing more from you, you have my word.'

She caught his face in her hands and kissed him with such passion that he was lost. A groan caught in his throat and he returned her kiss, deepening it until his senses were soaring. Gasping, he broke off the kiss and he heard her give a little cry as she threw back her head. The slender column of her throat was a pale blur in the darkness and he trailed a line of kisses along its length, flicking his tongue into the hollow at its base. Her sigh was pure pleasure and his mouth moved on to the soft swell of her breasts. While his tongue flickered and circled one hard nub his fingers caressed the other. Her body arched towards him and she cried out as her body trembled and shuddered with ecstasy. Her passion delighted him, but all the time he was holding back, refusing to acknowledge his own needs and desires until he was sure he had sated hers. He continued to caress one pert breast with his mouth, eager to bring her to that point of white-hot heat again. Her fingers clutched at his hair and she murmured restlessly, but he did not stop. He caught her hands and pinned them against the pillow above her head, holding them fast with one hand while the other explored the soft curves of her body and his mouth and tongue played over her breast. Her hips tilted and he slid his fingers into her hot, slick core, stroking and circling until she was bucking and writhing against his hand.

With a cry Cassie arched her back and her body clenched around the long, gentle fingers that were causing such havoc inside her. Her hands were still clamped above her head, but she was not constrained, she was soaring, flying and falling all at the same time. At last the pulsing spasms ceased, every inch of her skin felt alive and sensitive to the lightest touch, but still the tongue circling her breast and the fingers stroking her core continued to move. They were feeding a fire deep inside and she could feel the pressure building again, but this time she wanted more, she wanted to feel Raoul's skin on hers, to join with him. She wondered how to tell him. Would he make her beg for the final union that she longed for so much? She licked her lips and managed to whisper his name. It was enough. While his fingers continued their inexorable rhythm he released her hands and stretched his hard, naked body against hers, at the same time seeking her lips with his mouth to join in a long, passionate kiss. He was so aroused she could not suppress a little mewl of delight deep in her throat. She clung to him, her body pliant, inviting, and when he rolled on to her she wrapped her legs around his waist and tilted her hips up to receive him. The invitation could not be resisted any longer. Their coupling was fast and furious, Cassie cried out, digging her nails into his shoulders even as his body tensed for the final push that carried her into oblivion.

They collapsed back against the pillows, gasping. Raoul kept his arms about Cassie, felt the tension leave her and he cradled her until she fell asleep. He rested his head against her hair and closed his eyes, reflecting ruefully that at the end his had not been the performance of an experienced lover. He had been as quick and hasty as a schoolboy, but he had wanted her too much, he had not been able to withstand the urgent demands of his own body. He smiled, planting a kiss on the dusky curls that tickled his chin. That did not matter. They would rest awhile and then he would take her again and show her just how skilled a lover he could be. But first he must sleep.

When Raoul awoke he was alone. Cassie was gone, but the memory of the night lingered, so fierce that he was sure he could smell her perfume. Daylight streamed in through the high little window and he lay very still, wondering if perhaps his longing had got the better of him and he had dreamed the whole thing. He quickly donned his clothes and went to the door. He knocked and hesitated briefly before entering the main bedchamber. It was empty. The door to the anteroom stood open and through it he could see Cassie, fully dressed and standing by the window. As he entered the little room she turned and one look at her face told him it had been no dream. Her cheeks were flushed and her lips had an added colour. She looked like a woman who had been loved.

Cassie had been dreading this moment. It was not that she regretted going to Raoul's bed. She had wanted a memory to take with her to England, but her longing for him had blinded her to the enormity of her actions. She had thrown herself at him, like a wanton. Was that the memory she wanted *him* to take away? She could not help the blood racing to her cheeks and hated the telltale blush. She eyed him warily: his bow was perfectly measured, his voice when he bade her good morning was coolly polite. He had hinted that he was an expert lover and most likely he was disappointed in her performance. She had wanted only to please him and had not intended to lose control so completely once she was in his arms. Just thinking about it made her body hot again. A searing disappointment swept through Cassie. She knew their lovemaking would not change the future, she and Raoul could never be together, but in her desperation to have him love her she had forfeited any respect he might have for her. She drew herself up. It was too late now to worry about that. Perhaps it was best if they ignored what had happened in the night.

She said, with a fair assumption of calm, 'I have sent down for breakfast. It should be here any moment.'

Raoul was regarding her solemnly.

'Milady, I think we should talk—'

Milady! Yesterday he had called her Cassie. If anything was needed to show how far they had moved apart that was it. She felt her panic rising and with relief heard the clatter of crockery outside the door.

'Ah, here is the servant now,' she cried gaily. 'I pray you sit down, sir, and break your fast with me.'

'As you wish.'

Raoul gave an inward shrug and closed his mind to his disappointment. She was an aristo, she had used him for her own amusement in the night, but with the day she had no wish to acknowledge what had happened. The hectic flush on her cheek and the way she avoided his eyes suggested she was ashamed of what she had done. Perhaps she was ashamed of him and he had to admit his performance had not been spectacular. Very well. It was forgotten.

But even as he watched Cassie pouring coffee for them both his body told a different tale. He could not forget those dainty hands clinging to him, the cherry-red lips fastened against his mouth, the slender body that was now clothed in demure linen pressed against his own, flesh upon flesh.

How he got through breakfast he could never afterwards remember. They talked of mundane matters like the weather, the possibility of rain, the excellence of their simple repast, but Raoul's head was bursting with words he dare not utter, lest he should see disdain or revulsion in her face.

As the breakfast dishes were being cleared away the landlord appeared and handed Raoul a note. 'This came for you, *monsieur*.' He dropped his voice. 'I brought it up myself, I would not entrust it to a servant in these uncertain times.'

Raoul pressed a coin into the landlord's hand and put the note in his pocket. He did not take it out again until the last of the servants had departed.

Across the table Cassie was impatient for information.

'What is it?' she asked. 'Is it from Wolfgang?'

'It is.' Raoul scanned the sheet, frowning. 'He says Valerin's men are patrolling the harbour and the guards have been doubled on all the roads out of Dieppe. Word is out that they are looking for a desperate criminal and they should not hesitate to shoot.'

A chill fear spread through Cassie.

'You think that means you?'

'Who else?'

She watched him tear the paper and throw it into the fire, where the pieces flared and burned.

'What will you do?' she asked him.

'Take you to the church of St Valery, as we agreed. Arrandale is sending someone to fetch us and show us a safe way out of the town.' He smiled. 'We will get you to your ship, never fear.'

'I am not worried for myself, Raoul.'

'You are all goodness, milady.' He picked up her hand and kissed it lightly. Cassie wanted to cling, to say something about what had happened in the night, but before she could find the words he had dropped her hand and was turning away, saying cheerfully, 'Now, we have the day to ourselves. Shall we sally forth and see how good Valerin's guards really are?'

'But if they are looking for you—'

'They will be looking for a skulking villain, not a

gentleman enjoying the sunshine with his lady wife. Come, put on your bonnet and veil and let us go out.'

The town was even busier than the previous day. They strolled towards the quay and Cassie discovered that if anything was needed to make her forget the wonder of the night it was the effort of walking past the numerous *gendarmes* as if she had not a care in the world. True, she had her veil to hide her countenance, but she had to work hard not to grip tightly to Raoul's arm every time an officer glanced their way. She was constantly on the alert, looking out for Valerin. Raoul, by contrast, appeared totally at his ease. They made no attempt to approach the *Prométhée*, but even from a distance Cassie could see two men lounging at the foot of the gangplank and whenever anyone approached the ship they immediately stopped and questioned them.

'It would appear Valerin is taking no chances,' Raoul murmured. He gently guided Cassie away from the waterfront. 'I am indebted to your cousin for visiting Captain Belfort in my stead last night. Let us take a look at the other routes we might use to leave this town.'

They spent the day wandering through Dieppe, listening to the gossip in the market and noting the number of *gendarmes* at each of the gates leading out of the town.

By the time they returned to the inn for dinner Cassie was exhausted and it was a struggle to eat the delicious meal put before them.

'There are some hours before we will be leaving here,' remarked Raoul, noting her fatigue. 'We should try to sleep.'

His words immediately brought back memories of being in his bed and she felt herself blushing.

'You think I want a repeat of this morning?' His lip curled. 'I may not be a gentleman in your eyes, milady, but I have my own code of honour.'

'Forgive me, I did not mean—that is—' She stumbled over the words, distressed that he should misunderstand her, but he was already walking away to the dressing room, closing the door firmly between them.

Cassie lay down upon the covers. The comfort she had gained in his arms and the embraces they had shared seemed long ago. It had been a mistake, to throw herself at him in that way. She curled herself into a ball and nestled her cheek on her hand. What a fool she was to give in to a passion she knew only too well would fade and die. Well, she had her memory and perhaps in time it would not matter that she had sacrificed his respect to get it.

'Wake up, milady. We must leave.'

Raoul gently touched Cassie's shoulder. He watched her stretch and roll on to her back as her eyes fluttered open. She gazed up at him, looking so innocent, so vulnerable in the golden glow of the candles that it was as much as he could do not to place a kiss on her lips, parted now in the beginnings of a smile. She would not welcome it, so instead he stepped back and held out his hand to her,

'*Madame?*'

Perversely she did not approve his polite behaviour. Her face became a mask. She ignored his hand and slid off the bed, shaking out her skirts.

'Very well. Give me five minutes to collect my things.'

'One small bag only,' he reminded her. 'We cannot carry more.'

The landlord's son, Gaston, was waiting for them in the stables.

'You are our guide?' asked Raoul.

The lad grinned.

'Trust me, *monsieur*, it is not the first time I have helped people to leave the town. Let us collect your horses.'

They discovered their mounts ready and waiting for them and Gaston quickly fixed Cassie's small portmanteau to her saddle. When he took Raoul's saddlebags he swore roundly.

'By our lady, this is too heavy. Do you want to kill the horse?'

Raoul thought of the surgeon's box squeezed into the saddle bag.

'It is the tools of my trade,' he said. 'I must have them with me.'

Cassie's spirits lifted a little at his words. Raoul would not be taking the tools if he did not truly value them. It was a small comfort, but comfort nevertheless. As they led the horses out of the stables she noticed that each hoof was wrapped in cloth.

'We must walk them through the town,' explained Gaston. 'Quietly now.'

They followed the boy through a series of dark, deserted alleys, keeping away from the main streets. The dirt from the day's traffic was thick beneath their feet and Cassie was grateful for her serviceable boots. The night was very dark, the moon no more than a thin line in the sky, and Cassie found herself thinking that in a couple more days there would be no moon at all to light their way. A final, noisome alley ended at a large ramshackle building.

'My uncle's house,' Gaston informed them in a whisper. 'You will not see him tonight, but he has a very useful barn.'

He led them towards a wooden outhouse and opened one of the large doors for them to pass inside. When the door closed behind them the darkness was almost complete. Cassie knew a moment of chilling fear before she felt Raoul's hand close around hers, warm and comforting.

Gaston's voice came softly through the blackness.

'Wait here.'

They heard the lad moving around and suddenly a large panel in the back wall slid aside to reveal a small orchard.

'Walk your horses through the trees to the gate on the far side. The track there leads to open ground and a coast path to the church of St Valery.'

'Thank you,' Cassie began, 'We are most grateful—'

'There is more,' the boy interrupted her. 'The open ground is overlooked by the castle and there may be lookouts keeping watch.' He pointed. 'Head *away* from the coast once you are in the open. That will take you over the rise and out of sight of the lookouts in the quickest possible time. Keep going until you reach the crossroads, you cannot mistake it, there is a gibbet swinging there. Only then should you head back towards the coast. Ride like the wind,' he told them.

'There is always a chance that the soldiers will not see you.'

He beckoned to them to follow him into the orchard and helped them remove the cloth from the horses' hoofs before wishing them *bonne chance* and disappearing into the black shadows of the barn. The barn wall slid back in place and they were alone amongst the apple trees. As they began to walk away from the buildings Cassie felt her anxiety growing about their forthcoming ride. She was reluctant to ask Raoul if he was nervous, but he said, as if reading her mind, 'If anything happens and we are separated, you know the directions. Head for the church of St Valery and meet your cousin there.'

'You think there might be trouble?'

She saw his teeth gleam in the darkness.

'When we ride across that open ground under the castle walls we will be perfect targets.'

She tried to smile. 'Let us hope they are very poor shots.'

They continued in silence until they reached the gate, where Raoul turned to Cassie.

'Let me throw you up.'

'No, wait.' She caught his arm. 'Raoul, in case…in case anything should happen, I wanted to thank you. For last night.'

The shadow cast by his hat was too deep for her to see his face, but she had to continue, to let him know what it had meant to her. She forced herself to continue.

'I d-did not know being with a man could be so… satisfying. Thank you.'

She was aware of how woefully inadequate the words were to express her feelings, but at least she had tried. She sighed and was about to turn away when Raoul's hand came out and cupped her cheek. Gently he drew her into his arms, but when their lips met there was nothing gentle about his kiss. It was ruthless, demanding and it left her breathless. As he raised his head she remained within the circle of his arms, her head thrown back against his shoulder, gazing up into his shadowed face. His eyes gleamed with a fiery spark.

'If you thought last night was good, milady, you are woefully mistaken,' he told her. 'Only let us get through this alive and I will show you how good lovemaking can be.'

With something that was halfway between a sob and a laugh Cassie threw her arms about his neck and dragged his head down for another bruising kiss. There would be no more lovemaking, they both knew it, but she was grateful and comforted by his teasing words.

The soft breeze rustled the leaves, a whispered reminder that time was pressing. Reluctantly they broke apart and Raoul threw Cassie up into the saddle. He waited for her to arrange her skirts and checked the girth before he mounted upon his own horse. They trotted along the narrow lane, but drew rein when the track petered out into open ground. Cassie glanced back. Now they were away from the houses she could see the massive black edifice of the castle looming behind them.

'Remember,' said Raoul, 'we go that way, up the rise and on to the crossroads. Do not stop. Whatever happens, you are to make your way to the church, do you understand me? Now, are you ready?'

Cassie gathered up the reins and dragged in a long, steadying breath. They would be riding for their lives.

'Ready.'

The horses sprang forward and they were away,

galloping across the springy turf. Cassie's cloak billowed out behind her, the strings tugging at her neck. Raoul's horse was bigger and stronger, but he remained at Cassie's shoulder and she realised that Raoul was deliberately holding back, putting himself between her and any marksman firing from the castle. The thought made her feel quite sick with fear and she fought against it, forcing herself to concentrate upon the ride ahead of them. The ground rose steadily, but to Cassie's overstretched nerves they seemed to be getting no closer to the top. Her heart leapt into her mouth when she heard the first crackle of shots behind them. She put her head down and urged the little mare to go faster, chillingly aware that Raoul presented the better target. Another brattle of musketry and she could not bear it, she had to take a quick glance behind. Raoul was still at her shoulder. His cloak, too, was flying out from his shoulders and she prayed any marksman taking aim would be distracted by its fluttering folds.

The shooting continued, but it was fading and she hoped they were out of range now. The mare was tiring, but they had at last crested the ridge and the land began to drop away. As soon as the town and the castle were hidden by the rise Cassie slackened her pace and turned to ask Raoul the question that was uppermost in her mind.

'Are you hurt?'

'Not a whit,' he said. The horses had slowed to a walk and he added, 'Would you care?'

A smile was growing inside Cassie, a mixture of relief that the immediate danger was past, elation from the gallop and the sheer joy of being with Raoul. Now as she turned to look at him that joy blazed forth and she did not care if he saw the raw emotion shining from her countenance.

'You know I would.'

She put out her hand and he took it, smiling at her in a way that set her heart pounding and it leapt into her throat, sending her senses reeling when she read the message in his eyes. Even in the faint light of the setting moon it was unmistakable. Love.

The shock of revelation took Raoul's breath away. Here, on a lonely, windswept heath in the dead of night, he knew with certain, blinding clarity that he loved Lady Cassandra Witney. For the moment nothing else mattered, only that searing, soaring realisation. His heart was almost bursting with the joy of it and it was with some difficulty that he dragged his thoughts back to the present. The blazing look had died from Cassie's face, replaced by a sadness that sobered him. He was still holding her hand and now he squeezed her fingers.

'Cassie, I—'

She shook her head at him. 'Please, do not say anything Raoul. We must part and nothing has happened to change that.' She was smiling at him and at first he thought her eyes sparkled with starlight, but a second look told him it was tears. When she spoke there was a brittle, self-deprecating lightness to her voice that he had never heard before. 'You need not worry about me. Why, 'tis only two weeks since I buried my husband, so you may believe me when I tell you this type of grand passion never lasts. Let us say no more about it, if you please.' She pulled her hand free. 'Do you think we are safe yet?'

Raoul shook his head to clear his thoughts. She had

retreated from him, but there was no time now to think of that or to consider her words. He must concentrate on their present situation. He looked about him.

'The danger is not over yet,' he said. 'They may have sent a party of riders after us, so we must push on. There is the crossroads ahead. We had best make haste to cover as much ground as we can before the moon sets.'

They turned their horses and cantered on towards the coast road. As they passed the crossroads Raoul glanced up at the gibbet with the caged remains of some poor soul swinging gently like a portent of doom.

Chapter Ten

Wolfgang had told them that the little church of St Valery was perched on the limestone cliff overlooking a sheltered cove with a pebble beach. Neither beach, cove nor the sea were visible when Cassie and Raoul reached the rendezvous shortly before midnight. The church was a black shape against the dark blue of the sky, but beyond it everything faded into blackness and only the fresh breeze and a muted roar told them that the sea was very close.

They had been riding hard, mostly in silence, and as they neared the coast Cassie was aware of the knot of unhappiness growing inside her. In a few more hours she would be leaving France, leaving Raoul. They must return to their own very different worlds, there was no other way. Occasionally she would glance across at Raoul and the set look on his face told her he, too, was not looking forward to their parting. He loved her, she had seen it in his face when they had slowed for a moment from their madcap ride, but following quickly on from the joyous realisation came the certainty that it could not last. Memories of the fierce passion she had shared with Gerald still haunted her. At first they could not bear to be parted for even a day, yet how soon their love had died, leaving only bitterness and pain. Just the thought of going through such agony again made Cassie shudder.

They tethered the horses in an old wooden shelter, as they had been instructed. Cassie was relieved to see Wolfgang's big black hunter was already there and she hurried after Raoul as he went softly into the church. Inside a single lantern burned near the altar, illuminating the scene. The lantern was held aloft by an elderly priest who was standing to one side while two men knelt over a prostrate figure. They were all so still that at first Cassandra thought she was looking at a religious sculpture, but at their entry the priest turned and the lantern's light fell more fully on the man lying on the ground. She ran forward with a cry.

'Cousin!' She fell on her knees beside Wolfgang. 'What has happened here?' she demanded. 'What has occurred?'

The two men rose, touching their caps instinctively and introduced themselves as the captain and first mate of the *Antoinette*.

'He collapsed,' said the captain. 'We met as agreed, came in and then he staggered, complaining of an old wound.'

Raoul gently moved Cassie aside and began to examine the unconscious form.

'It would appear he received more than a scratch at the harbour,' he muttered. 'He has a bullet in his shoulder and he has lost a lot of blood. Why in heaven's name did he not tell me?'

Cassie touched his arm. 'Can you help him, Raoul?'

'Of course. He is strong, but the bullet will need to come out and quickly.'

'No, no, *monsieur,* you cannot tend him here,' cried the priest in alarm. 'If anyone should see the light, if you were to be discovered—'

'Is your house nearby?' said Cassie. 'We could take him there.'

The priest recoiled even more.

'No, no, *madame.* It is not possible. The *douaniers* patrol here regularly. They already suspect me of having links with the smugglers. I cannot risk having an injured man in my house.'

'Then it must be here,' she said. 'We cannot let him *die*.'

'There's the vaults,' suggested the captain. 'No one would see the light down there.'

'Very well, let us get him there now,' said Raoul taking charge. 'Monsieur le Curé, if you would be good enough to light the way. Captain, can you and your man help me carry him? Carefully now!' He glanced at Cassie, his voice softening. 'It appears I shall need your instruments sooner than expected.'

She nodded. 'I will fetch them.'

The vaults were cold but clean, as if regularly used. Raoul said nothing but he noticed the marks on the wall, as if something had been stacked against it. Barrels, perhaps. A flat-topped tomb to some ancient dignitary filled the centre of the biggest vault and Raoul helped the two sailors to lay the unconscious form gently on the top. It provided a perfect operating table. Lighted candles from the church were brought down to illuminate the space and the priest hurried away to fetch hot water and sheets to make bandages.

'What can I do to help?' asked Cassie.

The captain stepped up. 'Begging your pardon, *madame*, but 'tis time to leave. The tide will be turning and we need to get back to the ship.'

Raoul had shut his mind to this moment but he could do so no longer. It was as if a band of steel was tightening around his chest.

'He is right, milady. You must go.'

They were on either side of the tomb, facing each other across Arrandale's near-lifeless body.

'I cannot leave my cousin like this.'

Her voice shook and Raoul tried to reassure her.

'I will not let him die, Cassie.'

Her eyes sparkled with unshed tears. 'I cannot leave *you* like this.'

Her words were like a knife, twisting in his gut.

'My dear, there is no choice. The ship must leave with the tide.'

'Then I shall not go.'

The captain cleared his throat.

'Monsieur Lagrasse has been a friend for many years, *madame*. I told him I would see you safely to England. He would not forgive me for breaking my word.'

'Then I am sorry for it, Captain, but Monsieur Lagrasse is my cousin and *I* will not leave him until I know if he will live. I beg your pardon for your wasted journey.'

The captain rubbed his chin. 'We *could* stand off another day, perhaps, and come back tomorrow night.'

One more day. Raoul clutched at it, although he knew

the parting would be no easier tomorrow. He looked at Cassie.

'You can help me tonight and nurse him tomorrow, until midnight. Then you must leave. Are we agreed?'

She nodded. 'Yes. Agreed.'

'Very well, then,' said the captain. 'I will return here for you at midnight tomorrow, *madame*. But you must be ready to leave; I put my men and my ship at risk coming back again.'

Cassie hesitated, wondering if Raoul would protest and beg her to stay. At that moment she knew she would willingly tell the captain not to return, she would remain in France and take her chances, but Raoul said nothing and she knew in her heart that it was for the best. She had said as much, had she not?

'Thank you, Captain,' she said at last. 'I will be ready.'

The sailors departed and she turned her thoughts to preparing Wolfgang for the operation. She had a few more precious hours here. She must try to remember everything.

Cassie worked with Raoul to remove Wolfgang's ruined coat and shirt, then she shifted the candles to provide the best light and prepared the instruments for him, making use of everything she had learned at Flagey. All the while the priest ran back and forth, bringing cloths and bandages from his house. He also brought a *réchaud*, or chafing dish, which not only kept the water hot but also provided a little warmth in the chill vault. She was relieved her cousin was oblivious when Raoul began to probe the wound, but by the time the bullet had been removed and the wound dressed, Wolfgang's continued unconsciousness was beginning to worry her.

'His heartbeat is strong,' Raoul reassured her, when she voiced her fears. 'If only he had let me look at his shoulder yesterday, instead of telling me it was nothing.'

She managed a little smile. 'We Arrandales do not like admitting our weaknesses.'

With the priest's help they moved Wolfgang to a bed of straw and blankets on the floor. Cassie wrapped herself in her cloak and sat down beside him, keeping watch. It was an anxious time, but there was little she could do save bathe his face and wait for him to come round.

She had dozed fitfully, waking once in a panic to find that she and Wolfgang were alone with a single lantern to light them. Her relief when Raoul reappeared must have shown on her face for he came over, directly.

'I have been to check on the horses and I helped the *curé* remove all evidence of his involvement. Now if we are discovered he can deny he knew anything about us being here.' He knelt beside the patient and laid a hand on his forehead. 'He is sleeping. There is no fever, that is a mercy, and his body will heal more quickly if he rests. Do not fret, Cassie, he will wake soon.'

He turned down the lamp and came around to sit beside her.

'Is it daylight now?' she asked.

'Yes, a fine day, too.'

She shivered. 'I do not like being here, I feel too... trapped. What if someone should come? What if Valerin should find us?'

'He cannot even be sure we were in Dieppe, unless

Captain Belfort gives me away, which I do not believe he will do,' he told her. 'The most likely thing is that the *douaniers* might arrive, searching for contraband, but the *curé* has promised he will keep a look out for us and will send his boy to warn us if he sees anything suspicious. You should sleep while you can.'

'And you?' she asked him.

'I shall try to sleep, too.'

He had put his cloak on the ground beside her and stretched out on it. Cassie lay down, taking care that their bodies did not touch as she turned this way and that, trying to get comfortable. Eventually she heard Raoul give a loud sigh.

'What is the matter?'

'I beg your pardon, I did not want to disturb you, but the ground is so hard...'

He reached out one arm and drew her to him.

'There,' he said, nestling her against his shoulder. 'Is that better?'

'Oh, yes,' she whispered.

Tired as she was she knew she would not sleep, not even with the regular thud of Raoul's heart against her cheek, but she kept very still and silent, knowing he must be exhausted. However, it seemed that Raoul could not sleep, either.

'I cannot help but remember the last time I held you like this,' he murmured. 'Did you mean what you said, that you found our lovemaking...satisfactory?'

She sighed. 'It was more than satisfactory, Raoul. I never knew such happiness before.'

'Then your lovers were sadly lacking.'

'I have had no lovers,' she confessed. 'Only my husband.'

'And he did not give you pleasure?'

'At first perhaps, there was something like it, when I thought we were in love, but I wonder now if he ever truly loved me. I think perhaps he married me for the fortune I would inherit when I reached one-and-twenty.'

Raoul's arm tightened a little. 'He was a scoundrel, then.'

'Yes, but I was a fool. He had no money of his own, you see, but that did not matter to me. When we ran away I took all my jewels to sell.' She exhaled sadly. 'You would indeed think me spoiled if you had seen how many jewels and trinkets my family had lavished upon me. It should have been enough to live comfortably for years, but by the time we were sent to Verdun the money was running low and my husband needed more. Gambling had become an obsession. My grandmother warned me how it would be, she knew he was weak, although thankfully she had no idea just how low he would stoop and I will never tell her. But I should have heeded her.'

'But you need not have stayed,' Raoul pointed out. 'Once you knew what sort of man your husband was, why did you not go home to your family?'

She said simply, 'It would have been very disloyal to leave my husband at such a time. Although, I began to wish I had done so. He…he changed.'

He took her hand and said gently, 'Would you tell me?'

Could she? Cassie let her breath go in a long, low sigh. She knew she would never confess the whole to Grandmama, but lying here beside Raoul, her hand resting safely in his grasp, she thought perhaps it was time to give voice to it all.

'Gerald courted me so charmingly and it seemed such an adventure to elope, and the idea of going to France was so exciting! By the time we reached Paris I realised I did not love him. However, we were married by then and I knew I would have to make the best of it. Everything was well as long as there was money, but when it ran out—' Her hand trembled and Raoul's grasp tightened, giving her the strength to continue. 'Gerald wanted me to ask Grandmama to send more funds, but I refused. I would not ask her to pay for his gambling. He did not like that, it made him angry and we argued constantly. He said I was a burden, that I must pay my way.' She stopped, recalling the revulsion and fear of those last few months. 'He began to bring his friends to our rooms and to hint that I should…entertain them. He wanted to share me with his friends. To—to sell my favours.' She closed her eyes. 'I dreaded those parties and took to retiring to my room and locking the door, but I knew, sooner or later, Gerald would catch me out and make me do what he wanted. If he had not died when he did—' She broke off as the hot tears began to slide over her cheek. 'And now I feel so guilty, because when they came to tell me I was a widow I felt nothing but *relief*!'

Raoul had listened with growing anger to her story, but now he could be silent no longer.

'Ah, my love.' The words were forced from him and he turned, gathering her into his arms so she might cry her heart out against his chest. When at last the wrenching sobs died away he murmured against her hair, 'You must not blame yourself. The man was a brute to treat you in such a way.'

'B-but he was my husband, and he always maintained he l-loved me.'

His arms tightened. 'That was not love, *chérie*. You are well rid of such a monster.'

'He—he said I was cold,' she whispered. 'He said I have no heart.'

'I can assure you that is not true.' He shifted his position, cupping her face with one hand and gazing into her eyes. 'Forget this man, *ma chère*. He is not worth a moment's regret.' He dropped a light kiss on her eyelids and another on her mouth, where he tasted the salt of her tears.

'Raoul, I—'

'Hush now.' He settled her more comfortably in his arms again. 'It is time to rest. Or are you afraid of your dreams?'

She gave a sigh of contentment.

'Not now. Not when I am with you.'

Raoul closed his eyes, satisfied.

'Thank you,' she murmured, so softly he could barely hear her. 'Thank you for listening.'

He held her close, overwhelmed by the urge to protect the dainty, fragile creature beside him. Once she was in the care of her family it would be a different matter, but he hated the thought of her being alone and defenceless, even for a single day.

Arrandale's low groans woke Raoul. He gently disengaged himself from Cassie's sleeping form and went to tend his patient.

'Where the devil am I?'

'In the vaults of the church,' murmured Raoul, making a swift examination of the wound. 'I have removed the bullet from your shoulder. You fool, why did you not tell me about this the other night?'

'I was anxious to be on my way.' Arrandale drew in a sharp, hissing breath as Raoul touched a sore spot. 'I did not want to bring the officers to your door.' He raised his head to peer at his shoulder. 'How is it now?'

'The bleeding has stopped. It will heal, given time.'

'Good.' He sank back, closing his eyes again. 'Speaking of time, did Cassie get away?'

'No.'

'What!'

'She stayed to help you.'

Arrandale followed Raoul's glance towards Cassie's sleeping form and he muttered angrily under his breath.

'Your captain friend says he will return for her tonight,' said Raoul .

'Aye, he's a good man—' Arrandale broke off as Cassie stirred and sat up.

'Wolfgang. You are awake. How do you feel now?'

'I'll live. But what the devil do you mean by staying here?'

'I wanted to help,' she said simply.

'Confound it, Cousin, you have jeopardised your chances of getting to England. What if the weather is bad, tonight? What if—'

'Hush,' said Cassie, putting a hand on his good shoulder. 'Do not concern yourself, Cousin. Your captain has promised to return, I trust that he will.' She added shyly, 'Will you not change your mind and come back to England with me?'

'You know I cannot do that, Cassie. I am a wanted man.'

She shook her head.

'Grandmama has never believed it, I am sure she will help you.'

'Nay, Cousin, it will need more than that to save me from the gallows.'

Raoul listened in silence to their exchange. He was sure now that Cassie was not in love with her cousin, but he could not help a prickle of jealousy at her concern for Arrandale's welfare. He said curtly, 'You should go with your cousin, sir. She should not be travelling alone.'

'If that's the case, then you should go with her, Doulevant.'

'Impossible,' said Cassie immediately. 'Raoul is going back to Brussels to join his family and take up his work again.'

'He could work in England, now he has his papers,' Arrandale pointed out. 'If anything, my friend, you would be safer there than here, for if Valerin finds you before you reach Brussels he will not let you live long enough to prove your innocence.'

Raoul said nothing. Arrandale was right. The journey to Brussels was fraught with danger and he might even bring more trouble to Margot. But to go to England, to be so close to Cassandra, knowing he could never have her—

A sudden noise at the door had Raoul reaching for his pistol, but it was the *curé*'s servant carrying a heavy pot from which emanated a most appetising aroma.

'*Mon père* has sent you dinner, *madame, messieurs.* And he says to tell you it is growing dark now.'

'A thousand thanks to him for his goodness,' said Raoul, going forward to relieve the man of his burden.

By the time they had finished their simple meal of stew and bread Raoul noted that Arrandale was looking much better and was even talking about getting up.

'You should rest a little longer,' Cassie advised him. 'You are very weak.'

'Nonsense, I am as strong as an ox.' He struggled to his feet, wincing a little. 'Although an ox has four legs, which would help considerably.' He looked about him. 'Where is my shirt?'

'The priest took it away to burn it, along with your coat. They were both beyond repair.' For the first time that day Raoul grinned. 'He has left you some clothes from the poor box.'

'What? They are mere rags!' Arrandale looked with distaste at the old shirt and badly patched jerkin that Raoul was holding up. 'Well, help me into the shirt, if you please, it will at least keep off the damp chill of this place.'

It was soon done and despite Arrandale's protests Raoul fashioned him a sling from the remains of the sheet they had been tearing up for bandages.

'You will need to keep that arm still and rest the shoulder.' He took out his watch. 'It is nearly midnight. Your sailor friends should be here soon.'

'Aye. I will see my cousin safely away before I set off. Can I ask you to saddle the horses for me, Doulevant? I doubt I will be able to do that tonight and we shall have to take Cassie's mount away with us.'

'Of course,' said Raoul absently. 'I will slip out and see to it shortly.'

'Where will you go?' asked Cassie.

'It is best that you do not know that.' Arrandale flicked her cheek with a careless finger. 'Trust me, I shall survive.'

'Perhaps Raoul will ride with you,' she suggested. 'At least for a few miles.'

'No.' Raoul had at last come to a decision.

You are a fool, man. You are only delaying the inevitable parting.

Perhaps he was a fool, but he could not bear to think of sending Cassie off alone into the night, with only strangers for company.

'If you will not go with your cousin to England, Arrandale, then I must go.'

'That is excellent news, my friend, and what I expected. You will find I have already paid for your passage, and sent instructions to the inn at Newhaven to expect you.'

Raoul's brow darkened and he scowled at Arrandale.

'You *knew* I would go?'

'I thought it very likely and made my plans accordingly.'

The tall Englishman was grinning broadly, but it was the soft shine in Cassie's eyes that alarmed Raoul. He should not be raising false hopes in her.

'It will be safer for me to quit France for a while. I will not risk leading Valerin to my sister.' He looked at Cassie and said meaningfully, 'This changes nothing between us, milady. I will stay with you only until you are safe in your grandmother's care.'

Cassie dropped her gaze.

'Of course,' she said quietly. 'I understand.'

She would have Raoul's company for another few days and she could not help herself, she was glad of it. She was not ready yet to say goodbye.

At a few minutes before midnight Cassie followed the men up the stairs, reaching the nave of the church just as the *Antoinette*'s captain and first mate entered.

Wolfgang cut short their expressions of delight at seeing him on his feet again.

'Never mind that, my friends. You have two passengers tonight. Make haste to get them away.'

He broke off as the church door was flung open. The priest's servant stood in the doorway.

'*Messieurs*, you must leave, now. This instant. There are riders approaching!'

'Are they customs men?' demanded the captain.

The servant bent over his knees, gasping for breath. 'No, no, they are not *douaniers*. They are in uniform and look more like soldiers, or *gendarmes*. It is difficult to see in the dark. There are a dozen of them at least.'

'Valerin,' muttered Raoul, drawing his pistol. 'Captain, take milady and get her down to the beach. Arrandale and I will cover your escape—'

'No,' gasped Cassie.

Wolfgang caught Raoul's arm. 'Do not be foolish man, what do you expect us to do, fight them all?'

'Yes, or die in the attempt.'

Wolfgang put his hand on Raoul's shoulder, saying urgently, 'If we stay here we are all lost. Get Cassie away while you can, man. The path to the beach is perilous and she will need your help. I cannot manage it in my present condition, but I *can* ride. I am well acquainted with this coast, I'll take the horses and draw them off.'

'Quickly, quickly,' cried the servant, his voice rising with panic. 'They will be here any moment!'

Cassie held her breath. Time seemed to stand still as she waited in an agony of suspense for Raoul's answer.

'Very well,' he said at last. 'Take my pistol.'

'Aye, your hat and jacket as well,' said Wolfgang. 'If

I hunch low in the saddle it should be enough to fool them that I am the man they want.'

Hastily Raoul exchanged his riding jacket for the worn leather jerkin. Wolfgang fixed the hat on his head.

'Goodbye, Doulevant. I rely on you to get my cousin safely to her grandmother.' He gripped Raoul's hand for a moment, then turned to Cassie.

She hugged him fiercely, being careful to avoid his injured shoulder.

'Goodbye, Cousin.' He held her close with his one good hand. 'Give my daughter a kiss from me.' He turned and grabbed the servant by the arm. 'Come along, my man, you can help me with the horses. Thank heaven Doulevant has already saddled them.'

He went off, dragging the protesting servant with him, while Cassie and Raoul followed the sailors out of a side door and through the graveyard to the cove path.

At the cliff edge Raoul stopped, a stifled exclamation escaping him.

'My papers,' he muttered. 'Arrandale has them, they are still in my coat pocket.'

Cassie gave him a little push.

'Go after him, quickly,' she urged him. 'We will wait for you. Captain—'

The sounds of shouts and hoofbeats filled the night as Wolfgang rode out of the stable, leading the two spare horses.

'Too late,' said Raoul.

The captain gave a little grunt of satisfaction.

'It's so dark now the *gendarmes* might well think you are all riding away. Yes, look, there they go, after him.' He turned back to Raoul, saying urgently, '*Monsieur*, we must go.'

Raoul took Cassie's hand. 'Come on.'

They stepped on to the path. It dropped steeply away and the church was soon lost to sight. The descent was steep and they went slowly, picking their way in the darkness. Cassie held her cloak tightly about her with one hand, the other clinging to Raoul's fingers. They had not gone far when a shot sounded, quickly carried away by the breeze. They all stopped as several more followed, a distant sharp crackle of sound in the night.

'It looks like Lagrasse has got their attention,' muttered the captain.

Cassie said nothing, she felt sick with worry for her cousin, but there was nothing to be done now, except go on. By the time they reached the beach her whole body was aching from the strain of negotiating the steep path in near darkness. Every step was fraught with danger on the rocky, uneven path and without Raoul's firm clasp on her hand Cassie thought her legs might seize up altogether. On the beach they were sheltered a little from the stiff breeze, small waves lapped softly against the shore, and Cassie could just make out a small rowing boat pulled up out of the water, little more than a blacker shape against the darkness. As they scrunched across the pebbles several shadowy figures loomed up and pushed the boat back into the waves.

Without ceremony Raoul lifted Cassie into his arms and waded out to place her in the boat. Everyone else jumped aboard, she heard the scrape and splash of the oars, and they were moving swiftly away from the shore. A dark shape loomed up ahead of them and she guessed they had reached the *Antoinette*. She suffered in silence the indignity of being thrown over Raoul's shoulder as he climbed aboard and she sat with him in a sheltered spot on deck while the crew raced around them, weighing anchor and setting the sails.

'As long as we avoid the British warships we should make good time,' said the captain, coming up. 'We have a fair wind and the tides are in our favour. I expect to be putting you ashore near Newhaven early tomorrow evening.' He grinned. 'The gods are smiling on us; the weather is unusually good for this time of the year. You should enjoy an easy crossing.'

'Thank you, Captain.' Cassie put up her hand to smother a yawn.

'We have very few luxuries aboard this vessel,' he said, 'but there is one cabin below, if you would like to rest there?'

'Yes, indeed,' said Cassie. 'We are both in need of sleep.'

She reached for Raoul's hand, but he moved away from her.

'I will sleep on deck. Milady can have the cabin. Perhaps, Captain, you would show her the way?'

There it was again, that note of steel in Raoul's voice that told her he would not be moved. Silently she followed the captain down the ladder-like steps to the lower deck and resigned herself to a long, lonely night.

Chapter Eleven

England. Enemy territory. Raoul stood beside Cassie on the shingle beach as the rowing boat that had brought them to this shore slowly drew away. The moon was just rising and the *Antoinette* was no more than a shadow against the starry sky. A chill wind was blowing, cutting through the worn leather jerkin and making him shiver.

'We will be warmer if we walk,' said Cassie. 'And we must speak English now.'

'As you wish,' he replied in her own language. 'I do not speak it quite like a native, but enough to get by, I think.'

'You speak it very well, Raoul.'

They set off along the beach, heading for the distant lights that the captain had told them were from the port of Newhaven.

Raoul reached for her hand.

'You are tired, milady?'

'No.'

'Then what is it, why are you so quiet?'

'I am…sorry that this will soon be over.'

He laughed, deliberately misunderstanding. 'I am not. I cannot wait to get into clean clothes and a real bed!'

'Not that. Our time together.'

'Ah.' The lead weight that had settled in his gut that morning grew heavier. Perhaps it was better to speak the truth now and get it over with. He said gravely, 'After all that has occurred I should ask your *grandmère* for your hand in marriage, but she would not allow it. I have nothing to offer you, *ma chère.*'

'I do not expect you to marry me,' she replied quietly. 'I am a widow, not some innocent virgin that you have deflowered.' She fell silent. Then, 'What will happen to you, Raoul?'

'It is most likely that I shall be locked up.'

'But you are not French. You are not an enemy!'

'Who will believe that, when I have no papers to prove it? War, she is cruel, my love.' He tightened his grip on the leather-bound case in his hand. 'But look, I have my surgeon's tools now. It is possible I shall be allowed to tend the other prisoners of war.'

'What if...?' She hesitated. 'What if I am with child?'

He hesitated, torn between desperately wanting her to be carrying his baby and fear for a child he could not protect.

Misunderstanding his silence, she hurried on. 'You need not worry if that is the case. I am sure Grandmama will take care of matters.'

'I am sure she will,' he answered bitterly.

It took them an hour to reach Newhaven and they soon found the Bridge Inn, a busy hostelry where they discovered that they were expected. The landlord greeted them in person, bowing low.

'Good evening, my lady, sir. Your rooms are ready. I hope you will find everything is in order. Pray send word when you wish dinner to be sent up.'

They were escorted to an impressive suite of rooms on the first floor. Servants were waiting to show them to their separate bedchambers. Cassie followed the maid into a large chamber with a cheerful fire blazing in the hearth, hot water in a jug on the washstand and a clean set of clothes spread out on the bed. There was even a truckle bed made up in the corner for the maid, a tacit reminder to Cassie that the proprieties were to be observed now she was back in England.

When she emerged some time later she found Raoul waiting for her in the sitting room. He was attired in riding jacket, buckskins and top boots, the epitome of English country fashions, and with his sleek, dark hair, near black eyes and lean cheeks freshly shaved, he looked every inch a gentleman.

He turned to her and bowed.

'Your cousin, he surpasses himself with the arrangements,' he said, putting a hand to his snowy neckcloth. 'The coat, it is a little tight across the shoulder, but overall it looks very well, I think?'

He looked so handsome that Cassie felt almost sick with longing for him, but she hid it behind an even brighter smile.

'From the maid's chatter I believe he sent a full purse here with instructions for our every comfort. I have no idea where he came by so much money.'

'I think it is best not to enquire too closely into the affairs of your cousin,' said Raoul.

'Very true. I do hope he managed to get away.' Her smiled faltered, but after a brief pause she recovered, saying brightly, 'And this gown suits me very well, does it not?' She glanced down with satisfaction at her walking dress of pale-pink muslin over white cambric. 'In truth, it was too big at first, but with a little judicious pinning and tucking it now fits me perfectly. There are gloves, too, and a pelisse and bonnet for me to wear, when we go out.'

'Your cousin has truly thought of everything,' remarked Raoul. 'The landlord tells me the—what did he call it?—the *shot* here is paid until Lady Hune's coach arrives to fetch you, however long that may be.'

She looked up quickly. 'To fetch *me*? You will come with me to meet Grandmama, Raoul, will you not?'

The look he gave her tore at her heart.

'We must part sometime, milady.'

'Not yet,' she begged him. 'Please, Raoul, do not leave me until you have met the marchioness. She will be able to help you, I know she will.'

He inclined his head and said politely, 'As you wish. Shall I send down for dinner?'

Two days later Lady Hune's travelling chaise arrived to carry them to Chantreys.

'At least it is closer than Bath,' Cassie remarked as they set off. 'We should be no more than three nights on the road.'

Raoul said nothing, but kept his eyes fixed on the window as the houses dwindled and they rattled through the open countryside. How was he to survive another three nights, knowing Cassie was so close, but that he could not hold her? It must be done. They were both agreed there could be no future for them, but it cut him to the heart to see Cassie trying to be so brave. They were perfectly civil to one another, but occasionally he would look up to find her watching him, such sorrow in her eyes that he could hardly bear it.

Yet bear it he must. His mother had died as much of a broken heart as the growth in her body, pining for the man she loved. Raoul knew he was his father's son, he was committed to his work and he would not risk making the same mistake, of neglecting those he loved until it was too late. It was better that he left Cassie now, while she was young enough to find another man to love her, to cherish her. One who could give her the life she deserved, the life of a lady.

By the time they reached Chantreys, Raoul was exhausted. He and Cassie had maintained the pretence of being nothing more than acquaintances, retiring each night to their separate beds, but at one of the inns the walls were so thin that he had caught the sound of muffled sobs coming from her room. And in the morning she was looking so wan and hollow-eyed only his strong conviction that it was for the best kept him from taking her in his arms and kissing away her sadness.

As the chaise bowled up the drive he studied the house. It was a fine building, but it was not the grand palace he had been expecting. Cassandra had informed him that Chantreys was not the Earl of Davenport's principal seat, yet it was where he and his family had chosen to make their home. A house suitable for a gentleman, certainly, but with none of the magnificence

Raoul thought essential for a peer of the realm. He wondered if he would ever understand the English.

When they alighted at the door they were met by the butler, Fingle, who informed them that the dowager marchioness was resting and would see them later. He then passed Lady Cassandra over to the care of the housekeeper and personally escorted Raoul upstairs to his bedchamber. The significance of this gesture was not lost on Raoul, who had half-expected to be treated as a hired courier and lodged in the servants' quarters. When a footman came in carrying a supply of fresh linen for him and asking if he would like hot water brought up for a bath, Raoul accepted readily. He was anxious to wash away the dirt of the road and refresh himself before his meeting with Lady Hune.

'There you are, my lady, this is your room.' The motherly housekeeper showed Cassie into a light, airy bedchamber overlooking the gardens. 'The fire has been burning all morning so 'tis nice and warm in here. Her ladyship's maid said she would come in when you are ready to dress, but perhaps you would like to rest, first?'

'Thank you, Mrs Wallace, I think I would like to lie down for a while. Tell Duffy I will send for her when I am ready.'

The housekeeper had been chattering non-stop and Cassie felt the beginning of a headache nagging at her temples. As soon as the woman left her she lay down on the bed and closed her eyes. Unhappiness weighed upon her like a heavy cloak. She felt so *tired*. Her body ached with longing for Raoul, with the effort of keeping that longing hidden from him. They had agreed that they must part and she was determined not to make it more difficult for him than necessary.

She heard a soft knock at the door and sat up. Had she slept without knowing it? Another knock followed and the door opened. A golden head appeared and a pretty, musical voice spoke.

'Ah, you are not asleep, Lady Cassandra. Good. May I come in?' Hardly waiting for Cassie's assent the young lady slipped into the room. 'I wanted to introduce myself to you, my lady. I am Ellen Tatham.'

'Ah yes. Of course.' Reluctantly Cassie slid off the bed. 'Will you not sit down, Miss Tatham?'

When they were sitting down on either side of the fireplace, Miss Tatham continued.

'Pray, do call me Ellen. Your grandmother has been kind enough to take me under her wing for my come-out. She has looked after me in London for most of the Season, but I wanted to assure you that I have not in any way usurped your place in her affections, Lady Cassandra. She has been so worried for you, but I hope I have helped her to bear it.'

'Thank you,' said Cassie politely. 'I am sure you have helped to divert her mind. But you must be sorry to have left London.'

'Not a bit of it,' Ellen reassured her. 'I had had quite enough of balls and parties. I was delighted to come here while Alex and Diana are away. And you must not think I allow Lady Hune to tire herself out running after the children. They spend most of their day with Nurse and myself.'

'Ah, yes, the children. I have not seen them for some years. How are they?'

'Quite delightful, and they are growing so fast, Florence especially. She celebrated her ninth birthday recently and is going to be very tall, I think.'

'Like her father,' murmured Cassie.

'I beg your pardon?'

'Oh, nothing. When do you expect Lord and Lady Davenport to return?'

'Lady Hune had a letter from them only today: they are even now on their way back to Chantreys and should be with us in two weeks. As soon as they return I shall rejoin my stepmama and the marchioness plans to take you to Bath with her.' Miss Tatham rearranged the folds of her white-muslin skirts. 'And the gentleman who escorted you to England—Monsieur Doulevant, is it not? Will he accompany you to Bath?'

'Oh, no, I would not think so.' Cassie hoped she sounded indifferent. 'Although I shall ask Grandmama to give him her patronage. He will require help, I think, if he is to avoid being taken as a prisoner of war. Not that he is French,' she hurried on. 'He is from the Southern Netherlands, which was under Austrian rule for a long time. Raoul deeply resents Bonaparte claiming his country as part of France.'

She felt the heat in her cheeks when she realised she had used Raoul's name, but her visitor feigned not to notice and she was grateful for that.

'And is he from a noble family?'

Cassie could not prevent a heartbeat's hesitation before she responded.

'No. He is a surgeon. A very skilled surgeon.'

'Ah. I see.'

Cassie doubted it, but she said nothing more.

'I had best go.' Miss Tatham rose gracefully. 'I am so pleased to have met you, Lady Cassandra.'

'Please, call me Cassie.'

'Very well, then, Cassie. We will meet again at dinner, when you shall introduce me to your very skilled surgeon.'

'Of course. Tell me, which room is Lady Hune occupying?'

'Her door is the last one on this passage and she may well be awake by now.' Ellen twinkled at her. 'You need not be afraid to go and see—her terrifying dresser will soon send you about your business if she is asleep!'

With that she whisked herself out of the room and Cassie was alone again, but she no longer wished to lie down. Quickly she washed her face and hands and went off to find her grandmother.

Duffy opened the door to her and Cassie was well enough acquainted with her grandmother's dresser to recognise the relief and affection behind the woman's brusque manner.

'Oh, so you've come back to us, have you, my lady? And about time, too, if you forgive my saying so.'

She was interrupted by an imperious voice.

'Who is it, Duffy? Is it Cassandra? Let her come in.'

The dresser stepped back and Cassie entered the room. Lady Hune was sitting in a wing chair by the window, regally attired in her customary black with white-lace ruffles at her neck and wrists.

'Yes, Grandmama, I am here.'

'Then come closer, where I can see you.'

Cassie took a few slow, hesitant steps forward, but then the marchioness put out her hands and with a sob Cassie threw herself on her knees before her chair and buried her face in her skirts. Her grandmother gently stroked her curls.

'Well, my love, what is the matter this time?'

Cassie gave a watery chuckle.

'You used to say that to me whenever I was in a scrape.'

'And is that not the case now?'

'No. *Yes!* Oh, Grandmama, I am so unhappy!'

Between gulping sobs and fresh tears Cassie told the marchioness what had happened since she had left Bath a year ago. The narrative was not quite complete; she spoke of Gerald's gambling, but not his weakness for women, nor did she describe those final few months in Verdun when money was short and Gerald's mood had changed. When it came to explaining her meeting with Raoul she said merely that he had been her escort. She did not mention the heavenly night she had spent in his arms, but Lady Hune was not deceived.

'This Monsieur Doulevant...' Lady Sophia handed Cassie a fresh handkerchief. 'You think you love him?'

'Yes.'

'You thought yourself in love with Witney.'

Cassie wiped her eyes.

'He is nothing like Gerald, Grandmama. Raoul is good and generous and so very kind. If you could have seen how he toiled to save those poor souls at Flagey! I love him so much.'

'And what is his family?'

'His father was a doctor in Brussels—'

'He is not French, then?'

'No, ma'am. His family are from the Netherlands.'

'Well, that's a mercy. I lost too many friends during the Terror to feel any warmth towards the French.'

Cassie gave a little huff of impatience.

'All this makes little difference, ma'am, since we are not to be married. We are both agreed on that.' Cassie tried to smile but it went sadly awry. 'We have known each other for such a short time, it is inconceivable that we can have formed a lasting attachment.'

If Cassie expected her grandmother to contradict her she was disappointed. Lady Hune gave a loud sigh of relief.

'Well, I am glad you both have the sense to see that.'

'That is what I have been trying to tell myself.' Cassie's head bowed and she said in a small voice, 'But he loves me, Grandmama.'

'Has he said as much?'

Cassie paused. There had been endearments, but no outright declaration.

'Not exactly.'

'Then I will give him credit for that, too.'

'He is a good man, an honourable man, Grandmama. He risked his life to help me, but he will not marry me, even though he has no money and he knows I shall come of age in a few months and will then have control of my own fortune. I will have enough money to keep us both.'

'I like him better and better!'

'Pray, ma'am, do not jest with me.'

'I have never been more serious, my love. Even if he were not from a country that is now annexed by France and therefore our enemy, to marry a man who is so far outside your sphere, a man with no money, no expectations—it would be a disaster. You would hate one another within the year.'

Cassie's head dropped even lower. She had tried to tell herself the very same thing. She wiped her eyes.

She must try to forget her own unhappiness and think of Raoul.

'I want you to help him, Grandmama. I cannot bear the thought of his being locked away as a prisoner of war.'

'What do you expect me to do, child?'

'I do not think he will accept money, he is too proud for that. But perhaps you could use your influence to keep him from prison and perhaps to find him a position. Or help him to return to Brussels.' Cassie looked down at clasped hands. 'I quite see that we cannot marry, I am resigned to that, but I owe him a great debt, Grandmama.'

Lady Hune pursed her lips, considering. At last she nodded.

'I shall talk to Monsieur Doulevant at dinner and I will see what I can do for him.'

'Thank you, ma'am.'

Cassie leaned against the marchioness's skirts again and felt her grandmother's frail fingers smoothing her hair. It did not take away the ache that gnawed at her, but it was comforting.

'Let us move on to other matters,' said Lady Hune at last. 'You saw my great-nephew, Wolfgang Arrandale? I am glad my letters reached him.'

'So, too, am I,' said Cassie. 'We could not have escaped without his help, only I fear it might have cost him dear.' She raised her head and directed an anxious look at the marchioness. 'I have no idea if he is safe. We were pursued by French officers and he rode off to draw them away. We heard shots—'

'Worrying about him will do no good,' said Lady Hune prosaically. 'Wolfgang Arrandale has lived on his wits for the past nine years, we can only hope he has survived.'

'The thing is,' said Cassie, frowning, 'he did not know he had a daughter, for he has avoided all contact with his family until now. He told me to give her a kiss from him.' She looked up. 'Should we tell Florence, Grandmama? It would be heartbreaking to raise false hopes in such a little girl.'

'Then let us wait until we have word that he is safe,' said Lady Hune. 'Wolfgang was always a wild one, but I am grateful to him for helping to send you back to me.' She looked at Cassie, her eyes suspiciously bright, before saying in her usual sharp tone, 'But enough of this. It will soon be time for dinner and you must change, my dear. There was no time to send for your clothes from Bath—oh, yes, Cassandra, I have kept everything, just as it was when you eloped—but my protégée has looked out a couple of her dresses for you and Duffy will bring them to your room. Ellen is about your size, as you will see when you will meet her at dinner.'

'I have already done so, ma'am. She came to my room a little while ago. I thought her very charming.'

'She is a baggage,' said Lady Hune, not mincing her words. 'She reminds me very much of you, which must be why I like her so much.'

Cassie picked up one of the gnarled hands and kissed the beringed fingers. She said penitently. 'I am very sorry to have caused you so much trouble, Grandmama.'

'Yes, yes, well, be off with you now, or we shall both of us be late for dinner! And dry your eyes, Cassandra. An Arrandale does not show a woebegone face to the world!'

* * *

Raoul received the summons to join the Dowager Marchioness of Hune and he made his way immediately to the drawing room. He passed a large mirror in the hall and it took a conscious effort not to stop before it and make a few final adjustments to his neckcloth. He was no lackey to fawn and cower before an English aristocrat. He entered the room to find the marchioness alone and sitting in a chair beside the fire. Her back was ramrod straight and her black dress was as severe as her countenance. She had an abundance of silver hair crowned by a cap of fine Mechlin lace and she held a black cane in one hand while the other rested on the arm of the chair, a king's ransom in jewels sparkling on her fingers. A matriarch, if ever he had seen one! She regarded him as he approached, her blue eyes sharp and assessing.

'I must thank you, Monsieur Doulevant, for escorting my granddaughter safely to England.'

He made his bow. 'It was a pleasure, Lady Hune.'

'My nephew Arrandale said in his message to me that you are a doctor.'

'No, ma'am. I am a surgeon.'

'Ah. That makes all the difference.'

'I am aware.' His pulled himself up a little straighter. 'In France, my lady, surgeons are beginning to receive the recognition they deserve.'

Those sharp eyes snapped at him.

'But we are in England, *monsieur*, and presently at war with France.'

Raoul held his tongue. It would do no good to antagonise the marchioness. He would be gone soon enough.

He did not speak again until he was once more in control of his temper.

'Lady Hune, I do not know how much your granddaughter has told you of our journey together.'

'Enough.'

His neckcloth felt too tight, but he resisted the temptation to run a finger around it.

'I am aware, ma'am, in such circumstances, a gentleman should make an offer of marriage to Lady Cassandra, but as you say so truly, we are in England now and I am not regarded as a gentleman here. I believe you would think me presumptuous to aspire to the hand of your granddaughter.'

'You are correct, *monsieur*, I would. But it is not only the disparity in your birth that makes it an ineligible match. There is another, and to my mind an even more important, reason you should not offer for her.' Those sharp old eyes regarded him steadily. 'I do not believe you could make Cassandra happy. If she married you, society would turn its back on her. Would you really wish to remove her from the comfort of her family and friends, from the life she has known since birth?'

'No, ma'am, I would not.'

'We are agreed, then.'

He met her gaze.

'And if there should be…consequences of the time we spent together?'

'Let us speak plainly, Monsieur Doulevant. If my granddaughter should be carrying a child I shall deal with it. You need not fear that Cassandra will be cast penniless into the world, after all she is only recently widowed and might pass the child off as her late husband's.'

The idea filled Raoul with abhorrence and he said quickly, 'I do not believe she would do that.'

'Then she will be confined in the country until after the birth. There would be some talk, but it would pass.' She added with a hint of bitterness, 'The Arrandales are no strangers to scandal.'

'And the child?'

'Would be put with a good family.' The dowager marchioness regarded him for a moment and said in a softer tone, 'Do not worry, *monsieur*, whatever her decision I shall ensure that neither Cassandra nor her child shall want for anything. But all this is conjecture. There may be no baby—'

The old lady broke off as the door opened and Cassandra came in, looking very demure in a gown of pale-blue muslin, her dusky curls confined by a matching ribbon. She was looking down, her thick dark lashes accentuating her pale cheeks, and Raoul's heart contracted painfully. He wanted to take her in his arms, promise her that all would be well, but he could not. At this moment he could not promise her anything at all.

Cassandra looked quickly from the marchioness to Raoul, trying to read their faces, but both were inscrutable. She longed to ask Grandmama if she had agreed to help Raoul, but Lady Hune was already saying something innocuous about the weather. Raoul responded politely and Cassie joined in the conversation. She knew her grandmother too well to press her. She must bide her time and hope that over the course of the evening Raoul would make a good impression with the marchioness.

Miss Tatham's arrival lightened the mood slightly. She announced cheerfully that she and Cassie were now good friends and she greeted Raoul with un-feigned friendliness. She even cajoled Lady Hune into a smile within minutes of entering the room. Never-theless dinner was a strained affair. Conversation was stilted. Raoul no longer supported the French, but his dislike of the aristocracy had not waned and Cassan-dra was careful to avoid any topics that were likely to put him at odds with her grandmother. The effort was quite exhausting and frustrating, too, for at the end of dinner Lady Hune announced that after such a long day the ladies would go directly to bed.

The following morning Cassie rose early. Her hope was to find Lady Hune alone and ask her what she thought of Monsieur Doulevant, but when she glanced out of the window and saw Raoul walking alone in the gardens, she quickly grabbed her shawl and ran down-stairs to join him.

When he saw her on the path she stopped, suddenly feeling shy.

'May I walk with you, Raoul?'

He inclined his head and she fell into step beside him. He did not offer her his arm, and she kept both hands firmly holding her shawl about her shoulders.

'The sun is very pleasant,' she said, desperate for something to say, 'but it is has grown much colder these last few days.'

'Yes.'

His brief response was daunting.

'Would you rather be alone?'

He shook his head. 'I have been thinking that it would be best if I leave here.'

'No!' She stopped, turning to look up at him. 'I

would like you to become acquainted with my grand-mother.'

'To what end, milady, so that she might approve me as a husband for you?'

Cassie flushed and looked away. He was right, al-though she had hardly admitted it to herself.

'To stay would only bring us more pain, *ma chère*,' he said, smiling in a way that pierced her heart. 'You know there is no future for us. I cannot give you the things you deserve and I do not talk of just the things that money can buy,' he added quickly. 'You know my profession is my life.' He took her hand and pulled it on to the crook of his arm before starting to walk again.

'I have been thinking a great deal about this, Cassie, and I would not ask any woman to suffer as my mother did. To be sure my father was dazzled by the English lords and ladies in Brussels, but it was not for their titles and money that he attended them. He could not ignore those in need, any more than I could ignore those poor crushed men at Flagey.'

'You know I would not ask you to do so, Raoul.'

'I do know it, but I have told you, surgery is every-thing to me. I have dedicated my life to my profession and there is no room for a wife. I could not bear to think I would neglect you, as my father did *Maman*.'

Cassie drew a breath. 'I would take that chance, Raoul.'

'But I will not. That is why I must leave.'

'But not yet,' she begged him. 'Do not leave me just yet!'

With something between a sigh and a groan he stopped and pulled her round to face him.

'Ah, Cassie, do you think this is easy for me? I should

have left you at Dieppe, but I was too weak. I told myself you needed me to see you safe to England, and when we reached Newhaven still I could not leave you. But now you are safe, there is no reason for me to stay longer.'

'But there is!' She clutched at his jacket. 'Grandmama will use her influence to help you find a position here in England, I know she will. At least stay here until we have secured you a place in a hospital. Please, Raoul.'

She was begging him, but she did not care. Perhaps if she kissed him he would give in. She reached up to cup his face, but he caught her hands, shaking his head at her.

'Do not do this, Cassie, in the end it will make no difference, I must go.'

'At least stay until the end of the week,' she said desperately. 'That will give Grandmama time to write letters of introduction for you. It is the least you deserve after all you have done for me.' She placed her hands on her stomach. 'And if I *am* with child, I would rather its father was not locked up like a common felon.'

She was being cruel and the shadow of pain in his eyes tore at her heart, but it was her last argument.

He exhaled, a long, sighing breath. 'Very well. I will remain here until the end of the week, but not a moment longer.'

'Thank you.'

She closed her eyes. Four more days. It was not long, but it was something. All she could do now was pray for some miracle.

Cassandra made her way back indoors alone. She could not help thinking that there was something she had missed, that somehow there was a way for them to be happy together. She did not see Raoul again until late in the afternoon, when her grandmother asked her to accompany her for a stroll on the west lawn. She was aware of a stab of jealousy as she watched Raoul joining in a lively game of cricket with Ellen and her two young charges.

'Miss Tatham is certainly at ease with little Meggie and Florence,' she observed, trying hard to sound unconcerned.

'I am much indebted to her,' replied Lady Hune. 'I was at first against the idea of our looking after the little girls while my nephew and his new bride went away, but it has indeed been more restful than escorting Ellen to an endless round of parties in town. And now she is initiating Monsieur Doulevant into the mysteries of cricket.'

Cassandra saw her chance.

'What do you think of him, Grandmama?'

'Is it right to judge a man on such short acquaintance, Cassandra? I am naturally disposed to like him because he has brought you home to me and I think at heart he is a good man.'

'He *is*, Grandmama,' said Cassie. 'He is the bravest man I have ever met and also very kind, and honourable—'

'My love, he may be all those things, but he is still not the husband for you.' Lady Hune took her hand. 'We may be able to keep him out of prison, but he still has nothing to live on.'

'I know it,' said Cassandra unhappily. 'He has told me he will only remain at Chantreys until the end of the week.'

'I respect him all the more for curtailing his visit here. Forgive me if I speak frankly, Cassandra, but I believe he knows in his heart that you would make a disastrous wife for him. He needs someone of his own rank, someone who understands his world and can support him in his work.'

Cassie nodded and glanced down at her hands, encased in chicken-skin gloves to protect them while the blisters and cuts of the past few weeks healed.

'What a useless creature I am, Grandmama.'

'Nonsense. You have all the accomplishments of a lady and in time I do not despair of you finding another husband, this time one who will make you happy.'

Cassie did not attempt to argue, but at that moment she doubted she would ever be happy again. She must not think of that.

'But you will help Monsieur Doulevant, Grandmama, will you not?'

'Certainly, my dear, if I can. Now, this wind is too chill to remain out of doors for long, even with the sunshine. We shall go in. That is, unless you wish to remain here and join in their game?'

Cassie glanced at the laughing group running happily about the lawn and resolutely looked away again.

'No, Grandmama, I shall come indoors with you.'

Raoul watched Cassandra walk off with the marchioness and the unhappy droop of her shoulders tore at his heart. Having delivered her safely into Lady Hune's care he should have left Chantreys immediately. Now he had promised Cassie he would remain, when every day was torture for them both. He decided he must break that promise, since remaining here was merely prolonging

the agony. He fixed his smile in place and tried to concentrate upon this foolish English game. He still had
a little money left from the purse Cassie had shared
with him, he would use that to hire a chaise and leave
at first light in the morning. Where he did not know
and did not care.

As soon as he had changed for dinner Raoul went off
in search of Fingle. He ran lightly down the stairs to the
hall, turning the last corner just as the butler appeared.

'Ah, Monsieur Doulevant. Her ladyship would like
you to join her in the drawing room.'

'But certainly,' replied Raoul, descending the last
few steps. As he accompanied Fingle across the marble
floor he quickly explained his requirements for a carriage the following morning.

'I wish to be leaving at dawn,' he reiterated as they
reached the drawing room door. 'Is that understood?'

Fingle bowed. 'Perfectly, *monsieur*. Allow me to announce you to her ladyship.'

Lady Hune was sitting in her customary chair, but
Raoul's eyes were drawn immediately to Cassie, who
was standing by the window and outlined by the late
afternoon sun that was pouring in through the glass.
She was wearing the pale-blue gown again, the muslin
so fine that the sun shone through it and he could see
the slender body beneath. Quickly he averted his gaze
and turned away from her to greet his hostess.

'Ah, Monsieur Doulevant.' Lady Hune held out her
hand to him and he bowed briefly over her fingers. She
continued without preamble. 'I am under an obligation
to you and I need to repay it. I have been making en-

quiries and I understand a medical degree may be obtained quite easily from some universities, especially those of Aberdeen or St Andrews. I am willing to purchase such a degree for you and to give you my support to set up a practice in Bath—'

He stepped back, frowning.

'I have heard what it is to be a doctor in Bath, madam. To quote your granddaughter, they have grown fat giving out pills and placebos to the rich and privileged. No, I thank you!' He pressed his lips together to prevent any further outburst and took a few slow, steadying breaths so that he could say politely, 'I am obliged to you, my lady, but I will make my own arrangements.'

'Oh? And just how will you to that, *monsieur*? Do you have papers, proof that you are not a Frenchman?'

'Grandmama!'

He heard Cassie's anguished whisper and curbed his temper.

'You know I do not, Lady Hune. I served with distinction in the French Navy for six years—'

'That is hardly going to recommend you to the English government! You are most likely to be taken up and imprisoned the moment you leave Chantreys.'

'So be it. I will ask them to contact my captain. He would vouch that I was conscripted into the navy and that I was honourably discharged.'

'My grandmother will help, will you not, ma'am?' He looked down to see Cassie standing beside him. 'She managed to get word to my cousin so I am sure she could find Captain Belfort. She will not let the war prevent her from doing so, will you, dearest Grandmama?'

'We can try,' admitted Lady Hune. 'But that may take months if the man is at sea.' She stared pointedly at Cassandra, who refused to move from Raoul's side. 'In the meantime,' she continued, 'what is to become of Monsieur Doulevant?'

Raoul said quickly, 'I will not live as your pensioner, ma'am!'

'No, I did not think that would be acceptable to you.'

With Cassie beside him he was emboldened to give voice to a plan that had been forming.

'I know that there is now a Royal College of Surgeons in London, Lady Hune. If I could gain membership *there*—members have to pass an examination, I believe, but I have no fear of failing. I studied at the Hôtel Dieu before I entered the navy, and went back there upon my return to Paris. In time I could prove myself, I could even make a reasonable living.'

'Then you could come to Bath and call at Royal Crescent to keep us informed of your progress,' put in Cassie.

Lady Hune put up her hand.

'You do not understand, Cassandra. A doctor might be considered acceptable as a visitor, but a surgeon's presence would never be countenanced in our circles.'

'No, Grandmama, forgive me, but *you* do not understand,' cried Cassie. 'Raoul is very skilled at his profession, I have seen him at work, he has saved many lives—'

Lady Hune's ebony cane banged on the floor.

'That is not the point, Cassandra. One might invite a doctor to dine with us, to visit. But a surgeon—it is an admirable trade, I am sure, but it is a trade nevertheless. Let me speak plainly, my child, as a surgeon's wife you would never be acknowledged in society. You would do as well to marry a shopkeeper!'

Raoul looked into the haughty face of his hostess.

'If we are speaking plainly, ma'am, permit me to ask: are you saying that if I were to become a doctor you would allow me to marry Lady Cassandra?'

The marchioness compressed her lips and after a long silence she pronounced judgement.

'Once your practice was established and if the attachment between you proves lasting, then, yes. You have charm, *monsieur*, I can see that. It will not take you long to make a success in Bath and with success comes money. And in the meantime I would sponsor you and introduce you to my acquaintance.'

Raoul said nothing. It was a compromise, but would it be so very bad? He would be at the beck and call of just the sort of persons he most despised, but he would be able to practise a little medicine. At least he would have Cassandra and he would not feel the same obligation towards his pampered patients so there was little chance of his neglecting her. She would be his whole world.

She would have to be.

'Lady Hune, there is something you should know.' He glanced towards Cassie. 'When I left the French Navy and joined my sister in Paris, she had just received word from our father's lawyer in Brussels. It concerned an English countess.'

'The one who ruined your lives?' put in Cassie.

He nodded. 'The very same. It appears that when she died she remembered me in her will. She has left me a house in England. Perhaps at the end her conscience pricked her.'

'Perhaps she had fond memories of your father,' said Cassie. 'It may have been that she was lonely in Brussels.'

'Perhaps. I was so young then. The situation may not have been quite as I perceived it.'

'But what of this property?' demanded Lady Hune. 'Where is it, what is it?'

'That I do not know, the lawyers mentioned a small bequest, probably not enough to provide an income. At that time I wanted nothing to do with the lady or her money and I never made enquiry. Now, however...' He turned to the marchioness. 'I know I have no papers, ma'am, but with your help perhaps, I might go to London and approach the lawyers.'

'That is possible,' replied Lady Hune. 'Certainly a doctor with property would be a more acceptable suitor for my granddaughter.'

He bowed. 'That is what I thought, ma'am.'

Cassie caught her breath. Could Raoul truly love her so much that he would consider giving up his work, his vocation, to marry her? That was a sacrifice indeed. She closed her eyes. Gerald had wanted everything from her, no compromise, no sacrifice on his part at all. She had happily given up everything, her family, friends and her fortune, to be with him. It had been an unequal partnership and inevitably it had ended in disaster.

Suddenly she knew what must be done. She forced her unwilling limbs to move across the room until she was standing beside her grandmother.

'No, Raoul,' she said quietly. 'I will not let you sacrifice yourself in this way. It would destroy you to give up the work you love.' She met his eyes steadily, drawing on all her Arrandale blood and breeding to get her through the next few minutes. 'You told me yourself you had no choice, that being a surgeon is what you are. You *must* be allowed to practise. I have seen the good work you can do. I cannot allow you to give that up for me. You said yourself there could be no happiness for us. You would resent me and I could not blame you.' She took a deep breath. 'Before you came into the room, my grandmother was telling me that she has an acquaintance who is patron of a hospital on the coast, near Portsmouth. I am sure Grandmama would be willing to write to him and together they could help you become a member of the Royal College of Surgeons and find you a post at the hospital. With the Dowager Marchioness of Hune as your sponsor they are unlikely to turn you away.'

Raoul's dark brows snapped together.

'Cassie, I—'

She put up her hand. 'We are at war again and it is unlikely to be over quickly. Your services will be in great demand, I am sure, and your skills would save many lives.'

There, it was done. Raoul was looking stunned, Grandmama was silent but approving. Cassie felt her spirit disintegrating. She must go if she was not to disgrace herself. She forced a smile to her lips.

'Now, I pray you will both excuse me if I do not join you for dinner tonight. I shall lie down for a little while and ask Fingle to send me up a supper tray. So I will say goodbye to you now, Monsieur Doulevant, but believe me when I say I wish you every happiness.'

With that Cassie gave a little curtsy and, keeping her head high, she walked quickly from the room.

* * *

Raoul stared at the closed door, trying to bring his chaotic thoughts into some sort of order. He was hardly aware of the marchioness's deep sigh.

'My granddaughter must love you very much to put your happiness before her own.'

There was a rustle of silks as the old lady hunted for her handkerchief.

She gave a little *tsk* of impatience, 'Oh, go after her, sir. Ask her to be your wife. Tell her if she wishes to marry a mere surgeon I will not stand in her way.'

Slowly Raoul shook his head.

'Lady Cassandra deserves better than to take second place to my work.'

'I doubt she would agree with you,' replied Lady Hune.

'She will, in time. Whatever I choose to do I will hurt her, but if I may use the analogy, I know that sometimes one must lose the limb to save the life.' He was still staring at the door, but slowly his thoughts settled and he turned to face the marchioness. 'Very well, then, ma'am, if you can help me to find a post as a surgeon I will accept your help and I will thank you for it.'

Her hand clenched upon the black cane and she said sharply, 'Let us understand one another, *monsieur*. I will fund you while you obtain the necessary membership of the College of Surgeons and I will do what I can to find you a position. You will be paid adequately, I have no doubt, but there can be no advancement in society, no opportunity to make a fortune.'

'I do not want a fortune.'

'But without the means to support her you cannot hope to marry my granddaughter.'

'I understand that, ma'am. I have no hopes in that quarter.'

'And you will not try to contact Cassandra again?'

'You have my word.' Raoul met the faded old eyes steadily. 'It is over.'

He left Chantreys the following morning, driving away into a grey dawn with the first chill of winter frosting the grass.

Chapter Twelve

Gosport, Hampshire—February 1804

'I have shut up the house, sir, and made up the fire in your bedchamber. If that is all, sir, I will bid you goodnight.'

'Yes, thank you, Slinden. Goodnight.'

As the servant closed the door Raoul leaned back in his chair and stretched his feet towards the crackling blaze in the hearth. Perhaps he would have just one more glass of wine before he went to bed. Only one, though, because he would have to rise betimes and return to the hospital. He had received word only this evening that another ship had docked and the wounded would be transported to Gosport overnight.

Even in the few months he had been at the small hospital the number of injured men returning from the ongoing war with France had risen. It was already being suggested that he should be promoted to chief surgeon, the trustees recognising his superior knowledge and ability, but the daily round was gruelling. He and his fellow medical staff—surgeons, physicians and medical assistants—worked through all the daylight hours and often Raoul would continue far into the night. Even when he had finished at the hospital local people would turn up at his door with a variety of injuries and ailments, for word had soon spread that kind-hearted 'Mr Doolevant', as they called him, would help them if he could. And without charge, too, if they had no money. He rarely had a moment to himself.

One would have thought that such a busy life would leave him little time to think of Cassandra, but it was not the case. He missed her so much it was a physical pain. She was like a ghost at his shoulder; whenever he was operating he remembered how she worked with him at Flagey, if he saw a pretty brunette in the street he would think of Cassie and when he lay down each night she haunted his dreams. Cassie as he had first seen her, fighting off her attackers; Cassie laughing and teasing him; Cassie naked in his arms...

It was five months since he had driven away from Chantreys and the heartache was as strong as ever. Impatiently he pushed himself out of his chair and poured a glass of wine from the decanter on the table. It was contemptible to feel so sorry for himself when the hospital was full of men who were injured or dying. He heard the faint thud of the knocker and closed his eyes. Another poor soul requiring his help. In the past months he had become adept at setting bones and stitching broken heads, not to mention advising his neighbours on all sorts of bodily ailments from chilblains to childbirth. He had never wanted to become a doctor yet here he was administering to the sick, albeit those who were too poor to pay for medical help. At first Raoul had thought his services might offend the local physician, but Dr Radcliffe was sanguine.

'There's more than enough sickness and ailments to go round, young man,' he had said, when Raoul had voiced his concerns. 'These unfortunates cannot afford to pay, so you are not robbing me of my livelihood.'

They had discussed the possibility of setting up a charitable trust to help the townsfolk. Nothing had come of it yet, but it was something Raoul was determined to pursue, when he was not so overworked. The knock sounded again and he closed his eyes. Let them go away. He was too tired to deal with anything more tonight.

He was refilling his glass when Slinden came in.

'Mr Doulevant, sir, there is a lady wishing to see you.'

Raoul turned, intending to rebuke his servant for disturbing him, but when his eyes fell upon the figure standing beside Slinden the words died away.

Cassandra pushed back her hood and looked nervously at Raoul.

'I beg your pardon for calling so late.'

Perhaps she should have waited until the morning. He was frowning so direfully that she was about to withdraw when he came towards her, hands held out.

'No, no, it is not yet ten. Come, sit here by the fire, let me get you a glass of wine. Have you eaten? Slinden shall bring you bread and cheese, or there is a little chicken broth—'

'No, no, I dined on the road,' she told him, relief at his reception making her laugh a little.

She sank on to a chair and accepted a glass of wine.

'Please sit down, Raoul. You look so tired, are you working very hard?'

'Yes, but it is very rewarding.'

'I am glad.' She fell silent, sipping her wine while the servant withdrew and closed the door upon them. Raoul was devouring her with his eyes like a starving man might survey a banquet.

'Why have you come here?' he demanded.

She saw his glance drop to her stomach.

'Not to tell you I am carrying your child.'

She watched him carefully and was heartened when he looked a little disappointed at her words. He frowned at her.

'Have you come from Bath, alone?'

'No, no, I have my maid with me.' She added, when he raised his brows, 'I left her at the Globe.'

'You should not be here.'

'We made very good time and spent only one night on the road,' she said, ignoring his comment and untying the strings of her cloak. 'Grandmama's chaise is prodigious comfortable and very swift.'

'And does Lady Hune know you are here?'

He was still staring, as if memorising every detail, and her heart fluttered. His eyes were every bit as dark and intense as she remembered, but then it was hard to forget him when he filled her thoughts by day and haunted her dreams every night.

She said now, 'I came of age last month, Raoul, I do not need Grandmama's consent, but, yes—' she smiled at him '—she knows I am here and I have her blessing.'

She waited expectantly, hoping he might drag her

out of her chair and kiss her. Instead he looked down into his wine, scowling.

'I thought she had more sense than that. Finish your wine, milady, and I will escort you back to the Globe. I take it you have bespoke rooms there?'

Cassie was disappointed, but not downhearted. She had been thinking about this meeting for the whole of her long journey and his reaction could have been so much worse. She took another sip of her wine.

'Very well. But first I must give you this.' She reached into her reticule and pulled out a bundle of folded papers which she handed to him.

He opened them and studied the contents in silence.

'This is my testimonial from Captain Belfort. And the copy of my discharge papers…'

'Yes. Grandmama received them two days ago.'

He looked up. 'But how?'

'They arrived with a note from my cousin.' Her smile grew. 'Wolfgang is alive. He successfully escaped from Valerin's men, but a bullet grazed his temple and eventually he collapsed. He was taken in and nursed by some kind villagers, but when he came round he had no knowledge of who he was. They found these papers on him and assumed he was you. As did Wolfgang.' She chuckled. 'He says in his letter he knew something was wrong when he was confronted with his first patient and had not the smallest idea of what to do! Thankfully, a few weeks ago, his memory returned and as soon as he was able he sent the papers to my grandmother.'

She waited, but when he said nothing she continued. 'It means that you can claim the house that was left to you by the English countess.' She saw his mouth twist in distaste, observed the slight shake of his head and said quietly, 'Or you could go home, now you have proof against Valerin's lies.'

'Home?' He shook his head. 'Brussels is no longer home, it is under French rule and Bonaparte is greedy for more power. He has already established his own system of law and made his brother-in-law Governor of Paris. It would not surprise me if Bonaparte declared himself king. It seems no one can stop him, but at least the English are trying to do so. I shall remain here, where thanks to Lady Hune I can continue my work. And there is much to do. The trustees here are forward-thinking men and I hope eventually we may establish a medical school.'

Cassie noted how the tiredness left him and his face lit up with enthusiasm as he spoke of his plans.

'For that you will need money,' she said. 'And perhaps someone to help you.' She sat forward, saying in a rush, 'My fortune is mine to control, or my husband's—'

'No! I have told you, Cassie, we cannot marry. It is impossible.'

'Why is it impossible, unless you do not love me?' She held her breath waiting for his answer.

He exhaled, something between a sigh and a groan as he said, 'Oh, my dear, I love you more than I can say, but I cannot give you the life you need.'

'How do you know what I need? I have tried to re-sume my old life in Bath, a social round of parties and concerts and balls, but it all seems so, so *meaningless*.' She clasped her hands together, saying earnestly, 'I was never happier than when we were together, Raoul. I know that now. Remember how we worked together in

Flagey? When you were saving the lives of those poor people and I was helping you? For the first time in my life I was doing something useful, not merely giving out alms or delivering a basket of food to the hungry. Let me help you again, Raoul. I have been told that the army allows soldiers' wives to nurse the injured, so why not the wife of a surgeon? There must be *something* I can do.

'It will be hard work, I am not afraid of that, and I know I shall make mistakes because this life is very new to me, but I cannot go back to my old one, the past months have taught me that much.'

'No,' he said, jumping up. 'It is impossible.'

Cassie rose and placed herself before him. She had rehearsed the arguments so often in her head, now she must use them to convince him.

'You say we are too different, Raoul, that we cannot live happily together, but the world is not as it was. The revolution in France has turned the old order on its head. And things are changing in England, too. In marrying you I do not consider I would be marrying beneath me.' She smiled up at him, cupping his dear face with her hands. 'I have no doubt that your colleagues here would think it was you who had the worst end of the bargain.'

He reached up and drew her fingers gently but firmly away.

'No, Cassandra, I cannot do it. I *will not* ask you to marry me.'

'That is why I had to reach you tonight.' She glanced towards the clock ticking quietly on the mantelshelf. 'It is not yet midnight and today is the last day of February. Leap Day. It is an old tradition in this country that on this day a lady may ask a gentleman to marry her and if he should refuse she can demand a forfeit.' She sank to her knees before him. 'And so, Raoul Doulevant, will you do me the very great honour of becoming my husband?'

He drove one hand through his hair as he gazed down at her, consternation in his face.

'Get up, Cassie, you must not kneel to me. You are a lady!'

She smiled up at him. 'You told me once you did not believe my birth made me superior.'

'Not your birth, no.' He reached down and lifted her bodily on to her feet. 'But everything else about you— your bravery, your goodness—you are too far above me, my love. I cannot make you happy.'

His hands were on her shoulders, his grip firm, as if despite his words he could not bear to let her go and it gave her hope.

'How do you know that?' she challenged him. 'Will you not give me the opportunity to show you that I am not the silly, simpering female you think me?'

'That is not how I think of you and you know it!'

She waited patiently, watching the play of emotions in his face. At last he released her and gave a hiss of exasperation.

'And if I refuse, what forfeit will you demand of me?'

Cassie had spent the journey considering that, too, and now she gave her head a tiny shake.

'Why, none, my love, but I shall *"make me a willow cabin at your gate"*.' She smiled. 'To be serious,

I shall buy myself a house here and use my money to ingratiate myself with the trustees. I shall help them to expand the hospital here, perhaps I will even invest in their medical school.'

Raoul listened to the reasoned voice, saw the stubborn determination in that beautiful face. His defences were crumbling, but he was not yet ready to give in.

He said dismissively, 'You have no idea how to go about these things.'

'I will learn,' came the calm reply. 'There are always plenty of people ready to advise an heiress how to spend her money. Alternatively, you could marry me, and we could discuss all these matters of an evening.' She put her hands against his chest. His heart reacted immediately, thudding heavily as if it was trying to break out from his ribs and reach her fingers. Her smile told him she was well aware of the effect she was having on him. She stepped closer and murmured, 'When we are in bed, perhaps.'

Raoul's iron control snapped.

'The one thing we will *not* do in bed is discuss business!'

He dragged her into his arms and with something between a laugh and a sob Cassie flung her arms around his neck and turned her face up to receive his kiss. It was hard, demanding and ruthless, everything she had hoped it would be and she responded eagerly. When he broke off and held her away from him she had to stifle a sigh of disappointment.

He frowned at her. 'Are you sure you want this, Cassie?'

'Very sure.' She felt a smile tugging at her lips. 'So sure that I sent the cab away.'

'You are quite shameless.'

Her smile grew. 'Utterly beyond redemption, my darling!'

With a growl he swept her up into his arms and carried her out of the room. Her hands were around his neck and she laughed up at him as he climbed the narrow staircase.

'You are going to marry me, then, Raoul?'

'That depends.'

'Oh? On what?'

He paused, his eyes burning into her in a way that set her pulse racing.

'It depends, *ma chère*, upon what you think of my lovemaking.'

He negotiated the last of the stairs and the doorway into the bedroom. A small fire was burning in the hearth, sufficient for Cassie to see that the room was sparsely furnished, but her only concern was the bed, and that looked wide enough for two. Without ceremony Raoul dropped her on to the covers, but her arms were around his neck and she dragged him down for another deep, passionate kiss.

Raoul could not stop the sense of urgency that overcame him, but it was not just his blood that was heated. Cassie moaned in his arms; she was already plucking at his shirt, as eager as he to feel flesh on flesh. They scrabbled to discard their clothes while all the time those hot, frantic kisses continued. They were consumed with a need to touch, to kiss. At last they fell back together on the bed, a frenzied tangle of limbs.

Their coupling was as fierce and urgent as the first time, their cries a mixture of laughter and tears until they collapsed, sated and exhausted, to fall asleep in each other's arms.

Cassie stirred. She did not want to leave this dream, for she was in a comfortable world where she was lying with her lover. Slowly the truth dawned. She was not dreaming, this was not her bed but Raoul's and he was asleep beside her, one arm thrown possessively across her body. It felt so peaceful, so *right*. It was very dark, but she could feel a slight chill on her naked skin and she reached down to the tangle of sheets and blankets they had pushed aside during their fevered lovemaking. Smiling at the memory, she pulled a thin coverlet over them. Raoul stirred, reaching for her, and she went willing back into his arms, kissing the line of his jaw, rough with overnight stubble, before sinking once more into a deep slumber.

When she woke again it was to the delicious sensation of a hand gently caressing her breast. Raoul. She gave a little sigh as she stretched luxuriously. The hand moved down over the curve of her waist. When Raoul's fingers slid through the curls at the apex of her thighs her body arched. She was offering herself to him, inviting him to explore her core. She opened her eyes. It was still dark with a sprinkling of stars shining in through the window.

'Do you have to go to the hospital in the morning?' Raoul's lips grazed her neck.

'I do, but we have plenty of time yet.'

'Are you sure?' She held him off. 'I want to be a good wife to you, Raoul. I do not want you to say I am keeping you from your work.'

'I will not let you do that, my love.'

He kissed her mouth and she felt her body liquefying with anticipation. She put her hands on his chest, revelling in the feel of his skin with its covering of crisp hair against her palms. She smoothed over the hard contours, tracing the muscle. She trembled as his fingers began to move again, slipping inside her and slowly, gently stroking until her body began to respond. She moved her own hands down over his torso, exploring his aroused body, watching his reaction and repeating any touch that made him groan with pleasure, sliding her fingers across the silky skin, feeling her own power over him.

His caresses were growing quicker, deeper, rousing her own body to frenzy with the sweet torture of his questing fingers. Suddenly she threw back her head, giving a little scream as she lost control. She shuddered, her whole being rocked with ripples of pleasure evoked by his remorseless stroking. She writhed, arched and cried out as wave after wave of sensual delight coursed through her. And still his gentle inexorable pleasuring continued, until her body was a trembling mass of sensations and she thought her mind would explode. Even when at last his fingers stilled the spasms continued, but she was not afraid because Raoul was holding her close and he continued to hold her until the last shudder of ecstasy died away.

'Oh, Raoul that was…exquisite,' she breathed, when at last she could command her voice.

She heard him laugh softly, felt it rumble deep in his chest.

'I am glad you enjoyed it, milady, but I am not done with you yet.'

She sighed and snuggled closer. 'I think you are. I do not think I could endure anything more.'

Another soft laugh reverberated through him and she felt his hands begin to move again.

'Raoul, no, I cannot...'

She trailed off with a sigh of sheer pleasure. Her body was giving the lie to her words. It was softening, yielding, her skin supremely sensitive to the lightest touch. When he began to kiss her breast she pushed against him and when his kisses moved down over her belly she almost swooned with the delight of it. Gently he eased her thighs apart and she felt the gentle rasp of his stubble as he brought his mouth upon her. Then he was kissing her, his tongue flicking, stroking and setting her body on fire all over again. The swelling wave of excitement was building and she reached for him, driving her fingers through his hair, wanting him to stop, to go on.

He brought her to the crest again, but before she splintered he drew away and shifted his body over hers. She took him into her, wrapped her arms about him and lifted her face to his kiss. Her body flexed and gripped him as they moved together, faster and more urgent until, with a triumphant shout he gave one final thrust and they shuddered against one another, minds and bodies joined as one.

Cassie woke as the first grey fingers of dawn crept into the room. Raoul was lying on his side, watching her.

'What time must you be at the hospital?'

'Not for a few hours yet.'

She snuggled closer.

'Oh, Raoul, it has been five months! I have missed you.'

'And I you,' he muttered, covering her face with kisses. 'How soon can we be married?'

'Within weeks. As soon as the banns are called.' She felt the familiar knot of desire unfurling again as his hands moved over her body. It was difficult to concentrate. 'Grandmama would like us to be married in Bath, but I told her that would depend upon your work.'

'I am sure I can be spared for a little while.'

'Good.' She sighed with satisfaction as he began to nibble her ear. 'Then Grandmama and I will organise everything.'

'Everything?' Cassie opened her eyes as he stopped his delicious onslaught and held her away from him. He was regarding her with undisguised suspicion. 'It will be a very quiet wedding, I hope.'

She lay back against the pillows, smiling up at him. 'Why, yes, of course,' she murmured, her eyes shining with love and mischief. 'That is, as quiet as a wedding can be for the daughter of a marquess.'

'Cassandra…'

She laughed at him. 'Do not fret, my dearest love, there is not time to arrange a vast ceremony. And once it is over we may return here.' She put a hand up to his face. 'I am impressed with our marital bed. It is extremely comfortable.'

'It is not the bed that is important,' he growled, rolling on top of her. 'It is how one performs in it, as I am about to demonstrate. Again, if milady is willing?'

'I thought you would never ask me.' She sighed, gazing up at him lovingly. 'Yes, Raoul darling, milady is *very* willing!'

* * * * *

THE OUTCAST'S
REDEMPTION

For TGH
Thank you.

Chapter One

March 1804

The village of Arrandale was bathed in frosty moonlight. Nothing stirred and most windows were shuttered or in darkness. Except the house standing within the shadow of the church. It was a stone building, square and sturdy, and lamps shone brightly in the two ground-floor windows that flanked the door. It was the home of Mr Titus Duncombe, the local parson, and the lights promised a welcome for any soul in need.

Just as they had always done, thought the man walking up the steps to the front door. Just as they had done ten years ago, when he had ridden through the village with the devil on his heels. Then he had not stopped. Now he was older, wiser and in need of help.

He grasped the knocker and rapped, not hard, but in the silence of the night the sound reverberated hollowly through the hall. A stooping, grey-haired manservant opened the door.

'I would like to see the parson.'

The servant peered out, but the stranger kept his head dipped so the wide brim of his hat shadowed his face.

'Who shall I say is here?'

'Tell him it is a weary traveller. A poor vagabond who needs his assistance.'

The servant hesitated.

'Nay, 'tis late,' he said at last. 'Come back in the morning.'

He made to shut the door but the stranger placed a dirty boot on the step.

'Your master will know me,' he stated. 'Pray, take me to him.'

The old man gave in and shuffled off to speak to the parson, leaving the stranger to wait in the hall. From the study came a calm, well-remembered voice and as he entered, an elderly gentleman rose from a desk cluttered with books and papers. Once he had passed the manservant and only the parson could see his face, the stranger straightened and removed his hat.

'I bid you good evening, Mr Duncombe.'

The parson's eyes widened, but his tone did not change.

'Welcome, my son. Truscott, bring wine for our guest.' Only when the servant had closed the door upon them did the old man allow himself to smile. 'Bless my soul. Mr Wolfgang Arrandale! You are returned to us at last.'

Wolfgang breathed a sigh of relief. He bowed.

'Your servant, sir. I am pleased you remember me—that I have not changed out of all recognition.'

The parson waved a hand. 'You are a little older, and if I may say so, a little more careworn, but I should know you anywhere. Sit down, my boy, sit down.' He shepherded his guest to a chair. 'I shall not ask you any questions until we have our wine, then we may talk un-interrupted.'

'Thank you. I should warn you, sir, there is still a price on my head. When your man opened the door I was afraid he would recognise me.'

'Truscott's eyesight is grown very poor, but he prefers to answer the door after dark, rather than leave it to his wife. But even if he had remembered you, Truscott is very discreet. It is something my servants have learned over the years.' He stopped as the object of their conversation returned with a tray. 'Ah, here we are. Thank you, Truscott. But what is this, no cake? Not even a little bread?'

'Mrs Truscott's gone to bed, master.'

Mr Duncombe looked surprised. 'At nine o'clock?'

'She had one of her turns, sir.'

'Pray do not worry on my account,' put in Wolfgang quickly. 'A glass of wine is all I require.' When they were alone again he added drily, 'Your man does not want to encourage dubious fellows such as I to be calling upon you.'

'If they knew who you are—'

'They would have me locked up.'

'No, no, my boy, you wrong them. Not everyone in Arrandale believes you killed your wife.'

'Are you quite sure of that, sir?' asked Wolfgang, unable to keep a note of bitterness from his voice. 'I was found kneeling over her body and I ran away rather than explain myself.'

'I am sure you thought it was for the best, at the time,' murmured the parson, topping up their glasses.

'My father thought it best. He was never in any doubt of my guilt. If only I had called here. I am sure you would

have counselled me to stay and defend myself. I was
damned the moment I fled the country.'

'We cannot change the past, my son. But tell me where
you have been, what you have done for the past ten years.'

Wolfgang stretched his long legs towards the fire.

'I have been in France, sir, but as for what I did there—
let us just say whatever was necessary to survive.'

'And may one ask why you have returned?'

For a long moment Wolf stared into the flames. 'I have
come back to prove my innocence, if I can.'

Was it possible, after so long, to solve the mystery of
his wife's death? When the parson said nothing he continued, giving voice to the thoughts that had been going
round in his head ever since he decided to leave France.

'I know it will not be easy. My wife's parents, the
Sawstons, would see me hanged as soon as look at me. I
know they have put up the reward for my capture. Florence's death might have been a tragic accident, but the
fact that the Sawston diamonds went missing at the same
time makes it far more suspicious. I cannot help feeling
that someone must know the truth.'

The parson sighed. 'It is so long ago. The magistrate
is dead, as are your parents, and Arrandale Hall has been
empty for years, with only a caretaker there now.' He
shifted uncomfortably. 'I understand the lawyers wanted
to close it up completely, but your brother insisted that
Robert Jones should remain. He and his wife keep the
house up together as best they can.'

'Jones who was footman in my day?' asked Wolf.

Mr Duncombe nodded. 'Yes, that is he. I am afraid
your lawyers will not release money for maintaining
the property. Your brother does what he can to keep the
building watertight, at least.'

'Richard? But his income will not cover that.'

'I fear it has been a struggle, although I understand he has now married a woman of…er…comfortable means.'

'Ah, yes. I believe he is now step-papa to an heiress,' said Wolf. 'Quite a come-about for an Arrandale! Ah, you are surprised I know this. I met Lady Cassandra in France last year and she gave me news of the family. She also told me I have a daughter. You will remember, sir, that Florence was with child and very near her time when she died. I thought the babe had died with her but apparently not.' He gazed into the fire, remembering his shock when Cassie had told him he was a father. 'The child is the reason I must clear my name. I do not want her to grow up with my guilt hanging over her.'

'An admirable sentiment, but how do you begin?'

'By talking to anyone who might know something about that night, ten years ago.'

The old man shook his head.

'That will not be easy. The staff are gone, moved away and some of the older ones have died. However, Brent, the old butler, still lives in the village.'

He stopped as a soft, musical voice was heard from the doorway.

'Papa, am I so very late? Old Mrs Owlet has broken her leg and I did not like to leave her until her son came—oh, I beg your pardon, I did not know you had a visitor.'

Wolf had risen from his chair and turned to face the newcomer, a tall young woman in a pale-blue pelisse and a matching bonnet, the strings of which she was untying as she spoke to reveal an abundance of silky fair hair, neatly pulled into a knot at the back of her head.

'Ah, Grace, my love. This is Mr…er…Mr Peregrine. My daughter, sir.'

'Miss Duncombe.' Wolf found himself being scrutinised by a pair of dark eyes.

'But how did you come here, sir?' she asked. 'I saw no carriage on the street.'

'I walked from Hindlesham.'

She looked wary and he could not blame her. He had been travelling for over a week, his clothes were rumpled and he had not shaved since yesterday. There was no doubt he presented a very dubious appearance.

The parson coughed. 'Mr Peregrine will be staying in Arrandale for a few days, my love.'

'Really?' she murmured, unbuttoning her pelisse. 'I understand the Horse Shoe Inn is very comfortable.'

'Ah, you misunderstand.' Mr Duncombe cleared his throat again. 'I thought we might find Mr Peregrine a bed here for a few nights.'

Grace sighed inwardly. Why did Papa think it necessary to play the Good Samaritan to every stranger who appeared? She regarded the two men as they stood side by side before the fire, the guest towering over his host. She turned her attention to the stranger. The dust of the road clung to his boots, his clothes were positively shabby and as for his linen—the housewife in her was shocked to see anything so grey. Grace was not used to looking up at anyone, indeed she had often heard herself described as a beanpole, but this man topped her by several inches. His dark curling hair was as rumpled as the rest of him and at least a day's growth of black stubble covered his cheeks. She met his eyes and although the candlelight was not sufficient to discern their colour they held a most distracting glint. She looked away, flustered.

'I do not think…' she began, but Papa was not listening.

'And we have been very remiss in our refreshments, my love. Mrs Truscott is unwell, but I am sure you will be able to find our guest a little supper?'

'Why, of course,' she answered immediately, glad of the opportunity to get this man away from her father, who was far too kind-hearted for his own good. 'Perhaps Mr Peregrine would like to accompany me to the kitchen?'

'The kitchen?' her father exclaimed, surprised. 'My dear—'

'It will be much easier for me to feed Mr Peregrine there, sir, since he will be on hand to tell me just what he would like.' She managed a smile. 'I came in that way and noted a good fire in the range, so it is very comfortable. And you may finish your sermon in peace, Papa.'

Her father made another faint protest, but the stranger said, 'Pray do not be anxious for me, sir. If you have work to finish, then I must disturb you no longer.' He picked up his battered portmanteau and turned to Grace. 'Lead on, Miss Duncombe. I am at your service.'

It was most gallantly said, but Grace was not fooled. She merely inclined her head and moved towards the door.

'Oh, Grace, send Truscott to me, when you see him, if you please. I need to apprise him of the situation.'

She looked back in surprise. 'There is no need, Papa, I can do that.'

'It is no trouble, my love. I want to see him on other matters, too, so you had best send him up. As soon as you can.'

'Very well, sir.' Her eyes flickered towards the stranger. 'Come along.'

She crossed the hall and descended the stairs to the basement with the man following meekly behind. No, she amended that. There was nothing meek about *Mr Peregrine*. Hah, she almost laughed out loud. That was no more the man's name than it was hers. Clearly Papa had made it up on the spur of the moment to give him some semblance of respectability. It was the sort of thing her father would do. Papa was a scholar and Grace's own education was sufficient for her to know that the name meant traveller in Latin. No doubt Papa thought that a good joke.

She went quickly to the kitchen, despatched Truscott upstairs to see his master and turned to face the man.

'Very well, you may sit at the table and I will see what we have in the larder.'

'A mere trifle will do,' he murmured, easing his long legs over the bench. 'A little bread and butter, perhaps.'

She pursed her lips. Even sitting down he dominated the kitchen.

'I do not think *a mere trifle* will do for you at all,' she retorted, reaching for an apron. 'You look the sort of man who eats heartily.'

'You have it right there, mistress, but with your cook indisposed I would be happy to have a little bread and cheese, if you know where to find it. Perhaps your man Truscott will help us, when he returns.'

Grace had been thinking that she would serve him just that, but his words flicked her on the raw. She drew herself up and fixed him with an icy look.

'I am quite capable of producing a meal for you. It is a bad housewife who has to depend upon her servants for every little thing!'

* * *

Wolfgang rested his arms on the table as he watched Grace Duncombe bustling in and out of the kitchen. She must be what, twenty-three, twenty-four? He couldn't remember seeing her, when he had lived at Arrandale, but ten years ago he had taken very little notice of what went on in the village. He had been four-and-twenty, reluctantly preparing to settle down with his wife. He thought of Florence, lying cold and broken on the stone floor, and her daughter—their daughter. The baby he had always believed had died with her. He rubbed his temples. He would consider that tomorrow. For now he was bone-tired from travelling and ravenously hungry. From the delicious smells coming from the frying pan his hostess was rising admirably to the challenge of feeding him.

When Truscott returned, Wolf knew he had been informed of their guest's identity. The man was bemused and not a little embarrassed to find Arrandale of Arrandale sitting in the kitchen. Miss Duncombe was absent at that moment and the manservant stood irresolute, shifting uncomfortably from one foot to the other.

'Sir, I—'

Wolfgang stopped him. 'Hush, your mistress is returning.'

She came in from the yard.

'Truscott, pray fetch a bottle of wine for our visitor.'

'Nay, not just for me,' said Wolf quickly. 'Bring a glass for your mistress, too.'

He thought for a moment she would object, but she merely frowned and went back to her cooking. The kitchen was warm and comfortable and Wolfgang felt himself relaxing as he watched her work. She was well

named, he thought, there was a gracefulness to her movements, and an assurance unusual in one so young.

When Truscott went out again, Wolf said, 'Are you
only preparing a meal for me?'

'Father and I dined earlier,' she replied, dropping
pieces of lamb into the pan. 'Papa will take nothing more
than a biscuit or two until the morning.' She finished
cooking the meat and arranged it neatly on the plate.
'There,' she said with a hint of defiance. 'Your dinner.'

Wolf regarded the meal she had set before him. Besides the collops of mutton there was a dish of fried potato as well as cold potted hare and a parsnip pie.

'A meal fit for a lord,' he declared. 'Will you not join
me?'

'No, thank you. I told you I have already dined.'

'Then at least stay and drink a glass of wine with me.'
When she shook her head he murmured, '"*Better a dinner of herbs where love is, than a stalled ox and hatred
therewith.*"'

She glared at him, but at least she stayed. She slid on
to the end of the bench opposite. 'What an odd thing to
say. I do not hate you, Mr Peregrine.'

He poured wine into the glasses and pushed one across
the table towards her. She cradled it in her hands before
sipping the contents.

'Then what *do* you think of me?' he asked.

'To begin with,' she said slowly, looking down at her
wineglass, 'I do not think you are deserving of Papa's
best claret.'

'The best, is it?' Wolf murmured. 'Perhaps your man
made a mistake.'

'Truscott does not make mistakes.'

No, thought Wolf, but it would be his undoing if the

man showed him too much respect. For all that he could not help teasing her.

'Then clearly he sees the worth of the man beneath these sorry clothes.'

She put her glass down with a snap. 'Who *are* you?'

'What you see, a humble pilgrim.'

'Yes, I know that is what you would like me to think, Mr Peregrine, but I will tell you to your face that I find nothing humble about you!'

'Humility comes hard for a gentleman fallen on hard times.'

She was silent and Wolf gave his attention to the food. It was really very good, but it troubled him that she had been obliged to cook it.

'You have only the two servants?' he asked her. She bridled at his question and he went on quickly. 'You have a large, fine church here and this area is a prosperous one, I believe.'

'It was used to be,' she told him. 'There has been no one living at the Hall for several years now and that has had an effect. Without a family in residence our shop-keepers cannot sell their goods to them, the farmers do not supply them with milk and meat.'

'But the estate is very large, it must provide a good living for many local families.'

'With an absentee landlord the farms do not thrive and there is no money to maintain the houses. Many families worked at the Hall, when it closed they lost their positions. Some moved away and took up new posts, others found what work they could locally.' She looked across the table at him. 'There is much poverty here now. My father does what he can to relieve it, but his own funds are limited. We have very little of value in this house.'

Wolf understood her, but the fact she thought he might be a thief did not matter at that moment, what concerned him was that the people—his people—were suffering. Duncombe had told him the lawyers were being parsimonious with his money, but clearly they did not realise the effect of that. Richard should have started proceedings to declare him dead. Instead he preferred to put his own money into Arrandale.

He closed his eyes for a moment, as the weight of responsibility pressed down on him. He had thought himself unfairly punished, exiled in France for a crime he had not committed, but he saw now that he was not the only one to suffer.

'How long do you intend to stay in Arrandale?' Grace asked him.

'A few days, no more.' He glanced up at the clock. 'It is growing late and I should indeed be grateful for a bed, Miss Duncombe, if you can spare one.'

'My father does not turn away anyone in need.'

'Thank you.' He pushed aside his empty plate. 'Then with your permission I will retire now.'

'Of course.' She rose as the elderly manservant shuffled back into the room. 'Ah, Truscott, Mr Peregrine is to be our guest for a few days. Perhaps you would show him to his room. Above the stable.'

She took a large iron key from a peg beside the door.

'The…the groom's quarters, mistress?' The servant goggled at her.

'Why, yes.' She turned her bright, no-nonsense smile on Wolf. 'We have no stable hands now, so the garret is free. I have already made up the bed for you. Truscott will show you the pump in the yard and where to find the privy. I am sure you will be very comfortable.'

And I will be safely out of the house overnight, thought Wolf, appreciatively.

'I am sure I shall, Miss Duncombe, thank you.'

Truscott was still goggling, his mouth opening and closing like a fish gasping for air. Wolf clapped him on the shoulder.

'Come, my friend, let us find a lamp and you can show me to my quarters.'

The servant led him across the yard to the stable block, but when they reached the outer stairs that led to the garret, Truscott could contain himself no longer.

'Mr Arrandale, sir,' he said, almost wringing his hands in despair. 'Miss Duncombe's as kind as can be, but she don't *know,* see. I pray you'll forgive her for treating you like this.'

'There is nothing to forgive,' said Wolf, taking the key from the old man's hands. 'Your mistress is very wise to be cautious. I should not like to think of her letting any stranger sleep in the house. Now, go back indoors and look after her. And remember, tomorrow you must treat me as a poor stranger, no serving me any more of your best wines!'

Wolf climbed the stairs to the groom's quarters and made a quick inspection. Everything was clean and orderly. One room contained a bed, an old chest of drawers and a washstand, the other a table and a couple of chairs. Wolf guessed the furniture had been consigned there when it was no longer of any use in the house. However, it was serviceable and the bed was made up with sheets, blankets and pillows upon a horsehair mattress. He lost no time in shedding his clothes and slipping between the

sheets. He could not help a sigh of satisfaction as he felt
the soft linen against his skin. After a journey of twenty
hours aboard the French fishing boat that had put him
ashore near Eastbourne, he had travelled on foot and by
common stage to reach Arrandale. The most comfortable bed on his journey had been a straw mattress, so by
comparison this was sheer heaven.

He stretched out and put his hands behind his head.
He could not fault Miss Grace Duncombe as a housekeeper. A smile tugged at his mouth as he recalled her
shock when the parson said he was to stay with them.
She had come into the room like a breath of fresh air.
Doubtless because she brought the chill of the spring
evening in with her. She said she had been visiting a Mrs
Owlet. He frowned, dragging back old memories. The
Owlets had worked at the great house for generations. It
was a timely reminder that he would have to take care
in the village, there were many such families who might
well recognise his lanky frame. Grace Duncombe had
no idea of his true identity, but she clearly thought him
a rogue, set upon taking advantage of her kindly father,
which was why she was housing him in this garret. That
did not matter. He was here to find out the truth, but he
must go carefully, one false move could cost him his life.

It was Grace's habit to rise early, but this morning she
was aware of an added urgency. There was a stranger in
the garret. She was quite accustomed to taking in needy
vagrants at the vicarage, giving them a good meal and a
bed for the night, but Mr Peregrine disturbed her peace.
She was afraid her father would invite the man to breakfast with him.

As soon as it was light Grace slipped out of bed and

dressed herself, determined to make sure that if their guest appeared he would not progress further than the kitchen. When she descended to the basement she could hear the murmur of voices from the scullery and looked in to find Mrs Truscott standing over the maid as she worked at the stone sink in the corner. They stopped talking when Grace appeared in the doorway.

'Ah, good morning, Miss Grace.' Mrs Truscott looked a little flustered as she came forward, wiping her hands on her apron. 'I was just getting Betty to wash out Mr— that is—the gentleman's shirt. So dirty it was, as if he had been travelling in it for a week. We didn't heat up the copper, not just for one shirt, Miss, oh, no, a couple of kettles was all that was needed and look—hold it up, Betty—you can see it has come up clean as anything. All it needs now is a good blow out of doors and it will be as good as new.'

'Did Mr Peregrine ask you to do this?' asked Grace, astounded at the nerve of the man.

'Oh, no, Miss Grace, but I could see it needed washing, so I told Truscott to fetch it off the gentleman at first light, saying I would find him a shirt from the charity box to tide him over if need be, but he said he had another to wear today, so all we have to do now is get this one dry.'

Betty had been nodding in agreement, but she stopped, putting up her nose to sniff the air like a hound.

'Begging your pardon, Mrs Truscott, but ain't that the bacon I can smell?'

'Oh, Lordy yes.' The housekeeper snatched the wet shirt from the maid's hands and dropped it into the basket. 'Quick, girl, it will be burned to a crisp and then what will the master say? Oh, and there's the bread in the oven, too!'

Grace stepped aside and the maid rushed past her.

'Give me the shirt, Mrs Truscott, I will peg it out while you attend to Father's breakfast.'

'Oh, Miss Grace, if you are sure?'

'I am perfectly capable of doing it, so off you go now.' Smiling, she watched the housekeeper hurry back to the kitchen then, putting a handful of pegs in the basket on top of the shirt, she made her way outside. The sun was shining now and a steady breeze was blowing. Grace took a deep breath. She loved spring days like this, when there was warmth in the sun and a promise of summer to come. It was a joy to be out of doors.

A clothes line was fixed up in the kitchen gardens, which were directly behind the stable block. As she crossed the yard Grace heard the noise of the pump being worked and assumed it was Truscott fetching more water for the house, but when she turned the corner she stopped, her mouth opening in surprise to see their guest, stripped to the waist and washing himself.

Her first reaction was to run away, but it was too late for that, he had spotted her. She should not look at him, but could not drag her eyes away from the sight of his half-naked body. The buckskins covering his thighs could not have been tighter, but although he was so tall there was nothing spindly about his long legs. They were perfectly proportioned. He had the physique of an athlete, the flat stomach and lean hips placing no strain on those snugly fitting breeches, but above the narrow waist the body widened into a broad chest and muscled shoulders, still wet and glinting in the morning sun. He bent to pick up his towel, his movements lithe, the muscles rippling beneath the skin. As he straightened she noted the black beard on his cheeks and watched as he flicked the thick dark hair away from his face. Droplets of water flew off the tendrils, catching the light. Like a halo, she thought wildly. A halo for a dark angel.

'Good morning, Miss Duncombe.'

Her throat had dried. She knew if she tried to speak it would be nothing more than a croak so instead she inclined her head, frowning in an effort not to blush. She forced her legs to move and walked on, feeling very much like one passing a strange dog and not knowing if it was going to attack. The line was only yards away from the pump and, keeping her back to him, she concentrated on pegging out his shirt. Her fingers felt stiff, awkward and her spine tingled at the thought of the man behind her. She had noticed faint scars on his body, signs that he had not lived a peaceful life.

It was very quiet, perhaps he had gone, after all he had finished washing himself and it must be cold, standing in this chill wind, naked...

'Thank you for going to so much trouble for me.'

She jumped at the sound of his deep voice. She turned to find he was very close, towering over her. He was towelling his wet hair and with his arms raised he looked bigger and broader than ever. The skin beneath his ribcage was drawn in, accentuating his deep chest with its shadow of dark hair. What would it be like to touch him, to run her hands over his skin and feel those crisp, dark hairs curling over her fingers?

Shocked, Grace stepped back and hastily picked up the washing basket, holding it before her like a shield while she tried to gather her scattered wits. She must answer him.

'It was nothing. We c-cannot have you going about

the village like a beggar.' She began to move backwards, as if she was afraid to turn her back on him. 'Once you are dressed Mrs Truscott will serve you breakfast in the kitchen.'

He kept his eyes on her, his look dark, unfathomable. She felt like a wild animal, in thrall to a predator.

'Then I had best make myself presentable.'

She swallowed.

Pull yourself together, Grace!

'Yes. Please do. And do not take too long about it. My servants have a great deal to do today.'

From somewhere she found the strength to turn and walk away. She wanted to run, she could feel his eyes boring into her and a shiver ran the length of her spine. She had never met anyone who made her feel so ill at ease. Or so deliciously alive.

When Grace went down to the kitchen later she found their guest sitting at the table, enjoying a hearty breakfast. Mrs Truscott was also there, but Grace's relief at finding that she was not alone with the man was tempered by the housekeeper's behaviour. She was standing at one end of the table, watching the stranger with a look of motherly satisfaction while he addressed his plate of bacon and eggs. It was understandable, thought Grace, fair-mindedly, for the stranger had clearly made an effort to clean himself up. His hair was still damp but the dark curls were now brushed and gleaming and his lean cheeks were free of stubble, making him look much younger.

And much more attractive.

He looked up at that moment and she blushed.

'Good morning again, Miss Duncombe.'

He rose, but Grace quickly gestured to him to sit back

down. He was so tall she did not want him towering over her. Again.

'Pray, go on with your breakfast,' she told him, not meeting his eyes. 'I came to fetch tea. My father and I always enjoy a cup at this time, before he goes to his study to work.'

'I beg your pardon, Miss Grace. I've been that busy I forgot all about it. I will make it now, just as soon as I have cut some more bread for Master…er…Mr…um…'

'Peregrine,' said Wolf, as the housekeeper stumbled over how to address him. He gave her a reassuring smile, which would have included Grace, if she had been attending, but she was already busy at the range, preparing tea. He had noted the tell-tale flush on her cheeks when she saw him and thought how well the extra colour suited her. She was a long Meg, no doubt about it, but not thin. He watched her now as she bustled about gathering cups, milk and sugar. Her movements were actually very pleasing to the eye.

Wolf told himself this was no time to be considering a flirtation. But he could not resist one more small tease.

He said, 'I would very much like some tea, ma'am, if you can spare it.'

She was pouring tea into the two fine porcelain cups as he spoke and he saw her hand shake a little.

'You may have what is left in the pot.' Still she would not look at him. 'Mrs Truscott shall pour more water on the leaves for you, but if you will excuse me I must take these upstairs. Papa will be waiting.'

And with that she whisked herself out of the kitchen. The housekeeper let out a whistling breath.

'Well now, I've never known the mistress so curt before. I'll make fresh tea for you, master, don't you fret.'

'No, no, you heard Miss Duncombe. The remains of this pot will do well enough for me. And do you sit down and join me.'

'Nay, Master Wolf, that wouldn't be fitting, me being a servant and all.'

He pushed his plate away. 'I have sat at table with much worse company than honest servants, Mrs Truscott, believe me. And I pray you will stop treating me like some great gentleman.'

'But you are master of Arrandale, sir. How else am I to treat you?'

'Like the scrubby schoolboy that used to creep into the parson's garden and steal the best plums from the tree! Lord, how you used to scold me in those days. What a rogue I was.'

'Aye, a rogue, sir, but never a villain,' replied the old woman, her eyes unnaturally bright. 'That I will never believe.'

But could he ever prove it? thought Wolf. He saw the housekeeper surreptitiously wiping her eyes and he continued cheerfully, 'Now let us have that tea while it is still drinkable.'

'It will serve several times yet,' she told him, fetching more cups. 'I shall use the leaves again for Truscott and me, and then dry them and give them to the poor.'

'Times are hard here?'

'Times are hard everywhere, Master Wolf, what with the war and everything, but there's no doubt that since your parents died, life has become much more difficult in Arrandale. The steward was carried off in the same epidemic and that made matters even worse, for there was no one to run the estate. These London lawyers don't understand, you see. They expect their rents every Quarter

Day and make no allowances for bad harvests, or sickness. What charity there is in the village comes from Mr Duncombe and his daughter.' She hesitated. 'There is some hereabouts that blames you for the troubles, Master Wolfgang.'

'And with good cause. If I had not been so wild no one would have believed me capable of murdering my wife, I would not have fled the country and my parents would not have died.'

'You don't know that, sir.'

'No, but it is what many believe, is it not?'

'Aye, sir, it is. Which is why you must take care. There's some in the village as would give up their own mothers for a shilling.'

'I am aware of that, but I must talk to Brent, our old butler. Where will I find him?'

'He lives with his niece and her husband in the house beneath the elm trees, at the far end of the village. His sight is very poor now and he rarely goes out.'

'I need to see him alone, if possible.'

'Then this morning would be a good time, the others will be off to market.'

'Then I will go now.'

He rose and began to pack up the dishes, but Mrs Truscott stopped him.

'You be on your way, Master Wolf, but be careful. There's plenty hereabouts with long memories, and though you ain't dressed like your old self there's no disguising that tall frame of yours.'

'I have been disguising this frame of mine for years, Mrs T., but don't worry, I'll take the lanes and skirt the village.'

'Shall I tell Mr Duncombe you will join him for dinner?' she asked. 'He'd like that, I'm sure.'

Wolf paused at the door. 'I would, too,' he admitted. 'But what of his daughter?'

The housekeeper gave him an enigmatic look.

'Miss Grace will come round when she knows you better, sir, you'll see. You could always charm the birds from the trees and that's a fact!'

Chapter Two

Grace was in the morning room with her father when Truscott informed him that Mr Peregrine had gone out, but would join him for dinner. Mr Duncombe received the news with equanimity, but not so Grace.

'Mr Peregrine is very sure of his welcome,' she remarked, when they were alone again.

'And why not?' replied her father mildly. 'We have offered him hospitality, as we would any of God's creatures.'

'But we know nothing about the man.'

'He has a good heart.'

Grace shook her head. 'You are too kind, Papa, too trusting. I have put him over the stables.'

'Yes, so I understand.' Her father chuckled. 'I am sure he has slept in worse places.'

'But you will have him sit down to dinner with us.'

'Yes, dear, and I would remind you of what the Bible says: *"Be not forgetful to entertain strangers."* Hebrews, my love, Chapter Thirteen.'

She smiled. 'Somehow I do not think Mr Peregrine is an angel in disguise, Papa.'

'Perhaps not, but I can assure you he is a gentleman and, I think, a man worthy of our help.'

More than that he would not say and soon retired to his study to work on his sermon. Grace tried not to think that he was running away from her, but she was left with the uneasy suspicion that Papa knew more about this stranger than he would tell her. She glanced out of the window. It was a fine day, if she hurried through her household duties there might be time for a ride before dinner.

Wolf found the little house under the elms without much difficulty. He had taken the back lanes around the village, his hat pulled low on his brow, and he adopted a slouching, shambling gait so that anyone seeing him would not think him a gentleman, let alone Arrandale of Arrandale. The house appeared to be deserted, but Wolf kept his distance for a while, watching and waiting. It was no hardship, for the sun was high and it was a warm spring day. At length the door opened and an old man limped out. Wolf recognised him immediately. The butler looked no older than he had done when Wolf had last seen him ten years ago. The old man sat down on a bench against the wall of the house and turned his face up to the sun. Wolf approached him.

'Good day to you, Brent.'

'Who is that?' The butler peered up short-sightedly.

'Do you not know me?' Wolf dropped down until his face was level with the old man's. He smiled. 'Do not say you have forgotten me.'

'I know the voice, but...' The faded eyes stared into Wolf's face. 'Is it really you, Mr Wolfgang, after all these years?'

Wolf grasped the frail, outstretched hands. There was

no doubt of the old man's delight. He said gently, 'Yes, Brent, I am come back.'

'Lord bless you, sir, I never thought to see the day! Not that I can see very much, for my eyes ain't what they was.' He frowned suddenly. 'But 'tis not safe to be out here. Pray, step inside, sir.'

'Let me help you up.' Wolf took his arm and accompanied him into the house.

'Forgive me if I sit in your presence, Master Wolfgang, but I've got a leg ulcer that pains me if I stand for too long.'

'I think you have earned the right to sit down,' replied Wolf, helping him to a chair and pulling up one for himself. 'You served my family faithfully for many years.'

'Aye, I did, sir, and very sorry I was when the old master and mistress died and the house was shut up for the last time. Very sorry indeed.' He brightened. 'Are you come back to stay, master?'

'Not quite yet. First I have to prove my innocence. That is the reason I am here, Brent, I want you to tell me what you remember, the night my wife died.'

'I remember it as clear as day, sir, but I told it all to the magistrate and he said there was nothing in it to help you.'

'I would like you to tell me, if you will. Starting with the argument I had with my wife before dinner.' Wolf's mouth twisted. 'I am sure you heard that.'

The old man sighed. 'Aye, the whole household heard it, but if you will excuse my saying so, sir, we was accustomed to you and your lady's disagreements, so fiery as you both were. You went out and Mrs Wolfgang ordered a tray to be sent up to her room. That left only the master and mistress and Sir Charles to sit down to dinner.'

'Ah yes, Urmston, my wife's cousin.' Wolf sat back.

Sir Charles Urmston had always been received warmly at Arrandale. Personally, he had never liked the man. Wolf and Florence had never needed much excuse to hurl insults at one another and on this occasion she had accused him of hating Charles because he was the man Wolf's parents would have liked for a son, rather than the wild reprobate Wolf had become. The idea still tortured him.

'I went out for a ride to cool my temper,' he said now. 'What happened while I was gone?'

'We served dinner and Meesden, Mrs Wolfgang's dresser, took up a tray for her mistress. Mrs Wolfgang did not come downstairs again. About eleven the mistress prepared tea in the drawing room, just as she always did, to be served with cakes and bread as a light supper. Then, shortly after midnight, I was coming upstairs to the hall when I heard a shriek, well, a scream, more like.' The old man stopped, twisting his hands together. 'If only there'd been a footman at the door, he'd have seen what happened, but it was late and they was all in the servants' hall.'

'Never mind that,' said Wolf. 'Just tell me what you saw.'

'Mrs Wolfgang's body at the bottom of the grand staircase, her head all bloody and broken and you kneeling over her. I remember it so well. White as a sheet, you was. The master and mistress came running out from the drawing room and you said, in a queer sort of voice, "She's dead. She's dead."'

'Such a to-do as there was then. Mrs Arrandale fell into hysterics and we was all in a bustle. The doctor was sent for and the master sent word that your horse was to be brought round, as quick as possible.'

'How incriminating must that have looked,' Wolf

declared. 'If only I had waited, stayed and explained myself.'

'Ah but your father was anxious for you. Even if Sir Charles hadn't been pressing him I think he would have insisted—'

'Charles? You mean Urmston urged him to send me away?'

'Aye, sir. As soon as Sir Charles came in from the garden he told your father to send you off out of harm's way until they could find out what really happened. But they never did find out, sir. Instead…'

'Instead they found the Sawston diamonds were missing and I was doubly damned.' Wolf finished for him. 'Who discovered the necklace was gone?'

'Meesden, sir. She had been fetched down to her mistress, when it was found Mrs Wolfgang was still alive. The poor lady was carried to the morning room and Meesden stayed with her 'til Dr Oswald arrived. Fortunately he was dining at the vicarage and was soon fetched. Meesden went up to Mrs Wolfgang's bedchamber for something and came down screaming that the lady's jewel case was open and the necklace was gone.'

'And everyone thought I had taken it,' muttered Wolf.

'I never believed that, sir. Even though the evidence…' The butler's words trailed away.

'Aye,' growled Wolf. 'My wife always kept the key hidden behind a loose brick in the fireplace.' He was suddenly aware of his neckcloth, tight around his throat like a noose. 'To my knowledge only three people knew of that hiding place. Florence, her dresser and myself.' His mouth twisted. 'I have no doubt Meesden told everyone that fact.' The distress in the old man's face confirmed it.

Wolf reached out and touched his arm. 'Think, Brent. Are you sure there was no one else in the house that night?'

'Well, 'tis only a feeling…'

'Tell me.'

Brent paused, his wrinkled brow even more furrowed as he struggled to remember.

'I told the magistrate at the time, sir, but he made nothing of it. You see, once I had taken the tea tray into the drawing room for the mistress I prepared the bedroom candles. I was bringing them up to the staircase hall when I heard a noise upstairs. Voices.' The old man sat up straight. 'I thought it was Mrs Wolfgang talking to someone.'

Wolf's lip curled. 'Some would say it was me. That I returned and pushed Florence from the balcony.'

Brent shook his head. 'When I saw you kneeling beside Mrs Wolfgang's body I could tell you'd just come in. It was bitter cold that day and we had the first heavy frost of the winter. There was still a touch of it on the skirts of your coat, as there would be if you'd been out o' doors for a length of time. I told the magistrate, but he paid no heed to me. He thought I was just trying to protect you.'

'And no one else in the house saw or heard anything?'

Brent shook his head slowly.

'No, sir. Your father and the magistrate gathered everyone in the servants' hall and asked them that very question, but 'twere bitter cold that night, so those servants who had not gone to bed was doing their best to stay by the fire in the servants' hall.'

'But the voices you heard upstairs, could it have been my wife's dresser? Surely Meesden might have been with her mistress.'

'No, sir. When Meesden brought her mistress's tray

downstairs after dinner she said she was going to bed and she passed on Mrs Wolfgang's instructions that on no account was she to be disturbed again until the morning. Quite adamant about it, she was, and then she went to her room. The maid who sleeps next door heard Meesden pottering about there, until she was sent for, when it was known her mistress was still alive.'

Wolf frowned, wondering if there was some little detail he was missing. He said, 'I must visit the house. Jones is living there, I believe.'

'Aye, Master Wolfgang, he is, and he would be willing to talk to you, I am sure, but take care who else in the village you approach, sir. There's many who lost their livelihoods when Arrandale Hall was shut up and they would not look too kindly upon you.'

'That is understandable, but if I do not try I shall not make any progress at all.' Wolf rose. 'I must go. Thank you, Brent.' He put a hand on the old man's shoulder. 'No, don't get up. I will see myself out.'

'You'll come again, sir. You'll let me know how you get on?'

'I shall, you may be sure of it.'

Wolf walked back through the lanes, going over all the old man had told him. He would not risk going through the village in daylight but he would make his way to Arrandale Hall later, and perhaps, once it was dark, he might call upon one or two of the families that he knew had worked at the house, the ones he felt sure would not denounce him. The pity of it was there were precious few of those. He had spent very little of his adult life at Arrandale. Some of the old retainers would remember him as a boy, but most of the newer staff would have little loyalty to him, especially if they believed he was the reason Arrandale was closed up.

The thud of hoofs caught his attention and he looked round to see Grace Duncombe riding towards him on a rangy strawberry roan. She sat tall and straight in the saddle, made taller by the very mannish beaver hat she wore, its wispy veil flying behind her like a pennant. Wolf straightened up and waited for her. She checked slightly, as if uncertain whether to acknowledge him, then brought her horse to a stand.

He touched his hat. 'That is a fine mare. Is she yours?'

'Yes.' Her response was cool, but not unfriendly. 'Bonnie is my indulgence. I have a small annuity from my mother that I use for her upkeep.'

He reached out and scratched the mare's head.

'You need not excuse yourself to me, Miss Duncombe.'

She flushed and her chin went up. 'I do not. But people wonder that I should keep my own horse when we have had to make savings everywhere else.'

'I imagine she is useful for visiting your father's parishioners.'

Her reserve fled and she laughed. 'With a basket of food hanging on my arm? I cannot claim that as my reason for keeping her.' She smoothed the mare's neck with one dainty gloved hand. 'I have had Bonnie since she was a foal and cannot bear to part with her.'

'I understand that. I had such a horse once. A black stallion. The very devil to control.'

'Oh? What happened to him?'

'He died. I am on my way back to your father's house now. Shall we walk?'

Grace used the gentle pressure of her heel to set Bonnie moving.

Perhaps he is a highwayman and his horse was shot from under him. That might also account for the scars on his body.

She quickly curbed her wayward imagination. She had seen a shadow cross the lean face and guessed he had been very fond of his black horse, so it was no wonder he did not wish to talk about it. She must follow her father's example and be charitable.

'You would find it quicker to cut through the village,' she said, waving her crop towards a narrow path that wound its way towards the distant houses.

'Not much quicker.'

'Ah. You are familiar with Arrandale?'

'I can see the church from here, Miss Duncombe, and it is clear this way will bring us to it almost as quickly as cutting back to the village.'

'And you would rather avoid the villagers,' she said shrewdly.

He shrugged. 'You know how these little places gossip about strangers.'

Grace pursed her lips. He frustrated every attempt to learn more about him.

She said now, 'That should not worry you, if you have nothing to hide.'

'I am merely a weary traveller, taking advantage of your father's hospitality to rest for a few days.'

'I fear *taking advantage* is just what you are doing,' she retorted, nettled.

'I mean no harm, Miss Duncombe, trust me.'

'Impossible, since I know nothing about you.'

'You could ask your father.'

'I have done so, but he will tell me nothing.' She

paused. 'I understand you are dining with us this evening.'

'Yes. Do you object?'

She stopped her horse.

'I would worry less if I knew something about you.'

He looked up and she had her first clear view of his eyes. They were blue, shot through with violet, and the intensity of his gaze was almost a physical force. Her insides fluttered like a host of butterflies.

'One day I will tell you everything about me,' he promised. 'For the present I would urge you to trust your father's judgement.'

'He seems to have fallen completely under your spell,' she snapped, seriously discomposed by the sensations he roused in her. 'You might be an out-and-out villain for all we know.'

Grace inadvertently jerked the reins and Bonnie sidled. Immediately he caught the bridle, murmuring softly to the mare before looking up again.

'Your father knows I am no villain, Miss Duncombe.'

He placed his hand on her knee as if in reassurance, but it had quite the opposite effect on Grace. Her linen skirt and several layers of petticoats separated them, but the gesture was shockingly intimate. Waves of heat flooded her, pooling low in her body. Her alarm must have shown in her countenance, because his hands dropped and he stepped away.

'Perhaps you should ride on, if you are afraid of me.'

Afraid? Grace's head was full of chaotic thoughts and feelings. He unsettled her, roused emotions she had thought long dead, but, no, she was not *afraid* of him. Quite the opposite.

'I should,' she said, gathering her reins and her disordered senses at the same time. 'I *shall*!'

And with that she set Bonnie cantering away.

Wolf watched her go, the skirts of her russet riding habit billowing and accentuating the tiny waist beneath her tight-fitting riding jacket. He had to admit it was a fine image. He had thought when he first saw her that her hair was the colour of pale honey, but out of doors, with the sun glinting on her soft curls, it reminded him more of ripe corn. And those eyes. They were a rich, deep blue. Dark as sapphires.

With a hiss of exasperation he took off his hat and raked his fingers through his hair. Bah, what was this, was he turning into some foppish poet? And, confound it, what had come over him to talk to her like that? He had said he was a lowly traveller, he should have touched his cap and kept a respectful silence.

It might be wiser to eat in the kitchen this evening, but Wolf knew Mr Duncombe would be able to tell him more about his family. Ten years was a long time and Wolf wished now that he had kept in touch, but it had been his decision to cut himself off. He had thought he would never return to England, but that was changed now. He had a daughter, a responsibility. Settling his hat more firmly on his head, he set off once more for the vicarage. As the good parson said, the past was gone. He must look to the future.

Grace was determined to wear her most sober gown for dinner that night, but when Betty came up to help her dress, she rejected every one pulled out for her as too tight, too low at the neck, or too *dull*. In the end she settled for a round gown of deep-blue silk gauze with turban sleeves. Its severity was relieved with a trim of white silk at the neck and ankles and a run of seed pearl buttons down the front. She found a white shawl with blue embroidery to keep off the chill and, throwing this around her shoulders, she made her way downstairs to the drawing room.

'Oh.'

Grace stopped in the doorway when she saw their guest was alone. She had deliberately left her entrance as late as possible to avoid just such a situation.

'Do come in, Miss Duncombe. Your father has gone to his study to find a book for me. He will be back immediately, I am sure,' he said, as she came slowly into the room. 'I hope you will forgive me dining with you in my riding dress, but I am…travelling light. And I had not noticed, until I changed for dinner, that this shirt is missing a button.' Again that dark, intense look that did such strange things to her insides. 'I hope you will forgive me. It hardly shows beneath the cravat, and at least, thanks to your housekeeper's services, it is clean.'

Her training as a vicar's daughter came to her aid.

'If you will give it to Truscott when you retire this evening I will see that it is repaired. I will have your other shirt laundered, too.'

'Thank you, ma'am, but Mrs T. is already dealing with that.'

Mrs T.! She bridled at his familiarity with her servants, but decided it was best to ignore it. She turned thankfully to her father as he came back into the room.

'Here you are, my son.'

He held out a book and Grace's brows rose in surprise. *'The Mysteries of Udolpho?'*

'Mr Peregrine wanted something to amuse him if he cannot sleep,' explained her father. 'And he is unfamiliar with Mrs Radcliffe's novel.'

'I do not see how you could have failed to hear of it. It was a huge success a few years ago,' remarked Grace.

'I was out of the country, a few years ago.'

Heavens, thought Grace. *It gets worse and worse. Are we harbouring a spy in our midst?*

'Ah,' cried Papa. 'Here is Truscott come to tell us dinner is ready. Perhaps, Mr Peregrine, you would escort my daughter?'

Grace hesitated as their guest proffered his arm, staring at the worn shabbiness of the sleeve.

Oh, do not be so uncharitable, Grace. You have never before judged a man by his coat.

And in her heart she knew she was not doing so now, but there was something about this man that disturbed her peace.

'Do not worry,' he murmured as she reluctantly rested her fingers on his arm. 'I shall not be here long enough to read more than the first volume of *Udolpho*.'

'I am relieved to hear it,' she retorted, flustered by his apparent ability to read her mind.

His soft laugh made her spine tingle, as if he had brushed her skin with his fingers. When they reached the dining room and he held her chair for her the tiny hairs at the back of her neck rose. He would not dare to touch her. Would he?

No. He was walking away to take his seat on her father's right hand.

Wolf wanted to ask questions. Coming back here had roused his interest in Arrandale. His eyes drifted towards

Grace, sitting at the far end of the table. It would be safest to wait until he and the parson were alone, but after ten years of resolutely shutting out everything to do with his family, suddenly he was desperate for news.

'So Arrandale Hall is shut up,' he said.

'But it is not empty,' said Grace. 'A servant and his wife are in residence.'

Wolf's mouth tightened at her swift intervention and the inference that he wanted to rob the place. He kept his eyes on the parson.

'Do you hear anything of the family, sir?'

'Alas, no, my son. I hear very little of the Arrandales now.'

'There was something in the newspapers only last week,' put in Grace. 'About the Dowager Marchioness of Hune's granddaughter, Lady Cassandra. She was married in Bath. To a foreign gentleman, I believe.'

Wolf laughed. 'Was she indeed? Good for her.'

Grace was looking at him with a question in her eyes, but it was her father who spoke.

'Ah, yes, you are right, my love, but that can hardly interest our guest.'

'No, no, of course I am interested.' Wolf hoped he sounded politely indifferent, as befitted a stranger. 'I take it there are no Arrandales living in the area now?'

'No. The house was closed up in ninety-five. There was a particularly bad outbreak of scarlet fever that spring and old Mr Arrandale and his wife died within weeks of one another.'

'Is *that* what they say killed them?' Wolf could hardly keep the bitterness from his voice.

'It was indeed what killed them, my son.' The parson turned his gentle gaze upon him. 'Nothing else.'

'There had been some trouble earlier that winter, had there not, Papa? At the end of ninety-four,' remarked Grace. 'I was at school then, but I remember there were reports in the newspapers. The older son killed his wife for her jewels and fled to France. It was a great scandal.'

The old man shook his head. 'Scandal has always followed the Arrandales, my love. Not all of it deserved.'

'You say that because your living is in their gift,' muttered Wolf.

'No, I say it because I believe it.'

'But, Papa,' said Grace, 'you believe the best of everyone.'

Wolf did not look up, but felt sure her eyes were on him. Mr Duncombe merely chuckled.

'I look for the best in everyone,' he said mildly, 'and I am rarely disappointed. Do pass me the fricassee of rabbit again, my dear, it really is quite excellent.'

Wolf wanted to ask about the child, his daughter. Had the parson seen her, was she tall, like him, or small-boned like her mother? Was she dark, did she have his eyes? The questions went round and round in his head, but he knew he must let the matter drop. When Mr Duncombe began to talk of more general matters he followed suit, but his long exile had left him woefully ignorant.

'You appear singularly ill informed of how matters stand in England,' observed Grace, clearly suspicious.

'I have been living in the north country, they have little interest in what goes on nearer London. That is why I have come south, to take up my life again.'

She pounced on that.

'Oh, are you a local man, then, Mr Peregrine? I do not recall any family with that name hereabouts.'

'No, the Peregrines are not local,' he replied truthfully.

The parson shifted uncomfortably.

'My dear, it grows late and I am sure Mr Peregrine would like to join me in a glass of brandy. I do not often indulge the habit, sir, but since you are here…'

Grace rose immediately. 'Of course, Papa.'

'If you wish to retire, Grace, I am sure our guest will not mind if we do not send for the tea tray.'

Wolf knew he should agree with his host. They could bid Miss Duncombe goodnight now and he would be free of her questions and suspicions, but some inner demon made him demur.

'If it is no trouble, a cup of tea before I retire would be a luxury I have not enjoyed for a very long time.'

Grace looked at him, eyes narrowed.

'You seem to be inordinately fond of the drink, Mr Peregrine.'

'I believe I am, Miss Duncombe.' He met her gaze innocently enough and at length she inclined her head, every inch the gracious hostess.

'Of course Mr Peregrine must have tea if he wishes it, Papa. I will await you in the drawing room.'

With that she swept out of the room.

As soon as the door was closed Mr Duncombe said, 'Was that wise, sir? My daughter is no fool.'

'I am aware of that, but I was not funning when I said I have missed life's little luxuries.' The old man's brows rose and Wolf's mouth twisted into a wry smile. 'Not tea-drinking, I admit, unless it was in the company of a pretty woman.' Wolf saw the other man draw back and he hurried on. 'Pray, sir, do not think I have any thoughts of *that* nature towards your daughter, I would not repay your hospitality so cruelly. No, I have no interest in anything save clearing my name.' He looked around to check again that they were alone. 'On that subject, sir, what do you know of my own daughter?'

'Alas, my son, I cannot help you. She lives with Lord and Lady Davenport, I believe. Doctor Oswald was dining here the night your wife died and a servant came to fetch him. When we met again Oswald said it was a miracle the baby survived. Your wife never regained consciousness.' In the candlelight Mr Duncombe's naturally cheerful face was very grave. 'He told me, in confidence, that if it had not been for the missing diamonds the magistrate would have recorded your wife's death as a tragic accident. Alas, both the doctor and the magistrate are now dead.'

'So you have a new Justice of the Peace?'

'Yes, Sir Loftus Braddenfield of Hindlesham Manor,' the parson informed him. 'And that is another reason you might wish to avoid being in Grace's company, my son. She is betrothed to him.'

Chapter Three

Grace blew out her candle and curled up beneath the bedcovers. She really could not make out Mr Peregrine. She turned restlessly. In general Papa was a very good judge of character, but he seemed to have fallen quite under this stranger's spell.

She had to admit that dinner had been very enjoyable, the man was well educated and there had been some lively discussions of philosophy, religion and the arts, but he lacked knowledge of what was happening in the country. Surely the north was not that backward. Fears of Bonaparte invading England were never far away, but she thought if the man was a spy he would be better informed. Had he been locked up somewhere, perhaps? She was more thankful than ever that he was in the groom's accommodation and that she had reminded Truscott to check the outer doors were secure before he went to bed.

Perhaps he had been in the Marshalsea. Many men of good birth were incarcerated there for debt, or fraud. With a huff of exasperation she sat up and thumped her pillow.

Such conjecture is quite useless. You will only end

*up turning the man into a monster, when he is probably
nothing more than penniless vagrant, for all his talk of
having business in Arrandale.*

But would he be in any hurry to leave, if they continued to treat him like an honoured guest? She settled
down in her bed again. The man had clearly enjoyed his
dinner and he had been eager to take tea with her after.
A knot of fluttering excitement twisted her stomach as
she remembered his glinting look across the dining table.
It was almost as if he was flirting with her.

Yet he barely spoke two words to her in the drawing room. Once the tea tray appeared he lost no time in
emptying his cup and saying goodnight. She tried to be
charitable and think that he was fatigued. Sleep crept up
on Grace. No doubt matters would look much less mysterious in the daylight.

'Good morning, Mrs Truscott.' Grace looked about
the kitchen. 'Is our visitor still abed?'

'Nay, Miss Grace, he went out an hour ago.'

'Goodness, what can he be up to?'

Mrs Truscott smiled. 'Well, you know what your father always says, miss. Only those who rise early will
ever do any good.'

Grace laughed.

'It is quite clear you approve of Mr Peregrine! But
never mind that. I have come down to fetch tea for Papa.
We are taking breakfast together and then I am going to
visit Mrs Owlet. Perhaps you would pack a basket for
me to take to her.'

'I will, Miss Grace, but it goes against the grain to be
helping those that won't help themselves.'

'Mrs Truscott! The poor woman has broken her leg.'

'That's as may be, but if she hadn't been drinking strong beer she wouldn't have tumbled off the road and down the bank, now would she? And that feckless son of hers is no better. I doubt he's done an honest day's work in his life, not since the hall closed and he lost his job there.' The older woman scowled. 'It's said there's always rabbit in the pot at the Owlets' place, courtesy of Arrandale woods.'

'I am sure young Tom isn't the only one to go poaching in the woods and there is more than enough game to go round, since the woods are so neglected.'

'That's not the point, Miss Grace. It's breaking the law.'

'Well, if the law says a man cannot feed his family when there is such an abundance of rabbits on hand, then it is a bad law.'

'Tsk, and you betrothed to a magistrate, too!' Mrs Truscott waved a large spoon in her direction. 'Don't you go letting your man hear you saying such things, Miss Grace.'

'Sir Loftus knows my sentiments on these things and I know he has some sympathy with the poorer villagers, although it would never do for him to say so, of course, and I suppose I should not have said as much to you.'

'Don't you worry about me, Miss Grace, there's many a secret I've kept over the years. Now, let's say no more about it, for the kettle's boiling and the master will be waiting for his tea.'

Later, when she had seen her father comfortably ensconced in his study, Grace set off with her basket. Mrs Owlet lived at the furthest extremity of the village, at the end of a small lane backing on to Arrandale Park.

Grace stayed for some time, trying to make conversation, although she found the widow's embittered manner and caustic tongue very trying. The sun was at its height when Grace eventually emerged from the ill-kept cottage and she stood for a moment, breathing in the fresh air. Having spent the past hour sympathising with Mrs Owlet, Grace was not inclined to walk back through the village and listen to anyone else's woes. Instead she carried on up the lane into the park. There was a good path through the woods that bounded the park itself, and from there she could walk past the hall and on to the vicarage. It was a well-worn path that cut off the long curve of the High Street.

It was a fine spring morning and the woods were full of birdsong. Grace's sunny nature revived and she began to feel more charitable towards Mrs Owlet. She had fallen on hard times when Arrandale House had been closed up. Now she lived a frugal existence with her son in what was little more than a hovel. It was no wonder that she was bitter, but Grace could not help thinking that less indulgence in strong beer and more effort with a broom would have improved her condition. Seeing her now, with her grubby linen and dirty clothes, it was difficult to think that she had once been laundress in a great house.

Grace recalled Mrs Truscott's dark mutterings about young Tom Owlet poaching in these very woods and she looked around her. Not that anyone could mistake her tall form in its blue pelisse for a rabbit, but she strode on briskly and soon reached what had once been the deer park. Arrandale Hall was ahead of her, but her path veered away from the formal gardens and joined an impressive avenue of elms that lined the main approach to the house and would bring her out very close to the vicarage.

She had walked this way many times and always thought it regrettable that such a fine old house should stand empty. It was looking very grand today in the sunshine, but there was something different about the building that made her stop. She frowned at the little chapel beside the main house: the wide oak door was open.

Grace hurried across to the chapel. It was most likely Mr Jones had gone in there for some reason, but it could be children from the village, up to mischief, and the sooner they were sent on their way the better. She stepped inside and stood for a moment, while her eyes grew accustomed to the gloom. Someone was standing by the opposite wall, but it was definitely not a child.

'Mr Peregrine! What on earth are you doing here?'

Wolf turned. Grace Duncombe stood in the entrance, a black outline against the sunshine.

'The door was open and I was curious to see inside.' He saw the frowning suspicion in her eyes. 'I have not been stealing the church silver, Miss Duncombe, if that is your concern.'

'There is nothing of that sort left in here now,' she replied. 'But what business can you have at the Hall?'

'Curiosity,' he repeated. 'After what your father said last night I was interested to see the house, but you may be easy. The caretaker knows better than to let strangers into the house.'

Aye, thought Wolf, Jones would turn a stranger away, but the man had been happy enough to let Wolf wander through the familiar rooms. If Grace had arrived ten minutes earlier she would have found him in the entrance hall of the house itself. That would have been more difficult to explain away.

'It was remiss of Mr Jones to leave the chapel open,' she said now. 'I must remind him of his duties.'

'Must you?'

'Why, yes. While the family are absent we must respect their property.'

'Very commendable, Miss Duncombe, but since we are here, would you object if I took a moment to look around? You may stay, if you like, and make sure I do no damage.'

'I shall certainly do so.'

Silently he turned to study an ornately carved edifice with its stone effigies. A curious stranger would ask whose tomb this was, so he did.

'That is the tomb of Roland Arrandale and his wife,' said Grace, stepping up beside him. 'He was the first Earl of Davenport. The second and third earls are buried here, but the Hall was not grand enough for James, the fourth earl. He built himself a new principal seat and bequeathed Arrandale Hall to his younger son, John. His descendants are buried in the vault below us and you can see the carved memorials on the walls.'

'Including these,' murmured Wolf, looking up at two gleaming marble tablets.

'They are recent additions. For the late Mr and Mrs Arrandale, and Florence, the poor wife of Mr Wolfgang Arrandale. I believe the younger son arranged for these to be installed at his own expense when the trustees refused to pay.'

Wolf kept his face impassive. What were those cheese-paring lawyers about to deny money for such things?

And Richard—confound it, his little brother should not be bearing the cost. This was his fault. All of it.

'It was fortunate there were no children,' he said, keeping his voice indifferent.

'Oh, but there was,' she corrected him, as he had hoped she would. 'There was a little girl. She was adopted by an Arrandale cousin, I believe.'

'I am surprised her maternal grandparents did not bring up the child.' He glanced at Grace, hoping she might answer the question he dare not ask. She did not disappoint him.

'The Sawstons moved away from the area after their daughter's death. They wanted nothing more to do with the Arrandale family, nor their granddaughter.' Disapproval flickered over her serene countenance. 'It was cruel of them to abandon the baby at such a time. The poor child had done nothing to warrant it, except to be born.'

And that was his fault, too. A shudder ran through Wolf and he turned away, saying curtly, 'There is little of interest here.'

'Unless you appreciate craftsmanship,' she told him. 'The font cover is by Grinling Gibbons.'

'Is it now?' Wolf went to the back of the church where the stone font stood behind the last box pew. He ran a careful hand over the elaborately carved wooden cover. 'What a pity I did not know that earlier, I might have carried it off to sell in the nearest town.' His mouth twisted. 'Is that not what you think of me, Miss Duncombe, that I am a thief?'

'I do not know what you are.'

'Your father trusts me.'

'Father trusts everyone.'

'True. He is a saint and I will not deny that I am a sinner. But I am not here to steal from the chapel.' Her darkling look was sceptical. He shrugged. 'I have seen enough here now. Shall we go?'

She indicated that he should precede her out of the church, then she carefully locked the door. She stood on the path, as if waiting for him to walk away.

He said, 'If you are going to the vicarage, I will escort you.'

'Thank you, but before I leave I am going to take the key back to Mr Jones.'

'Very well, I will wait for you.'

She looked dissatisfied with his answer, but she turned on her heel and hurried away to the house. Wolf followed more slowly. He could only hope that Jones would not give him away.

A few minutes later she returned and he was relieved by her exasperation when she saw him. Clearly she had no idea of his real identity.

'Yes, I am still here,' he said cheerfully. 'I shall escort you back to the vicarage. It is not at all seemly for a young lady to walk these grounds alone.'

'I have done so many times without mishap.'

'So you are an unrepentant trespasser.'

'Not at all, there is a right of way through the park.'

'And you walk here for pleasure?' he asked her.

'Not today. I have been visiting an old lady. It is much quicker to walk home this way than through the village.'

'It would be quicker still to ride. And having seen you in the saddle I know you ride very well, Miss Duncombe.'

'One cannot live within twenty miles of Newmarket *without* riding.' He detected the first signs of a thaw in her response. 'However, riding today would not have been so convenient. You see, I came through the village and carried out several errands. I passed on Mrs Truscott's recipe for a restorative broth to one family, called in upon a mother with a newborn baby to see how they go on and took a pot of comfrey ointment to old Mr Brent, for his leg. That would have been much more difficult if I had been riding Bonnie. I would have been forever looking for a mounting block to climb back into the saddle.'

'I quite see that. But do you never ride here, in the park?'

'I would not presume to do so without the owner's permission.'

'Are you always so law-abiding?'

'I am the parson's daughter and betrothed to Sir Loftus Braddenfield. I am obliged to set an example.'

'Of course.'

She looked up. 'I think you are laughing at me.'

'Now why should I do that?' He saw her hesitate and added, 'Come, madam, do not spare my feelings, tell me!'

'I think...' she drew a breath '...*I think* that you have very little respect for the law!'

His lip curled. 'You are wrong, ma'am. I have a very healthy respect for it.'

Grace did not miss the sudden bitterness in his voice. A convict, then. She should be afraid, he might be dangerous.

Not to me.

A strange thought and one she was reluctant to pursue. Instead she looked about her as they made their way through the avenue of majestic elms that led to the main gates and the High Street.

'It is such a pity that the park is now turned over to

cattle,' she remarked. 'It was a deer park, you know. I used to love watching them roaming here.'

'You remember the house as it was? You remember the family?'

'Of course, I grew up here. At least, until I was eleven years old. Then I was sent off to school. As for knowing the family, my father may be a saint, as you call him, but he was careful to keep me away from the Arrandales. The old gentleman's reputation as a rake was very bad, but I believe his two sons surpassed him. Thankfully for Papa's peace of mind, by the time I came back the Hall was shut up.'

'And just when did you return?'

'When I was seventeen. Seven years ago.'

His brows went up. 'And you are still unmarried?'

She felt the colour stealing into her cheeks.

'I came home to look after my father, not to find a husband.'

'The local gentlemen are slowcoaches indeed if they made no move to court you.'

He is flirting with you. There is no need to say anything. You owe him no explanation.

But for some inexplicable reason she felt she must speak.

'I *was* engaged to be married. To Papa's curate, but he died.'

'I am very sorry.'

For the first time in years she felt the tears welling up for what might have been. She said quickly, 'It was a long time ago.'

'And now you have a new fiancé,' he said.

'Yes. I am very happy.'

* * *

There was a touch of defiance in her words, but Wolf also heard the note of reproof. He had been over-familiar. She was the parson's daughter and not one to engage in flirtatious chatter, but he had been curious to know why she was still unmarried. She was very tall, of course— why, her head was level with his chin!—and she had no dowry. Either of those things might deter a suitor. But they should not, he thought angrily. She was handsome and well educated and would make any man an excellent wife. Any respectable man, that is.

When they reached the park gates he saw they were chained, but there was a stile built to one side. Wolf sprang over it and, having helped Grace across, he pulled her fingers on to his arm. Silently she disengaged herself. Understandable, but he could not deny the tiny pinprick of disappointment.

Grace was relieved to be back on the High Street and with the vicarage just ahead of them. This man was far too forward and the tug of attraction made her feel a little breathless whenever she was in his company.

You are very foolish, she told herself sternly. *His only advantage is his height. He is the only man in Arrandale taller than you and that is hardly a recommendation!*

'You are frowning, Miss Duncombe. Is anything amiss?'

'No, not at all.' Hastily she summoned a smile. 'Here we are back at the vicarage. It will be quicker if we walk up the drive rather than going around to the front door and summoning Truscott to let us in.'

Grace pressed her lips together to prevent any further inane babbling.

* * *

She is uneasy, thought Wolf. *But how much worse would she feel if she knew I was a wanted man?*

A large hunter was standing in the stable yard and Mr Duncombe was beside it, talking to the rider, but seeing them approach he smiled.

'So there you are, Grace, and in good time.'

The rider jumped down. 'My dear, I am glad I did not miss you altogether.'

Wolf watched as the man caught Grace's hand and raised it to his lips. He looked to be on the shady side of forty, stocky and thick-set, with a ruddy complexion and more than a touch of grey in his hair. His brown coat was cut well, but not in the height of fashion, and he greeted Grace with an easy familiarity. Even before they were introduced Wolf had guessed his identity.

'Sir Loftus Braddenfield is our local Justice of the Peace.'

It did not need the warning note in the parson's mild words to put Wolf on his guard. Some spirit of devilry urged him to tug his forelock, but he suppressed it; Sir Loftus Braddenfield did not look like a fool. The man was coolly assessing him as Wolf made a polite greeting.

'So you are on your way to London, eh? Where are you from, sir?'

'I have been travelling in the north for some time,' Wolf replied calmly.

'And you thought you'd break your journey in Arrandale. Friend of Mr Duncombe's, are you?'

'I knew the family,' explained Mr Duncombe. 'A long time ago.'

Sir Loftus was still holding Grace's hand and it occurred to Wolf that he did not like seeing his fiancée escorted by a stranger. Wolf excused himself and as he walked away he heard Sir Loftus addressing Grace.

'I wish I could stay longer, my dear, but I have business in Hindlesham. I merely called to invite you and your father to dinner this evening. But if you have visitors…'

Grace's reply floated across the yard to Wolf as he ran lightly up the garret stairs.

'Mr Peregrine is not a visitor, Loftus. More one of Papa's charitable cases.'

He winced. That cool description should allay any jealous suspicions Braddenfield might have. Clearly the lady had a very low opinion of 'Mr Peregrine'. He went inside, but as he crossed the room he could not resist glancing out of the window, which overlooked the yard. The little party was still there, but the parson and Braddenfield appeared to have finished their discussion, for the magistrate was taking his leave of Grace, raising her hand to his lips. Wolf scowled. She was smiling at Braddenfield more warmly than she had ever smiled at him.

Kicking off his boots, he threw himself down on the bed. It did not matter what Miss Grace Duncombe thought of him. There were more pressing matters requiring his attention. Putting his hands behind his head, he thought of all he had heard from old Brent and from Jones, the caretaker at Arrandale Hall. He closed his eyes and conjured his own memories of the tragedy. He remembered the servants coming up to the hall while he knelt beside Florence's almost-lifeless form. Jones had added one small detail that Wolf had forgotten. It had been Charles Urmston who pulled Wolf to his feet, saying as he did so, 'You have done it this time, Arrandale. Your temper has got the better of you.'

Everyone would think Florence had met him on the landing, ready to continue their argument, and he had pushed her away so that she had fallen to her death. There were witnesses enough to their frequent quarrels. And the theft of the necklace was also laid squarely at his door.

He sat up abruptly. Whoever stole the diamonds knew the truth about Florence's death, he was sure of it. Wolf glanced out of the window again. The stable yard was empty now. Mr Duncombe and his daughter were invited to dine with Sir Loftus, so he was free to patronise the local inn this evening.

'Well, well, that was a pleasant dinner.'

Grace wished she could agree with her father, but if she were truthful, she had found the evening spent with Sir Loftus and his elderly mother a trifle dull. Mrs Braddenfield was a kindly soul, but her interests were narrow and her son, although well educated, lacked humour. Grace supposed that was partly to do with his being Justice of the Peace, a position he took very seriously. They did not even have the company of Claire Oswald, Mrs Braddenfield's young companion, to lighten the mix, for she was away visiting relatives.

The conversation over dinner ranged from local matters to the weather and the ongoing war with France, but it had all been very serious. Grace compared the evening to the previous one spent in the company of their mysterious guest. They had discussed a whole range of topics and her own contributions had been received without the condescension she often detected in her fiancé's manner. Berating herself for being so ungrateful, she sought for something cheerful to say.

'It was very kind of Loftus to put his carriage at our disposal.'

'It was indeed. It would have been a chilly ride in the gig.'

She heard the sigh in her father's voice. At times like these Papa felt the change in their circumstances. The tithes that provided a large proportion of his income as rector of the parish had diminished considerably since Arrandale Hall had been shut up and when their ancient coachman had become too old to work they had pensioned him off. Grace had persuaded her father that a carriage was not a necessity; they could manage very well with the gig and the old cob. And so they could, although she could not deny there were benefits to riding in a closed carriage during the colder months of the year.

Sir Loftus owned the manor house in the market town of Hindlesham. It was only a few miles, but Grace was thankful when they reached Arrandale village, for they would be home very soon. It was nearing midnight and most of the buildings were in darkness, no more than black shapes against the night sky, but light spilled out from the Horse Shoe Inn, just ahead of them. With her head against the glass Grace watched a couple of figures stagger on to the road without any heed for the approaching vehicle. The carriage slowed to a walk, the coachman shouting angrily at the men to get out of the way. From the loud and abusive response she was sure they had not come to harm beneath the horses' hoofs.

Grace was relieved her father was sleeping peacefully in his corner of the carriage, for he did not like her to hear such uncouth language. Dear Papa, he was apt to think her such a child! Smiling, she turned her gaze back to the window. They were level with the inn now and there was someone else in the doorway. As the carriage drove by, the figure turned and she saw it was Mr Peregrine.

There was no mistaking him, the image was embedded in her mind even as the carriage picked up speed. He was hunched, his coat unbuttoned and he was wearing a muffler around his throat rather than the clean linen she had taken the trouble to provide for him. His hat was pulled low over his face and it was the merest chance that he had looked up at just that moment, so that the light from the inn's window illuminated his face.

Why should he be skulking around a common inn at midnight? And had he recognised her? Grace drew herself up. She was not at fault. If he had seen her, then she was sure he would be at pains to explain himself. She was more than ever relieved that he was not sleeping in the house. When they reached the vicarage she gently roused her father and accompanied him indoors. She decided not to say anything to him about their guest tonight, but unless the man had a satisfactory explanation for his activities she would urge her father to tell him to leave.

The following morning she found their guest breaking his fast in the kitchen, freshly shaved, a clean neckcloth at his throat and looking altogether so at ease that for a moment her resolve wavered. But only for a moment.

'Mr Peregrine. When you have finished your breakfast I would be obliged if you would attend me in the morning room.'

Those piercing violet-blue eyes were fixed upon her, but he waited until Mrs Truscott had bustled out of the room before he spoke.

'You wish to see me alone?'

She flushed, but remained resolute.

'I do.'

'Is that not a little…forward of you, Miss Duncombe?'

Her flush deepened, but this time with anger.

'Necessity demands that I speak to you in private.'

'As you wish.' He picked up his coffee cup. 'Give me ten minutes and I will be with you.'

Grace glared at him. Mrs Truscott had come back into the kitchen so she could not utter the blistering set-down that came to her lips. Instead she turned on her heel and left the room. How dare he treat her thus, as if she had been the servant! If he thought that would save him from an uncomfortable interrogation, he was sadly mistaken.

Wolf drained his cup. The summons was not unexpected. It was unfortunate that Grace had seen him last night and it was his own fault. A carriage rattling through the main street at any time was a rare occurrence in Arrandale and he should have realised that it was most likely to be the Duncombes returning from Hindlesham. If only he had kept his head down, remained in the shadows, instead of staring into the coach window like a fool. Even now he remembered the look of shocked recognition on Grace's face. Well, he would have to brazen it out.

He made his way to the morning room where Grace was waiting for him, her hands locked together and a faint crease between her brows. She was biting her lip, as if she did not know quite how to begin. He decided to make it easy for her.

'You want to know what I was doing at the Horse Shoe Inn last night.'

'Yes. You are, of course, quite at liberty to go wherever you wish,' she added quickly. 'It was rather your appearance that puzzled me.'

'My appearance, Miss Duncombe?'

She waved one hand towards him. 'Today you are dressed neatly, with propriety. Last night you looked like a, like a…' He waited, one brow raised, and at last she burst out, 'Like a ne'er-do-well.'

He shrugged. 'I have always found it expedient to adapt to my surroundings. I had a sudden fancy for a tankard of home brewed and I did not want to make the other customers uncomfortable.'

It was not a complete lie. It had been a risk to go into the taproom at all, but the parson had told him the landlord was not a local man and would not know him. Wolf had hoped that with his untidy clothes and the ragged muffler about his neck no one would associate him with the Arrandale family.

Grace looked sceptical.

'Since the inn supplies us with our small beer I can only assume you had a sudden fancy for low company, too,' she said coldly. 'Forgive me if I appear uncharitable, but I think you have imposed upon our hospitality long enough.'

The door opened and the parson's soft voice was heard.

'Ah, Mr Peregrine, there you are.' Mr Duncombe came into the room, looking from one to the other. 'Forgive me, am I interrupting?'

Wolf met Grace's stormy eyes. 'Your daughter thinks it is time I took my leave.'

'No, no, my dear sir, there is no need for that, not before you have finished your business in Arrandale.'

Wolf waited for Grace to protest, but although her disapproval was tangible, she remained silent.

'Miss Duncombe is afraid I am importuning you, sir.'

'Bless my soul, no, indeed. I am very pleased to have you here, my boy.'

'But your daughter is not.' His words fell into a heavy silence.

'Perhaps, my son, you would allow me to speak to my daughter alone.'

'Of course.' As Wolf turned to go the old man caught his arm.

'Mark me, sir, I am not asking you to quit this house. In fact, I strongly urge you to stay, for as long as you need. You are safe here.'

'But if Miss Duncombe is not happy about it—'

'Let me talk with Grace alone, if you please. We will resolve this matter.'

Grace frowned. She did not understand the look that passed between the two men, but the stranger went out and she was alone with her father.

'Now, Grace, tell me what is troubling you. Is it merely that you think Mr Peregrine is imposing upon me?'

'I do not trust him, Papa.' She saw his look of alarm and said quickly, 'Oh, he has not acted improperly towards *me*, but—' She broke off, searching for the right words to express herself. 'Yesterday, when I was coming home after visiting Mrs Owlet, I came upon him in the Arrandale Chapel, and I saw him again last night, outside the Horse Shoe Inn when we drove past at midnight.'

'Ah.' The parson smiled. 'These are not such great crimes, my dear.'

'But you must admit it is not the behaviour of an honest man.'

'It may well be the behaviour of a troubled one.'

'I do not understand you.'

'No, I am aware of that. I am asking you to trust me in this, Grace.'

'Papa!' She caught his hands. 'Papa, there is something you are not telling me. Do you not trust *me*?'

He shook his head at her.

'My love, I beg you will not question me further on this matter. One day, I hope I shall be able to explain everything, but for now you must trust me. It is my wish that Mr Peregrine should remain here for as long as it is necessary.'

He spoke with his usual gentle dignity, but with a firmness that told her it would be useless to argue.

'Very well, Papa. If that is your wish.'

'It is, my child. Now, if you will forgive me, I am off to visit the Brownlows. They sent word that the old man has taken a turn for the worse and is not expected to last the day.'

'Of course. I must not keep you from your work.'

'Thank you. And, Grace, when you next see Mr Peregrine I want you to make it plain to him that we want him to stay.'

With that he was gone. Grace began to pace up and down the room. Every instinct cried out against her father's dictum. The man was dangerous, she knew it, to her very core. So why was her father unable to see it? Grace stopped and pressed her hands to her cheeks. The image of Mr Peregrine filled her mind, as he had been that day by the pump, droplets of water sparkling on his naked chest like diamonds. That danger was not something she could share with her father!

There was a faint knock on the door. She schooled her face to look composed as Truscott came in with a letter for her. The handwriting told her it was from Aunt

Eliza, but her thoughts were too confused to enjoy it now. She would saddle Bonnie and go for a ride. Perhaps that would help her to see things more clearly.

Wolf heaved the axe high and brought it down with more force than was really necessary. The log split with satisfying ease and even as the pieces bounced on the cobbles he put another log on the chopping block and repeated the action. It was a relief to be active and he was in some measure repaying his host's kindness. The vision of Grace's stormy countenance floated before him and he pushed it away. He wanted to tell her the truth, but Mr Duncombe had advised against it. He must respect that, of course, but there was something so good, so honest about Grace that made the deception all the more abhorrent.

The axe came down again, so heavily that it cleaved the log and embedded itself in the block. He left it there while he eased his shoulders. He had discarded his coat and waistcoat, but the soft linen of his shirt was sticking to his skin. It would need washing again. A reluctant smile tugged at his lips as he recalled Grace tripping out into the garden and seeing him, half-naked, by the pump. He remembered her look, the way her eyes had widened. She had not found his body unattractive, whatever else she might think of him.

The smile died. There was no place in his life for a woman, especially one so young. Why, he was her senior by ten years, and her innocence made the difference feel more like a hundred. No, Grace Duncombe was not for him.

There was a clatter of hoofs and the object of his reverie approached from the stable yard. Her face was solemn, troubled, but the mare had no inhibitions, stretching her neck and nudging his arm, as if remembering their last meeting. Idly Wolf put a hand up and rubbed the mare's forehead while Grace surveyed the logs covering the cobbles outside the woodshed.

'My father wishes me to make it clear that you are welcome to remain here as long as you wish.'

'Thank you, Miss Duncombe.'

She looked at him then.

'Do not thank *me*. You know I would rather you were not here.'

She went to turn the mare, but Wolf gripped the leather cheek-piece.

'Grace, I—'

The riding crop slashed at his hand.

'How dare you use my name?'

He released the bridle and stepped back. Fury sparkled in her eyes as she jerked the horse about and cantered away.

'Hell and damnation!' Wolf rubbed his hand and looked down at the red mark that was already appearing across the knuckles.

'Is everything all right, sir?' Truscott appeared, looking at him anxiously. 'I just seen Miss Grace riding out o' here as if all the hounds of hell were after her.'

Wolf's eyes narrowed. 'I need a horse. A fast one.'

Chapter Four

The frantic gallop did much to calm Grace's agitation, but it could not last. She had already ridden Bonnie hard for a couple of hours that morning and the mare needed to rest. She had returned to the stables, determined to carry out her father's instructions and speak to their guest. She thought that, perched high on Bonnie's back, she would be able to remain calm and aloof, but the sight of the man had caught her off-guard. The white shirt billowing about him accentuated his broad shoulders and sent her pulse racing. And when he fixed her with those eyes that seemed to bore into her very soul, she panicked. Her reaction to his presence frightened her and his hand on the bridle was the last straw for her frayed nerves. She had thought only of getting away. But now, as she slowed Bonnie to a walk, she was filled with remorse. She hated violence and was ashamed to think she had struck out so blindly. She would have to apologise.

With a shock Grace realised she was on the outskirts of Hindlesham. Having come this far she should carry on to the Manor and give her thanks for last night's dinner. Loftus might well be out on business but his mother would be there. The very thought had Grace turning and cantering back towards Arrandale. Mrs Braddenfield frequently urged Grace to look upon her as a parent, since her own dear mother was dead, but Grace could no more confide in her than a stranger. Besides, Mrs Braddenfield would agree that Papa was far too trusting, that this 'Mr Peregrine' should be sent away immediately and perversely Grace did not want to hear that. Oh, heavens, she did not know what she *did* want!

She eased her conscience with the knowledge that Mrs Braddenfield was not in want of company. The lady had told them herself that her neighbours were being very attentive during the absence of Claire Oswald, her excellent companion. No, Mrs Braddenfield did not need her visit and, in her present agitated state, Grace would be very poor company indeed.

Grace had reached Arrandale Moor when she saw someone galloping towards her. She recognised Mr Styles's bay hunter immediately, but the rider was definitely *not* the elderly farmer. He was tall and bare-headed and she thought distractedly that he looked as good on horseback as he did chopping wood. Her mouth dried, she had a craven impulse to turn and flee, but she drew rein and waited for horse and rider to come up to her, steeling herself for the apology she must make to the man calling himself Mr Peregrine.

It took all her nerve to keep Bonnie still, for it looked at first as if horse and rider would charge into her, but at the last moment the bay came to a plunging halt, eyes wild and nostrils flaring. The rider controlled the powerful animal with ease, his unsmiling eyes fixed on Grace.

'Sir, I must apologise—'

'You said you want the truth,' he interrupted her. 'Very well. Follow me.'

Without waiting for her reply he wheeled about and set off back towards the village. Intrigued, Grace followed him. They passed the vicarage and took the narrow lane that bordered Arrandale Park until they came to a gap in the paling. As soon as both horses had both pushed through they set off again, galloping towards the Hall. The pace did not ease until they reached the weed-strewn carriage circle before the house itself. Grace saw her companion throw himself out of the saddle and she quickly dismounted before he could reach her. He looked to be in a fury and even as she slid to the ground she wondered if she had been wise to follow him.

'Come along.'

He took her arm and escorted her up the steps, arriving at the door just as Robert Jones opened it. With a curt instruction to the servant to look after the horses, he almost dragged Grace inside.

She had never been inside the Hall before. She wanted to stop and allow her eyes to grow accustomed to the shuttered gloom, but her escort led her on inexorably, through what she could dimly see was a series of reception rooms to the narrow backstairs. Fear and curiosity warred within her, but for the moment curiosity had the upper hand.

'Where are we going?'

'You will soon see.'

He marched her up the narrow, twisting stairs to a long gallery that ran the length of the building. After the darkness of the shadowy stairwell, the light pouring in from the windows was almost dazzling.

'Why have you brought me here?'

A prickling fear was already whispering the answer.

'You will see.' He strode along the gallery and stopped at one of the paintings. Only then did he release her. Grace resisted the urge to rub her arm where his fingers had held her in a vice-like grip.

They were standing beneath a picture. A family group, an older man with powdered hair in a dark frock coat and a tall crowned hat, a lady in an elegant muslin dress with a blue sash that matched her stylish turban. Between them, in informal pose, stood their children, a fair-haired schoolboy and beside him, his arm protectively resting on the boy's shoulder, a tall young man dressed in the natural style that was so fashionable ten years ago, a black frock coat and tight breeches. But it was not the clothes that held her attention, it was the lean, handsome face and the coldly cynical gleam in the violet-blue eyes that stared out defiantly beneath a shock of thick, curling dark hair. She glanced at the man beside her and involuntarily stepped away.

'Yes, that is me.' There was a sneer in the deep, drawling voice. 'Wolfgang Charles Everdene Arrandale. Not-so-beloved son and heir of Arrandale. This was painted to celebrate my twenty-first birthday. Not that it was much of a celebration, I was a rakehell even then, in true Arrandale tradition. Is it any wonder my father thought me capable of murder?'

'And the boy?' It was all she could think of to say.

'My brother Richard, seven years my junior. He could have inherited Arrandale. When I left England I deliberately cut myself off from the family, ignored letters and messages, even the news that my parents were dead. I wanted everyone to think I had died, too, but it seems Richard would not accept that. Consequently the miserly lawyers have held the purse strings at Arrandale and my foolish brother has dipped into his own pocket to pay for necessary maintenance work here.'

Surely a murderer would not say such things.

Grace needed to think, so she moved along the gallery, studying the portraits. There were signs of Wolfgang Arrandale in many of them, in the shape of the eye, the strong chin and in most of the men she saw that same world-weary look, but the lines of dissipation were etched deeper. Reason told her she should be frightened of this man, but she felt only an overwhelming sadness and an irrational, dangerous wish to comfort him.

At the end of the gallery she turned.

'Why have you come back now?'

'I learned I have a daughter.'

'You did not know?'

'No. I thought when I left England I had no commitments, no responsibilities. I had brought enough shame on the family and thought it best if I disappeared. Now, for my daughter's sake, I need to prove my innocence.'

She forced herself to look him in the eye. 'Are you a murderer?'

'I have killed men, yes, in duels and in war. *But I did not kill my wife.*'

He held her gaze. Grace desperately wanted to believe him, but she could not ignore the portraits staring down at her from the walls, generations of rogues, rakes and murderers going back to the time of good King Hal. Everyone in the parish knew the history of the family. Why should this Arrandale be any different to his ancestors?

Her legs felt weak and she sank down on to a chair, regardless of the dust. She should have known who he was. It made such *sense*, she should have known.

He began to pace the floor, his boots echoing on the bare boards.

'There is a warrant for my arrest and a price on my head. If I am caught, your father could be charged with harbouring a criminal. He did not want you to have that on your conscience, too. But he was afraid you might guess.'

'Why should I do that?' She was answering herself as much as him. 'I was at school when your wife died. By the time I came home to look after Papa it was old news and the Arrandales were rarely mentioned.'

'Except to curse the name for bringing hardship and poverty to the village.'

She heard the bitterness in his voice and said quietly, 'Will you tell me what happened?'

He stared out of the window.

'I do not know. We argued, I rode out to cool my heels and when I came back I found her lying at the bottom of the stairs.'

'Could she have fallen?'

He looked at her then. 'Judge for yourself.'

He strode off towards a door at the far end of the gallery. Grace knew this was her chance. She could go back the way they had come, escape from the house and from Wolfgang Arrandale. That would be the safe, sensible thing to do.

It took only a heartbeat for Grace to decide. She followed him out of the gallery and down a different set of stairs, wider and more ornate than the ones they had ascended.

'This is the grand staircase,' he said, as they reached the first floor. 'My wife's room was there, the first door on the far side of the landing.'

The lantern window in the roof threw daylight onto the cantilevered stone staircase. It incorporated two half-turns and landings, so that it occupied three sides of the square inner hall. Grace looked at the shallow steps and elegant balusters. There was a smooth wooden handrail that would provide a good grip for the daintiest hand. Grace imagined herself emerging from the bedroom to descend the stairs. Her fingers would be on the rail as she crossed the landing, long before she reached the top step. Her companion let his breath go with a hiss.

'I have had enough of this place. Let us go.' He put out his hand, but let it drop, his lip curling when Grace shrank away. 'No doubt you will feel safer if I go first.'

Silently she followed him down the stairs. When they reached the bottom he stood for a moment, looking down at the flagstones as if reliving the awful sight of his wife lying there.

'You said you had just come in,' she said, trying to think logically. 'From the front entrance?'

'No, the garden door, that way.' He indicated a shadowy passage set beneath the stairs. 'I had taken the key with me. I was in a foul temper and wanted to avoid seeing anyone.' He looked down at the flags again. 'I found her just here, on the floor.'

Grace looked at the spot where he was standing, then she looked up at the landing almost directly above them.

'You are thinking, Miss Duncombe, that she might have fallen from the balcony, rather than tumbled down the stairs. I remember the injuries to her head were commensurate with such a fall.'

Grace put her hands to her mouth.

'That could not have been an accident.' She read

agreement in his eyes and closed her own, shuddering. 'Oh, poor woman.'

'Quite.' He sighed. 'I beg your pardon, I have said too much. I never intended you to know the full horror of it. Come, let me take you outside.'

She did not resist as he caught her arm—more gently this time—and led her to the door. When they reached the front steps she stopped and dragged in a long, steadying breath. The sun still shone brightly, a few feet away Robert Jones was holding the two horses. It was only minutes since they had gone into the house, but she felt as if she had come out into a different world. When she spoke she was surprised at how calm she sounded.

'Thank you, Mr Arrandale, you may release me now, I am not going to faint.'

His hand dropped. 'I am glad to hear it.'

Grace set off towards the horses. Without a mounting block she had no choice but to allow him to throw her up into the saddle and she made herself comfortable while he scrambled up on to his borrowed mount. When he thanked Jones for holding the horses the servant lost himself in a tangle of words.

'It was nothing, Master—Mr Arr—I mean...'

'You may be easy, Jones. Miss Duncombe knows who I am now.'

The man looked as if a great weight had been taken from his shoulders.

'Well that's a mercy. I'll wish 'ee both good day, then, sir. Miss Duncombe.'

They trotted away. Grace's head was bursting. Speculation, arguments, doubts whirled about and they were halfway across the park before she broke the silence.

'If you are innocent, you should have stayed and defended yourself.'

'I know.'

'So why did you flee the country?'

'My father insisted I leave. He and my wife's cousin bundled me out of the house before I could think clearly. My father had...connections at Sizewell who would take me across to France.'

'Do you mean smugglers?'

He nodded. 'The weather was bad so I remained at an inn on the quay for a few days. It gave me a chance to think it all through. I had just decided to turn back when word reached me that the diamonds were missing and the Sawstons were bringing a prosecution against me for theft and murder. Thus I am as you see me, Miss Duncombe. A fugitive with a price on his head.'

They had reached the gap in the paling and Wolf stopped to let Grace go first. He wondered what she thought of him now. He was somewhat encouraged when she waited on the road for him to join her.

'Well,' he said, as they moved off towards the vicarage. 'You now hold my life in your hands.'

She threw him a troubled look. 'Pray do not joke about it, Mr Arrandale. It is not a responsibility I want, I assure you.'

She tensed and he looked up to see Sir Loftus trotting out of the vicarage drive. He nodded at Wolf before turning to address Grace.

'This is the second day in a row that I have missed you, my dear. If I were the suspicious sort I should think you were avoiding me.'

She laughed and replied with perfect calm, 'Now how can that be, sir, when I had no idea you were going to call today? I have been taking advantage of the fine weather to show our guest around the area.'

'Indeed? And how much longer do you intend to remain in Arrandale, Mr Peregrine?'

'Oh, I hardly know, a few days, a week.'

Wolf waited for Braddenfield to ask him the nature of his business here, but Grace gave the man no chance. She reached across and put a hand on his arm.

'It must be nearly dinner time, Loftus. Will you not stay and take pot luck with us? It will give me the opportunity to make amends for not being in when you called.'

Wolf held his breath. The last thing he wanted was to spend the evening in the company of a Justice of the Peace. Not by the flicker of an eyelid did he show his relief when Braddenfield declined the invitation.

'Another time, perhaps,' he said, patting Grace's hand. 'My mother is expecting me.'

'Of course.' Smiling, Grace gathered up her reins. 'Pray give her my regards.'

'That was close,' murmured Wolf, as they watched Sir Loftus ride away.

'Not at all,' she replied. 'I learned last night that his mother's companion is visiting her family and I knew he would not leave his mama to dine alone. It was quite safe to invite him.'

A laugh escaped Wolf. 'By Gad, then it was very coolly done, ma'am.'

Two spots of colour painted her cheeks.

'It was very badly done,' she retorted, kicking her horse on. 'Do not think I take pleasure in deceiving an honest man!'

It was at times such as this that Grace regretted they only had the Truscotts at the vicarage to help them. She would have liked to hand her horse over to a groom and disappear to her room; instead she had to stable Bonnie herself. In normal circumstances she did not object, Truscott already worked very hard and she could not expect him to look after her mare as well as the old cob they kept to pull the gig.

She had just finished rubbing down Bonnie when Wolfgang Arrandale came into the stable.

'I have brought a bucket of water for your mare.'

'Thank you, but there was no need,' she told him coldly. 'What have you done with Mr Styles's bay?'

'I have returned him and paid Styles handsomely for the loan of his horse.'

'And now you are back to plague me.'

'That is not my intention. I beg your pardon.'

She sighed. 'No, I beg *yours*, Mr Arrandale. You are my father's guest and I have behaved very badly to you.'

'That is understandable, if you think me a murderer.'

'Papa believes you are innocent.'

'But you do not, do you?

She eased herself out of Bonnie's stall only to find him blocking her way. She knew he would not move until she gave him an answer.

'I do not know *what* to believe. You…' She locked her fingers together. 'You frighten me.'

'I do not mean to.'

He took her hands. His grasp was gentle, but it conveyed the strength of the man. Odd that she should find that so comforting.

'Believe me, Miss Duncombe, I mean you no harm.'

'No?' She looked up at him. 'But just your being here might harm us. Harbouring a criminal is an offence, I believe.'

'Is that why you said nothing to Sir Loftus?'

Was it? She didn't know any more.

He was still holding her hands and gazing down at her with no hint of laughter in his face. Her mouth dried. Suddenly everything seemed sharper, she was aware of the dust motes floating in the band of sunlight pouring in through the window, the soft noises from Bonnie as she munched the hay from the rack, the faint cries of a shepherd and his lad driving their sheep through the village.

Then everything around them faded into nothing. She was aware only of the man holding her hands, his powerful presence calling to something inside. It set her heart pounding so heavily she thought she might faint. His eyes bored into her and, fearing he could read her thoughts, she dragged her gaze away, but only as far as his mouth. Strong, unsmiling, sensual. She wondered what it would be like to have those finely sculpted lips fixed on hers. As if in answer his hands slid up her arms, pulling her closer and she leaned into him, her face turned up to receive his kiss.

It was no gentle, reverential salute, it was rough and demanding and Grace responded instinctively. She clung to him, her lips parted. Following his lead, she let her tongue dip and dance and taste. She felt intoxicated, an explosion of excitement ripped through her, leaving her weak, and when Wolf raised his head to drag in a deep, ragged breath she remained in his arms, her head thrown back against his shoulder, gazing up at him in wonder.

Fear rushed in. With a little cry of alarm Grace pushed herself free and ran from the stable. He overtook her as they reached the house.

'I frightened you, I am sorry,' he murmured, stepping past her to open the door.

She did not pretend to misunderstand him. 'I frightened myself.'

'Grace—'

She put up her hand and shook her head. Tears were very near. 'I am not free to, to *like* you!'

And with that she fled.

Wolf stood and watched her disappear into the house. *Like* him? Like was too mild a word for what had passed between them and he cursed himself for allowing it to happen. He must concentrate on clearing his name. There was no time for dalliance and certainly not with a gently bred vicar's daughter. What if she developed a *tendre* for him? He glanced down at his hand. The weal where her riding crop had caught him was still bright, a testament to the passion he knew she possessed. His mouth twisted. She was one who would love fiercely and he had no wish to break her heart.

He exhaled, the breath whistling out. That would be a dastardly way to repay all the kindness the parson had shown him. No, he had learned all he could in Arrandale and it was time he moved on and forgot all about Miss Grace Duncombe. Closing the door carefully behind him, Wolf went in search of his host.

Grace summoned Betty to help her out of her riding habit. She was still shaking and her lips still burned with the memory of that kiss. It frightened her that she could lose control so easily. Perhaps she was like those wanton women of the Bible such as Jezebel or the daughters of Zion. A dispiriting thought and it made her ask Betty to look out her grey silk. It was her most sober dress, a plain, high-necked gown with long sleeves and only a tiny edging of lace at the neck and cuffs. Even Papa had joked that it made her look like a nun.

Once she was dressed she dismissed Betty and sat down before her looking glass to re-pin her hair, but for some moments she did nothing but gaze at her reflection. There was no doubt she looked very severe. Some months ago Mrs Braddenfield had commented favourably upon the grey silk and in a rare moment of rebellion Grace had put it away, determined never to wear it again. However, this was a necessity, she thought, picking up her hairbrush and dragging it through her hair with quick, jerky movements. She needed to be covered from neck to toe from the glances of men, glances that could bring the blush not only to her cheeks but to her whole body.

Her hand stilled. No, it was not men in general. Loftus had never made her blush in that way. In fact, it had never happened before in all her four-and-twenty years. What was it about Wolfgang Arrandale that caused her pulse to race and the blood to sing in her veins?

'It is because he is so tall,' she told her reflection. 'Not since you were a child have you had to look up to a man. It is a novel experience, and you have allowed your fancy to run away with you.'

Yes, that was it. She finished brushing her hair and quickly pinned it up. It was the novelty of the man. He was so tall and dark and…

'And dangerous.'

Her words echoed around the bedchamber. She had so little experience of the world. Of men like Wolfgang Arrandale. She gave a sigh. Mama had died when she was a baby and Grace had never felt her lack, until now. Now she wished quite fervently that she had a mother to advise her. She glanced at the small writing desk in the corner, where she had tossed her aunt's letter before going out for her ride. Aunt Eliza had stood in place of a mother once, until she had married Mr Graham. Grace had felt bereft then, and a little aggrieved, but her aunt had never stopped loving her. And Aunt Eliza was so much more worldly-wise than Papa. That was the solution. Grace moved across to the writing table and sat down.

Grace went downstairs just in time to go in to dinner. The conversation was desultory while Truscott placed the last of the dishes on the table, but once they were alone Grace braced herself for the inevitable.

'So, Grace,' said her father. 'You know our guest's little secret.'

'Not such a *little* secret, Papa.'

'No, indeed, my dear. I would rather he had not told you, but perhaps you now understand a little better the need for secrecy.'

'I do understand it, Papa, but I could wish Mr Arrandale had not put such a burden upon you.'

'Believe me, Miss Duncombe, if I thought I could trust anyone in Arrandale half so well I would not have done so.'

Enveloped in her grey gown and the width of the dining table between them, Grace thought she might risk a glance at the speaker. A mistake. He looked dark and saturnine in the dim light. There was a pent-up energy about him, like a wild animal poised and ready to spring. Having raised her eyes to his, she found it difficult to look away.

Her father gave one of his mild exclamations.

'My dear sir, I am *glad* you came to me and, despite my earlier concerns, I cannot regret that Grace knows the truth.' He put out his hand to her. 'We have never had secrets from each other, have we, my dear?'

She reached for his fingers and gave them a squeeze. 'No, Papa, we have not. And that reminds me, there is something I have to tell you.' She paused as Truscott and Betty came in to clear away the empty dishes, but only for a moment. After all, what she was going to say was not really a secret. 'I have had a letter from Aunt Eliza.'

'My sister,' Papa explained to their guest. 'She kept house here and looked after us until Grace went off to school. Then she left to get married.'

'I remember Miss Eliza Duncombe from my visits to Arrandale as a boy,' he replied, when the servants had withdrawn again. 'How is she, sir?'

'My sister is a widow now, alas, although her husband provided for her very well. She has a house in Hans Place and lives there very comfortably, I believe.'

Grace nodded. 'Her letters are always cheerful, however I think she is a little lonely since Mr Graham's death a few years ago. You will know, Papa, that whenever she writes she invites me to visit. Indeed, you have been urging me any time these past twelve months to do so.' She took a breath. 'I have just now sent off a note, accepting her invitation. I plan to join her within the week. I hope you do not mind, Papa?'

Grace looked up, expecting surprise from her father and even a little regret that she would be leaving him. She had mustered her arguments: if he said he would be lonely she would point out that he had Mr Arrandale to keep him company, and if he expressed concern at her going away when they had a visitor she would have to explain that she could not be easy in her conscience, harbouring a fugitive.

In the event, her preparations were unnecessary. Papa looked surprised, but only for a moment, then he gave a wide smile.

'Why, that is excellent news, my love. I am delighted for you.'

She gave a sigh of relief. 'I thought perhaps you would wonder at my going now…'

'Not at all, my dear, not at all. In fact, the timing could not be more propitious. You see, Mr Arrandale is off to London, too, so you may travel together.'

Chapter Five

Wolf almost laughed at the look of horror upon Grace's face.

He said drily, 'I think you will find Miss Duncombe's intention in leaving Arrandale is to remove herself from my presence.' He added with a touch of bitterness, 'She does not share your belief in my innocence, sir.'

'That may be,' said the parson, 'but I am sure Grace is as keen as I am to see justice done.'

'Yes,' said Grace. 'Of course, Papa, but...'

'It would be quite ridiculous for you to travel to London separately. Why, you would be following one another within a matter of days, and what is the sense in that? And, Grace, I would be much happier to know you had a gentleman to escort you to your aunt's door.'

'Not if that gentleman is wanted for murder!' Grace looked shocked by her outburst and said immediately, 'I beg your pardon, but I do not need a gentleman to escort me, Papa. I thought I might take Betty.'

The parson laid down his knife and fork. 'And how, pray, do you expect the poor child to get back? Why, she has less sense than a peahen.'

Wolf watched as Grace opened her mouth to protest, then closed it again. He felt a certain sympathy for her.

'I understand your concerns, Miss Duncombe, but your father is right, I had already decided to go to London within the next few days. In fact, we were discussing the matter before dinner. However, I shall not inflict my company upon you if it is so abhorrent.'

'Thank you, sir, but Papa is correct,' came the stiff reply. 'It would be sensible to travel together.'

'Then perhaps a private chaise might be in order.' Wolf saw her brows go up and added coldly, 'The burden for this extravagance would not fall upon your father, my funds are more than sufficient.'

Her response was equally chilly.

'You must excuse me if your dress and your manner of arrival caused me to doubt that.'

'When I landed in England I wanted to attract the least possible attention. Thus I travelled as a gentleman of middling fortune, and with only one portmanteau. Going to London is another matter.' She looked sceptical and, goaded, he went on, 'Be assured, madam, I could hire a dozen private chaises to convey me there if I so wished!'

Wolf clamped his jaws together. He thought he had learned to govern his hot temper, but this woman brought out the worst in him. He wondered if he should apologise to his host, but the parson was unperturbed and helping himself to another portion of lamb from the dish at his elbow.

'Where will you stay, my son? I am sure my sister would put you up.'

'But, Papa, Hans Place is very out of the way. Even Aunt Eliza admits it is not convenient for the fashionable shopping areas such as Bond Street.'

'Do I look as if I wish to shop in a fashionable area?' Wolf retorted. Those dark eyes flashed with anger, but she made no response. He said stiffly, 'Thank you, sir, but I shall arrange my own accommodation when I reach town.'

'As you wish, my boy, but I shall send an express to Eliza, so she may expect you. She would never forgive me if she learned you had been so close and had not visited her.' He sat back. 'Now, if we have all finished shall we retire to the drawing room? I will ask Truscott to serve our brandy there and we can discuss the details of your journey.'

Grace put down her napkin. So she was to be allowed no respite. If only she had not been so precipitate! She had dashed off her reply to her aunt and asked Truscott to send one of the village lads to Hindlesham with it, to catch the night mail. It would look very odd if she were to cry off now.

'Miss Duncombe?'

She heard Wolf Arrandale's voice behind her and realised he was waiting to escort her from the room. There was nothing for her to do but rise and put her fingers on his sleeve.

'This has put you in an awkward situation,' he said as they entered the drawing room. 'If I had not agreed the whole with your father before dinner I might have told him I needed to remain here a little longer.'

'And if I had not been so quick to write to my aunt.' She gave a little smile as she released his arm and walked to a chair beside the fire. 'I fear Fate has conspired against us, sir, and I for one am not disposed to fight it any longer.'

'Will you cry friends with me, then?'

She said cautiously, 'Not friends, but not enemies, either.'

'That will do for me.'

He held out his hand and instinctively she put up her own. She stared at the red mark across his knuckles and said remorsefully, 'That looks very sore.'

'I do not notice it, I assure you.'

'You did not deserve that. I am sorry.'

'Not then, perhaps, but later…'

Grace felt the heat burning up through her again.

'What happened in the stables was not entirely your fault,' she admitted. 'I fear we bring out the worst in each other, Mr Arrandale.'

She thought he was about to agree, but her father walked in and the moment was lost.

Truscott brought in the decanters and they talked of innocuous matters until each had a full glass, brandy for the gentlemen and madeira for Grace. Papa looked askance when she requested it, but she felt in need of something stronger than ratafia to get her through the evening. As soon as Truscott closed the door upon them her father turned to her.

'Now, my dear,' he said, his eyes twinkling. 'We must decide how best to get you two to London. I would not want Sir Loftus to think you were running away like star-crossed lovers.'

Lovers! A shiver of excitement scurried through Grace at the thought. She swallowed and tried to concentrate.

'Indeed not, Papa,' she agreed. 'And, sadly, I do not think we can take Loftus into our confidence.'

'Good heavens, no. A very worthy man, but he is, after all, a magistrate.'

She said awkwardly, 'He has been pressing me to order my wedding clothes, so he will not object to my going to town for that purpose.'

'Have you set a date then, Miss Duncombe?' asked Wolfgang politely.

'No, but Loftus is keen to do so.' She wrapped her hands around the wineglass and stared down at it. 'I shall tell him we will be married as soon as I return from London.'

'An excellent suggestion,' agreed Papa. 'If you will forgive me saying so, my dear, you have kept the poor man waiting quite long enough.'

Grace continued to stare into her glass. She had expected to feel nervous at the thought of getting married, but not this sick, unhappy dread.

Do not think of it, then. Concentrate instead upon getting safely to London.

Wolfgang's deep voice interrupted her thoughts. 'If you will tell me where I can hire a travelling chaise, I will arrange everything.'

'If I might suggest...' She looked up. 'I think we should take the mail coach. Loftus is bound to enquire and he will not expect me to travel by private chaise.'

'Will he not want to escort you himself?'

'I was about to ask that myself.' Papa turned his gaze upon her. 'Is that not a possibility, Grace?'

'Yes. But we could travel on Friday. Loftus will be engaged at Hindlesham market on that day. And...' She paused. 'Perhaps Truscott could drive us to Newmarket. I know the mail picks up from Hindlesham after that, but we need not alight, so there is less chance that anyone would see us, or think that we were travelling together.'

'You are a born conspirator, Miss Duncombe.'

The admiration in Wolf's voice only flayed Grace's conscience even more. Her father declared it an excellent plan and the two men discussed the final arrangements. However, when everything was settled and their guest had retired, Grace remained seated, gazing into the fire and twisting her hands together.

'Something is troubling you, my child.' Her father drew a chair up beside her and reached out to take her hands. 'You do not like this business, do you?'

She shook her head.

'No, Papa, I do not like it. My conscience is not easy. And after what happened to Henry…'

'That is why I was loath to share Mr Wolfgang's secret, my love. I am convinced of his innocence, but I knew for you it would bring back painful memories of Henry's tragic death.'

She shuddered and he gave her hands a comforting squeeze.

'I know it is difficult for you, my love, but when Wolfgang Arrandale came to me for help I could not refuse him.'

'And you truly believe he is innocent?'

'I do, Grace. Even more, I fear someone has deliberately put the blame on him. The tragic events of Mrs Wolfgang's death might have been used to cover the theft of the necklace, but it could be something much more sinister.'

A cold chill ran down Grace's spine.

'He showed me the spot where he found her. Papa, it was directly beneath the balcony. What if…what if he lost his temper with his wife and pushed her over the balcony? It *is* possible, is it not, Papa?'

'Yes, it is possible,' he replied. 'But he has returned here to prove his innocence. Surely that is in his favour?' He gripped her hands. 'He asked for my help, Grace, and I cannot deny him.'

No more can I.

Grace felt a band tighten around her heart. Papa was such a good man he would not think ill of anyone. She was far less sure of her own reasons for wanting to help Wolf Arrandale.

'No, of course not, Papa.' She kissed his cheek. 'Tomorrow I shall see Loftus and tell him I am going to London.'

Grace was not looking forward to her visit to Hindlesham and she delayed it as late as possible the following morning by taking baskets of food to the needy. The last of the baskets was for Mrs Owlet, the widow who had broken her leg. The visit was not strictly necessary and Grace admitted it was an attempt to learn more about the Arrandales, but if she was hoping for reassurance then she was sadly disappointed. When Grace broached the subject the widow was scathing in her condemnation of the family.

'The old man was a villain,' she said, almost spitting with hatred. 'Dying like that and leaving us all to fend for ourselves.'

'He could hardly be blamed for that,' said Grace, recoiling a little from such vehemence.

'His sons are as bad. Rakes, both of 'em. The whole family is damned.'

It was not what Grace wanted to hear.

'Oh, surely not,' she murmured, preparing to take her leave.

The old woman clutched her arm, fingers digging in like claws. 'And the oldest boy, the wife-murderer, well, he's turned out worst of all. He walks with the devil.'

Grace made her excuses at that point and hurried back to the vicarage, but however much she told herself Mrs Owlet was embittered because the Hall had closed and she had lost her position, the words haunted her.

The visit to Hindlesham could be delayed no longer. Grace changed into her riding habit and went to the stableyard, where she found Wolfgang leading out Bonnie.

He walks with the devil.

'You have been busy, so I saddled the mare for you,' he said. 'I thought you would go in the gig, but your father told me you would prefer to ride.'

'He sees no harm in my riding alone here, where I am so well known. Besides, Truscott needed the gig to go to Newmarket and book our places on the mail.'

She allowed him to keep the mare steady while she used the mounting block and he held Bonnie while Grace arranged her skirts.

'Thank you.'

She gathered up the reins, but he did not release the mare.

'No,' he said quietly. 'Thank *you*, Miss Duncombe. I appreciate what you are doing for me.'

'For my father,' she corrected him. She glanced around to make sure they were alone. 'He believes you are innocent.'

'And you do not?'

His look sent the butterflies fluttering inside again.

She knew where this man was concerned her heart was ruling her head. The only defence she could summon up was anger.

'I would rather not think of you at all, Mr Arrandale!'

He nodded and stepped away from the mare's head. 'Do not tarry, Miss Duncombe. It looks like rain.'

Grace trotted out of the yard, resisting the temptation to look back. One more day and she would not have to see Wolfgang Arrandale again. A few weeks in London with Aunt Eliza, then she would return and marry Loftus. Safe, dependable Loftus. The marriage settlements had been agreed: they would secure her future and that would be a great comfort to Papa.

It would be a comfort to her, too. It had to be. Her betrothal was a promise to marry and she had been raised to believe a promise was sacred.

Once they reached open ground, Grace set Bonnie galloping, but for once the exhilaration of flying over the moor did not banish everything else from her mind. If Wolfgang was innocent, as her father believed, then she prayed he would be able to prove it. But what then? Would he return to his old rakehell life, or would he marry and settle down at Arrandale? That would be an advantage for the parish and it was what her father wanted, so she should want it, too. After all, it could make no difference to her. She would be married to Loftus and living at Hindlesham.

As if conjured by her thoughts the manor house appeared ahead of her and she was momentarily daunted by the necessity of explaining her sudden departure to her fiancé. Grace sat a little straighter in the saddle. It must be done, there was no going back now.

* * *

Upon her return to the vicarage Grace ran upstairs to change before going in search of her father. She found him in his study with Wolfgang. They rose when she entered, her father exclaiming in some alarm, 'My dear, never tell me you rode back from Hindlesham in this rain?'

'I was obliged to do so, Papa, unless I wanted to remain at the manor all day.' She smiled. 'Do not fret, sir, Betty has taken my riding habit to dry it in the kitchen and apart from my hair still being a little wet, I am perfectly well, I assure you.'

'Nevertheless, you should sit by the fire,' said Wolfgang, vacating his chair for her.

'Yes, you must,' agreed her father. 'I cannot have you catching a chill. How did you get on at the manor?'

Grace sank down gratefully and held her hands out to the flames.

'Fortune favoured me,' she said. 'Loftus has gone to Cambridge and will not be back until late, so I spoke to his mother. I did not rush away, Papa, I was not so impolite. Miss Oswald, her companion, has returned from visiting her sister in Kent and we spent a pleasant hour conversing together.'

'Oswald?' Wolf looked up. 'Dr Oswald's daughter?'

'Yes. She kept house for her father, but when he died several years ago she was left with very little to live on. Papa knew Mrs Braddenfield was seeking a companion and he suggested Claire for the post,' Grace explained. 'Miss Oswald virtually runs the manor and is sincerely attached to her employer. They deal extremely well together. Much better than I shall ever do!'

She ended with a rueful laugh, but her father did not notice.

'There was some speculation that she and Sir Loftus would make a match of it when his wife died,' he said. 'But instead he turned his attention to Grace.'

'Does she resent you?' Wolf asked her.

'I hope not. She is a sensible woman and we get on very well.'

'I am glad,' he said. 'She could make life uncomfortable for you when you are married. I would not like to think of you being unhappy.'

Grace looked up quickly. The idea that he should care about her future was unsettling. She pushed herself out of the chair.

'If you will excuse me, I had best go and pack.'

'Would you not like to sit by the fire a little longer?' asked her father. 'Your hair is still damp.'

Grace shook her head. Much as she liked the warmth of the blazing fire she needed to be away from Wolfgang Arrandale. She needed to decide how best to deal with him and the confusing feelings he aroused in her.

Wolf noted that Grace was subdued at dinner, and as soon as the meal was over she announced that she was going out.

'Must you?' Mr Duncombe glanced towards the window. 'Your hair is barely dry from this morning's soaking.'

'It is not raining very hard now, Papa, and there is a visit I must pay. Perhaps Mr Arrandale would escort me.'

The parson's brows went up, but he was not nearly as surprised as Wolf. It was the last thing he expected, but he rose at once.

'Of course,' he said. 'Give me a moment to fetch my greatcoat from the garret.' He hurried away, returning moments later to find Grace waiting for him at the door, her heavy cloak about her shoulders. He said, as they stepped outside, 'I have taken the liberty of borrowing your father's umbrella. It is sufficiently wide for two.'

He offered her his arm, noting the tiny pause before she rested her fingers on his sleeve. The rain was little more than a fine drizzle as they set off and since there was no wind the umbrella kept them both dry.

'Where are we going?'

She lifted the spring flowers she was holding in her free hand. 'To the church.'

The High Street was deserted. Doors were closed against the chill of a damp spring evening and the smell of woodsmoke pervaded the air. Wolf felt a definite lightening of his spirits. She had invited him to come with her. How normal it seemed to be walking along with Grace at his side, how *right*.

'You are standing too tall, sir. Do not give yourself away!'

The urgent whisper reminded him that he was a fugitive with a price on his head. Every hint of pleasure fled as bitterness and regret welled up. He wanted to rail against the world for the injustice of it but really, who was there to blame but himself? He had been a wild youth and the world was only too ready to believe he had capped his misdemeanours by murdering his wife.

Turning that around would take a miracle and Wolf did not believe in miracles.

It did not take them long to reach the churchyard. Grace dropped his arm and went before him, taking a narrow path between the graves. It was barely raining now and Wolf closed the umbrella. She had stopped beside one of the headstones when he came up to her.

'Your mother,' he said, reading the inscription.

'Yes. I never knew her, she died when I was a babe, but I come here to pay my respects, especially if I am going away.'

She stooped to lay a bunch of flowers at the base of the stone and paused for a moment, resting her gloved fingers on the carved lettering. Wolf was silent, unwilling to intrude upon what was clearly a private moment and wondering why she had invited him to join her. When she rose he noticed that she was still carrying flowers.

'Two bunches, Miss Duncombe?'

'Yes. This way.'

She led the way to a far corner of the graveyard where a small, square stone marked a plot beneath an ancient yew tree, whose overhanging branches made the twilight so deep that Wolf had to bend close to read the inscription.

'"Henry Hodges. Curate of this parish. Twenty-six years."'

'My fiancé.' She placed the flowers on his grave and straightened. 'He died five years ago. We were going to be married at Christmas, on my nineteenth birthday.'

Wolf knew he should say something consoling. Instead he found himself asking her how he had died. She did not answer immediately, she was staring fixedly at the grave and he wondered if she had heard him.

'Violently,' she said at last, her voice very low. 'Henry was on his way home late one evening after visiting a sick parishioner. He saw a w-woman being attacked, robbed. Henry intervened and…and was stabbed.' She shook, as if a tremor had run through her. 'He was brought to the vicarage, but we could not save him. He died in my arms.'

Wolf struggled not to reach out to her. He said curtly, 'And the man who killed him?'

'Hanged. Not that I wanted that.'

'You could forgive him, after what he had done?'

'Not forgive, no. But I did understand.' She took a deep breath. 'My father spoke for the man at the trial. He was one of our parishioners and Papa said he had been a good man, a stable hand at the Hall until it closed. Since then years of poverty and want had driven him to despair.'

'Is that why you wanted me to accompany you? That I might more fully appreciate the harm my family did by closing the Hall?'

'No. You are not responsible for that. As I understand it your father's profligate ways had long made the estate's downfall inevitable.' Her dark, troubled gaze was fixed on him. 'I wanted you to understand that my heart is here, with Henry. Anything else is just…just earthly desire.' She turned and began to retrace her steps, saying over her shoulder, 'That k-kiss. It should not have happened. I should not have allowed it.'

So that was it. She was warning him off. Not that there was any reason to do so, he had already decided Grace Duncombe was a complication he did not need in his life.

'Sometimes these things catch one out,' he replied lightly.

'Apparently so.' She glanced at him. 'I wanted to explain, before we set off for London tomorrow. I do not hold you wholly responsible for what occurred in the stable, and…and I want to think no more about it.'

'Consider it forgotten, Miss Duncombe.' A few fat

drops of rain splashed on the path and he raised his umbrella again. 'Shall we go back now?'

Grace took his arm and Wolf led her back to the vicarage, wondering why he did not feel more relieved that she was in no danger of losing her heart to him.

It was almost twenty miles to Newmarket and Grace spent the journey squeezed between Wolfgang and Truscott, in a gig only intended for two people. Wolfgang rested one arm along the back of the seat to make more room for her, but it felt to Grace as if he had his arm *around* her. She tried not to lean against him, but it was impossible to sit bolt upright for the whole time, and as the gig bowled along the road through the early morning darkness the rocking motion made her sleepy. At one point she awoke to find herself snuggled against him. When she tried to sit up his arm pulled her gently back against his shoulder.

'Hush now,' he murmured into her hair. 'Truscott needs room to handle the reins, even though the horse sees the road better than he does.'

And Grace allowed herself to believe him. She sank back against his convenient shoulder and dozed contentedly until they reached their destination.

A grey dawn was just breaking when they alighted at the inn, but even at that early hour the place was bustling. Grace was thankful that they could go into the dining room, where a few coins soon procured them two cups of scalding coffee.

It put new heart into her, so much so that she could almost forget her embarrassment at having virtually slept in Wolfgang's arms. She looked up to ask him what time the mail was due in and found he was gazing at her. A slow, lazy smile curved his lips.

Two thoughts raced through her head. She could not remember him smiling, really *smiling* before. And how much she wanted to smile back. That would never do, one could not share smiles with a suspected murderer!

She said crossly, 'Pray sir, why are you laughing at me?'

He immediately begged pardon but that only made her glare at him.

'What were you thinking?' she asked suspiciously.

'That no other woman of my acquaintance has ever looked as neat as you do at this ungodly hour.'

'Any woman of sense would be in bed at this hour.'

'There is that, of course.'

Grace had answered without thinking, but his response made her choke on her coffee and a blush of mortification burned her cheeks.

'You should not say such things,' she told him, wiping coffee from her lips.

'Why not? I was complimenting you on your appearance.'

She was not deceived by his innocent reply, but decided it would be wiser not to pursue the subject. She heard the laugh in his voice when he spoke again.

'I know you are trying to maintain a dignified silence, but you have coffee on your cheek. Here, let me.'

He reached across, cupping her chin with his fingers and drawing his thumb gently across her cheek. Grace wanted to close her eyes and rest her face against his hand. When she looked at Wolfgang there was no mistaking the heat in his gaze. Her breath stopped. She could not look away, his eyes were violet-black in the lamplight and they seemed to pierce her very soul.

'London mail!'

The landlord's strident call broke the spell. Grace looked up to find the dining room had emptied.

'You'd best be quick,' the landlord warned them, standing by the door. 'The mail don't wait for no one.'

Wolf rose and put his hand under her elbow. 'Come along, Miss Duncombe.'

She would have liked to shake him off but really, she was not at all sure that her legs would support her.

There were only two places left in the mail coach. Grace took the window seat and Wolf climbed in to sit beside her. She pulled her cloak about her. At least she could lean into the corner of the carriage. There would be no need for her to fall asleep on his shoulder, as she had done in the gig.

Soon they were rattling over the open road, swaying and jolting so much there was no chance for Grace to rest, she was afraid her head would crash against the window.

'This 'un's a bone-shaker and no mistake.' A motherly woman sitting opposite grinned at her. 'Never you mind, dearie, the road is a vast deal better on t'other side of Hindlesham, you wait and see.'

Grace nodded. She hoped so, for she had no idea how she would endure a whole day's travel.

By the time they reached Hindlesham the sun was creeping over the horizon. As they clattered through the streets, two of the passengers began to gather up their things ready to alight at the Golden Lion. The coach swept into the inn yard and even before it stopped the

ostlers came running to change the horses. The early
morning sun was low enough to shine through the arch
and on to the side of the coach where Grace was sitting,
illuminating her through the window. She decided that
as soon as the passengers had alighted she would change
seats, but even as the motherly woman heaved herself
out of the door Grace spotted Claire Oswald standing
in the yard and knew she had been recognised. It would
be pointless to move now. Claire waved and came up to
the open door.

'I wondered if you would be here, Miss Duncombe.
When I did not see you in the coffee room I thought
perhaps I had been mistaken and you were catching the
night mail.'

Claire was looking rather fixedly at Wolfgang and
Grace sat forward to block her view.

'Good morning, Miss Oswald.' She glanced around
the yard, hoping she did not sound as anxious as she felt.
'Is Sir Loftus with you?'

'No, he is busy in the market. Mrs Braddenfield had a
letter for the mail and I said I would deliver it.'

The ostlers had finished their work and the shout went
up to stand clear. Miss Oswald stepped back.

'I wish you a good journey, Miss Duncombe.'

The door slammed and Grace waved through the glass
as the coach began to pull away.

'Well, that was unfortunate,' murmured Wolfgang. 'I
presume that was Claire Oswald.'

'Yes.'

The other passengers were busy making themselves
comfortable and did not appear to be taking any notice,
but Grace was wary of saying more.

* * *

She and Wolfgang passed the rest of the journey in near silence and when they eventually alighted at Bishopsgate the sun had already set. Grace stood in the yard with her small trunk at her feet and feeling bone-weary.

She said, trying to be cheerful, 'I would not have believed sitting down all day could make one so tired.'

'We have a little further to go yet,' Wolf warned her. 'Wait here while I find someone to take us to Hans Place.'

'There really is no need for you to accompany me across London,' she replied. 'You had much better find yourself lodgings.'

'I promised your father I would see you safely to your aunt's house.'

There was a note of finality in his voice and Grace did not argue. If truth were told she was too tired to make the effort. However, as she waited for him to find a cab she remembered something that had been nagging her at the outset of the journey and once they were in the hired carriage she asked him the question.

'The lady we saw at Hindlesham, Miss Oswald. Can you remember meeting her when you were at Arrandale? She looked at you most particularly.'

He frowned.

'I do not think so. I was rarely at Arrandale before my marriage. My father decided that the future heir should be born at the Hall. Having chosen my wife for me, he thought he was entitled to rule my life.'

'Chosen? Did you not have any opinion?'

'Oh, yes, I had far too many opinions! But I always knew I would have to knuckle down some time. Florence Sawston came from a good family and brought a fortune with her. It was a provident match and approved by both families. When it was clear she was carrying our child it seemed sensible to move to Arrandale and acquaint myself with my inheritance, but Father and I had never dealt well together. It was a disaster. He saw my attempts to familiarise myself with the running of the estate as interference, every suggestion was scorned. I was a dissolute wastrel with no idea what was due to my name.' His lip curled. 'And that from a man who had lived for years on the profits of Arrandale, squandering his money on mistresses, gambling and high living. It was clear almost as soon as I moved in that we could not work together. We could never meet without arguing.'

'That must have been very uncomfortable for your wife,' she murmured.

Wolf gave a bark of laughter, but there was little humour in it.

'Florence thrived on conflict. She was an expert at stirring the coals, setting me even more at odds with my father. Sometimes I think it was a match made in hell.'

'And your mother, did she not support you?'

'My mother was only interested in her own comforts. Richard and I had learned long ago not to worry her with our concerns.'

'I am sorry. I cannot imagine how it must be to live in a house of strife.'

'Do not pity me, madam. It was a bed of my own making. Arrandales are masters of it, we go through life raking hell, so we should not complain when we get burned.'

Grace wanted to reach out to him, to comfort the lonely boy he must have been and the angry, wayward young man growing up without a parent's love. She gripped her hands tightly together in her lap. Ten years in exile had made him bitter and he would not want her comfort, or her sympathy.

And whatever Papa said, she was not even sure that he deserved it.

They came to a halt and by the light of the streetlamps Grace could see they were in a square surrounded by terraces of tall, new buildings. As they alighted from the cab the door of one of the houses was thrown open and Aunt Eliza came flying out.

'Dear Grace, how happy I am to see you and in such good time, too. I have been looking out for you this past hour, but I really did not expect you to arrive so soon. Come in, my dear, come in. And Mr Peregrine, too. Come in, sir, we cannot welcome you properly while we are standing on the street!'

Wolf thought it was like being taken up by a small whirlwind. Mrs Graham ushered them inside, talking all the time and never pausing until they were in the welcome warmth of her elegant drawing room.

'Now then, a little refreshment. Jenner, fetch the tray, if you please.'

'Thank you, ma'am, but I will not stay,' said Wolf. 'I came only to see Miss Duncombe delivered safely to you. The cab is waiting.'

'Nonsense, Mr…Peregrine.' She was smiling and looking at him with a decided twinkle in her sharp eyes. 'My brother mentioned that you were an old acquaintance and I see it now. Yes, I remember you very well, sir, and I will not allow you to go anywhere else tonight. You shall stay here, as my guest. No, not another word. I insist. Jenner, send Robert to pay off the cabbie and fetch in Mr Peregrine's bags. He is to take them to the blue room, if you please, and do you bring in the refreshments.

Wine, I think, and a little bread and butter. Unless you would like Cook to find you something hot for supper?'

Wolf shook his head and Grace said politely, 'Thank you, no. We dined on the road.'

'Oh, I should have had Jenner take your greatcoat, sir, but never mind, take it off and throw it over the chair over there, with Grace's cloak, then come and sit by the fire, do.'

The lady was already pulling Grace down on to a sofa beside her, so Wolf took a chair opposite. He glanced at the door, to make sure it was firmly shut.

'So you know me, Mrs Graham?'

'Lord bless you, sir, I remember you very well,' came the cheerful reply. 'You were always in a scrape as a boy and it seems to me that nothing has changed.'

'I fear this time it is more than a scrape, ma'am—' He broke off as the butler returned.

'Yes, well,' said his hostess, 'we will discuss everything as soon as we are settled comfortably. Thank you, Jenner, that will be all. I shall ring when I need you again.' She paused just long enough for the butler to withdraw before saying, 'Now, why has my niece brought you to London, Mr Wolfgang?'

'I did not bring him, Aunt!'

'I have come to find my late wife's dresser,' he said, when Mrs Graham waved aside Grace's indignant protest. 'I believe she may be able to help me discover the truth about my wife's death and the theft of the Sawston diamonds.'

'And about time, too.'

'You believe he is innocent, Aunt?'

Wolf winced at Grace's surprised tone. It was clear what she thought of him.

'Those of us acquainted with Wolfgang Arrandale as a boy know he is no villain, my love.' Mrs Graham turned her eyes towards him and added drily, 'However, from what I heard of the situation at the Hall ten years ago, I could understand if you *had* murdered your wife.'

'You are frank indeed, madam! I did not do so, however.'

'And how do you intend to prove it?'

'I need to find out what happened to the necklace. Its loss was reported by my wife's dresser. I know Meesden came to London after my wife's death and set herself up in a little shop. She could not have done so on the salary my wife paid her.'

'And where is this shop?' asked Mrs Graham. 'Perhaps we could help you find this woman.'

'Aunt, no!' exclaimed Grace.

'Thank you, ma'am, but your niece came here to get away from me,' said Wolf.

'I am sorry, sir, if I appear unfeeling, but—'

'Not at all, Miss Duncombe, I understand that I have put you in a difficult situation.' He turned back to Mrs Graham. 'I will accept your hospitality for tonight, ma'am, but only for tonight.'

'My dear sir—'

He cut off the widow's protests with a shake of his head.

'You are very kind, madam, but your brother has already put himself at considerable risk to help me. I must pursue my enquiries alone.' He glanced at Grace, who was stifling a yawn. 'I fear we have exhausted Miss Duncombe. We have been travelling since dawn, you see.'

As he had hoped, Mrs Graham was immediately distracted.

'Oh, of course. Poor Grace, you have scarcely eaten a crumb. You must be ready for your bed. I will take you up immediately and send Robert to show our guest to his room.'

Wolf rose to bid the ladies goodnight and when they had left the room he sank wearily back in his chair. Mrs Graham's unquestioning belief in his innocence had lifted his spirits, but now he felt exhausted and not just from the physical exertion of the journey. It had been a trial to maintain the polite, distant friendliness with Grace in front of their fellow passengers. Several times they had started a conversation, only to break off the moment it became interesting, aware that they were not alone. Which was a pity, because they had much in common, if only they could talk. He closed his eyes. The only time he had spoken freely was in the cab to Hans Place. For a moment he had let down his guard and given her a glimpse of his early life. He should not have done so, because if there was one thing he was certain of, it was that he did not want Grace Duncombe to pity him.

Grace followed her aunt to a pretty yellow guest chamber at the front of the house. A good fire burned in the hearth and Aunt Eliza left her with Janet, the maid appointed to attend her, promising to look in a little later, to make sure she had everything she required. Grace felt herself relaxing. She had fulfilled her own and her father's obligations to Wolfgang Arrandale. She could let him go with a clear conscience. And she had no duties here. All that was expected of her was that she should enjoy herself. She was determined to do so; she would take a little holiday before she returned to the vicarage and her wedding to Sir Loftus.

* * *

When her aunt knocked softly on the door a little while later Grace was propped up against the bank of pillows, reading one of the novels thoughtfully provided for her entertainment.

'May I come in, my love? I wanted to make sure you were comfortable.'

'Extremely comfortable, Aunt, thank you.'

'Good, good.' Aunt Eliza shut the door and came across to stand by the bed. 'I am so pleased that you are come to stay at last. But I was a *little* surprised at the speed of your reply. I hope there is nothing wrong at home?' She added quickly, 'I know your father must be in good health or you would not have left him. But…is all well between you and Sir Loftus?'

'Why, yes.' Grace carefully placed a bookmark on her page and closed her book. 'In fact, that is the reason for my coming to London, to buy my bride clothes. Will you help me?'

'Nothing would give me greater pleasure, my dear.' Aunt Eliza fell silent. She sat on the edge of the bed and plucked at a loose thread in the embroidered coverlet. 'What Mr Wolfgang said, about you coming to London to escape him…'

'When I learned his identity I was uneasy about his presence at the vicarage,' said Grace. 'There is a reward offered for his capture, you know.'

'Yes, I did know that, my love. It must have been very difficult for you, engaged as you are to Sir Loftus.'

Grace nodded. 'Papa is convinced of Mr Arrandale's innocence, but you know my father is so good he cannot believe ill of anyone.'

'Titus is so unworldly I wonder more people do not

take advantage of him,' replied Mrs Graham frankly. 'However, in this instance I agree with him. Wolfgang Arrandale was always a wild boy, but I think it was more an attempt to gain his parents' attention rather than any inherent wickedness. His father was much worse in his day and, unlike dear Titus, Mr Arrandale could never see *good* in anyone, even his own sons. As I understand it he was convinced Wolfgang had murdered his wife and shipping him off to France only helped to confirm the boy's guilt.' She sighed. 'It is very commendable of Mr Wolfgang to come back now and try to find out the truth, but it was all so long ago. I fear he is unlikely to succeed.'

'I pray that he does, Aunt,' said Grace earnestly.

'Yes, I hope so too, my love, but if not…well, we must not let it concern us overmuch. These great families all have their trials and tribulations.' She leaned forward to kiss Grace's cheek. 'Now, you must rest and in the morning we will decide just what bride clothes you should have!'

Chapter Six

The noise from the square woke Grace. Carriages rattled on the cobbles, hawkers shouted and there was the faint ring of hammers. She smiled. Aunt Eliza's letters had mentioned the incessant building work taking place as London expanded.

She dressed quickly and made her way downstairs, where she found her aunt at breakfast. She was not alone, a pug dog with an incongruous collar of sparkling gems was on the floor beside her, eating pieces of ham and chicken from a silver dish. Aunt Eliza smiled when she saw Grace.

'Meet Nelson. I bought him as a companion when dear Mr Graham died. He is named after our heroic admiral.'

Grace looked at the overweight little dog snuffling in the dish and wondered if the heroic admiral would consider it a compliment.

'Mr Peregrine was up betimes and is even now preparing to leave,' her aunt continued, with a warning glance towards the butler. 'I was a little concerned that the poor young man might be a little, indigent, but he assures me he has sufficient funds. One would never think it, to look at him.'

Grace was silent while Jenner served her with coffee and bread rolls.

She said, as the door closed behind him, 'He paid for everything on the journey here, ma'am, including the tickets. I believe he made his present fortune abroad, although it might be unwise to enquire too closely into his methods of acquiring it,' she added darkly.

'Very true! The boy was always a scapegrace. My dear, what is the matter? You are looking very censorious.' Aunt Eliza put down her cup. 'Pray do not say you have grown into one of those disapproving females who finds no fun in anything.'

Grace waved her hand, unable to express herself. How was she to explain the confusion she felt about Wolfgang Arrandale? There was a darkness about him. It was like an aura. She had felt it from the first moment they had met. He had lived outside the law for so many years that perhaps he no longer knew the difference between right and wrong. He reminded her of an animal, a panther, lithe, alert and ready to spring. He was dangerous, she knew it in every fibre of her being. He fascinated her and that was dangerous too.

Her aunt sighed.

'You were such a lively little girl, Grace. You were forever climbing trees and tearing your gown, reading books full of knights and princes, always looking for adventure. What happened to that love of life, my dear?'

'I grew up,' Grace replied stiffly. 'And I am now engaged to a Justice of the Peace.'

When she had finished breakfast Grace took her reading book into the drawing room, but she left the door open, and as soon as she heard Wolfgang's deep voice in the hall she went out.

'So it is time for you to leave us, sir.'

'It is.' He turned to her. 'I am very grateful to your family for your hospitality. You need not be polite and say it was nothing. I am aware it was a great deal.'

'No more than any Christian would do,' she murmured. 'Shall we see you again?' The enormity of the task he had set himself filled Grace with dread and she had to ask, 'What will you do, if you are not successful?'

He shrugged. 'Go abroad again. Make a new life elsewhere.'

She put out her hand. 'I wish you good fortune in your endeavours, sir.'

'And I wish you good fortune in your marriage, Miss Duncombe.'

She watched as he raised her fingers to his lips, a last chance to memorise every detail of that darkly handsome face, then he was gone.

Wolf heard the door behind him close as he walked away. It was a sound he had heard many times in his career, physically and metaphorically. As a wild young man, respectable mamas had shut their doors on him to protect their daughters, even though those daughters were only too eager to fall into his arms. Friends of his schooldays had turned their backs on him when his exploits became too outrageous, so he had entered doors that were never closed to a rich young man, those belonging to ladies who lived in discreet little houses in Covent Garden, the less reputable gambling dens and the dingy drinking taverns, where the night invariably ended in a bloody brawl. The only one that had ever hurt was the door to his father's study, resolutely shut upon his sons unless they were hauled in for a reprimand. Even the beating that regularly ensued was preferable to the cold indifference his parents usually showed him. They saw him as a commodity, a means of continuing the family name, and Wolf was mostly referred to as a confounded nuisance. And his father believed him capable of murder.

Wolf felt the familiar black depression creeping over him. It had overwhelmed him during those early years in exile when his innocence seemed far less important than the shame he had brought on the family. He had decided then that it was his turn to shut the door. He made it clear he wanted to hear nothing more about England and the Arrandales. He had gone his own way, survived, prospered by fair means or foul and had expected to spend the rest of his life wandering through Europe as Monsieur Georges Lagrasse. Until last winter, when he had learned he had a daughter.

Florence. Named after her mother. Did she look like her namesake, or was she a dark, thin child, as he had been? Was she happy? It was most likely she did not know what had happened to her mother, for she was only a child, but that would change. When she grew up and took her place in society the gossip mongers would not hesitate to drag up all the sordid details of her parents' tempestuous marriage and its tragic end.

When he had learned of his daughter's existence he had realised it was impossible to shrug off all responsibility for the past. He must prove his innocence. If he could not do so then she, too, would find that many doors were closed to her, save those of generous, kind-hearted people like the Duncombes.

The thought brought him back to Grace. She would

not close her door to his daughter, he was sure, but he wanted her to know he was innocent, too. The thought took hold; he imagined how it would be to have her trust him. Perhaps even to like him. He remembered when she had come upon him washing himself at the kitchen pump, the hectic flush that had disturbed her calm serenity. Even now the thought made him smile. She was such an innocent he doubted she had ever seen a naked chest before! She had been shocked, but not frightened.

He had wanted to pull her against him then and there, so she could feel his skin against her breast while he kissed that luscious mouth. And later, in the stable, he had allowed himself to give in to temptation. Why, he had no idea. She was not his type at all, far too tall and willowy for his taste. And far too respectable. Dammit, he didn't *like* good women!

But there was no denying that he wanted her approval. Wolf gave a little grunt of annoyance. It made no sense. She was about to be married to a man as good and respectable as Wolf was bad. But he could not bear the thought of her thinking ill of him.

Wolf emerged on to Sloane Street and moved his portmanteau to the other hand, looking for a cab to hire. He must not allow thoughts of Grace Duncombe to distract him, nor could he afford to give in to the melancholia that had paralysed him for those first few years in France. He needed to find out the truth of what had happened at Arrandale Hall ten years ago. He had to right some of the wrongs that had been caused by his long absence.

A battered hackney carriage slowed in response to his signal. He gave the driver directions to his lawyers' offices in the city and climbed in. His investigations could take months and it might all come to nought. He must forget all about Miss Grace Duncombe and her family.

Two weeks later he was back in Hans Place, pacing up and down on the expensive Aubusson carpet in Mrs Graham's drawing room and anxiously chewing his lip. This was hard. He had sworn he would not return, but he needed help and could think of no one else.

When Jenner came to tell Grace that 'Mr Peregrine' was waiting downstairs in the drawing room, she could not stop the sudden, soaring elation. She had tried to put Wolf from her mind, but he was there, at her shoulder every waking moment. Even in her dreams. She had known him such a short time, but it felt like for ever. In the two weeks since she had last seen him she had gone over and over every moment they had spent together, every look, every word and now she was quite certain he had not killed his wife. Such certainty was quite unreasonable, but in her defence, Papa and Aunt Eliza were both convinced of his innocence, too, and they had known him for much longer. After ten years there was only the smallest of chances he could clear his name, so she had to reconcile herself to never seeing him again, but it was very hard.

Not that they could ever be anything other than friends. She was about to become Lady Braddenfield and as such, even if Wolf did clear his name and return to Arrandale, they would rarely meet. But for the moment, just the thought of seeing him again was enough to raise her spirits. She ran to her looking glass and patted her hair, but what she saw there gave her pause. She must not show Wolf this glowing face. He might misunderstand

and think that she cared for him, that she could offer him more than friendship. Schooling her countenance to show only cautious reserve, she went slowly downstairs.

Wolf's heart lurched when Grace entered the room. She looked more beautiful than ever in a pale-blue redingote over her cream gown. A matching bonnet swung from its ribbons held in the fingers of one hand. She did not smile at him and her dark eyes still held that wary look.

'I am afraid my aunt is out, *Mr Peregrine*.' Jenner had deliberately left the door open, but after a brief hesitation she closed it before turning to look at him. 'You have not yet succeeded, then.'

'No.' He took another turn across the carpet and came back to stand before her. 'I need help.' Her brows rose a fraction. 'I need the help of a lady,' he explained. 'A lady of unimpeachable reputation.'

She stared at him for a moment, then walked back to the door. She was going to refuse. She was going to ask him to leave. Why should he be surprised? He had no right to expect more help from her.

'Then to preserve my unimpeachable reputation we should not remain in here alone. I was about to take my aunt's dog for a walk. Will you join me?'

'Of course.'

He followed her into the hall and watched her place the straw bonnet over her curls, tying the ribbons beneath one ear in a jaunty bow, quite at variance with her solemn look. The tip-tap of clawed feet on the marble floor made him turn. A wooden-faced footman was leading a small and very ugly lapdog into the hall.

'Thank you, Robert.' Grace took the lead from the footman. 'Come along, Nelson, it is time for your walk.'

'Nelson!' Wolf could not help the exclamation.

'Yes.' There was a definite twinkle in her deep-blue eyes now. 'Shall we go?'

They stepped across the road to the railed garden in the middle of the square.

'As you can see, the gardens are very new,' she said. 'Once all the houses have been built I am sure it will become much busier, but presently there are very few of us who use this area. It is ideal for walking Nelson. I like to bring him out for an airing at least twice a day. My aunt indulges him dreadfully.'

He glanced down at the little pug waddling beside her.

'So I can see,' he muttered.

'He was much fatter than this when I arrived and wheezed most horribly. My next task is to convince my aunt to exercise him. I think it would be beneficial to them both.'

'You have changed.'

'Changed, sir? I should think so. My aunt has been spoiling me, buying me I do not know how many new gowns.'

'No, it's not that.' He frowned. 'You are less...' *Repressed,* he wanted to say. *Not so starched up. Not so prim and proper.* Impossible. 'You are more cheerful.'

'Perhaps that is because I no longer have a wanted man under my roof.'

'Is that it? Did you feel the weight of my presence so very much?'

She shook her head, a smile lilting on her generous mouth.

'No, that is not the whole of it, but I could not help teasing you a little. As you teased me, did you not?'

'I did and I point to this as proof of how different you are. You never laughed at me in Arrandale.'

'No.'

'Has being in London made you so much happier?'

'I was not unhappy in Arrandale,' she said quickly. 'Merely in need of a holiday.'

'Are you regretting your betrothal to Sir Loftus?'

'Not at all.'

Her answer was a little too quick. He said, 'But you do not love him.'

'You know I do not. But there is affection and respect. That is a good foundation for a happy marriage.'

Perhaps, thought Wolf. It was certainly something he had never had in his own marriage.

'You said you needed my help,' she prompted him.

'Yes.' Where to begin? Now it came to the moment he was loath to continue, to embroil her in his sordid affairs.

'We are alone here, sir, you can speak freely now. Perhaps you should start by telling me what you have been doing for the past two weeks.'

'Perhaps I should. The day I left you I went first to the city, to see my lawyers. Old Mr Baylis was on the point of retiring when I married. His son has now taken over and he is a very different character, I could see that the moment I walked into his office. He would not have acknowledged me, but his two clerks recognised me instantly. He has sworn he will not inform upon me, but I do not know if I believe him. However, I am still a free man at the moment and I have instructed him to draw up papers giving my brother power of attorney. I shall also write to Richard, telling him of the matter, so the rascally lawyer cannot worm out of it.'

They stopped while the pug relieved himself against a convenient bush.

'So three more people now know you are in England.'

'Many more than that. As soon as I arrived in town I looked up my old valet, Kennet. His brother owns a tavern in Bench Lane so he was not difficult to track down. Fortunately he was unhappy with his current situation and delighted to give notice and join me. I also discovered my tailor and my barber are still in business and visited them, but I am confident they will not give me away.' He glanced down at Nelson, who was sniffing at his new Hessians and leaving a slobbery trail across their shiny surface. 'The bootmaker was a different matter. The staff there were all unknown to me, so I thought it prudent to be Mr Peregrine, a rich gentleman from the country, intent on cutting a dash in town.'

And he will certainly do that, thought Grace as they began to stroll on again. Today she had hardly known him for the same man. With his cutaway coat that fitted without a crease across his shoulders, pale pantaloons, tasselled Hessians and a tall beaver hat set at a rakish angle on his head, he looked the epitome of a man of fashion. She had seen any number of them in town, but in her opinion none had looked quite so handsome. She was glad that in the transformation he had not allowed his barber to cut his thick dark hair into the famous Brutus crop, she liked the way it curled over his collar.

Grace quickly pulled herself up. What was she thinking? His appearance was nothing to her. Just as her new style of dress could mean nothing to him. She had objected strongly when Aunt Eliza had taken her to the fashionable modistes in Bond Street, but her aunt had been very persuasive, telling her that it was her duty to look her best.

'A man wants to be proud of his wife, Grace. Soon you will no longer be the parson's daughter, but Lady Braddenfield, a prominent member of the local society. Your neighbours will expect you to bring a little town bronze to Hindlesham. You must not disappoint them.'

To every argument Grace put forward her aunt had an answer and to her final protest, that Aunt Eliza should not be spending her own money on such finery for her niece, she had responded with a clincher.

'And what else should I spend it on, pray? I give generously to charity and I am a great supporter of the Foundling Hospital, but it is not the same as having *family*. You will be doing me a kindness, my love. I have no children of my own to spend my money on, no one except Nelson, and there are only so many diamond-studded collars one can buy for a pug.'

Grace pulled on that diamond-studded collar now as she dragged her attention back to the reason she was walking here with Wolfgang Arrandale.

'And how does your turning into a man of fashion affect me, sir?'

'It doesn't. At least, I needed to smarten myself up. A fashionable gentleman attracts little attention in Bond Street. From the servants at Arrandale I had learned that my wife's dresser, Annie Meesden, bought a milliner's shop there. She told them her uncle had died and left her some money. No one knew quite where the shop was and it took me a week to discover that she is no longer there. The shop failed within a year and Meesden was forced to find work again as a lady's maid. Luckily the registry office that she approached keeps very good records and I was able to trace her to a house in Arlington Street, the home of an elderly widow, one Mrs Payne.

'The problem is, Miss Duncombe, I have been unable to learn anything more. Mrs Payne's staff are very tight-lipped. None of them will impart any information at all, either out of loyalty or for fear of losing their position. Short of keeping vigil outside the house in the hopes of seeing Meesden I am at a stand.'

'Could you not write to this Mrs Payne, or ask your lawyer to do so?' she suggested.

'I did. I sent a letter, posing as Mr Peregrine, which received a terse reply to the effect that Mrs Payne does not correspond with unknown gentlemen and to approach her son, who deals with all her household affairs. I duly wrote to the fellow, only to receive a note from his secretary, saying he is on business in Scotland and will be out of town for several months.'

'And this is why you require a lady of, er, unimpeachable reputation. To contact Mrs Payne.'

'You have it precisely, ma'am.'

'No doubt your acquaintance with such ladies is limited,' she murmured.

'Very limited,' he replied frankly. 'There is no one else in town I can trust with this task, saving yourself. Or your aunt.'

They walked on in silence while Grace considered everything he had told her. She could of course decline to help him. Aunt Eliza would be only too pleased to step into the breach, but her aunt was so garrulous who knew what she might let slip?

Do not make excuses, my girl, you want to do this. Admit it, you have had enough of shopping and paying

*visits to Aunt Eliza's friends. You want a little adventure
before you settle down.*

Grace ignored the demon who whispered such scur-
rilous things in her ear. It was her duty to assist a fellow
creature in need. Papa would understand, he would never
refuse a plea for help. Neither should she.

'So, Miss Duncombe. Will you help me?'

'I will, sir.' She looked across the square. 'I think that
is my aunt's carriage at the door now, which is excellent
timing, for we have completed two full circuits of the
gardens, sufficient exercise for Nelson, and we may now
return to the house. Will you come in and take tea with
us? Then you may tell me all I need to know.'

Grace went to Arlington Street the following afternoon, but her call proved fruitless. In her efforts to look
as respectable as possible Grace took her maid with her,
but even this did not help. The old lady was every bit as
irascible and uncooperative as Wolf had led her to believe
and after less than ten minutes Grace found herself being
shown to the door. As she paused in the hall to collect
her muff and umbrella from her maid, the tomb-like silence was shattered by a series of yaps and a lively little
brown-and-white spaniel dashed up to Grace and began
to fawn about her.

'Lottie, Lottie, come here, you *naughty* dog!'

A flustered maid appeared, saying breathlessly, 'I am
ever so sorry, ma'am. She's ready for her walk, you see,
and that always makes her so lively that she can't help
herself.'

'That is no trouble at all,' said Grace, stooping to fon-
dle Lottie's ears. 'I am sorry if my visit to your mistress
has delayed their walk.'

'Oh, no, ma'am, I always takes Lottie out.' The maid tucked a grey curl back under her cap and bent to scoop up the little dog.

'You are very fortunate to have the park so conveniently close,' said Grace, smiling.

'Oh, yes, ma'am, that we are. I takes Lottie there twice a day. Every morning, afore breakfast and then again about now, so she will sit quiet with the mistress for an hour afore dinner.' With a bob of a curtsy the maid retreated to the nether regions of the house and Grace made her way back to Hans Place. Her aunt pounced on her almost as soon as she walked through the door.

'Well, have you found Meesden?'

'No. All I could discover was that Meesden left Mrs Payne's service two years ago. More than that the lady would not say.'

'Oh, that is annoying,' exclaimed Aunt Eliza. 'I was hoping we would be able to further Mr Wolfgang's investigations. He will be so disappointed to find we have learned nothing.'

'But all is not yet lost,' said Grace. 'I am not prepared to give up yet. Tomorrow I shall take Nelson walking in Green Park!'

Early the following morning Grace lifted the little pug from Aunt Eliza's carriage when it drew up at the edge of the park. She had no idea what time Mrs Payne took breakfast and in preparation for a long vigil she had put a thick cloak over her redingote to keep out the cold and the threatened showers. Nelson was also wearing a woollen coat. Grace thought it made him look like a cushion on legs, but her aunt had insisted that May had not yet begun and Nelson, too, should be protected from the inclement weather.

They were strolling along the Queen's Walk for the second time when Grace saw a small figure in a red flannel cloak emerge from a gate in the wall just ahead, and she had a little brown-and-white spaniel with her.

Fortune favoured Grace, for the maid was walking towards her. Despite Nelson's new exercise regime, she knew that if her quarry had been heading away from them the pug's short legs would never have been able to catch up. Nelson was showing little interest in his surroundings, but the spaniel was very inquisitive and as they drew closer she made prancing overtures towards the pug. Grace feigned a start of surprise and stopped squarely before the maid, blocking the path.

'Oh, surely that is Mrs Payne's little dog. Lottie, is it not?'

'Why, yes, ma'am.'

The maid bobbed a polite curtsy and Grace turned and fell into step beside her, saying with a little laugh, 'How strange that we should meet again so soon. Do you mind if I walk with you? Poor Nelson would be glad of the company, I am sure.'

'Poor Nelson' was doing his best to ignore the spaniel's friendly overtures, but the maid was clearly dazzled by the pug's sparkling collar and could not deny any request his owner might make.

Grace marvelled as she listened to herself chattering on, drawing the maid out by degrees, until she admitted that she had been in Mrs Payne's service for nigh on twenty years.

'Indeed? Then you must be a very loyal and trusted servant,' said Grace. 'Your mistress is fortunate to have you.' She dropped her voice a little. 'In fact, you may be able to help me. You see, the reason I called upon Mrs Payne yesterday was to learn information about her lady's maid. Mrs Meesden.'

'Annie Meesden? Why she's been gone from this house these two years or more.' The maid clapped a hand over her mouth. 'Not that the mistress likes us to talk about these things.'

'I quite understand,' Grace responded smoothly. 'However, Mrs Meesden has applied to me for a position. Mrs Payne made it quite clear to me that all such matters are dealt with by her son, but you see, my dresser has given notice very suddenly and I am *desperate* to replace her. Mrs Meesden seems quite perfect for the role, but she has no references and I should so like to hear some good word of the woman, before I take her into my household.'

The maid had her lips firmly shut and Grace gave a little sigh.

'Your mistress is quite right to insist that you do not give away any secrets, so I will not ask you to say anything. But I am sure you understand my anxiety. Being unmarried and alone I am very anxious to avoid taking on someone who may prove unreliable.' She then turned the subject, talking about such innocuous topics as the weather and the trials of running a house in town.

Goodness, Grace Duncombe, you sound very much like a lonely spinster, desperate for company!

She finally ran out of words and fell silent. Nelson and Lottie chose that moment to move to one side of the path to investigate some interesting smells at the base of a tree. Grace and the maid both stopped and after a moment the maid let out a hiss of breath, as if she had been searching her conscience and had come to a decision.

'I don't see what harm it can do for me to tell you, ma'am,' she burst out. 'Mrs Meesden was turned off, you see. That's why she has no reference from Arlington Street. Rude to Mr Payne, she was, and although the mistress said she was an excellent dresser, she couldn't allow insolence towards her son.'

'No, I should think not,' said Grace, shaking her head. 'Very bad indeed.'

'Well, from what I heard in the servants' hall afterwards, it wasn't the first time she'd been turned off. And she was never married, neither, even though she called herself "Mrs".' The maid was in full flow now and Grace let her talk, she would sift out the important points later. 'Seems she couldn't abide men. Well, that's understandable.' The maid sniffed. 'Being in service can be hard for a woman, ma'am. Some of the tales I've heard would make your hair stand on end and that's the truth. Not that there's anything of that sort at Mrs Payne's house, which is why I've stayed so long. She's a strict mistress and she don't allow no goings on.'

'I am very glad to hear it,' Grace said warmly. As they began to stroll on again she said casually, 'Do you know what became of Mrs Meesden?'

The maid shook her head.

'Bad business, ma'am. I heard she couldn't get another position and is now taking in sewing.'

'Oh, the poor creature,' exclaimed Grace, thinking how far the woman had fallen since being lady's maid at Arrandale. She said, in perfect sincerity, 'I do hope her fortunes can be improved.'

'Ah well, ma'am, p'raps they can be, if you was to take her on, you not having a gentleman in the house for her to take against.'

'Where is she living now, do you know?

'That I don't, ma'am, but Mrs Payne must know, because she sometimes sends gowns to her for mending.'

'That is very charitable.'

The maid gave a snort. 'Not her! It's more that Meesden's the best needlewoman she's ever known. The mistress ain't the charitable sort, for all she's patron of the Foundling Hospital. The Lord helps them as helps themselves, she says.' She looked up guiltily. 'You won't tell the mistress I told you any o' this, will you, ma'am?'

'No, of course not,' replied Grace. They had reached the southern end of the Queen's Walk and she could see her aunt's carriage in the distance.

'Thank you for the information, you have been most helpful.'

The maid was gazing round-eyed at the silver coin Grace had pressed into her hand. 'Ooh, ma'am, I shouldn't—'

'Nonsense, that is for allowing Nelson to have Lottie's company on his morning walk, nothing more,' said Grace, thankful that the two animals were actually walking together quite amicably.

'Yes, yes, of course.' The maid nodded. She added ingenuously, 'But I shan't tell anyone who gave it to me, ma'am.'

'No, that might be best,' said Grace, stifling her conscience. 'You could merely say a lady pressed it upon you, when you gave her directions.'

With another friendly smile Grace scooped Nelson into her arms and set off briskly for the waiting carriage, pleased with her morning's work.

Chapter Seven

Wolf left the premises of Baylis & Thistle and paused on the flagway to pull on his gloves. There was a chill wind blowing and he decided to walk back to town rather than take a cab. The exercise would warm him up after sitting in his lawyer's cold offices for so long. It was not only the building that was cold, he thought grimly, the lawyer's greeting was only marginally warmer than at his first visit two weeks earlier. He knew he should expect nothing else. After all, both the original partners were long dead and young Mr Baylis knew him only as a fugitive from justice. However, the fellow had drawn up the power of attorney as instructed and it was signed now, so whatever happened to him, his brother would be able to administer the estate. He must write to Richard and tell him.

He tensed when he saw a fashionably dressed gentleman approaching. There was no mistaking Sir Charles Urmston, his dead wife's cousin. Wolf cursed under his breath. There was no point in turning away, Urmston had seen him. The man's start of surprise was followed very quickly by a delighted smile.

'My dear sir, I had no idea you were back in England.'

Wolf had no option but to stop.

He said coolly, 'It is not generally known.'

'Ah, quite, quite.' Urmston's smile disappeared and he shook his head. 'Bad business, very bad business. Poor Florence.'

Wolf would have walked on, but Urmston put up his hand.

'Pray, sir, do not think I ever blamed you for her death.' Wolf could not hide his look of disbelief and Urmston hurried on. 'Good heavens, no. I admit it was a shock, when I first saw you leaning over her, but I think I know you better than that! But we cannot part again without some discussion.' He turned and slipped his arm through Wolf's. 'Let us drink coffee together.'

Wolf fought down the instinct to pull free. He had never liked Urmston, but the man might have some useful information and he had learned precious little so far. Urmston suggested a nearby coffee house. Wolf would have preferred them to be a little further away from the city, for the place was full of clerks and lawyers, but at least there was little chance of anyone recognising him here.

They found an empty table and Urmston ordered coffee before sitting down opposite Wolf.

'So, my friend, what brings you back to England?'

Urmston's florid countenance showed only a look of innocent enquiry, but Wolf was cautious.

'I needed to see my lawyer.'

'About what?' When Wolf did not reply Urmston sat back, spreading his hands. 'Surely you know you can trust me, my friend.'

'Can I? You were damned eager to hustle me out of the country.'

'No, no, that was your father's doing, I assure you. He thought if you remained you might be clapped up. He was adamant about it and it seemed a sensible idea, to get you out of the way until things calmed down.'

'The consequence of which is that everyone thinks I am guilty,' retorted Wolf.

Urmston shook his head. 'If it had not been for the diamonds going missing at the same time...'

'I did not take them.'

'No, I believe you,' muttered Urmston, chewing his lip. 'I think Florence's dresser took them.'

'But she was devoted to her mistress.' Too devoted, thought Wolf. He had caught her out on more than one occasion lying to protect Florence.

'Have you seen Annie Meesden?' enquired Urmston, staring into his coffee cup. 'Have you spoken to her?'

Wolf had lived by his wits for the past ten years and they were screaming at him now not to trust this man. He answered one question with another.

'Do you know where I might find her?'

Urmston shook his head. 'No, she has given me the slip.'

'Then you *have* been looking for her.'

For the merest instant Urmston looked uncomfortable, as if Wolf had caught him out. Then he was smiling again.

'Naturally, at the beginning. I would have done anything to prove your innocence.'

Lies, thought Wolf. Urmston would not go out of his way for anyone but himself. If he wanted anything it was the necklace.

Wolf took another sip of his coffee. 'What can you tell me about the night Florence died?'

'Why, nothing,' said Urmston. 'I was out on the terrace and came in only when I heard your mother shrieking. I rushed into the hall and there you were, crouched over Florence's body.'

'And you thought I had killed her.'

'Never!'

Wolf looked at him steadily. 'You said I had allowed my temper to get the better of me.'

'Did I? I was upset. Upon reflection I realised you were innocent.'

'And the reward for my capture?'

'That was Sawston's doing. If I had gone to see him immediately I might have prevented that, but I had business in Newmarket. By the time I returned to Arrandale a week later, my uncle had offered a reward for your capture.' Urmston leaned forward, saying in an urgent under-voice, 'Trust me, Arrandale, I only want to help you. If there is anything I can do, you only have to ask it.'

'Thank you.'

Wolf rose, but his companion put a hand on his arm.

'At least tell me where you are staying!'

Wolf looked down at him.

'If you need to contact me, a message for Mr Peregrine at the Running Man in Bench Lane will reach me.'

With that he turned on his heel and walked out.

Wolf went quickly back to his lodgings, packed up his bags and paid his shot. He was taking no chances, he did not believe that Urmston had *just happened* to bump into him. He hailed a cab, then another to take him across town, making sure he was not followed before he set about finding himself fresh rooms. By the time he had secured new lodgings in Half Moon Street the day was well advanced. He remembered Mrs Graham's invitation to call and take pot luck at any time and he decided to do that. After all, he needed to see Grace, to find out if she had been able to discover anything about Annie Meesden. Not just need, he admitted. He wanted to see her.

His welcome at Hans Place was as warm as ever. Mrs Graham ordered another place to be laid at the dinner table and invited him to sit down and take a glass of wine.

'Grace is still in her room, but I expect her any moment.'

Wolf nodded and studied his wine rather than face the twinkle in his hostess's eye. He felt a spurt of irritation. The lady knew what he was; she could not possibly condone any connection between him and her niece. Even if everything went his way and it was proven that he was neither a thief nor a murderer, he was no match for Grace Duncombe. She was too good, too sweet.

She came into the room at that moment and the sight of her in a simple cream dress with her golden hair glowing like a halo about her head confirmed his thoughts. She was virtue incarnate. He rose and braced himself to greet her. Confound it, why could she not remain by the door and give him a cool and distant nod? But it seemed any reservations she had about him had been swept away. She was positively glowing with excitement and came forward, holding out her hand to him as if they were the best of friends.

'Good evening, sir.' Her soft musical voice had an added note, as if it incorporated her smile. 'Has my aunt told you about my visit to Mrs Payne?'

He kissed her fingers with punctilious politeness, but for the life of him he could not let her go. Instead he held on to her hand as he raised his head and looked at her. There was a faint blush on her cheek, but it could not be because of him. Rather, it was because she was happy. It radiated from her. With an effort he released her and moved away.

'She has told me nothing, so you had best sit down and do so.'

He had not intended to be so curt, but the sunshine in her smile was destroying the armour he had put around his heart. Desperately he tried to shore it up. He could not afford distractions and Grace Duncombe was most definitely a distraction. She sank down on to a sofa and folded her hands in her lap, apparently not offended by his abrupt manners.

'It was not very successful,' she admitted. 'When I called upon the lady yesterday she told me very much the same as she had written to you, that I should talk to her son and not bother her with matters of staff. However, I managed to speak to one of the housemaids.'

'Grace took Nelson to Green Park where a maid walks Mrs Payne's lapdog every morning,' put in Mrs Graham. 'Once the dogs were acquainted the maid could hardly avoid speaking to her. Was that not ingenious?'

'It was, if it persuaded the maid to talk to you.'

'It did.' Grace sat forward, her eyes shining. 'She told me the dresser was turned off two years ago, but Mrs Payne still sends sewing work out to her.'

'And you have her direction?'

Grace shook her head. 'Not yet, but I feel sure we will have it very soon.'

'How so?' Wolf frowned, trying not to think how alluring Grace looked with that gentle smile and her eyes twinkling with mischief.

Mrs Graham gave a little tut. 'Pray do not keep poor Mr Wolfgang in suspense, my love.' She turned to him. 'There is a ball tomorrow night to raise funds for the Foundling Hospital and since Mrs Payne is a patron, I feel sure she will attend. I had been disinclined to go. These affairs are always the same, no matter how many donations one has made in the past one feels obliged to pledge more. However, it will be a perfect opportunity to talk to Mrs Payne, so I have purchased tickets for us to attend.'

'How fortunate that you insisted I buy a new ball gown, Aunt!'

Grace's light-hearted laugh caught Wolf off guard. It hit him like a wave, battering against him, breaking down the last of his defences. Something in her was calling to him, like a kindred spirit. A companion in adversity.

'You are enjoying this,' he said.

It was more of an accusation than a statement, but she merely lifted her shoulders and let them fall again.

'I confess it is a little more exciting than the life I have been used to.'

He frowned. 'I would not have you put yourself in danger.'

Again that merry laugh, clear and bright as a bell.

'What danger can there be in attending a ball? Unless I trip and sprain my ankle.'

Dinner was announced and they said no more on the subject, but the change in Grace fascinated Wolf. A few weeks in her aunt's house had transformed her. It was not merely that she had left off the soft greys she had worn at the vicarage and was dressed more fashionably, she looked more alive, her eyes sparkled, her generous mouth had an upward tilt, as if a laugh was never far away, and her light gold hair was piled loosely about her head with the odd little curl escaping to rest like a kiss upon her neck. He imagined that if he pulled just one pin from those heavy tresses they would cascade over her shoulders like a waterfall.

It was a beguiling image and it stayed with Wolf throughout dinner. Grace at her dressing table, dragging a brush through those golden locks. Grace undressed.

Grace undone.

His fork clattered on to the plate and he muttered an apology. He signalled to the hovering waiter that he might remove the dishes. Thank heaven there was only the dessert course to endure, then the ladies would retire and leave him in peace for a while. He was uneasy in polite society. He had forgotten how to behave.

Sitting in solitary state and enjoying brandy from Mrs Graham's excellent cellar, Wolf calculated how long he would have to remain before he could leave without giving offence. Ten minutes, would do it, he thought. Long enough to thank his hostess for her hospitality. But when he returned to the drawing room he found himself wrapped in a cocoon of domestic comfort. The fire was blazing cheerfully, candles cast a golden glow over the room and the two ladies were at their ease, Mrs Graham flicking through a copy of the *Ladies' Magazine* and Grace with an embroidery frame in her hand.

Mrs Graham put aside her magazine to make him welcome. She ushered him to a chair by the fire, sat down opposite and proceeded to talk to him about Arrandale as she remembered it. Wolf answered her politely, but only half his mind was on the subject. From his seat he had a good view of Grace, who continued to set neat stitches in her embroidery, joining in very little with conversation. Even when her aunt left the room she did not look up from her work. He watched her in silence for a while.

'The last time we met I said you had changed,' he remarked. 'Now you are different again.'

The needle hovered about the cloth.

'My aunt is giving me what she calls a little town bronze.'

'That is not it. You are more at ease in my company. Why is that?' She began to ply her needle again, but Wolf could not let it go. 'Do you, can I hope you no longer think me guilty?'

She bent her head even lower over her embroidery.

'My father and aunt are convinced you are not guilty, so I am willing to give you the benefit of the doubt.'

She answered very quietly, but her words lifted a weight from Wolf's shoulders. A weight he had not been conscious of until now. When had her opinion become so important to him? She picked up a pair of silver scissors to cut her thread, then began to pack away her sewing.

'That is the only reason I am helping you to find Mrs Meesden.'

'Admit it, you are enjoying yourself.'

'There is a certain satisfaction in it.' He saw the faint but unmistakable upward curve of her mouth. Her eyes lifted to his, but only for a moment. 'It is part of my holiday, before I go home. To my fiancé.'

'And will you tell Sir Loftus what you have been doing in London?'

She raised her head at that.

'Of course,' she said. 'I shall tell him everything.'

Grace had replied with a touch of hauteur but later, when Wolfgang had gone and she had retired to her bed, she admitted to herself that it was not true. She could not tell Loftus quite everything. Not the way her pulse jumped whenever she saw Wolfgang, nor how the days seemed to drag when he was not with her. She certainly could not tell Loftus about the inordinate rush of happiness she had felt when she learned Wolf was to take dinner with them that evening. And certainly not the trembling excitement she felt whenever he looked at her.

No, she thought sleepily. Those were memories to be locked away, along with childish dreams of adventure and knights in armour.

'Mrs Graham, welcome. How good of you to support our little ball.'

Grace stood by silently as her aunt returned their hostess's greeting. Lady Hathersedge was a cheerful lady with a determined gleam in her eye that said she would be asking for large donations of funds from her guests before the end of the evening. When Grace was presented she felt obliged to explain that her father was a mere country parson.

'Indeed?' Grace could almost see Lady Hathersedge writing her off. 'It is a pleasure to have you with us, Miss Duncombe.'

'Goodness,' murmured Grace, as she accompanied her aunt into the drawing room. 'I feared for a moment I might be turned out of doors when she realised I am as poor as the proverbial church mouse.'

'Not at the price we paid for the tickets,' muttered Aunt Eliza behind her fluttering fan.

'*You* paid, Aunt. I feel quite guilty about asking you to spend so much.'

'Nonsense, what else were we going to do this evening? No, I am delighted to be helping you and Mr—our friend,' she corrected quickly. 'Now, if you will point out Mrs Payne to me, I will do the rest. Heavens, but it is a crush in here. Thank goodness you are so tall, my love, you should be able to spot our quarry if she is here.'

Grace laughed, in no way offended by this frank reference to her height. She was accustomed to being the tallest person in the room.

That is why you are so attracted to Wolfgang Arrandale.

Grace gave her head a little shake. It was unworthy of Papa's daughter to like a person for their physical attributes such as their height, or the width of their shoulders. One should like a person because of their character, because of their kindness and goodness, not because they made one feel dainty and petite. And alive.

'Mrs Payne is over there.' She touched her aunt's arm, forcing her thoughts back to the present. 'The lady in the black bombazine.'

'Ah, yes, I see her. And I am slightly acquainted with the lady beside her, so that will give me an introduction. You had best let me deal with this alone, my love. Off you go and enjoy yourself.'

With that she sailed away to confront Mrs Payne, leaving Grace slightly bemused. How was one to enjoy oneself in a room full of strangers? The orchestra were striking up for the first of the country dances, but one could not dance without a partner.

However, Grace had not been her father's hostess for years without learning a degree of self-sufficiency. She watched the first dance and when the music began again she made her way slowly around the room, smiling vaguely whenever anyone looked her way. The reception rooms were very grand and had a number of smaller apartments leading off, the largest of which was set out in readiness for supper. Grace had made a full circuit when a flurry of activity near the main entrance doors attracted her attention. She was close enough to hear a stentorian voice announce, 'Mr John Peregrine!'

Her heart leapt to her mouth when she recognised the tall figure in the doorway, but it was with fear rather than any warmer emotion. He was so tall, so distinctive, his dark hair curling over the collar of his black coat and providing a stark contrast to the snow-white shirt and neckcloth. She glanced around, wondering why no one was staring at him, surely they would recognise Arrandale of Arrandale, even after ten years? But to her relief the music was starting again and everyone was bustling and pushing towards the dance floor. A nervous laugh shook her. What effrontery, to stand there for all the world to look at him while he lifted his quizzing glass and cast an arrogant and slightly weary eye over the assembly.

He should not be here, courting danger so brazenly. The quizzing glass stopped at Grace and as he moved towards her she lost all desire to laugh. Her nerves were on edge and she was afraid she might do or say something to betray him.

'Mr Peregrine.' She held out her hand.

'Miss Duncombe. I thought I might find you here.'

'What are you doing here?' She hid her words behind a smile as he bowed over her fingers. 'What if you are recognised?'

'In this company? There is little chance of it. My family is not renowned for supporting good causes. Although in the past we might well have added a few foundlings to the hospital.'

His eyes glinted with wicked humour and she felt the tingle of excitement running through her. It was quite reprehensible.

'Pray do not try to shock me,' she retorted in a low, angry under-voice. 'I cannot believe you would put your-self in such danger.'

'I am flattered by your concern. Where is your aunt?'

'Over there, by the window. Talking to Mrs Payne.'

'Ah, yes, I see.' When she tried to pull away his grip tightened on her fingers. 'Are you as friendless here as I am? Perhaps you would like to dance.'

'And attract even more attention? No, I thank you!'

'Then we shall take a stroll about the room.' He placed her hand on his arm. 'I shall keep you company until your aunt is free.'

'I wish you would not,' she said, unable to hide the note of desperation in her tone.

'Very well, if you prefer, I shall take you in to supper.'

She gave a little sigh of exasperation. 'I cannot think it is safe for you to be here at all.'

'Miss Duncombe, after so many years, do you think anyone will—'

'Hush,' she hissed at him. 'Our host is bearing down upon us.'

'Ah, Mr Peregrine! Forgive my not being at the door to greet you.' Lord Hathersedge bowed and introduced himself. Almost without pausing he said, beaming at them both, 'So you have met Miss Duncombe? Capital! Perhaps you are acquainted with her aunt, too? Mrs Gra-ham is one of our most generous supporters.'

'I do indeed know her, my lord.' Wolf inclined his head, wondering if the twenty guineas in his pocket would be enough to make the fellow go away. He wanted to talk to Grace. She was the reason he had come here this evening. He wanted to see her in her finery. And by heaven she did look fine, her blonde hair sprinkled with tiny pearls and an apricot silk gown that somehow gave her clear skin a golden sheen, as if she had been kissed by the sun. She took his breath away.

'My lady tells me you are new in town, sir.' Their host had planted himself before them, barring their way. Wolf could see he was determined to say his piece before he allowed them to escape. 'Perhaps you are not familiar with the sterling work of the Foundling Hospital.'

'Oh, I am aware of it, my lord. My family have been great contributors over the years.'

Wolf heard Grace's sudden intake of breath, felt her fingers pinch his arm. He wanted to be alone with her, to dance or drink wine. Perhaps he might even feed her peaches and cream and make her blush by telling her they could not bear comparison to her lovely complexion.

He said, 'Believe me, my lord, first thing in the morning I shall instruct my bankers to send a hundred guineas to you.'

'A hundred guineas!'

Wolf waved a languid hand. 'Is that not enough? Let it be two hundred then. I feel sure you can put it to good use.'

I must be dreaming, thought Grace.

This was not how people in her world behaved. She wanted to laugh out loud at Wolf's cool assurance. Lord Hathersedge was staring at him, goggle-eyed, and Wolf put out his hand to gently move him to one side, murmuring apologetically that he wanted to take his partner in to supper. They had moved only a step when Grace noticed that their way was blocked again, this time by a gentleman in a blue coat and his fair-haired lady coming out of the supper room. What held Grace's attention was their height. The gentleman was easily as tall as she was, the lady a little less, but they made a strikingly handsome pair and there was something familiar about the gentleman, the way he walked, the world-weary look about his eyes. The man stopped, a look of shock upon his face. At the same time she heard Wolf bite off a muttered exclamation.

To Grace everything was frozen, like a tableau. Wolf and the man were staring at one another while Lord Hathersedge stood beside them, a look of bemusement on his ruddy countenance. Then the gentleman in the blue coat put out his hand.

'By heaven! Wol—'

Immediately Grace gave a little cry and lurched against Lord Hathersedge.

'Oh, do forgive me, I feel a little faint.'

'What? Oh, oh, my heavens!' He patted Grace awkwardly on the shoulder as Wolf quickly put his arm about her and pulled her back against him, holding her close.

Grace sagged against his arm and gave a little moan. 'Mr Peregrine, perhaps you could take me somewhere a little quieter…'

The fair-haired lady sprang forward, as if released from a spell.

'Yes, yes, sir, let us do that. Lord Hathersedge, is there not a room where we may be quite private?' She directed a look towards her host, who started, frowned, then nodded.

'Yes, yes, of course. That door over there, madam,

you will find it leads to a sitting room. It should be quite empty.'

'Excellent.' The lady moved beside Grace. 'We will take her there immediately. Richard, my love, you will fetch a little wine, if you please, and bring it to us. Richard?'

From beneath her lashes Grace could see that the man was staring open-mouthed at Wolf. A little push from his lady made him start and he lounged away. Grace directed a wan smile at Lord Hathersedge.

'I beg your pardon for being such a nuisance, my lord, but you can see I am in good hands now. You may safely leave me and return to your other guests. I know you have much to do.'

She was obliged to repeat her assurances before her host would leave her, but at last he allowed Wolf and the lady to bear Grace away from the ball room. They found the sitting room empty, candles glowing in the wall sconces and a good fire in the hearth. The lady released Grace and gave a little sigh of relief.

'This is perfect,' she said. 'We shall be able to talk in here quite freely.'

It was only then that Grace realised how tightly Wolf was holding her. She put one hand against his chest. 'Thank you, sir. I am very well now, I assure you.' He was still pale and when he looked at her his eyes were oddly bright. She said gently, 'The gentleman is your brother, is he not?'

'Yes,' said the lady, when Wolf remained silent. 'He is Richard Arrandale, and I am his wife, Lady Phyllida.' She chuckled. 'I vow I have never seen two men so dumbfounded.'

'Nor I,' murmured Grace.

The door opened and Richard Arrandale came in, kicking the door closed behind him.

'I thought we might all need to be revived,' he said, nodding at the tray in his hands. It held a decanter and four glasses.

Lady Phyllida went across to take the tray from her husband, murmuring, 'I will deal with this while you greet your brother in a more fitting manner.'

Grace eased herself free of Wolf's arm and stepped away. For a moment the two men stared at each other before coming together and embracing silently. Lady Phyllida caught Grace's eye and smiled.

Wolf cleared his throat. 'By George, Brother, this is the last place I expected to find you. Atoning for past sins, Richard?'

They were sitting opposite one another, a glass in hand. Emotions were running high, and Wolf kept his tone light. Richard answered in the same vein.

'It is my wife's doing. I am a reformed character.' He smiled and put out his hand to Lady Phyllida.

'How long have you been in England, Mr Arrandale?' she asked as she sat down beside her husband.

'Pray, ma'am, call me Wolf,' he said. 'I have been in the country just over a month.'

'A month!' exclaimed Richard.

'I want to prove my innocence. I wrote to you two days ago, but I sent the letter to Brookthorn Manor. By heaven, Richard, when I met Cassandra in Dieppe last autumn she said you had just become a father. I did not expect you to be jauntering to London so soon!' He added awkwardly, 'I should congratulate you.'

'You should indeed. We have a healthy son, who I

hope is sleeping peacefully in his crib in Mount Street. We had business in London and did not intend a long visit, but we did not wish to leave little James behind us.' The soft look fled from Richard's eyes and he frowned again. 'You have been in England for *a month*, Wolf, and you did not think to inform me before yesterday? I don't doubt it will be another week before your letter reaches us in Mount Street!'

'I told no one, save Miss Duncombe's father.'

'And Miss Duncombe, apparently.' Richard exhaled, as if reining in his temper. His blue eyes moved to Grace and a smile flickered. 'Forgive me, ma'am. I am a little acquainted with your father, but you and I have never met before tonight. I have no doubt Mr Duncombe would prefer to keep you away from the infamous Arrandales.'

'No, sir. It was his wish that we should help your brother prove his innocence, if we can.'

Wolf glanced up at Grace, who was standing beside his chair. She was on his side, supporting him. He felt a sudden tightening of his chest at the thought, but there was no time now to consider if it meant anything.

'You recognised Richard?' he asked her.

'I did, sir. At the same moment your sister-in-law recognised you.'

'And your quick thinking put us to shame, ladies,' said Richard, smiling and raising his glass in salute.

'I hope no one else made the connection,' Grace murmured.

Richard shook his head. 'I made a point of speaking to Hathersedge again when I fetched the wine. He was still congratulating himself for extracting such a generous pledge from Wolf. Two hundred guineas, Brother. Are you good for it?'

'I am, but I pray you will not ask me where I acquired my funds.'

'No. I shall ask you instead how you plan to clear your name.'

'By finding out what happened to the Sawston diamonds. I feel sure they hold the key to my wife's death.'

'Talking of Florence, I saw her cousin last week,' said Richard. 'Sir Charles Urmston. He stopped me in St James's Street and asked after you. Coincidence, do you think?'

'I doubt it.' Wolf frowned. 'He was hovering about when I came out of our lawyer's offices yesterday. If you didn't tell him I was in England—'

Richard scowled. 'Since you had not deigned to tell me you were here I could hardly do so!'

'Well, someone told him I was in England,' said Wolf. 'He asked me about Annie Meesden, my wife's dresser.'

'Perhaps he thinks she knows something,' suggested Grace.

'It is possible, I suppose,' agreed Richard. 'I saw her soon after she had moved to London and she appeared to be genuinely distressed about the death of her mistress. She blamed you for it, Wolf.'

'That does not surprise me.'

'If you did not do it, could it have been an accident?'

Wolf shook his head. 'The more I have thought of it the more certain I am that someone pushed her over that balcony. Florence hated carrying my child, she was always complaining of her swollen body, and how ungainly it made her, but I do not think she would have taken any risks. And I think Urmston is involved in this somehow. His coming up to me yesterday was just too convenient.'

'Well, I never liked the fellow,' stated Richard. 'I suspected him at the start, especially when I discovered he had come into a fortune within a week of the necklace going missing.'

'Did he now? That is something I did *not* know, and it sounds very promising.'

Richard raised one hand. 'Sorry to disappoint you, but it appears there is nothing in it. I made my own enquiries into the matter. Oh, I know it was some years later, but the facts are indisputable. The day after the tragedy Urmston left Arrandale and went to Newmarket. He met a young man there, a Lord Thriplow. He had just inherited the title and arrived in Newmarket eager to spend his money. Urmston took his whole fortune in one sitting. Poor boy blew his brains out the next day, but that didn't worry Urmston. It's an unedifying tale, but there are plenty of witnesses to it.'

Wolf grimaced. 'Yes, people remember that sort of thing.'

'Thriplow's money did not last him very long,' Richard continued. 'Urmston soon gambled it away, as he did his wife's dowry.'

Wolf's brows rose. 'So he married, did he?'

'Aye, but his wife died soon after the wedding,' said Richard. 'Rumour has it he mistreated her. One thing is certain, he has no fortune now.'

'And he told me he thought Meesden had taken the diamonds.' Wolf frowned. 'Perhaps he is not our villain after all.'

'Or he and Meesden were in it together and she tricked him,' suggested Richard.

Lady Phyllida shuddered. 'I do not know Sir Charles Urmston well, but I never liked him, and not merely because he wanted to seduce my stepdaughter. I could easily believe he would steal from his own cousin.'

'And at the time he did not *know* he was going to win a fortune at Newmarket, did he?' Grace reasoned.

'That is true,' Wolf conceded. 'But if Meesden did hoax him, why wait until now to find her?'

There was a soft tap on the door and Mrs Graham peeped in.

'Grace, my love. Lord Hathersedge told me you had been taken ill.' She came in, carefully closing the door behind her.

Wolf jumped up. 'Pray be easy, ma'am, your niece is very well. Her *malady* was a ruse to throw our host off the scent of what could have been an embarrassing meeting.'

Mrs Graham's anxious look disappeared as he made the introductions.

'I would not have recognised you,' she said, smiling at Richard. 'But then, I have not seen you since you were a schoolboy. I hope you will be able to help your brother, sir.'

'Aye, if he will let me.'

'I would rather none of you were involved in this,' declared Wolf quickly.

'Pho,' cried Richard. 'That is uncharitable of you, Brother.'

'None of you seem to appreciate the danger of associating with a felon.'

'You have not yet been proven guilty.'

Grace's gentle reminder did nothing to alleviate the black mood that was gathering like a storm cloud over Wolf. Richard had a wife and baby now. What right had he to involve him in his problems? It was bad enough he had already involved Grace.

'Well, I have news about Annie Meesden,' declared Mrs Graham. She hesitated and looked at Wolf. 'Perhaps you would rather wait until we are away from here.'

'By no means,' said Richard firmly. 'Tell us now, ma'am. You may depend upon our discretion.'

Wolf sighed and put up his hands in a gesture of defeat. 'Very well. What did you learn, Mrs Graham?'

The widow sat down on a chair, beaming widely.

'I think I managed it very well,' she said. 'I talked to Mrs Payne about the hospital, pledged a little money then discussed with her the difficulties of finding a clever needlewoman to do one's mending these days. As I hoped, she immediately suggested Mrs Meesden. It appears the woman has sunk very low and lives in a single room in Leg Alley, off Long Acre, north of Covent Garden. A very insalubrious area, but it seems one of the reasons Mrs Payne uses the woman is that not only is her sewing excellent, but she charges very little.' Her mouth turned down in a little grimace of distaste. 'I was shocked at her nip-farthing ways, but I thought it best not to say so.'

'No, indeed, Aunt,' said Grace. 'And how clever of you to find out her direction so adroitly.'

'Yes, thank you, ma'am,' said Wolf. 'I am in your debt. I shall call in Leg Alley first thing tomorrow.'

'You should lie low and let me go,' offered Richard.

'You do not know the woman, Brother. No, I must speak with her.'

'But you should not go alone, sir,' said Grace.

'Of course, alone.' Wolf gave an impatient huff. 'It will not be the first time I have ventured into such a place.'

She shook her head at him. 'That is not what I mean. When I talked to the maid she told me Mrs Meesden dislikes men. She was turned off for insolence towards Mr Payne. I do not think she will talk to you.'

'Wolf will make her talk,' said Richard grimly.

'I am sure he could do that,' murmured Grace. 'But will it achieve the result we want?'

Wolf scowled. 'Then what do you suggest, Miss Duncombe?'

'Let me come with you. She does not know me, but she will know my father, from her months at Arrandale, and she may be more willing to talk to me.'

Wolf acknowledged the truth of this. Even after ten years he could still remember the dresser's barely concealed contempt for him. She was unlikely to fall upon his neck and reveal all. He might use threats or bribes, but even then he could not be sure she would tell him the truth.

'Very well,' he said at last. 'We will go to see her together.'

'You must take my carriage,' put in Mrs Graham. 'And I shall send a footman. No, two. Those alleys around Covent Garden are little better than rookeries.'

Grace looked at Wolf. 'Come to the house tomorrow at ten, sir, and we will set off from there.'

Mrs Graham sighed. 'Oh, dear, perhaps I should not let you go, my love. What your father would say if he knew of it I do not like to think.'

Grace laughed. 'It was his idea that I should help Mr Arrandale, ma'am, so he could hardly complain!'

The carriage drew to a halt at the entrance to a grim little alley. It was so narrow Grace doubted the sun ever reached the lower windows.

'You do not have to do this,' muttered Wolf.

She squared her shoulders. 'Nonsense. We are agreed.' She picked up the package beside her. 'I have brought one of my old gowns that needs mending. It is the perfect excuse for seeking out Annie Meesden.'

Filth and detritus covered the cobbles and blocked the gutter that ran through the centre of the alley. Grace wrinkled her nose, thinking how much worse the place would smell in high summer. A slatternly woman with a baby at her breast was sitting in a doorway and Wolf asked her if she knew of Mrs Meesden.

'She is a mending woman,' added Grace, indicating the package in her hand.

The woman sniffed and jerked her head.

'Next door but one. Top floor.' She grabbed the coin Grace was holding out to her and a sly look came in her bloodshot eye. 'Thank 'ee, madam. That'll buy some milk for the babe, but if you could spare a few more pennies, I ain't eaten fer a week.'

Wolf pulled Grace away.

'It will only go on gin,' he muttered.

'I know.' Grace sighed, glancing back at the woman, who was already making her way unsteadily along the alley. 'I thought we had suffering enough in Arrandale, but it is nothing to this.'

She followed him to the house where they hoped to find Annie Meesden. The door was open and they went in. If there was a landlady she was nowhere in sight.

'At least the stairs have been swept,' Grace remarked. 'That is a good sign.'

There were two doors on the top floor, one stood open to reveal a wretched woman sprawled on the bed and snoring loudly. Wolf looked at the woman's face, then knocked at the closed door. A female voice demanded to know who was there. Wolf nodded to Grace.

'Mrs Meesden?' she called. 'I have some mending for you.'

The door opened a fraction to reveal a small, thin woman in a white cap. Her eyes widened when she saw Wolf and she tried to close the door, but his arm shot out and stopped her.

'What's wrong, Annie?' he drawled, pushing his way in. 'Are you not pleased to see me?'

The woman stepped back as he moved into the room. Grace followed him.

'What do you want?'

The woman retreated behind her little table, hissing like a wildcat. Grace closed the door.

'Please, Mrs Meesden, we mean you no harm. I am Grace Duncombe. You may remember my father, he is the vicar at Arrandale.'

Grace noticed a worn Bible on a shelf by the bed and she hoped the information would reassure the woman. Meesden spared her no more than a quick, contemptuous glance before turning her attention back to Wolf.

'How did you find me?'

'That is not important. I want to know the truth about what happened to my wife.'

The woman glared at him and Grace was chilled by the hatred in her eyes.

He said again, 'How did she die, Annie?'

'It's your fault,' she spat. 'If she hadn't married you she would be alive now.'

'But I did not kill her, Annie, so who did?'

'If *you* didn't, then it must've been an accident.'

The woman sat down on a chair, her mouth stubbornly closed.

'And what happened to the necklace?' Wolf demanded. When she did not reply his fist banged on the table. 'Did you steal it and use the money to set up your milliner's shop? If so, you were sadly duped. It was worth more than enough to keep you living comfortably for the rest of your days.'

'No, I didn't take it,' she said, goaded. 'Like I told 'em, my uncle died and left me money to buy the shop.' Her face twisted into a look of disgust. 'Only it wasn't enough to keep it going through the hard times. Still, it was more than I got from the Arrandales. My mistress never left me a penny, not that she was expecting to die so early, poor lamb.'

'Mayhap you thought the necklace would recompense you for that.'

'I tell you I didn't steal it.'

'But you know who did.'

'I don't know anything. Miss Florence dismissed me early on the night she died, but when I left her the necklace was in her jewel box. I saw it. The next time I went to her room it was missing. 'Tis the truth.' She waved her hand at them. 'You can leave now. I've nothing else to tell you.'

Wolf shook his head. 'You know more than you are saying, Annie.'

'No, I don't.' She wrapped her arms around her skinny frame. 'I told you, I don't know anything. Now go away and leave me in peace.'

She sniffed, staring doggedly at the floor.

'Very well, we'll go.' Wolf hesitated, his fingers tapping thoughtfully on the table. 'My lawyer is presently arranging pensions for staff at Arrandale who were turned off when the house was closed up. I will instruct them to add you to the list.'

Her eyes flew to him, a mixture of hope and suspicion in her ravaged face.

'Are you trying to bribe me?'

'You will not be paid one penny until you have told me the truth about the night my wife died.'

'Let him help you, Mrs Meesden,' Grace urged her, coming up to the table.

'What's it to you?'

The question was flung at her with such malice that Grace flinched, but she kept her voice calm as she replied.

'I want to see justice done and I would like to see you move on from this place.'

'Justice? That won't bring my mistress back. And you...' her hate-filled eyes fixed on Wolf again '...you are as guilty as anyone. No.' She hunched on her chair. 'My mistress's secrets will go with me to the grave.'

'Even the name of her killer?' said Wolf.

Grace saw a flicker of fear in the woman's eyes.

'And what of the necklace?' he went on. 'Who stole your mistress's diamonds?'

With a cry that did not sound human the woman flew out of her seat.

'No one stole the diamonds!' She stood behind the little table, her thin chest rising and falling with each angry breath. 'Get out before I screams the house down. That wouldn't look good for you and Miss Charitable Duncombe here, now would it?'

'Think it over, Annie.' Wolf moved to the door. 'I

know you could help me and you would. You can leave
a message for me at the—'

'I'll see you hang first.'

'Surely you do not mean that,' exclaimed Grace and
felt the full force of those malevolent eyes turned upon
her.

'Oh, yes, I do. Miss Florence never loved him. She
shouldn't have married him. She would've been happier
with—' Her voice broke and she dragged up the corner
of her apron to wipe her eyes. 'A curse on all men! Go
away, the both of you. Get out.'

Grace reached into her reticule.

'I hope you will reconsider Mr Arrandale's offer,' she
said quietly. 'But whatever you decide, this may help.'

She placed a silver coin on the table and the woman
stared at it. Grace stepped away, wondering whether she
had offended her even more.

Annie Meesden nodded to the parcel Grace was carrying. 'What's that?'

'A gown for mending,' said Grace. 'It is only a torn
hem, but I thought it might allay suspicions if I brought
something.'

The woman put out her hand.

'If you leave it I'll see to it, in exchange for your
half-crown.' She added, when Grace gave her the parcel, 'Come back the day after tomorrow and I'll have it
ready. Now get out.'

Without another word Grace and Wolf left the room.

Grace and Wolf did not speak until they were in the
carriage and on their way back to Hans Place, then Wolf
let out a long breath.

'You were right when you said she dislikes men.'

'And you in particular.' Grace clasped her hands together. 'Will she help, do you think?'

'Perhaps, when she has thought it over.'

Grace frowned, going back over everything she had seen and heard in Leg Alley. She said slowly, 'She is frightened, but I do not think she stole the necklace.'

'Then how did she find the money to set up her own business? Unlike Urmston, there is nothing to verify her story.'

'I do not know, but you saw that rather than accept charity she has taken my gown to repair. Her appearance, too, is in her favour. Despite the squalor of the house her room was clean, and her cap and apron were spotless. I find it hard to believe she is dishonest. And besides, she said no one had stolen the necklace. That was an odd thing to say, do you not agree?'

'There is that.'

Grace sighed. 'Whatever the truth of it, I do not like to think of her living in such penury. Could you not instruct your lawyers to pay her a pension immediately?'

'And if I do that, how am I supposed to persuade her to confide in me?'

'You forget, she said she would see you hang, first.'

'She may well do so.'

Grace flinched at his savage laugh.

'Pray do not jest about that.'

He reached out and covered her hands for a moment with one of his own. It was large and strong and she had to resist the temptation to cling on to it.

He turned his head to look down at her. 'You would have me pay an annuity to a woman who clearly hates me?'

'Your wife left her nothing. That was not kind.'

'My wife was never kind. Very well, I will visit Baylis in the morning and instruct him.' His brows went up. 'Now what is the matter, madam?'

'We have the carriage at our disposal, should we not do it now?'

'No. Emphatically not. Your aunt is anxious enough about your coming here today without delaying your return.'

'You could drop me at Hans Place first. I am sure my aunt would not object to you using the carriage for such a good cause.' She paused a moment before adding, 'It would then be done, sir, and you need not worry about it.'

A moment's silence then his breath hissed out and he gave a ragged laugh.

'By heaven but you are persistent, Miss Duncombe! Very well, I will impose upon your aunt's kindness and borrow the carriage to call at the offices of Baylis & Thistle today. There, will that do?'

'Why, yes, sir, that will do very well.' She could not help smiling. 'And perhaps you would like to join us for dinner, afterwards?'

'Thank you, but I am engaged to dine with my brother and his wife. We have a great deal to catch up on.'

'Oh, of course. That is perfectly understandable.'

Grace tried to keep the wistful note from her voice as she enquired when they might expect to see him again.

Wolf did not reply and she felt the sudden tension in the air, as if harsh reality must be faced.

He said at last, 'It would be safer for you and your aunt if I did not call again.'

'We are too involved now for you to leave us without a word.'

'Then I shall contact you, when I have any news.' He

turned away to look out of the window. 'Have you ordered your wedding clothes?'

'Not all of them. My aunt is taking me to Bond Street tomorrow.'

'And when do you return to Arrandale?'

'In two weeks.' Grace bit her lip, thinking of the latest letter from Hindlesham. It was polite, cheerful and expressed Loftus's wish for her speedy return, but there was nothing of the lover in the carefully penned lines and his news seemed dull and colourless compared to the past few weeks in London.

'I shall be glad to go back,' she remarked, as much to convince herself as her companion. 'I fear too much time spent in the metropolis could be injurious to one's character.'

As could too much time spent in Wolf Arrandale's company.

The carriage turned into Hans Place and drew up at Aunt Eliza's door. Wolf leapt out.

He said, as he handed her down, 'I do not believe you are in danger of being corrupted by the metropolis, Miss Duncombe.'

She stumbled and his grip tightened on her fingers. To steady herself, Grace put her free hand against his chest, it was hard as rock beneath the silk of his waistcoat. He was so close she could smell him, an alluring trace of scents that made her want to cling to him. Or to run away.

'On the contrary, sir, I think I am in very great danger of being corrupted!'

Oh, heavens, had she really said that? The heat rushed to her face, she dared not look at him, but snatching her hand from his grasp she picked up her skirts and fled.

* * *

Grace went directly to her room. She did not ring for Janet, but paced the floor, confused by the conflict warring inside her. Wolf Arrandale was dangerous, but there was no doubt she enjoyed his company. When he looked at her she found it was all too easy to bury any doubts about his innocence. But even though she believed he was no criminal he was not a good man. He drew her like a moth to a flame and there was only one way that could end.

And she could not ignore the price on his head. The longer she and Aunt Eliza continued to assist him, the deeper they were drawn into the dangerous world of subterfuge. With a little cry of frustration she made a very unladylike fist and punched it into her palm. Before meeting Wolf she had been a truthful, respectable parson's daughter. She had never lied, never been kissed.

Never lived.

'No!' She stopped her perambulations, head up, a new determination building inside her. She had a good life waiting for her. As Lady Braddenfield she could continue her father's work of looking after the poor, nursing the sick. She could be a wife and mother. It was what she had been born and bred to be. A good woman.

Grace made her way to dinner that night, resolved upon her course of action. This new restlessness, this longing for excitement and adventure, it would pass, given time. Naturally, she hoped Wolfgang Arrandale would find a way to prove his innocence, but she would play no further part in his life. However, when Jenner brought her a note and she saw her name written in a bold scrawling hand she knew it was from Wolf and she almost snatched it from the tray.

The message was short, merely telling her that a small regular pension would be paid to their mutual acquaintance and that the lawyer was writing to the recipient to inform her of the details.

I would she could know that she has you to thank for this kindness, but that is not possible. Not yet. W.

She looked at the single letter that passed for a signature. There was no address, nothing incriminating and no polite meaningless phrases of the writer being hers to command. Nor was there any indication that he would write again. She folded the note carefully and tucked it away. It was very likely the next she heard of Wolf Arrandale would be through the newspapers.

Wolf enjoyed the evening with his brother and sister-in-law more than he had expected. Richard was eager to learn how he had lived for the past ten years, but he took the little information that Wolf offered and asked for nothing more. They discussed politics, family, the lusty baby boy sleeping peacefully upstairs in the nursery. And the future of Arrandale.

'You talk as if you will never be master there,' Richard objected, when Wolf told him of the measures he wanted to see put in place. 'I know I have your power of attorney, but that is only a temporary measure, until you can clear your name. In fact, we should start on that immediately. We will find the best lawyers to represent you. And our great-aunt Sophia, Lady Hune, will help us, I am sure. She has connections.'

Wolf gave a faint, derisory smile.

'Do you tell me you have not already tried to prove my innocence?'

'You know I have, but that was before we had your testimony.'

'And what good do you think that will do?' Wolf replied bitterly. 'No, I have considered everything. The only witnesses to Florence's death are those who heard us arguing on the night she died and then saw me kneeling over her body with her blood on my hands.'

'But you have found your wife's maid, have you not? Perhaps she knows something.'

'I am sure she does, but whether her testimony would acquit or damn me I cannot say. I will have to talk to her again.'

Lady Phyllida had been sitting silently beside her husband, but now she leaned forward.

'You must have a care, sir.'

'I am always careful.'

'Not careful enough.' She handed him a folded newspaper. 'There is a piece here about you.'

Wolf read the report, his frown deepening.

'It claims you have been sighted in town,' said Richard. 'It also says the reward still stands. With such an incentive to find you, it can only be a matter of time before posters for your arrest are seen on the streets again.'

'You are quite right.' Wolf threw the paper aside. 'My guess is that Urmston has a hand in this. For all his weasel words to me I believe he wants me hanged.'

'What will you do?' asked Phyllida.

Wolf shrugged. 'If it was not for my daughter I would return to France now.'

'And leave Arrandale without a master?'

'You could fulfil that role, Richard.'

'Dam—dash it all, Wolf, I do not want it!'

Phyllida laid a hand on her husband's arm as she turned to address Wolf.

'Let us help you, sir, for your daughter's sake.' She added quietly, 'Little Florence is a lovely child and she looks a great deal like you.'

'You have seen her?' said Wolf eagerly.

'Yes.' Phyllida nodded. 'We have been to Chantreys to visit the Davenports.'

'And…' Wolf bit his lip '…is she happy?'

'She would be happier if she knew her papa, I am sure.'

Wolf stared at his sister-in-law. He did not want to involve them, but what choice did he have? At last he nodded.

'Very well, Richard. Write to Lady Hune, let her contact her lawyers, but if they say there is no hope then I will leave England. I would prefer to end my life in exile than on the gallows.'

It was gone midnight when he left Richard's house and hailed a hackney coach. He instructed the driver to drop him on the corner of Bench Lane. Halfway along the narrow passage the lights of the tavern were still burning. Muffled in his greatcoat and with his hat pulled low over his brow, Wolf entered and sought out the landlord. A short while later he was making his way to his lodgings, a folded note in his pocket and the first stirrings of hope that his luck was about to change.

Chapter Eight

Grace planned to spend the next day shopping for bride clothes with her aunt. She was obliged to remind Aunt Eliza several times that gowns such as those described in the society pages were not at all suitable.

'I am marrying the squire of Hindlesham, ma'am, not the Prince of Wales,' she declared over breakfast, when her aunt was once again poring over the latest newspaper to be delivered. 'You have already squandered enough of your money on me and I would not have you waste more buying gowns I will never wear.'

'Oh, very well.' Aunt Eliza sighed, closing the newspaper and placing it on the table beside her. 'But you must have a new silk for the wedding day, then you will need bonnets and reticules and a new redingote. Not to mention nightclothes.'

Grace concentrated fiercely on her breakfast. She did not want to think about nightclothes. She was resolved to do her wifely duty, but the idea of being intimate with Loftus was quite, quite different from the excitement she felt when she thought of Wolfgang. She closed her eyes.

It could not last, this foolish infatuation that she had conceived. She did believe that. She did.

Grace was suddenly aware that a silence had fallen over the breakfast room. Opening her eyes, she saw her aunt staring in consternation at the newspaper.

She said sharply, 'Aunt Eliza?'

Silently her aunt passed the paper across the table. Grace looked at the closely printed words and felt a chill as one paragraph stood out from the others. It was slyly phrased, calling Wolf 'Mr W— A— of A—le', but there could be no mistake. There could not be many men charged with murdering their wife ten years ago and stealing a valuable necklace. And a reward. Two hundred guineas in exchange for a man's life.

'Oh, my dear.' Aunt Eliza's anguished whisper brought Grace's head up.

'What can we do?' she asked bleakly. 'I do not even know how to reach him.'

Grace wanted to stay at home, in the hope that Wolf might call and she could warn him, but her aunt did not agree.

'We are not expecting him and your nerves would be in shreds by the end of the day, my love. Let us instead write a note for Mr Peregrine. Jenner will see that he gets it, should he call. Trust me, my love, we are much better distracting ourselves in Bond Street. Now, you take Nelson for his morning walk and I will order the carriage.'

Grace wondered how Aunt Eliza could think of shopping at such a time, but a little reflection persuaded her that there was nothing to be gained by remaining in Hans Place. However, it was difficult to concentrate on silk or muslin or lace when she was constantly looking about her in the hope of seeing a very tall, dark gentleman on the street.

* * *

They returned to Hans Place to discover there had been no callers during their absence. Grace tried to hide her anxiety as she and her aunt went over their purchases, checking to see if there was anything else she required.

'We have done very well,' declared Aunt Eliza, ticking another item from her list. 'The gowns we have ordered should be ready for you to take back to Arrandale with you. Indeed, we have ordered so much I wonder if we should hire a second carriage to carry it all. Grace?' She put down her pen and paper. 'Dearest, I do believe you have not heard a word I have said!'

'I beg your pardon, Aunt. I was thinking that perhaps we should seek out Mr Richard Arrandale. I remember him saying they were in Mount Street.'

'Grace, my love.' Aunt Eliza reached out and put a hand on her arm. 'If someone is searching for Mr Wolfgang they will be watching his brother's house, too. If you begin sending urgent messages to him it may well alert the watcher to *us* and whoever it is might well begin to ask questions about a certain Mr Peregrine. Mr Wolfgang did not give you his direction because he did not wish to involve you.'

'I know, but if he is in danger—'

'I have no doubt that he is aware of what is in the newspapers and is taking extra care.'

'Do you really think so, Aunt Eliza?' Grace looked at her doubtfully.

'I do, my love, but if we have heard nothing by the morning I will pay a call upon Mrs Richard Arrandale. After all, there would be nothing untoward about that, since we met at the Hathersedges' ball the other night.'

* * *

Grace agreed and tried to be content, but there was no denying the relief she felt when her aunt received a letter, just as they finished dinner. As soon as they were alone Aunt Eliza tore open the sheet and confirmed that it was from Mr Wolfgang. She read it quickly.

'Well, I am very encouraged by his cheerful tone.'

'What does it say?' demanded Grace, trying to read over her shoulder.

'Meesden has agreed to talk to him. He says they are to meet in Vauxhall Gardens at eleven o'clock tonight.' She gave a little laugh. 'Listen, my love, "...that she is willing to pay the admission price tells me she is not quite so lacking in means as she would have us believe!"'

'Or perhaps she has learned of the pension he has settled upon her.' Grace smiled. 'He went back to the lawyers yesterday especially to arrange it...' Her smile faded. 'May I look, Aunt?'

She took the letter and scanned it, a tiny crease settling between her brows.

'What is it, my love? Is this not good news?'

'I do not know,' said Grace slowly. 'He writes that she sent him word last night, but how?'

'He gave her his direction, naturally.'

'No, he did not.' Grace shook her head. 'I was with him when he tried to tell her how she could reach him. I remember it distinctly because I thought that I should discover it, too, but she cut him short.' She handed back the paper. 'Oh, Aunt, I very much fear that this is some sort of trap!'

Wolf kept his domino close about him as he climbed out of the coach at Vauxhall. The Season had only just begun, but already the gardens were thronging with crowds and that made him uneasy. He had not been here for over ten years and ticket prices had increased significantly, but it appeared to have made no difference to the popularity of the gardens.

He pulled out his watch as he made his way towards the Italian Walk. It wanted but fifteen minutes to eleven and Meesden might already be waiting for him. He thought it odd that she should want to meet south of the river, but perhaps she was as keen as he not to be recognised and that was definitely easier amongst this vast, masked crowd. An avenue of trees led to the Italian Walk, a series of arches and pediments built in the Roman style with statues placed at intervals along its length. Lamps twinkled from the trees and between the pillars. By their dim light Wolf strode on, looking for the statue of Minerva. Had Meesden known, when she chose the venue, that the goddess was said to have conferred upon women the skills of sewing and spinning? He had not thought her so well educated.

The statue he sought was set in a recess at the very end of the Walk, where there were plenty of people, but not the crush to be found around the orchestra and the supper boxes. Several couples were strolling along and a chattering group of ladies and their escorts tripped past as he stepped off the path.

A sudden breeze carried away the noisy chatter and set the leaves rustling on the thick bushes that enclosed three sides of the recess. Wolf had a sudden premonition of danger. He heard a cry and turned as a cloaked woman staggered from the bushes, her hands reaching out before her. It was only as she collapsed against him that he felt the hard projection of the knife handle beneath her ribs.

Quickly he laid the woman on the ground, her cloak falling away as he did so. The lamplight showed him it was Annie Meesden, a stain blooming around the knife and spreading over the front of her gown like a huge, blood-red flower. Wolf pulled the knife from her with one hand while with the other he drew his handkerchief from his pocket and pressed it over the wound, although he knew it was too late. There was no life in the sightless eyes that stared up at him.

'Murder, murder!'

Wolf heard the cry and looked up to find a crowd gathering on the path, staring at him in horror. Four men jumped forward to lay hands on him.

'Not me,' he cried, struggling against them. 'Her killer is back there, in the bushes. Quickly, go after him!'

'Oh, no, you won't trick us with that one!' Leaving three of his comrades to hold Wolf, one of the men knelt by the stricken woman. 'She's dead.' He looked up. 'And here you are, with the knife in your hand and her body still warm.'

The commotion had drawn more people. There was no escape and Wolf could hear their voices clamouring for the constable to be fetched.

His eyes returned to the bloody body on the ground and with a sickening certainty he knew he had been tricked.

From the far side of the walk Grace watched in horror as the crowd grew around Wolf, their cries and shrieks like the baying of hounds.

'No. No!'

She wanted to run towards him, but Richard held her back, saying, 'There is nothing we can do for him here.'

'But they will kill him!'

'No, they won't. They have sent for the constable.'

'Can we not go to him?'

'No,' said Richard. 'He is incognito. If I rush to his support it is very likely someone will make the connection.'

'If only we had come earlier!'

'You came to Mount Street as soon as you realised the danger,' muttered Richard. 'I am only thankful that we were at home.'

Grace nodded. They had arrived at Vauxhall in time to see Wolf heading for the Italian Walk. There had been no mistaking his tall figure, even in the black domino.

'I do not understand,' she said now, trembling with the shock of it. 'The arbour was empty when he stepped into it. And the next moment he is kneeling over a body.'

'There is a certain familiarity with that scenario,' drawled Richard.

Grace turned to stare at him. 'You do not believe he murdered her?'

'Do you?'

'No.' She shook her head emphatically. 'No, I do not. I was watching closely. She was not there when he walked in and I did not see her enter from the path.'

Her companion relaxed just a little.

'That is what I thought, too,' he said. 'It's damned suspicious. Come on, we need to know if the woman is Mrs Meesden.' He took her arm and led her to the edge of the crowd. 'What is going on here?'

The authority in Richard's voice caused some of the onlookers to move aside. He pushed into the crowd, Grace close beside him. It was impossible to get to the front, but Grace was tall enough to see Wolf being held by two burly individuals. A sudden shifting of the crowd gave her a glimpse of a woman's body lying on the ground. Grace forced herself to look at the dead woman's face. There was no mistaking Annie Meesden's gaunt features. Pressing her handkerchief against her lips, Grace nodded to Richard.

'It is her.'

'What has happened?' he demanded, loudly enough for his brother to hear.

Wolf looked towards them and briefly met Grace's eyes.

He said, as if addressing his captors, 'The woman was stabbed before she came out of the bushes behind the statue. Her killer must have been back there.'

A large woman in a mob cap and torn coat laughed scornfully.

'A likely tale!' she scoffed. 'The poor besom fell foul of her beau, plain as day.'

Several constables had arrived and were pushing their way through the crowd to take charge.

Grace pressed Richard's arm. 'Let us look around the back and see if there are signs that anyone has been there.'

It was much darker away from the main walk. Richard unhooked one of the lamps and led the way. It was too much to expect to find anyone lurking behind the little recess, but the lamplight showed them where the smaller branches had been snapped off and the ground was trampled.

'The bushes are much thinner here,' observed Grace. 'It would not be difficult to get through.'

'I think you are right,' muttered Richard. 'The killer stabbed her here, then pushed her forward. I can even see through to the path.' He stepped back. 'One of the constables is coming around here to look for himself. We must go.'

'What about Wolf?'

'There's nothing we can do for him at present. We will find out where they are taking him and I will go to see him in the morning. You need not be anxious about my brother, Miss Duncombe. They will lock him up securely, but I have no doubt it isn't the first time he has spent the night in a prison cell.'

Wolf was marched away and bundled into a carriage for the short journey to the prison. He cursed himself for being so easily fooled. He had let down his guard, allowed himself to believe that Annie Meesden truly wanted to help him. Had she conspired with the killer to lure him to the gardens? If so she had paid for it with her life. His jaw clenched. How foolish he had been to believe she wanted to meet him. He thought of seeing Grace and Richard in the crowd; she must have read his note and rushed here to support him, bringing Richard with her as the only man she could trust. He hoped, nay, he was sure his brother would realise there was some deep game afoot, but what would Grace think of him now that she had seen him in that incriminating situation? A chill went through him. Henry Hodges, the love of her life, had died from a stab wound. What had it done to her, seeing him there with a bloody knife in his hand? As the carriage rattled on his thoughts were as gloomy as the dark streets. It was too much to expect her to believe he was innocent now.

New Gaol in Horsemonger Lane was less than twenty years old and rose like a solid black square against the darkness. As the carriage pulled up Wolf was surprised to see the double doors were open. He frowned.

'I thought I'd be in a lock-up until I had seen the magistrate.'

'He's waiting for you,' was the gruff response. 'Just your misfortune that it's Hanging Hatcham on duty tonight!'

The constables roughly manhandled him out of the carriage on to the cobbled yard of the prison. He was escorted into a reception room where a portly figure in a powdered wig was sitting at a desk.

'I am Gilbert Hatcham, magistrate here.' The man introduced himself. 'I was told I might expect you this evening, Mr Wolfgang Arrandale.'

'You are mistaken,' said Wolf coolly. 'My name is Peregrine. John Peregrine.'

The magistrate gave a fat chuckle.

'Is that what you are calling yourself?' He lifted a printed sheet from the desk and glanced at it. Even in the lamplight Wolf could see that it was creased and yellow with age. The only word he could read from this distance was the one in large thick letters stretched across the page. 'Reward'.

Hatcham continued to scan the sheet. 'It says a tall man, six feet five inches, near black hair and violet-blue eyes.' He came around the desk and stared up into Wolf's face. 'Well, I can't see the colour of your eyes in this light, but I think the description is sufficiently close. Put him in a holding cell.'

'Will you not grant me bail?' demanded Wolf as the constables began to hustle him from the room.

'You are wanted for the murder of your wife and the theft of her diamonds, and now you have been caught red-handed taking the life of another poor wretch. No, sir, you will not be granted bail!'

Wolf woke up in near darkness, feeling parched and uncomfortable. He was wrapped in his black domino and lying on bare boards that ran the length of the cell, but they were several inches short of his height, so he was not able to stretch out. His ribs hurt, too; his captors had been none too gentle in their treatment of him. The only sources of light were the grille in the door and a hole in the ceiling, too high and small for a man to climb through, but within minutes of his waking he discovered it was large enough for the guards to pass down a flask of small beer and a crust of bread for him to break his fast. A short time later the door opened and a guard appeared, a black outline against lamplight from the corridor.

'You have visitors. Upstairs.'

'I am glad you do not expect me to receive them here.'

Wolf took time to fold his domino and put it on the boards before he accompanied his gaoler up the stone steps. Above ground the sun flooded in through the windows and he blinked uncomfortably in the light. His escort ushered him into a small panelled room, sparsely furnished with a square wooden table and four chairs, where he found his visitors waiting for him; his brother and a tall veiled lady that Wolf knew immediately was Grace. His spirits leapt, but plunged again when she lifted her veil. She looked so pale and drawn he guessed she had not slept and it was as much as he could do not to reach out for her. His frustration manifested itself in a scowl.

'You should not have brought her here, Richard.'

It was Grace who replied, saying quietly, 'I insisted upon it.'

Wolf's scowl deepened. 'You were at Vauxhall—can you doubt the evidence of your own eyes and believe me innocent?'

'Your brother and I were watching more closely than the others. You did not stab that woman. Your past may be very dark, sir, but you are no murderer.'

He was shaken by his sense of relief. It flared like a torch, but he could not bring himself to admit to it. He responded gruffly.

'I still say you should not be here. You should not be alone with any Arrandale!'

Richard scowled back at him. 'You need not concern yourself with the propriety, Wolf, Phyllida accompanied us. She is waiting in the carriage.'

'Trying to distance herself from her wicked brother-in-law,' said Wolf bitterly.

'No, she is trying to spare you embarrassment, you ungrateful cur!'

Wolf put up his hand, at last acknowledging his ill humour.

'I beg your pardon,' he said. 'Forgive me, Richard. I am grateful, truly.'

'Aye, well,' growled Richard, rubbing his nose. 'It isn't only that. She is in a delicate condition.'

'Then I am obliged to her for coming even as far as the gates with you,' exclaimed Wolf. He gripped his brother's hand. 'I felicitate you, Richard, and I am even more grateful that you should be here. But I am surprised. I expected to see my rascally lawyer.'

'I sent word to Baylis to come as soon as he can,' Richard replied shortly. 'We have just had a most unsatisfactory interview with the magistrate.'

'Gilbert Hatcham?'

'Yes. He refused bail for you.'

'He told me as much last night.' Wolf glanced to check that the door was closed and that they were alone before inviting them to sit down. 'How much did it cost you for this meeting?'

'Enough. This may be a new model prison, but a few pieces of silver can still achieve a great deal. Although not your freedom, Brother.'

Wolf grunted. 'Hatcham said he was expecting me. He had an old poster on his desk. Odd, do you not think, that he should have a ten-year-old notice so readily to hand?'

'Damned suspicious,' muttered Richard.

'How are they treating you?' asked Grace.

Wolf shied away from the concern in her voice.

'As you would expect them to treat a murderer,' he replied lightly. 'They barely gave me time to wash the poor woman's blood from my hands before they hustled me into a cell.'

He knew they must both have seen the dried blood on his clothes, although no one mentioned it.

Richard said, 'You were lured to that meeting, Wolf.'

'Yes, and I think I know by whom, although I cannot prove it while I am locked in here.'

'Then we must do it for you,' declared Grace.

Her vehemence touched him, but he hid it behind a rueful smile and a light word.

'I fear I have led you woefully astray, Miss Duncombe. What would your fiancé say if he knew you were here?'

'He would want justice, as I do.'

'But not at the expense of your reputation.'

'At any expense!'

She looked so resolute that his heart swelled.

'Why were you both at Vauxhall last night?' he asked.

'Miss Duncombe suspected a trick.'

A tinge of colour stole into Grace's cheeks. 'Your note said Annie Meesden had sent you word, but I distinctly remember she cut you off before you could tell her how to contact you.'

'Yes, I realised that, too, but only later, after I was locked up. A stupid error on my part.'

'So who did know how to contact you?' asked Richard. 'Apart from myself?'

Wolf met his eye. 'Sir Charles Urmston. I foolishly thought he might have information that could help me, so I told him how to reach me.'

'By Jove, that makes perfect sense!' exclaimed Richard. 'But how did he know where to find the woman?'

'I am not sure,' said Wolf slowly. 'I know he was looking for Annie Meesden, because he asked me if I knew anything of her. I did not tell him and I made sure we were not followed when we went to see her the other day. So either he picked up her trail or—'

He broke off, but it was too late.

'Or someone told him her direction,' said Grace. She put her hands to her face, a look of horror shadowing her eyes. 'If only I had not pressed you to set up a pension for her.'

Richard looked from one to the other. 'What is this?'

'After we had seen Meesden I persuaded your brother to arrange a small annuity for her,' explained Grace. 'For that he had to tell his lawyer where she was living.'

'There is nothing to say Baylis passed on that information,' said Wolf quickly.

Grace shook her head. 'You said yourself this man, Urmston, first came up to you directly outside the offices of Baylis & Thistle and at that stage—apart from

Aunt Eliza and myself—the only person who knew you were in London was your lawyer. Perhaps it was inadvertently done.'

'Whatever it was I think the Arrandales will be finding themselves another lawyer,' exclaimed Wolf wrathfully.

'Yes, well, I have been thinking that myself,' said Richard. 'I have suspected for years that Baylis has been creaming off the profits from your estate but nothing could be proved, and with you still nominally head of the family I couldn't turn him off, either. I will deal with him, don't worry, but for now we need to get you out of here.'

'You won't do it. Hatcham as good as told me last night I am here until my trial.'

And he expects me to hang.

He stopped himself from saying the words aloud and he met Richard's eye, sending him a silent message not to give Grace any more reason to worry.

His brother nodded. 'We shall make enquiries on your behalf, Wolf. Our first call will be Meesden's lodgings. Miss Duncombe has a gown to collect and we shall see if we can learn anything there.'

'Good,' said Wolf. 'You had best find Kennet, too. He will be at my rooms in Half Moon Street. Tell him what has occurred and ask him to bring some money. At least I may buy some comforts in this hellhole.'

He was giving them directions when a burly turnkey came in to tell them their time was up.

Wolf rose. He nodded to Grace, not trusting himself to go near her. Then he turned and gripped his brother's hand. 'Do what you can for me, Richard, and you had best engage another lawyer with all speed!'

* * *

Grace pulled her veil over her face and accompanied Richard Arrandale from the building. Her legs felt very weak and she was relieved when they were once more sitting in the carriage with Lady Phyllida. The sight of Wolf, unshaven, his eyes troubled and still wearing his bloody evening clothes, had shaken her to the core. Until then his predicament as a wanted man had seemed a distant threat, but as they drove away her eyes were drawn upwards to the roof of the prison and the black timbers of the scaffold, outlined against a lowering sky.

'We cannot let him hang.'

She did not realise she had spoken the words aloud until Richard replied.

'He won't, you need not worry about that. The Arrandales have had plenty of practice at cheating the gallows.' When her eyes flew to his face he added quickly, 'We will do the thing by fair means, if we can, but if not—'

She put up her hand.

'Please, do not tell me anything more.'

'I agree,' said Phyllida. 'Pray do not burden us with unnecessary conjecture, Richard.' She turned to Grace. 'Would you like to go back to Hans Place now? We can collect your gown for you, if you would rather not be mixed up further in this affair.'

Grace clasped her hands together and stared out of the window, but all she could see was Wolf's haunted eyes.

'I do not have any choice,' she murmured, almost to herself. 'I must see this through.'

They drove quickly to Half Moon Street to speak to Wolf's valet and then went on to Leg Alley. It was just as grim and daunting as it had appeared at Grace's first visit. Richard insisted his wife remain in the carriage while he and Grace picked their way through the rubbish to the house. The door was closed, but Richard's firm rap upon the weathered boards brought a plump, sharp-eyed woman in a grubby apron to open it. She declared she was the landlady and demanded to know their business.

'I have come to collect a gown from Mrs Meesden,' Grace explained.

The woman shook her head.

'She's dead. Murdered.' She said it with such relish that Grace did not have to feign her look of horror.

'Good heavens, when was this?'

'Last night. She went off to Vauxhall with her man friend and never came back. He's been arrested for her murder.'

Richard's brows went up. 'The fellow came here?'

The landlady leaned against the wall and folded her arms.

'Aye. I told the constables as much. He called late in the afternoon and they stayed upstairs 'til about nine o'clock. *She* said she had work to finish, but if you ask me they was carousing, for she was so drunk she could hardly get down the stairs when they left. He almost carried her out.'

'How dreadful, but I should still like to retrieve my gown,' said Grace. 'It is a yellow muslin with green embroidery at the hem. Perhaps I might step in and look for it?'

Richard held out a coin. 'I assure you, madam, we want only to collect the lady's property.'

The landlady's hand darted out to take the coin.

'Aye, well, I don't suppose it will do any harm if I takes you up there now.'

She waddled away and they followed her up to Annie Meesden's tiny room. Grace tried to take in as much detail as possible. It looked more untidy than she remembered, a chair was tipped over and on the table stood two glasses and an almost empty bottle that Richard picked up and held to his nose.

'Was the lady in the habit of drinking brandy?'

'Not that I knew of. If she had been I'd have sent her packing long ago. This is a respectable house.'

'And the man who came to see her, was he a regular visitor?' he asked.

'Never seen him before, but then I don't see everyone who comes and goes. As long as my tenants is quiet and pays their rent I don't interfere.'

'But you saw the man who called yesterday,' Richard pressed her. 'Was he as tall as I am? Taller, perhaps?'

The landlady regarded him with her sharp eyes but said nothing. Richard pulled another coin from his pocket. 'Well?'

'No, sir, he wasn't as tall as you.' The money disappeared into her pudgy hand. 'Fashionable swell, though. Handsome. Black shiny hair and a fine set o' whiskers.'

'And you would be willing to swear to this in court?'

Immediately the woman looked wary and Richard said impatiently, 'Surely the constables asked you to describe the fellow?'

'No, sir. They said there was no need. They said her killer was locked up right and tight. Now, is that your dress on the table, madam? Yellow muslin with green stitching, you said. Mrs Meesden was working on it when I showed her gentleman friend upstairs.'

'Yes, that is it,' said Grace.

The gown was neatly folded and weighted down with Meesden's Bible.

'Well, you should take it and go. I've got to clear this room today, I've another tenant wanting to move in.'

The landlady ushered them out of the room and down the stairs, closing the door behind them with a bang. Richard took Grace's arm and escorted her back to their carriage.

'Well,' demanded Phyllida as they set off. 'What did you learn?'

Grace said slowly, 'Meesden's visitor was not your brother-in-law.'

Richard agreed. 'The description the landlady gave us *does* fit Charles Urmston, though. I think he wrote the note to Wolf, then came here to take Meesden to Vauxhall, where he killed her.'

Grace frowned. 'That is a serious allegation, Mr Arrandale.'

'I know but I believe he would do it.'

'Perhaps, if the dresser knew things that would implicate him in your sister-in-law's murder.'

'My thoughts exactly, Miss Duncombe.'

She sat upright and said with sudden decision, 'We must talk to Wolfgang again.'

'Now?' Richard looked at his watch. 'The day is well advanced. Your aunt will be expecting you.'

Wolf's image swam before Grace's eyes and she clasped her hands together, as if in supplication. 'I have the strongest feeling we should tell your brother our suspicions. Immediately.'

Phyllida touched her husband's arm. 'We have two footmen up behind us, my dear. One of them could be sent to inform Mrs Graham that we will be delayed.'

'But is it not too much for you, love?' he asked her. 'We have been gadding about all day.'

Phyllida smiled. 'I have been sitting at my ease in a coach, Richard. I am not at all tired, I promise you.'

With a nod Richard jumped out to issue instructions to his servants and Grace gave Phyllida a grateful look, then was immediately assailed by doubt. Was she allowing her growing attraction to Wolf Arrandale to cloud her judgement? Perhaps she just wanted to see him again. It was late, she should go home, but the feeling persisted that they should talk to him. She comforted herself with the fact that the others had not argued strongly against it and soon they were crossing the river again, heading for the prison.

They travelled in silence, each lost in their own thoughts, but as they were approaching the Sessions House Richard sat up, staring out of the window.

'I think we might have to revise our plans.'

There was something in his voice that alerted Grace and she followed his glance. Coming out of the coffee house on the corner of the street was the magistrate, Gilbert Hatcham, accompanied by a fashionably dressed gentleman. They stopped on the pavement to take leave of one another and the gentleman removed his hat to display his thick black hair and a fine set of whiskers. A cold chill settled over Grace.

'Is that Sir Charles Urmston?' she asked, her throat growing dry.

'It is indeed,' muttered Richard. 'And he looks to be on the best possible terms with the magistrate.'

Chapter Nine

The officers in the prison were surprised to see Grace and Richard back again so soon, but a few coins slipped into waiting palms gained them immediate access. This time they were escorted to the cells, ranged along a corridor with numerous heavy wooden doors on one side, each with a small grille through which the prisoner might be observed.

'Welcome to my new abode,' said Wolf, when they were shown in and the door firmly locked behind them. 'Did you see Kennet on your way in? He left only a short time ago.' He looked about him. 'An excellent valet. He brought me fresh clothes as well as my purse, which has purchased me this cell. It isn't a palace, but at least it has a window and blankets on the bed. And I have a table and chair, so pray be seated, Miss Duncombe. Perhaps I could see if they can provide tea…'

'Stop playing the fool,' said Richard impatiently. 'We do not have time for this.'

'No, of course.' Wolf sobered immediately. 'Did you discover anything at Meesden's lodgings?'

Wolf listened intently to his brother's recital of what

they had found and at the end his countenance was forbidding.

'I am more than ever convinced that Urmston is behind all this,' he muttered.

'I am certain of it,' retorted Richard. 'We have just seen him coming out of the coffee house with the magistrate. They looked as thick as thieves.'

'Well, that explains why he lured me to Southwark to meet Meesden,' said Wolf. 'He wanted me delivered up to Hatcham, whom he could trust to keep me locked away until the trial. That way I have little chance to prove my innocence.'

'Then we must do so,' said Grace. 'We could advertise, put up bills asking for witnesses to the murder, offer a reward.'

'I doubt you would have any success,' Wolf replied. 'We would need nothing short of a full confession from the real killer for a jury to find me not guilty.'

'We are pretty sure who it is, so I will extract one from the villain!' was Richard's savage response.

Wolf shook his head. 'Urmston will have thought of that. He will be on his guard, ready to use any attempt to intimidate him as further evidence of my guilt. By heaven, I begin to think it will take a miracle to extricate myself from this fix!'

Richard laid a hand on his shoulder. 'We shall get you out of here, Wolfgang, never fear. I expect our great-aunt Sophia to be in London very soon.'

'That is good news,' declared Grace. 'The support of the Dowager Marchioness of Hune can only help our cause.'

She looked so much more cheerful that Wolf kept silent, but he doubted even Lady Hune's money and influence could help him now.

'If only we knew who stole the diamonds,' he exclaimed. 'That would be one less charge to contend.'

'But Meesden said they were *not* stolen,' Grace reminded him.

'Aye, so she did.' Wolf paced the small cell, his brow furrowing as the thoughts chased through his head. 'Perhaps…'

'Perhaps they are still at Arrandale,' said Grace, her face lighting up.

'But if Meesden knew where, Urmston may have forced her to tell him,' argued Richard.

'There is that,' said Wolf. 'But he won't have had a chance to get them. Richard, you must go to Arrandale immediately. Urmston will remain in town until his tame magistrate has committed me for trial, but once he knows I am safely locked up he will go in search of the necklace.'

Richard shook his head. 'I need to be here with you. I'll ask Lady Hune to go directly to Arrandale.'

'By heaven, Richard, you cannot do that, Sophia is an old lady.'

'But she is indomitable, Brother, and she has a large and impressive retinue to protect her. If I explain everything, she will keep the villain out.'

The distant chime of a clock floated in through the unglazed window. Wolf looked up.

'Is Phyllida waiting in the carriage, Richard? You should go. Do not worry about me, there is nothing more to be done tonight.'

Grace rose and held out her hand. It fluttered like a wild bird in his grasp.

'I shall come back tomorrow, sir.'

'You would be advised to stay away.' He saw the obstinate set of her mouth and added, 'Truly, such attention would give rise to speculation. I would not have you become the subject of such gossip.'

Her head went up. 'I will take that risk.'

Wolf knew he should forbid her to come, but for the life of him the words would not pass his lips. She was the one glimmer of light in his sorry, sordid history and he could not bear to lose it. Not yet.

When they had gone Wolf sat for a while, thinking over all they had told him, and when the warder arrived with his dinner he gave him a message for the magistrate.

Kennet brought Wolf's breakfast the following morning, together with the latest newssheets and more fresh clothes. Once he was washed and dressed, Wolf dismissed his man and settled down to await his visitor. Noon passed, then one o'clock. Two. Wolf was lying on his bed staring at the square of blue sky through the little window when at last the door of his cell opened. He sat up.

'Good of you to call, Sir Charles.'

Urmston sauntered in, a monogrammed handkerchief clutched in his hand. The cloying scent that wafted into the cell with him suggested he had soaked the linen in perfume as protection against the noisome odours of the prison. He glanced about him, a look of distaste on his florid features.

'Hatcham said you wanted to see me. I had an appointment with my tailor and could not come this morning. However—' he gave a mocking smile '—I knew you were not going anywhere.'

'Aye,' growled Wolf. 'Thanks to you I am incarcerated in this cell and likely to be here for some time.' He decided to go directly to the attack. 'Why did you give Hatcham that poster for my arrest?'

Sir Charles spread his hands.

'My dear Arrandale, I merely brought it to his attention, as any law-abiding citizen would do.'

'Law-abiding?' Wolf's lip curled. He rose, towering over the man. 'You killed Meesden, did you not?'

Urmston stepped back, but his cold, humourless smile did not falter.

'*You* were caught with the knife in your hand and her blood all over you. No one will believe you did not murder her.'

'But we both know I did not do it. And what about my wife?' asked Wolf. He glanced at the closed door. 'Come, man, now I am safely locked up, will you not tell me the truth?'

'I will tell you nothing!' Urmston spat out the words, his usual mask of urbanity slipping, but only for a moment. He looked down, tracing a crack in the floor with his silver-topped cane. 'Is this why you wanted to see me, to try to foist the blame for your crimes upon me?'

'I am innocent and you know it.'

'But who will believe you?' purred Urmston. 'There are at least a dozen witnesses to testify against you and I am sure by now some of them even believe they saw you plunge the knife into that poor woman. And what could any character witnesses say on your behalf? You were hardly a model of propriety before you fled to France, were you? No, Arrandale, you will hang. And soon, I promise you. Now, if that is all I am off to my dinner.' He lifted his cane to rap upon the door, then paused to say with studied indifference, 'By the by, when you called on Meesden, did she tell you what had happened to the Sawston diamonds?'

'Did she not tell you, before you killed her?'

Urmston's eyelids flickered, but he gave a little shrug.

'If you did not steal them, then I feel sure it was your wife's maid. But that need not concern you, Arrandale, the theft will be laid at your door.' Urmston called for the warder to let him out before he turned back to Wolf for one parting shot. 'That, added to the two murders, will be more than enough to hang you.'

Alone again, Wolf sat on the bed. So Urmston did not know where to find the diamonds. That was encouraging, but it was not enough to save him from the gallows. Frustration gnawed at him, he wanted to be out of this place, instead he had to rely on his brother and an aged aunt to search for the necklace and try to build a case for his defence. If they could not—well, he would find a way to escape and go back to France, but somehow the life of an outcast no longer appealed to him. He wanted to remain in England with his family. With Grace.

He pushed the thoughts away and went back over everything Urmston had said, looking for any little clue that might help. He was so engrossed in his thoughts that he did not hear the approaching footsteps, nor did he move when the key grated in the lock of his door. It wasn't until the tall figure in a cloak and veiled bonnet stepped into the cell that he looked up.

He was on his feet in an instant.

'You should not be here.' He tried to mean it, but his heart was drumming erratically against his ribs. He could not take his eyes off Grace as she put back her veil.

'I told you I would come.'

'Yes, and *I* told you it was dangerous. Urmston has just left me. Did he see you?'

'Yes, unfortunately. He was talking to Mr Hatcham when the warder was taking my details for the register.'

'The devil he was! Grace, it was bad enough that you should visit me with my brother, but to come alone—'

She was unmoved by his fury.

'I told them you are one of Papa's parishioners and it is my duty to visit you on his behalf. Sir Charles heard it, too, but he barely noticed me, I think I was very convincing as a reluctant and disapproving prison visitor.'

'Surely this is not the same lady who berated me so soundly for involving her father in this matter?'

He was shaking his head, but Grace saw that he was smiling. There was a mixture of admiration and disbelief in his look and she knew a tell-tale blush was not far away. Resolutely she fought it down.

'As I told the constable, one should never shirk from one's Christian duty, however unpleasant.' She nodded towards her basket, saying shyly, 'I am more used to taking food baskets to the poor, but I know you have funds and your man will fetch your dinner later, so I thought I might bring you books instead.'

'Thank you.'

Wolf's dark eyes were fixed upon her, unfathomable but disturbing. To cover her confusion she began to empty the basket.

'They are from my aunt's library. I have brought you some poetry, the *Gentleman's Magazine* and the last two volumes of *Udolpho*.' He had come closer and her skin prickled with awareness of him. She was trembling and her throat was dry, but she chattered on as she lifted the final book from the basket. 'I knew the guards would search the basket so I felt obliged to bring you a Bible, too, although I doubt you will read it.'

'Grace.'

His hand covered hers as she laid the Bible on the table. She had removed her gloves to sign the visitor register and his touch was like a spark on dry tinder. The shock of it set her heart hammering against her ribs. She fixed her gaze on the holy book lying beneath their hands and her mind was suddenly filled with thoughts of the marriage ceremony, of clamouring bells and bouquets of spring flowers. With a gasp she tried to pull away, but Wolf's grip tightened. He drew her fingers against his chest, forcing her to turn towards him. Grace kept her eyes lowered, staring at the top button of his embroidered waistcoat. Thoughts flashed through her mind with lightning speed. He was not wearing his coat and that was most improper. She thought how white his shirt was, how well his waistcoat fitted him, how it enhanced the flat stomach and narrow hips.

How much she wanted to put her arms about him.

'Grace, look at me.'

She heard his soft words but dared not obey. If she raised her eyes she would see the broad shoulders made even wider by the billowing sleeves of his shirt, the lean jaw, shadowed now with a fine, dark stubble, the sensuous mouth that only had to smile to send all sensible thoughts flying. She swallowed nervously and gave her head a tiny shake. She must not look into his eyes or she was lost.

Wolf growled. She felt the rumble against her hand, still captive on his chest. He caught her chin, gently but inexorably pushing her head up. She tried to close her eyes and pull away, but her traitorous body would not obey and she found herself gazing into his eyes. They were the violet-blue of an evening sky.

'I…' She ran her tongue over her dry lips. 'Must not.'

He was lowering his head and she could resist no longer. She had tasted his kiss before and was desperate to do so again. With a tiny cry she threw her free arm around his neck and reached up to kiss him. It was a fierce, reckless embrace and she felt clumsy, inexperienced, but only for a moment. Wolf's mouth was working over hers and her whole body shuddered with delight. His arms went around her, holding her tight as the kiss deepened. Her lips parted and his tongue darted and delved, drawing a response from deep in her core. She was melting against him while his muscled body only seemed to grow harder. He was like a rock and she clung to him as waves of desire swept over her, leaving her weak.

Wolf raised his head, gasping like a drowning man. His body was shaking with the powerful hunger that coursed through him. It was the second time he had held Grace in his arms. She leaned against him, eyes half-closed and a delicate flush on her cheeks. But even now the languorous glow was fading. She lifted her head, a tiny crease of dismay already furrowing her brow. Soon she would be pushing him away, as she had done before. He could not bear to wait for her rejection so he released her and walked across to the window, rubbing one hand over his face.

'Now do you see why it is so dangerous to come here alone?' he demanded harshly.

When she did not reply he turned around. Grace was staring at the floor, clasping and unclasping her hands in front of her.

'I have been fighting and fighting against this,' she muttered, as if to herself. 'It means nothing, save that I have been too many years alone. It *cannot* mean anything. Once Loftus and I are married all will be well.'

'Will it?' Wolf shook his head, as much to clear his thoughts as to contradict her. 'You are deluding yourself if you think Braddenfield will arouse such passions in you.'

She put her hands to her head, pushing her fingers against her temples.

'You misunderstand me,' she said slowly. 'I do not *want* him to arouse me in that way. I had hoped to share those appetites once, with Henry, my first, my only love, but, but *carnal* desires have no place in my life now.'

He could not allow that, not when she had been in his arms, matching him kiss for kiss.

'Well, they *should* have a place!' He reached out and caught her hands. 'Desire is not a sin, Grace, it is natural and you should not marry a man you do not desire.'

'No!' She backed away from him, crossing her arms over her breast. 'Henry and I loved each other, we longed for the day when we could consummate our love and when I lost him it was unbearable.'

'How old were you when he died? Eighteen, nineteen?'

She sank down on the edge of the bed, hunched over as if in pain.

'I was nineteen. We were very much in love. We were made for one another. I knew it, even though we had known each other for less than two years. Can you understand that?'

'Yes, I can.' He knew now it was possible to fall in love in less than two months.

'Henry was my life,' she said simply. 'When he was taken, a part of me died, too.'

'But *only* a part of you,' he said. 'For the past five years you have been afraid to live. You have been afraid to allow yourself to *feel* anything. Even your engagement to Braddenfield is a safe and sensible choice.'

'You make it sound like a crime.'

'It is, when you could do so much more with your life.'

'How dare you criticise me,' she retorted, stung. 'I was very happy, until I met you!'

'If I have made you feel again then I cannot regret it, Grace. Oh, I know I am not the right man for you, I have lived for too long with the devil at my shoulder, but there are other men, good men, who would love you and make you happy, if you would give them a chance. You are too young to bury yourself away in a loveless marriage. You should be out in the world, living. Loving.'

'I do not *want* that!'

Her anguished cry silenced him.

She dragged the back of her hand across her eyes.

'When you came into my life I knew you were dangerous, someone even said you walk with the devil, but I did not want to believe it. Papa was keen to help and I, well, I thought a little adventure might be enjoyable, but it isn't. Not at all. It has cut up my peace most horribly, not least because I know I will not be able to tell Loftus and one should not have secrets from one's fiancé. I shall have to live out my life with that on my conscience, but I am promised to Loftus and I shall stand by my vow. I *want* to marry him. I shall be situated near my father and my future will be secure. That will please Papa.'

'And will it please you, too?'

'Yes.' She took out her handkerchief to wipe a stray

tear from her cheek. 'I want a safe, quiet existence. I beg your pardon if my actions just now made you think otherwise, but that part of my life is buried with Henry.' She raised her solemn, resolute gaze to his. 'Henry was a paragon of goodness. He is the yardstick by which I measure all other men.'

Wolf had always known she was too good for him and now she had told him that her previous love was a saint. Very few men would match up to such a standard and certainly not an Arrandale.

He sighed. 'If I have caused you unhappiness I am very sorry for it and I beg your forgiveness. Believe me, you have done nothing for which you need reproach yourself. Go home and forget me, Miss Duncombe.'

Grace felt as drained and empty as the basket Wolf pushed into her hands. He hammered on the door and shouted for the warder. As the key grated in the lock she rose and he reached out to pull the veil over her face.

'Thank you for your kindness, ma'am, and allow me to wish you every happiness.'

Without a word Grace left the cell and made her way up the stairs. When she reached the office her hand was shaking so much she could barely write her name to sign out. Janet was waiting in the carriage, but although Grace could respond calmly to her anxious enquiries she kept her veil down, knowing that tears were not far away.

Grace had never told anyone how she had felt about Henry Hodges, the unfulfilled cravings and desires that had haunted her dreams. She had never even told Henry, when he was alive. She had always assumed he felt the same, but now she wondered. Henry's most daring move had been to kiss her cheek and when, on one occasion, she had tried to put her arms about him he had held her off, saying gently that there would be time for all that once they were married. In fact, there was no time at all. Within the month he was dead. A tear slipped down her cheek. She had loved Henry so much. No one could take his place. No one, least of all a man like Wolf Arrandale.

All the way to Hans Place Grace wondered what she should do. To stay away from Wolf, to abandon him to his fate, seemed like the coward's way out. She had thrown herself at him in a most shameful way and she must now atone for it. Wolf had been surprised into reacting, but *he* was the one who had pushed her away. And he had told her quite plainly that he was not the man for her, so it was not as if her lustful feelings were reciprocated. She must show him and the world that she was strong and compassionate, a suitable wife for a magistrate. Wolf might not want her in *that* way, but her visits would help to break up the long days of his incarceration. She would be doing her duty. Dear Henry had died doing his.

And what she felt for Wolf Arrandale would fade. Did not Papa say often and often, *'Blessed is the man that endureth temptation?'* She must face this temptation and overcome it.

She quelled the tiny, traitorous voice that suggested that she *wanted* to see Wolf, that the tug of attraction was too great to resist.

By morning Grace had convinced herself that she was making too much of what had happened at the prison. She had been overcome by the horrors of Wolf's situation and had wanted to comfort him, nothing more. Good heavens, if Daniel could walk into a lion's den and survive overnight, surely she could spend an hour visiting an innocent man in his prison cell.

* * *

Mrs Graham looked up from her breakfast to smile as Grace came in.

'What an energetic girl you are, my love,' she greeted her niece. 'I have only just left my room and you have already taken Nelson for his morning walk.'

'Then we may break our fast together, ma'am,' Grace replied, sitting down at the table.

'And I am very glad to see you up and about,' remarked Aunt Eliza, as Jenner filled their coffee cups. 'You were so quiet at dinner last night I was afraid you might have caught something in that dreadful gaol.'

'No, no, I am quite well,' Grace reassured her. 'I was merely troubled yesterday.'

'And no wonder,' said Aunt Eliza. 'Mr Arrandale's plight is indeed very worrying. I was horrified when you told me he had been locked up for the murder of that poor woman. I am as convinced as you are that he is innocent, but thankfully he has his brother to support him now, to say nothing of the rest of the Arrandale relations, so there can be no need for you to go to that horrid prison again.'

Grace helped herself to a bread roll. 'On the contrary, I intend to visit Mr Arrandale again today.'

'My dear girl, you cannot be serious!'

'Never more so,' she replied, not looking up. 'As Papa's daughter I must help those in need.'

'But you said yourself Mr Arrandale has funds enough to pay for his comforts; surely one visit to him is enough. Heavens, my love, you ransacked my library to find works he might enjoy. I will not say I begrudge him the books—after all they have been sitting on the shelves since Mr Graham died and *I* shall never read them—but surely there can be no need for you to go back again.'

'If Papa were here it is what he would do.' Grace felt the colour heating her cheeks as those disturbing doubts returned. Of course she did not *want* to see Wolf. Indeed, she would be far more comfortable if she could put him right out of her head, but how could she do that, when the shadow of the gallows hung over him?

She said aloud, 'My mind is made up, Aunt Eliza, I shall visit Mr Arrandale every day while he remains in prison. It is my Christian duty.'

'Well, you are of age and I cannot stop you. Although what your fiancé will say I am sure I do not know.'

Grace silently finished her breakfast. She would have to tell Loftus something of her activities in London and he might even decide to withdraw his offer of marriage. But that was for the future. For now, she could not abandon Wolf Arrandale, whatever it cost her.

Richard Arrandale was to see his brother every morning, so Grace timed her visit for later in the day. She took her maid, but Janet was reluctant to enter the prison and Grace left her in the carriage while she went in alone to see Wolf. She arrived to find Kennet with his master, playing backgammon. They both rose at her entry and although Wolf scowled and told her she should not have come, the glow in his eyes gave the lie. There was an awkward moment of silence. The valet coughed and muttered that perhaps he should go.

'Yes—no,' said Wolf. 'What do you say, Miss Duncombe, would you prefer Kennet to stay?' When she shook her head he waved a hand towards his man. 'Come back in an hour. No, make it a little longer.'

Wolf had not taken his eyes off her and Grace struggled to keep still under his scrutiny.

I can do this, she told herself. *It is no different from visiting any of Papa's needy parishioners.*

When they were alone he said again, 'You should not have come.'

'My father always asks after you in his letters.'

It was a poor enough excuse, but Wolf nodded.

'Very well, then, Miss Duncombe. Will you not sit down?'

The days fell into a pattern. Grace was at her aunt's disposal each morning, but every afternoon she made her way to Horsemonger Lane. Kennet was often in attendance, but as soon as Grace arrived he would excuse himself and leave them alone to talk. Grace had no fears for her safety, Wolf kept as much distance as possible between them during her visits. He might walk with the devil, but nothing could have exceeded his civility towards her.

The guards grew accustomed to Grace's visits and soon gave no more than a cursory glance at her basket filled with books and a few little delicacies to augment the meals Kennet brought in from the local tavern. She also included extra pastries for the guards, who fell upon them with relish and it earned her a smile and a cheerful word from the warders as they escorted her to the prisoner.

Grace knew Richard was trying to build a case for his brother's defence, but by tacit agreement she and Wolf never spoke of it. Instead they talked of unexceptional subjects such as books and art and the latest reports from the newspapers that Kennet brought for his master every day.

After an hour, or sometimes a little more, Grace would

take her leave, pulling down her veil to hide the despair that choked her every time she left Wolf's cell. Once a rogue tear escaped and splashed on to the page when she was signing out and after that the officer in charge waved her away, saying with gruff kindness that they could not have her spoiling their visitor register and he would sign her out in future.

Grace hoped that the parting would grow easier as the days went by, but at the end of the first week she felt more desolate than ever. She returned to Hans Place, hoping to slip upstairs unnoticed, but her aunt was waiting in the hall and asked her to step into the morning room.

'My love,' she said, as they sat down together on the sofa. 'Another letter has arrived for you, from Hindlesham Manor. No doubt your fiancé is anxious to hurry your return.'

'Quite possibly.' Grace knew she must leave London very soon, but the hours she spent with Wolf were too precious and she could not give them up. Not yet. Under her aunt's watchful eye she broke the seal on the letter and opened it.

'Loftus sends his regards to you, Aunt,' she said, reading quickly. 'And he writes to tell me that the reception for Mrs Braddenfield's birthday went off very well.'

'You missed his mother's birthday?' Aunt Eliza put a hand on her knee. 'Grace, my love, let me speak plainly. You should have been at Hindlesham for such an event.'

'Loftus quite understands that I have not yet finished my business in London. If we were married it would be different.' Grace glanced again at the letter. 'Besides, he tells me Claire Oswald arranged everything perfectly. Indeed, as his mama's companion she was by far the best person to do so.'

Aunt Eliza gave a little tut of exasperation.

'My love, tell me honestly, do you still mean to marry Sir Loftus? It is not kind of you to keep him waiting, you know, if you mean to jilt him.'

'Jilt him?' The letter slid from Grace's fingers and she bent to retrieve it. 'Good gracious, Aunt, why should I do such a thing?'

'Because you are showing more interest in visiting a prison than seeing your fiancé.'

'I…I want to help Wolf, that is all.'

Aunt Eliza's brows rose. 'So it is Wolf now. You are mighty friendly with that young man, Grace.'

'The injustice of his situation shocks me. Papa urged me to support him and I have done so.' She added, as much to convince herself as her aunt, 'It is not friendship or anything warmer that draws me to the prison, but duty.'

'Well, I am relieved to hear it,' said Aunt Eliza. 'I was afraid you were in danger of throwing away your chance of lasting happiness for a man who is not free, and who, barring a miracle, is like to hang before the year is out.'

Aunt Eliza's words haunted Grace as she made her way to Horsemonger Lane the following day. She lifted her eyes to the prison roof and a little shiver of foreboding ran through her as she stared at the scaffold. The feeling of disquiet grew even stronger when she found Richard with his brother, and looking grim. She stopped in the doorway, clutching her basket before her, until Wolf invited her to come in.

'Is there news?' she asked, as she took the proffered

chair. The men glanced at one another and she said quickly, 'Please tell me.'

Richard pulled up a second chair and sat down.

'Wolf is to be tried at the Sessions House in a se'ennight,' he said.

'So soon!' Grace looked at Wolf, who nodded.

'And Urmston is funding my prosecution for Meesden's murder.'

Grace frowned. 'Is that not unusual?'

'Florence was his cousin,' said Richard. 'And since Meesden was her dresser Urmston says it is his moral duty to see justice done.'

'Justice!' Wolf's lip curled. 'If there were any justice it would be Urmston standing in the dock. As it is he lays my wife's death and the theft of the diamonds at my door, too. A very neat end to his machinations.'

'Sophia has directed her lawyers to handle this case,' put in Richard. 'They approached Urmston to settle this privately, but he will not budge. He is determined to see you hang, Brother.'

'Of course. He wants me to take the blame for his crimes.' Wolf scowled. 'He knows what happened to Florence, I am sure of it. I have had plenty of time to think while I have been locked up here. When we went to see Meesden, Grace, do you remember her words? *"She would have been happier with—"* She did not say with whom, but I believe she meant Charles Urmston. He and my wife were very close, you see. Too close. That was the reason for our argument the night she died. I told her I was damned if I'd be cuckolded in my own house.'

He began to pace about the room, head down, thinking. 'It is all tied up with the diamonds. Urmston would sell his own grandmother for a groat. Perhaps he wanted the necklace and Florence did not want him to take it. I think Meesden, too, knew what happened that night. Urmston may well have paid her to keep quiet and her subsequent disappearance did not matter until I returned to England and began to ask questions. And Urmston now seems quite anxious to find the necklace. He asked me about it again when he came here.'

'Well, it is worth a fortune and his funds are certainly at low ebb again,' said Richard. 'When I ran into him in Bath the summer before last he was once more in need for a fortune and trying to find himself another heiress. Even tried to abduct Ellen. My stepdaughter,' he explained to Grace, adding with a grin, 'She's a minx, but fortunately too clever to fall for his tricks. She even bamboozled me into marrying her stepmama.'

Grace saw his face soften as he thought of his wife and felt a momentary pang of envy. Not that it was *Richard* Arrandale she wanted to think of her with affection. A glance at Wolf showed him lost in thought, his countenance very grim, and she sought around for some glimmer of hope.

'You say your great-aunt has hired lawyers to defend you? They will be the very best, I think.'

Wolf shook his head. 'With the evidence against me there is little hope of an acquittal, even in a fair trial. But here, where Urmston already has the magistrate in his pocket—' He leaned on the table. 'There is no alternative, I must get out.' His stormy eyes fell on Grace. 'You had best leave, my dear. I would not have you compromised by what we are about to discuss.'

'You plan to escape, sir?'

'I am going to try,' he said. 'I have done many foolish

things in my time, but I will not be hanged for crimes I did not commit.'

'Then let me help you.'

'No.' He shook his head. 'You have risked enough for me already.'

'But—'

'Go back to Arrandale and marry Sir Loftus. Then I need worry about you no longer.'

Grace winced as his words cut into her, but she would not let him dismiss her so readily. Her determination manifested itself in a steely calm. She gazed at the two men.

'Do either of you have a plan?' When neither of them spoke she said, with no little satisfaction, 'Well, I do.'

Chapter Ten

It took a while for the brothers to accept Grace's idea. Richard finally acknowledged that it might work, but Wolf stubbornly refused to agree.

'What you suggest is madness,' he declared. 'I cannot let you take such a risk for me.'

'The risk is all yours,' she replied. 'I shall be safely away from here before you make your escape.'

'No!' he said explosively. 'I cannot have you involved in this!'

Grace sat back on her chair. 'Can you think of a better plan?'

Wolf glared at her, his look a mixture of frustration and fury.

Richard laughed. 'I have to admit, Miss Duncombe, we cannot.'

'Then we must use mine.' She rose. 'It is time for me to go.'

As she walked to the door she heard Wolf's smothered exclamation behind her.

'No, Grace, I cannot let you do this!'

She looked back. 'I do not think you have any choice, sir, unless you want to hang.'

Grace hurried back to her carriage. The cool resolution she had shown in the prison had been replaced by a nervous energy that made her blood sizzle. How was she ever to explain this to Aunt Eliza, let alone to Loftus? The sad truth was that she had no intention of telling them of her involvement in this daring plan. Indeed, if everything went well there was no need for them to know anything about it. Her part in it was negligible. She would tell Papa and she prayed he would understand, even if he thought her misguided.

A memory stirred. When Henry had been brought back to the vicarage and it had been explained how he had been stabbed protecting a woman from her husband. Papa had given way to emotion then and for once he had railed, saying Henry had been impetuous and misguided to tackle the man alone. Now Grace remembered dear Henry's words as she nursed him through his final hours.

'I had to try, Grace. I could no more leave them to their fate than I could stop breathing.'

'That is it, exactly,' she murmured. 'Oh, Henry, you understand why I must do this, don't you?'

Wolf paced the floor of his cell. It was five days since they had agreed to Grace's idea and throughout each of them he had worried their plan would be discovered and she would be arrested. Richard had called this morning to tell him everything was in place, Kennet had been despatched with his instructions and now Wolf was waiting for Grace to make her final visit. He wished to heaven she need not come, but to all his protests she had calmly pointed out that it was necessary if their plan was to work.

'All your visitors save myself are searched upon entry here,' she had told him. 'The guards trust me and that is our advantage.'

And much as he disliked the idea of putting Grace in danger, for the life of him he could not think of any alternative.

When the door was unlocked and she stepped into the cell he fixed her with a grim stare. She put back her veil, pale but composed.

'Good day to you, Mr Arrandale. I trust you are well?'

Her greeting was the same every time and he replied with his usual scowl, which always made the guard grin as he locked the door upon them.

'I wish you did not have to come,' he muttered, as she put her basket down beside the table.

'I pray this will be the last time.'

Wolf walked to the door and looked out through the grille. The passage was empty, but he was not taking any chances and kept his voice low.

'Everything is ready?'

She nodded. 'A hackney coach will be waiting for you across the road from the gaol at the appointed time.'

'Kennet has found a couple of choice spirits who are even now spending money in the local gin house. Their customers should be roaring drunk and filling the cells within the hour. So you must go as soon as possible, the streets will not be safe.'

'I am aware. I have an extra footman on the carriage today.'

'And I have your word you will go home tomorrow?'

'Yes. That is all arranged.' She cast a shy glance up at him. 'Shall I see you, at Arrandale?'

Wolf had been expecting this and had his answer ready.

'No. I must go to the Hall, but I will not have you or your father involved any further in this business.'

'But if you can prove you are innocent—'

'It would take a miracle to get a confession from Urmston, and I have never believed in miracles.' He shook his head. 'If we can find the diamonds that will throw doubt upon my guilt. Not enough to convince a jury, I have no doubt that in their eyes the fact that I was found kneeling over the bodies of both my wife and her dresser, with their blood on my hands, would be enough to condemn me, but Richard might convince my daughter I am no murderer.'

'But we cannot give up hope.'

She looked at him, confident that justice could prevail. Experience had taught Wolf otherwise, but her faith was endearing. He wanted to kiss her, to lose himself in her soft goodness. She had responded to his kiss before, she would again, all he had to do was reach out and take her. Mentally he drew back, reining in his desire. She was betrothed to another man. He might seduce her, kiss and caress her until she was unable to resist him, but she would never forgive herself for breaking her vows. She was too good, too honest to bear the deceit. It would destroy her. *He* would destroy her.

'I shall not stay in England. Richard and I will appoint a good steward at Arrandale and I shall provide a dowry for little Florence, but then I shall go abroad.'

'Within the month I shall be married and living at Hindlesham.' Her eyes sparkled with tears. 'If your innocence is proved you need not leave Arrandale for my sake.'

He forced a laugh and said carelessly, 'Grace, m'dear, this isn't about *you*. The truth is I am too restless to stay in any one place or be faithful to any one woman. I have been a vagabond for too long. I shall never settle down.'

He looked away from the pain in her eyes. He was hurting her, he knew it, but it was for the best. He had never been anything but a wastrel and she deserved so much more than that.

He said, 'It is time for you to go. Let us get on with it. If you are ready?'

She nodded silently, looking so unhappy that he crossed the space between them in a single stride and took her hands, carrying them to his lips.

'I am more grateful than I can say for what you have done, Grace, believe me.'

'Thank you,' she whispered. The dark lashes swept down, shielding her eyes. Her fingers trembled in his grasp, he felt her steeling herself for what was to come. Gently she freed herself and gave a little nod. 'Now. Let us finish this.'

Wolf grabbed the chair and sent it crashing behind him, saying in a loud, angry voice, 'Damnation, woman, I am *sick* of your moralising!' He strode across the cell and pounded on the door, exclaiming, once the guard's footsteps rang on the stone flags, 'If all you can do is preach at me, madam, then you had best go now. And good riddance to you!'

As the guard opened the door Grace flicked her veil over her face and hurried out. As expected, the outer office was bustling. The usual officer was not yet on duty and she signed herself out. No one questioned that she was leaving within minutes of her arrival and she hurried away to her carriage, tears of despair welling in her eyes. She had been foolish enough to think she was the reason Wolf would not stay at Arrandale and he had lost no time in correcting her. It should not matter, she was marrying Loftus, if he would have her, so why should she care what Wolf thought of her? But she *did* care. Today in that cheerless little cell she had admitted to herself something she had been so resolutely ignoring for weeks. She was in love with Wolf Arrandale.

Wolf threw himself down on his bed while he waited for the hour to pass. He hated parting from Grace in so rough a fashion, even though they both knew it was contrived. He hated parting from her at all, but it had to be. There was no future for them and he consoled himself with the fact that she would soon forget him, once she was married to her magistrate.

From above came muted shouts and angry voices as drunken rioters were brought in to spend the night in the lock-up. That part of the plan seemed to be working and a few moments later he heard the jovial banter and rough insults that accompanied the changing of the guard. Wolf sat up. That was what he had been waiting for. The officers on duty now would not have seen Grace leaving early and with luck they would not question the veiled figure who would shortly be making her way out of the prison. Quietly, listening intently for any approaching footsteps, he gathered together the clothes Grace had smuggled in for him over the past five days.

Wolf's escape from the gaol was almost ludicrously easy. The guard was so used to Grace quitting Wolf's cell at this time that he hardly looked at the cloaked and veiled figure waiting to be let out and he barely glanced at the dark shape on the bed. The dim light helped to disguise the fact that there was nothing more than pillows and blankets beneath the covers.

Above stairs was a scene of uproar. Constables argued with their more drunk and belligerent charges and, as Grace had predicted, the beleaguered officer in charge merely waved the veiled figure on her way without even looking at the register. From beneath the veil, Wolf watched several drunken men crowd the desk, berating the guards. It might be hours before they discovered the deception. Wolf kept his large hands hidden inside Grace's swansdown muff and shortened his stride to a more ladylike step as he made his way out of the gaol. No one accosted him, but he did not breathe until he was in the coach and driving away from Horsemonger Lane.

Quickly he discarded the bonnet, cloak and skirts that had masked his identity and replaced them with the hat and riding jacket he found on the seat. Looking out of the carriage, he gave a small grunt of satisfaction. They were travelling south, away from the river. If anyone did remark them they would think he was heading for Dover. So far so good, but he would feel happier once he had reached New Cross, where Kennet should be waiting with the horses.

Darkness was falling by the time the coach pulled up at a busy inn. If the driver thought it odd that a heavily veiled lady had climbed into his carriage and a fashionable gentleman was leaving it, he showed no sign and Wolf tossed him a silver coin to add to the handsome payment he had already received for his services. Glancing back along the road, he caught a flash of movement on the horizon, riders outlined against the last remaining strip of daylight. Wolf's eyes narrowed. They were approaching fast. He had hoped for a little more time before his escape was discovered.

Recalling his brother's instructions, Wolf crossed the inn yard and out through a narrow gate on the far side, into a back lane. Once he was out of sight of any casual observer he began to run. In the dim light of the rising moon he could just make out a stand of trees a short distance ahead of him. As he approached he heard the faint snuffle of a horse.

'Kennet?' He spoke softly. 'Are you there?'

Two horses emerged from the black shadows of the trees but the figure leading them was not Kennet, it was too tall. The pale moonlight fell on a youth, a stripling dressed in riding clothes and a neat jockey cap. Wolf frowned. There was something familiar about the slender shape, the dainty profile.

'Grace! What the devil—!'

She cut him off. 'There is no time to explain. I saw the riding officers approaching the inn. They will be searching here very soon. We must go. There is a horse ferry waiting for us at Woolwich.'

Something blazed through Wolf. He ignored the reins she was holding out to him and dragged her into his arms.

Grace's nerves were at full stretch and she was defenceless against the onslaught of his kiss. It was fierce, ruthless and possessive. It promised everything she had dreamed of. Everything she knew she could not have. With a superhuman effort she kept her hands clenched on the reins and resisted the temptation to respond. It was over in an instant. Without a word he threw her up into the saddle and scrambled on to his own horse, wheeling the restive animal towards her.

'Woolwich, you say?'

She dragged her thoughts back, forcing herself to think. Wolf's life depended upon her now.

'Yes. Follow me.'

She headed into the trees. The path was barely discernible, but they reached the other side without mishap and she set her horse at a gallop across the open fields. The trees at their back screened them from the inn and as they crested a ridge she risked a quick glance behind. There were no signs of pursuit so Grace steadied the pace to a canter, avoiding roads and skirting villages until at length they reached a crossroads.

'You appear to know your way around here very well,' commented Wolf, as she slowed to a walk.

'Your brother supplied Kennet with very good directions, which I have committed to memory.' She looked around, then pointed north. 'That way, I think. You see the church tower over there? We head for that and it will bring us to a small dock, well away from the arsenal.'

'There is an *arsenal* at Woolwich?' Wolf cursed under his breath. 'That means the military. It is madness to consider crossing the river at this point.'

'And thus no one will expect it.'

As she gathered up the reins, ready to ride on, Wolf reached out and caught her arm.

'Go back, Grace. It's not too late. Let me go on alone, do not involve yourself with me.'

She shook her head. 'I *am* involved, Wolf. There is no going back for me now.'

Wolf's head was buzzing with questions as she cantered off along the road, but they must wait. For now all he could do was follow. They took a circuitous route around the town and approached the river through a series of narrow lanes.

'How the devil did my brother find this place?' he murmured as they rode between two derelict warehouses.

'I believe you are not the only Arrandale with dubious connections.' Grace reached into her coat and pulled out a pistol, which she held out to him. 'You should have this. It is loaded, but I am not familiar with firearms.'

'You surprise me,' said Wolf drily. He checked the weapon and carefully put it in his pocket. 'There is a light ahead. Could it be our ferryman?'

'It is certainly the signal,' she said, peering into the darkness.

'It could be a trap,' he muttered. 'Stay here in the shadows.'

She shook her head. 'We stay together.'

There was a stubborn note in her voice and he decided not to waste time arguing.

'Very well, but let me go first.' Wolf touched his heels to the horse's flanks and led the way towards the swinging light. His eyes darted about and he strained his ears for signs of danger, but there was no one save the ferryman, who silently beckoned them towards the waiting barge.

It took time and patience to persuade the horses to embark, but at last they were tethered securely and there was nothing for the passengers to do but to sit down out of the way while the crew plied their oars and rowed them across the wide expanse of the river. The night air was chill and they wrapped themselves in the thick cloaks that had been strapped to the saddles. They were far enough from the crew to talk without being overheard, and Grace braced herself for the questions she knew Wolf was burning to ask.

'So why are you here rather than my valet?'

'He can barely ride.'

'What? Why the devil didn't he say so?'

'He saw it as his duty to follow your brother's instructions.'

'But to let you take his place,' Wolf exclaimed wrathfully. 'Of all the cowardly—'

'Not at all. It was perfectly sensible that I should do so. I learned to ride astride as a child. You must admit I have not held you back.'

'I will admit nothing.'

He sounded so much like a sulky schoolboy that Grace laughed and was immediately shocked at her reaction. There was nothing amusing about their situation. It was perilous. Wolf's life was at stake, to say nothing of her reputation. Her amusement argued a most unfeminine lack of sensibility. Not what gentlemen wanted at all, she thought bleakly. Gentlemen liked weak, decorative females whom they could cherish and protect, not practical women with their own opinions. Years running her father's household had taught Grace to be strong and resourceful, and much as she enjoyed the romances that graced her father's library shelves she knew she was not suited to be one of those heroines who quailed in the face of adversity and turned to a hero to rescue her from danger. She was a practical female and there was nothing she could do about it. Thankfully, Loftus had not shown any romantic inclinations. Theirs would be a practical marriage and the most she expected from it was that her life would be useful.

Useful and dull.

'Where is Kennet now?'

Wolf's voice brought Grace back to the present.

'He is taking your things to Arrandale.'

He leaned closer and said menacingly, 'And just how, madam, did you discover he could not ride?'

Grace folded her hands in her lap.

'From my maid,' she said calmly. 'Kennet was in the habit of talking to her while she waited for me outside the prison each day. She quizzed him today because he was looking so unhappy and he confessed he had not been on a horse more than a dozen times in his life, but he was determined to do his duty. I, however, thought that might wreck everything, so we drove to New Cross and I persuaded him to give up his place to me.'

'No doubt you carry a set of boy's clothes with you, for just such an eventuality.'

His sarcasm made her smile.

'We were fortunate that it is market day. Janet purchased them for me.'

'And then Kennet and your maid left you alone to carry out this hare-brained scheme.'

'They were neither of them happy about it, but they could see it was for the best. I wrote a note for my aunt, telling her to send Janet and all my luggage on to the vicarage tomorrow and I will go there directly. No one will know I did not arrive by coach.'

'Unless we are caught.'

'Then we must make sure that does not happen.'

Her cool response shook a laugh from him. He reached for her hand and raised it to his lips.

'I begin to think you will be wasted as the wife of a magistrate.'

Grace pulled her hand away. His words stung her cruelly. Wolf did not want her so why should he mock her for her choice? And if Loftus discovered what she had done she doubted he would marry her. She would live out her days as her father's housekeeper. The choices were stark and neither of them appealing. The future stretched ahead of her, as dark and depressing as the river flowing silently around them.

Wolf rose. 'We are nearing the bank. Let us get to the horses.'

They disembarked into an eerie, midnight world. Not a light showed in any of the buildings as they cantered through the deserted streets, heading northwards and guided by the stars. Grace had been warned that the land was marshy on this side of the river and they would need to keep to the roads, but eventually they left the flat plains behind and found themselves hedged about by woodland. Grace hesitated, not sure of her direction.

'I had friends in this area as a boy,' said Wolf. 'We can ride cross-country and pick up the Newmarket road at Epping. I know the way.'

'Thank you.' Grace yawned and rubbed a hand across her eyes.

'You are exhausted. We must find somewhere to rest.' She tried to protest, but he cut her short, saying brutally, 'You are no good to me if you are too fatigued to ride hard. If my memory serves we shall soon reach the Colchester road. Let us cross that and we will find somewhere in the forest to sleep.'

Grace nodded, too tired to speak. They set off again. It took all her concentration to follow Wolf and keep her horse from stumbling on the uneven ground. Clouds scudded across the sky, hiding the moon and plunging them into an even darker night. Wolf rode without pause and Grace marvelled at his ability to find his way unerringly along the most twisting lane, heading ever northwards. They crossed a broad highway and plunged again into thick forest. Grace was nearly dropping with fatigue by the time they reached a small clearing and Wolf announced they would stop for the night.

Grace wrapped herself in her cloak and sank down against a convenient tree, apologising that she had not thought to include any food for their journey.

'No matter.' Wolf dropped down beside her. 'We will be in Arrandale in time for breakfast.'

The silence settled comfortably around them. An owl hooted softly in the distance and Grace instinctively moved closer to Wolf, who put his arm about her.

'Do not tell me you are afraid of the dark,' he teased her gently.

She chuckled. 'Not at all. You are softer to lean against than a tree trunk.'

Her head had fallen to his shoulder. It was so comfortable resting against him, breathing in the faint but unmistakable masculine scent. She must sleep now, but perhaps, when she woke, she might turn her face up to his for another kiss. A delicious sense of anticipation filled her at the thought. She put her hand against his chest and snuggled closer.

'Excuse me, I must check the horses.'

He eased himself away and Grace bit back a little mewl of disappointment. Hot tears pressed against the back of her eyes. She felt bereft, in need of comfort. Wolf was talking softly to the horses and she hoped he would come back to her soon. She felt safe when he was near, even though she knew she should not feel safe at all, especially when she was consumed by such a yearning to have him make love to her.

The memory of his kisses made her body hot then cold, as if a huge hand was squeezing her insides and turning them to water. She thought of what could happen here, in this sheltered glade. Helping her father in the parish, she knew the dangers of being too free with a man, but somehow that was of no consequence now. She wanted Wolf to lie with her and satisfy the aching longing that gnawed at her.

She would be ruined, of course. And there could be no question of marrying Loftus, but that seemed unimportant. She had always known she did not love Loftus, to cry off would hurt his pride, but not his heart. But what of her professed love for Henry? She had always believed she could never love anyone else but now she knew she loved Wolf Arrandale, and although nothing could come of it, she wanted to give herself to him, to feel the comfort of his arms, his body. Just once. Was that disloyal to Henry? It was strange that she should face this question now, when her mind and body were so tired, but perhaps that was why she could think of it, while her mind was clear of all the other obstacles.

Henry was dead. She had loved him, part of her would always love him, but Wolf had shown her that she could love again. What would Henry say to that, if he knew? She yawned and felt herself slipping further into sleep even as her imagination discussed it with him.

Wolf stood by his horse, smoothing the velvet nose and breathing deeply to fight down the desire that raged through his body. He had needed to get away from Grace and the almost unbearable temptation of having her in his arms, her body pressed so comfortably against his. She was a parson's daughter, a virgin. She had risked everything to help him and he would not repay her by seducing her.

Why not? whispered the devil on his shoulder. *She wants you, she was almost giving herself to you.*

He closed his eyes. She was a lady. He knew she would not be able to enjoy a brief liaison and then walk away without being hurt.

You could marry her.

No.

Even if by some miracle he could prove his innocence, the stains of his past life could not be eradicated. She was too good for him, he could never make her happy.

You do not know that.

The devil would not be silenced.

Put it to her. Lay your heart and hand before her and let her decide. She is a woman and capable of making her own choices.

He stilled.

'I could do that,' he murmured as the horse snuffled softly and pushed against his hand. For the first time he saw a glimmer of hope.

She believes I am innocent. She has risked everything to help me. Perhaps, after all, she might care enough to marry me.

He straightened his shoulders. It would be her choice. He would move heaven and earth to prove his innocence and make her mistress of Arrandale, but if not, if he failed, they could live abroad, content with each other's company.

If she truly loved him.

She certainly did not love her fiancé and Wolf decided if Grace was going to throw herself away on a man it should be him. He would love her as she should be loved. He would worship her.

Wolf's spirits rose higher than they had done for a long time as he walked back to Grace. In the darkness he could just make out her soft shape, wrapped in the cloak. Silently he lay down beside her and rested his hand on the swell of her hip, felt the dip where it fell away to the dainty waist and his blood heated again. He would wait for the parson to marry them, if she wished it, but if she wanted him now… He closed his eyes. It must be her choice.

'Grace, love.'

She stirred. 'You understand, do you not, my dear? Oh, Henry.'

The words were soft as a sigh but there was no mistaking them, or the name she spoke so tenderly.

Wolf rolled away. Disappointment, bitter as gall, flooded through him. Stifling a groan, he turned to look at her. In the darkness her face was no more than a pale blur, but in his mind it was clear. He knew every detail of it, the straight little nose, the determined mouth and those dark lashes that now fanned out over her ivory cheek.

'Oh, Grace.' Wolf dropped a kiss lightly on her sleeping head. 'That puts you out of my reach more surely than an ocean. I cannot compete with a dead man.'

Chapter Eleven

Grace awoke with a delicious sense of wellbeing, but as full wakefulness returned she realised she was lying on the ground, warm enough in her thick cloak, but very much alone. It had all been a dream, then, lying in Wolf's arms, feeling safe and secure and with the promise of delights to come, once they were both rested. She struggled to sit up, rubbing her eyes. It was early, the first grey fingers of dawn were creeping through the trees but everything was still and quiet. Not even the birds were singing yet.

She looked around and saw Wolf standing by the horses, strapping his cloak to the saddle. Somewhere in her foolish, naïve imagination she had expected to wake and find him lying beside her, that he would roll over and make love to her here in this forest glade. What a romantic notion for such a practical person!

A sigh escaped her and Wolf turned. The closed look in his face sent the rest of her happy thoughts crumbling to dust.

'It is time we were moving.'

'Of course.' Grace scrambled to her feet and shook

her cloak to shed the twigs and dead leaves that clung to the wool. The man was flying for his life. He had no time for dalliance, least of all with a woman who meant nothing to him. She should be grateful.

'Shall I pack up your cloak?'

'No.' She threw it back around her shoulders. The excitement of the adventure had gone, she felt exposed and rather foolish in her boy's clothes. 'I am cold.'

'The ride will soon warm you up.'

Silently Grace climbed into the saddle. It would take more than exercise to remove the ice in her heart.

Three hours hard riding brought them to the outskirts of Arrandale. They cut into the woods that bounded the park, where there was less likelihood of being seen than if they followed the road.

'You should go straight to the Hall,' Grace suggested. 'I will leave the horse at the stile and you can send someone to collect him.

'No, I will escort you.'

Wolf did not look at her. He did not want to see the pain in those lustrous eyes. Last night they had been so close, so companionable and he had almost succumbed to the temptation to make her his. Thank heaven he had moved away when he did. She still loved her precious curate, and although he might have made her forget the fellow for a time, in the days ahead she would measure Wolf against her saint and find him wanting.

When they reached the gates they were closed but unchained, suggesting Sophia had arrived. The village street was deserted, those who worked in the fields were already departed and the rest had not yet breakfasted. He turned to Grace.

'Give me the reins. I'll take the horse back with me.'

'Yes, of course.' She made no move to dismount.

'Go carefully. Grace.'

'I have only to cross the street. That back lane will take me directly to the vicarage garden.'

Wolf nodded. He had used it many times as a boy to steal fruit from the parson's orchard. What would Duncombe say, if he knew how close Wolf had come to stealing his daughter?

She sighed. 'So this is goodbye.'

'Yes.' He could not meet her eyes. 'We shall not meet again.'

'Will you not shake hands with me?'

After the long ride the animals stood quietly side by side. How could he refuse, after all she had done for him, risking her life, her reputation, to help him.

He took her hand, forced himself to look into her face.

Ah, Grace, if things had been different. If I had not led such a rakehell life. If we had met before you fell in love with your saintly curate. We might have stood a chance.

The words screamed in his head, but he could not say them.

'Goodbye, Grace Duncombe.'

She clung to his fingers. 'Wolf, last night—'

He shook his head at her. 'One day, my dear, you will thank me for my forbearance.'

She looked as if she might argue so he tore his hand free and caught her reins.

'Go now. Every moment you delay endangers us both.'

She recoiled from his harsh tone and he bit back the impulse to apologise. Without another word she jumped down and scrambled over the stile. Wolf watched her disappear into the lane, then he turned and headed for the Hall. If this was what it felt like, doing the right thing, he wanted none of it. Clearly he was not made to be a saint.

Wolf noticed the changes as soon as he approached the Hall. Two men were scything the lawn and they stopped to watch as he rode down the drive. When he reached the stables they were bustling with activity. An elegant travelling chaise was visible through the open doors of the carriage house and two young men were removing the weeds from between the cobbles in the yard. They were being watched closely by an older man who looked up as Wolf clattered in. He ran across to take the spare horse from him.

'Morning, Mr Arrandale. Welcome home.'

'Who the devil are you and what's going on here?' demanded Wolf.

The man touched his cap.

'I'm Collins, sir, groom to Mr Richard. He sent me here to meet you and to look after the stables. And not a moment too soon, if you'll excuse my saying so, sir, since Lady Hune is determined to set everything here by the ears.'

'So my great-aunt's installed herself at the house, has she?'

A wide grin split the groom's craggy features.

'Aye, sir, the dowager marchioness has brought her whole retinue with her, and then some. All trusted folk and loyal,' he added quickly. 'You needn't fear for your safety, sir.'

'Glad to hear it.' Wolf slid to the ground. 'I'd better go in and see what she has been doing with my property!'

'Just one more thing, Mr Arrandale.' The groom lowered his voice. 'Mr Richard ordered a fast horse to be kept saddled and ready in the stables at all times.'

Suddenly Wolf was twenty-four again, angry, confused and thrust out of the house by a father who was convinced he was guilty. If he had stood his ground ten years ago, this sorry mess might never have happened. And Richard was clearly prepared for the worst.

'Much obliged to him,' he said shortly and strode off towards the house.

He had not gone far before he was intercepted by Robert Jones.

'Her ladyship said she had orders from Mr Richard, there was nothing I could do,' he said, eager to explain himself. 'She just swept in and took over, sir, brought all her own people with her, too. Hundreds of 'em.'

'I doubt if anyone could withstand Lady Hune in full flow,' muttered Wolf.

'But I don't mind saying it's good to have the house staffed again, sir. 'Tis quite a responsibility, looking after a place this size. Why, I couldn't even offer Sir Charles any refreshment when he called.'

'Sir Charles Urmston was here?' Wolf stopped. 'When was this?'

Jones rubbed his nose. 'Oh, weeks back, sir. Just after you left. He came to the house, saying as how he was in the area and wanted to see where he had spent so many happy days.'

'You let him into the house?'

'I didn't see how I could stop him, his having been such a favourite of the old master and cousin to Mrs Wolfgang.'

'But you went with him?'

'Oh, yes, sir. He wandered through the reception rooms, sighing and lamenting.'

'And you were with him the whole time?' When the servant hesitated Wolf put his hand on his shoulder. 'Answer me honestly, man. It is important that I know the truth.'

'Well, sir, when we gets to the hall he looked at the spot where your poor wife died and he covers his face, upset-like. Then he asks for something to drink. I told him there was nothing fit and he says as how he would take a glass of water, if I would fetch it.'

'And where was he when you got back?'

'Sir?'

'Was he still in the hall when you brought the water?'

'No, sir, he was on the landing. Said he had been musing on how his poor cousin could've fallen from that very spot.' Jones shook his head, clearly disapproving. 'Didn't seem proper, sir, to be going over something that happened so long ago.'

'He was standing near the balustrade, was he? Could he have been in any of the bedchambers?'

'He might have done, sir, but I wasn't gone that long.' Jones screwed up his face in an effort to remember. 'And he was wiping his hands on his handkerchief, sir, as if they was dirty.'

'And what did he do then?'

'Well, he comes down and I gives him the water, which he took no more than a sip of before going off.'

'He didn't ask to see over the rest of the house?'

'Now you comes to mention it, Mr Wolfgang, he did say as how he thought his horse was going lame and could he stay the night, but I told him that wouldn't be possible, sir, not at all. I offered him the use of the old gig we keeps in the stables to take him to the Horse Shoe, if he didn't want to walk, but he said his horse would get him that far. I didn't see him again after that, sir. Nor anyone else, until her ladyship arrived. And now I'm not sure what I should be doing.'

Wolf squeezed his shoulder.

'Keep your head down, Robert. This will all be over soon.'

'And then will you be living here again, sir?'

The footman's hopeful look caused Wolf a pang of remorse.

'No, Robert, I won't. But I shall make better provision for you all before I go this time, you have my word on it.'

The house was even busier than the stables, with sounds of activity echoing around the hall, where Croft, his great-aunt's butler, was directing an army of servants. When he saw Wolf, the butler waved away his minions and bowed.

'Her ladyship is in the drawing room, sir. She is expecting you.' He added quietly, as he opened the door, 'May I say that we are all delighted to see you here safe, sir.'

Wolf nodded. He had no doubt of Croft's loyalty and he knew his formidable great-aunt would have brought no one to Arrandale who could not be trusted to keep his presence a secret.

Sophia, Dowager Marchioness of Hune, came away from the window as he entered, her bearing as upright and regal as he remembered, despite the use of a cane, but when he was close enough to press a salute upon her hand he could see how much she had aged, her face more lined and the blue of her eyes a little less intense, although the look she fixed upon him had lost none of its power to intimidate.

'I am delighted to see you here, ma'am,' he said politely.

'So you should be.' The claw-like fingers clung to him. 'Help me to a chair. Once Croft has brought in the refreshments we can talk.'

'You have lost no time in making yourself at home,' he observed.

'You could not expect me to stay in this barrack of a house without a few comforts.'

She fell silent when the butler came and served them both with a glass of wine. Wolf sipped it appreciatively.

'Did you bring this with you, ma'am? It is superior to anything I recall from these cellars.'

'Your father was always a nip-farthing when it came to good wine.'

'So you brought your own. And all your servants, too, by the look of it.'

'Not only *my* servants.' She looked up to make sure they were alone again. 'I had some idea what would be required to put the place in some sort of order, so I asked the family for assistance.'

'The family?'

'Your brother and his wife and Lord and Lady Davenport. The staff were all carefully chosen for their loyalty and discretion, I assure you.'

Wolf frowned.

'I do not doubt it, ma'am, but I would rather you had not dragged Alex and his new wife into this.'

'They are Arrandales and will wish to be involved. Do not worry, your secrets are safe enough, my boy.'

'I do not doubt it, but it comes hard to trust so many people, when I have been accustomed to fending for myself.' He looked up, one brow raised. 'The two fellows scything the lawns as I rode in. They looked useful fellows to have with one in a fight.'

He saw the familiar glint in those faded eyes. 'Your brother sent them, lest Sir Charles Urmston should turn up, although there has been no sign of him as yet.' She paused. 'They might also buy you a little extra time to make your escape, should it be necessary.'

'You have not discovered the Sawston diamonds, then?'

'No. I have had the house turned out of doors, but my people have found nothing.'

'Did Richard tell you to pay special attention to the dresser's room?'

'He and Phyllida are going over it. I presume they have found nothing or they would have come down by now.'

'What?' Wolfgang exploded. 'They are here?'

'They arrived last evening, although they have sent little James off to Brookthorn with his nurse.'

'Thank heaven they have shown some sense!' declared Wolf. 'I do not want the family interfering in my affairs any further.'

'I think you must accustom yourself to it, Wolfgang. These days Arrandales stick together. You should think yourself fortunate that Ellen Tatham, Phyllida's stepdaughter, is touring the Lakes with her old teacher at present or she would have been here, too, and she would set us all by the ears.'

'Even you, Sophia?'

Lady Hune allowed herself a faint smile. 'Even me. However, I think you should prepare yourself to see the

Davenports here tomorrow. And they *are* bringing the children with them.'

Wolf clapped a hand over his mouth, as if to hold back even more explosions, not so much of wrath as consternation.

'Send them an express,' he said at last. 'They should not come.'

'Do you not wish to meet your daughter?'

'Yes, very much, but I want to meet her as a free man. I do not want her to see me arrested and dragged off in chains.'

'Do you think that is likely?'

He nodded. 'If I delay here too long. Urmston will make sure Arrandale is searched, once the trail to Dover goes cold. If the necklace is not found within a day or two, then I must give up my plans to see little Florence and leave the country.'

'If that is the case then naturally you must go, but you may be sure we shall continue the search.'

'Thank you, ma'am, I—'

He broke off as the door opened and a cheerful, musical voice floated across the room.

'Go away, Croft, we will announce ourselves.'

'Cassandra!' The words had hardly left his mouth before a petite dark-haired beauty threw her arms about him. 'What the—the deuce are you doing here?' he demanded, frowning over her head at Raoul Doulevant, who had followed her into the room. Raoul merely lifted his shoulders in a very Gallic shrug.

'My wife, she thought we should support you.'

'You knew I was coming here?'

'I guessed,' said Cassie, twinkling up at him. 'As soon as Grandmama wrote to tell me she was coming to Arrandale I knew something was afoot. We set off as soon as Raoul had made arrangements for leave from his duties.'

'Then you can make yourself useful by helping to search the house for the Sawston necklace,' snapped Lady Sophia.

Wolf glanced at the dowager marchioness. Despite her sharp tone he could see she was delighted to have her granddaughter with her and she even greeted Raoul with more warmth than Wolf expected her to show to a mere surgeon.

'The diamonds?' said Cassie, going to sit on a sofa beside her husband. 'You think they are here?'

The dowager nodded. 'Wolfgang thinks so, although so far we have found nothing.'

Wolf exhaled fiercely. 'Perhaps I am wrong, but Meesden was adamant the diamonds had not been stolen. Grace and I both remember her saying so.'

'Grace?' Lady Hune pounced on the name. 'Your brother mentioned a young woman was helping you.'

'Miss Duncombe is the daughter of the local vicar here in Arrandale,' he said carefully. 'She was visiting her aunt in London.'

'Indeed?' Wolf found himself subjected to another of the dowager's piercing stares. 'I should like to meet her.'

'I think not,' he said quickly. 'She has had too much contact already with the Arrandale family. And she is about to marry the local magistrate.' Wolf stared moodily into the fire. The thought of Grace married to another man tore into him. It was made even more painful by the obvious affection that existed between Cassie and her husband. If only Grace could love him in that way, but her heart was buried in the Arrandale churchyard, along with her first love.

He rubbed a hand over his eyes, the long ride was catching up with him.

'I need to sleep,' he said, rising. 'Then I will help you search the house. The diamonds are here, I know it, and I am determined to find them.'

Grace slipped into the vicarage, thankful that there was no one on the stairs to see her in her boy's clothes. In her room she found the maid, humming tunelessly as she ran a cloth along the mantelshelf. On hearing the door open, Betty turned and immediately dropped the Dresden figurine she had been dusting.

'Ooh, Miss Grace, you did give me a scare!' She looked in dismay at the shattered porcelain pieces lying in the hearth. 'And what the master will say when he knows what I have done I don't know.'

Grace quickly closed the door.

'Leave that for now, Betty. I will make it all right with Papa, but first you must help me to change. I cannot go down to him dressed like this.'

'No, indeed.' The smashed figurine was forgotten as the maid put her hands on her hips and regarded her mistress. 'I thought I'd have time to clean your room before you got home and you turn up, bold as brass and dressed like a, well, like I don't know what.' She wrinkled her nose. 'And if you don't mind my saying, Miss Grace, you looks like you've been pulled through a hedge backwards.'

Grace stooped to look at her reflection in the mirror on her dressing table.

She gave a rueful smile. 'Perhaps it would be as well if you fetched me up some hot water.'

Betty hurried away and the smile faded. Although the

pain of the past few hours was lessened a little by being home, she felt so tired and unhappy that she wanted nothing more than to curl up on her bed, but that would have to wait. Papa would want to know why she had arrived in such a precipitous manner and she was not quite sure how much she could tell him.

'Papa?'

Grace peeped into the study. Her father was sitting at his desk, staring out of the window, deep in thought. At the sound of her voice he looked up and smiled.

'My love.' He rose and held out his arms. 'We did not expect you until dinnertime!'

'I rode on ahead,' she said, walking into his embrace and surreptitiously scrubbing away a rogue tear on his shoulder. 'I have such a lot to tell you...'

An hour later her tale was done. She was sitting on a footstool next to her father's chair. He had kept his hand on her shoulder throughout and shown no signs of censure or approval as she told him everything that had occurred since she had left Arrandale.

Well, not quite everything, she thought now, as she rested her head against his knee. She had not mentioned the way Wolf had held her, kissed her.

'So you helped Wolfgang Arrandale to escape, then rode through the night with him.'

'Yes, Papa. Was it very wrong of me?'

'I am sure you believed you had good reason, my love. How much of this do you intend to tell Sir Loftus?'

She looked up at that. 'Everything I have told you.'

'Oh, my love, he is a magistrate, and in helping Wolfgang to escape you have broken the law.' He sighed. 'I blame myself for this. It was I who insisted you and Mr Arrandale should travel to London together. I do not doubt you thought it your duty to help him, but I had not expected you to go this far.'

'You taught me it was my duty to fight injustice, Papa, and Wolfgang would surely hang if he was brought to trial in Southwark.' Her voice shook. 'We both hated the fact that poor Henry's murderer was hanged, imagine how much worse for it to happen to an innocent man, and I sincerely believe Wolf is innocent.' She took his hands. 'I could not in all conscience do other than help him, surely you must see that.'

He smiled sadly. 'I see a young woman who is very much in love.'

Grace quickly looked away.

'Do not say so, Papa.'

'After Henry died you shut yourself off from the world, Grace. I am glad to see that you can love again, I only wish it was your fiancé and not Wolfgang Arrandale.'

'I wish it, too, Papa.' She put her head back on his knee. 'What shall I do?'

'We shall pray, my child. And you must not show yourself until your carriage has arrived. Then I will write a note to Loftus telling him you are home and inviting him to dinner tomorrow. By then who knows what might have occurred at Arrandale?'

Grace went up to her room to rest. As soon as she lay down on her bed exhaustion overcame her and she slept soundly until Betty came in, telling her it was time to change for dinner.

'Have my trunks arrived?' asked Grace, rubbing her eyes.

'Aye, miss, they have, and Mrs Graham and her maid with them. Such a to-do there was, Mrs Graham not knowing whether you was safe, but the master put her mind at rest and now she's in the guest room, changing her gown, and Mrs Truscott's fretting about dinner and worrying that the capon she's got on the spit won't stretch.'

'I will go and talk to her. And I will arrange my own hair, Betty, so that you may be free to help in the kitchen. Now, have my luggage fetched upstairs and we will look out one of my new gowns to wear.'

Grace marvelled at how easily she was slipping back into the role of keeping house for Papa. There was at least some comfort in that.

Dinner was excellent, as Grace had known it would be, and if she had no appetite it was nothing to do with the quality of the chicken, nor the boiled tongue and potato pudding that accompanied it. She did her best to eat the lemon jelly that was served with the second course, knowing Mrs Truscott had prepared it especially for her homecoming, but in truth she tasted nothing. She spent most of the dinner hour in silence while her aunt discussed with Papa the best way forward.

'When Mr Wolfgang was clapped up Grace visited him every day,' said Aunt Eliza, casting a reproachful glance across the table at her niece. 'Perhaps you will say I should have stopped her, Titus, but I confess I do not know how I might have done so.'

'My daughter was merely doing her Christian duty,' murmured Papa and Grace threw him a grateful look.

'But then, when I received her note, saying she was

riding home and wanted her things sent on to you today I vow I could not sleep for worrying!'

Grace said softly, 'I am very sorry if I caused you anxiety, Aunt, but as you can see I am here, safe and sound.'

'Yes, yes, but what if it gets out that you have been aiding and abetting a felon?'

Grace sat up very straight. 'Wolfgang Arrandale is an innocent man.'

'I think we may be sure that Mr Arrandale will say nothing of my daughter's involvement in his flight,' said her father. 'We must hold to our story, that she left London with you this morning. But let us hope that no one asks.'

'I vow you are as bad as Grace,' declared his sister with a little huff of exasperation. 'After she lost her first fiancé we were all relieved when Loftus Braddenfield proposed.' She glanced at her niece. 'You will forgive me if I speak plainly, my love, but you are nearly five-and-twenty and unlikely to receive another offer. I very much fear all this has put the match in jeopardy.'

'Let us wait until tomorrow and see what Sir Loftus says,' replied Papa gently. 'After all, he is a reasonable man.'

'Not so reasonable that he will condone his fiancée careering around the country with a man,' muttered Aunt Eliza. 'Especially an Arrandale.'

Grace said nothing, but she very much feared her aunt was right. To the weight of her own unhappiness was added the knowledge that she had disappointed her family. By the time they retired to the drawing room she was feeling very low and she excused herself, saying she was going out.

'There is at least an hour's daylight left and a little fresh air will clear my head. I am only going to the churchyard, Papa, but I think I shall go straight to bed afterwards, so I will say goodnight to you both now.'

Grace went upstairs to fetch her cloak and found the maid turning out the trunks.

'You should have left that for me, Betty, I am sure you have been rushed off your feet today.'

'Nonsense, Miss Grace, it's been a pleasure to put away all the new clothes you bought in London. Well now, I never expected to see this old gown again.' She lifted out the yellow muslin. 'You must have had it for at least four years.'

'I had the hem repaired while I was in town,' said Grace, trying not to sigh at the memory. 'It was done by a lady who used to work up at the hall, you may remember her. Annie Meesden.'

'Oooh, yes,' said Betty, her face lighting up. 'She was brutally done to death, wasn't she? Mr Truscott read it in the master's newspaper. It said Mr Wolfgang Arrandale had been taken up for it.'

Grace did not know how to reply. She felt suddenly stifled by memories and her fears for Wolf. She needed to get out into the fresh air.

'So she was reduced to taking in sewing, was she?' said Betty, inspecting the gown. 'Well, she did a good job on this, I must say.' She frowned and peered closer at the muslin. 'Hmm, she thought a lot of herself, sewing her mark into the hem.'

'Yes, I saw that,' murmured Grace, hunting around for her cloak.

'But it's not her initials, is it?' Betty continued. 'That would be "A.M". And look, miss, she has embroidered "M.K. One-six, one-six". I wonder why?'

Grace barely glanced at the embroidery on the hem of the old gown. She did not want to think any more about the dresser, or murder. Or Wolf. At last she found her cloak and threw it around her shoulders as she hurried away.

Outside the house Grace took a deep, steadying breath. Even with a low blanket of cloud covering the sky it felt so much cleaner and fresher here than Hans Place, where the dust and dirt of the ongoing building work hung in the air. She walked briskly to the churchyard. Tomorrow she must see Loftus and explain everything, but tonight there was something equally important she must do, for the sake of her conscience.

The flowers she had laid by Henry's headstone before going to London looked withered and grey in the fading light.

'I am sorry I have not brought fresh ones,' she murmured, sinking to her knees. 'And I am sorry for a great deal more.' She gazed sadly at the ground. For five years she had thought her heart was buried here, with Henry. She knew that the innocent, girlish passion she had conceived for Henry Hodges was nothing to the love she now felt for the dark and brooding Wolf Arrandale.

'But he is as lost to me as you are,' she whispered, running her fingers over the rough lettering inscribed on the headstone. 'More so, because he does not want me. And even if he did, I am promised to Loftus. All I can do is to pray that Wolf will prove his innocence. I want him to be happy, that must be enough for me.'

There. She had made her peace with Henry. Grace blinked away the threatening tears, fixing her eyes on the final words engraved on the headstone.

We are the children of God
Rom 8:16

She froze. The air in the graveyard was very still. Nothing moved, there was no sound. In her memory she was seeing again the delicately embroidered numbers and letters on the yellow gown.

'It is not a seamstress's mark at all,' she muttered. 'It is a biblical reference!'

Wolf was in no mood for family reunions. The sight of Richard and Cassandra, both deeply in love with their partners, only intensified the aching emptiness of his own life. After dinner he remained in the drawing room for barely half an hour before retiring, declaring he was too tired to stay awake.

As he crossed the hall there was an urgent knocking at the door and he stepped into the shadows beneath the stairs. Had his pursuers caught up with him already? Croft opened the door and Wolf heard a familiar voice enquiring urgently for Mr Arrandale.

'Grace?' He strode forward and she ran past the astonished butler.

'Thank heaven I have found you! I must tell you—'

'Hush now, come into the library where we may talk privately.'

He led her across the hall. The library was in a state of disorder, for Sophia had ordered the servants to examine every book in their search for the missing necklace. Two servants were still going through the shelves, but Wolf dismissed them and gently guided Grace to a chair beside the empty fireplace.

'Have you run all the way here?' He asked, kneeling

before her and clasping her trembling fingers. 'Let me get you something to drink.'

'No, nothing, thank you.' She was still out of breath, but he noted now that her eyes were gleaming with excitement and not distress. 'I think, I am sure, Meesden left us a clue about the necklace. On the gown she repaired for me. Her landlady said she had been working on it when Urmston came to see her. It was neatly folded and left on the table with her Bible resting upon it. I think that in itself was a message.'

'Go on.' He watched her intently. Just seeing her lightened his heart.

'She had embroidered "M.K. Sixteen, sixteen" on the hem of the gown. I took it for some sort of trademark, but now I am sure it is something quite different.' Her fingers twisted and gripped his own. 'It is a biblical reference,' she explained. 'Mark, *Chapter* Sixteen, *Verse* Sixteen.'

'And do you know what it is?'

She shook her head. 'I am not familiar with that text.'

'And you a parson's daughter.'

Grace heard his teasing tone, saw the glint of amusement in his eyes and for the first time that day she felt like smiling. 'Surely the Arrandales are not so degenerate that they do not own a Bible.'

'Aye, of course we do!' He rose and looked around the room. 'The thing is, where to find it...' He grabbed one of the branched candlesticks from the mantelshelf and strode across to the desk, where several large leather-bound books had been piled up. 'Here it is... What was the reference again?' Quickly he turned to the pages. 'Mark... Mark... Chapter Sixteen, Verse Sixteen: *"He that believeth and is baptised shall be saved; but he that believeth not shall be damned".'*

Grace had jumped up to join him, but as she listened her excitement faded.

'Oh, dear. That is no use at all.'

'Isn't it?' said Wolf, with an intense look that sent her heart skittering. 'Baptism. She's telling us the diamonds are in the font.' He held out his hand. 'Come along.'

Chapter Twelve

They headed for the chapel, Wolf carrying a lantern to light their way through the heavy darkness that had descended. Grace pulled her cloak more tightly about her while he unlocked the chapel door and she followed him inside. The lantern threw grotesque shadows against the pale walls and she kept close to Wolf, resisting the temptation to clutch at the skirts of his coat. She took the lantern so he could use two hands to lift off the ornately carved wooden lid from the font and she peered in eagerly.

It was dry and empty.

Wolf lowered the heavy cover to the ground and ran his fingers around the rough grey stone of the basin as if he did not believe his eyes.

'It has been ten years,' she said gently. 'Perhaps someone took it.'

'Perhaps.'

He would not give up. Not yet. There were candles on nearby pricket stands, dusty with age, but once they were lighted he carried them closer and inspected the old stone font, looking for possible hiding places.

'My great-aunt said the chapel had already been searched, so if the diamonds are here they will not be easily found.'

He bent to inspect the base of the font. There was not so much as a crack where anything might be secreted. The cover itself looked more promising, but there was nothing hidden amongst the intricate carvings of fruit, flowers and cherubs.

'Nothing.' He picked up the cover to put it back on the font, twisting it to give a cursory glance to the base as he did so.

'Wolf!'

He had already seen it. The bottom of the cover had warped badly and split, providing a narrow pocket that stretched across the base. Carefully he reached in with a finger and thumb and tugged at the material tucked inside. It fell into his palm, weighted by something wrapped in its discoloured folds.

'Wolf, is it…?' Grace held up the lantern as he gently unfolded the linen.

'Yes,' he said, his voice not quite steady. 'It's the Sawston necklace.'

Grace reached out. He expected her to touch the diamonds twinkling on his hand, but instead she lifted a corner of the wrapping. It was a handkerchief with initials embroidered on the edge. The same letters and flourishing style he remembered seeing on Urmston's perfume-soaked handkerchief. From the other side of the font Grace was smiling, hope shining in her eyes.

'Do you still not believe in miracles? We can surely prove your innocence now.'

We. It was like a shaft of sunlight on a stormy day and it warmed his soul.

* * *

'I will take that.'

The words echoed around the darkened church. Urmston was standing just inside the door, the light glinting from the barrel of a pistol in his hand.

'I think not,' drawled Wolf, ignoring the weapon aimed at his heart. 'The diamonds are wrapped in your handkerchief. What more proof do we need that you stole them?'

'You are not a fool, Arrandale. You know I will not let you leave here alive.'

'Then you must kill us both,' declared Grace. 'I will not let you get away with murder.'

Urmston stepped a little further into the chapel.

'Brave words, my dear, but that is precisely my intention. Only I shall say that Wolfgang killed you, before I shot him. I have already informed the magistrate that the fugitive is here.'

Wolf's brain was racing. The lighted candles made him and Grace easy targets. He needed to catch Urmston off guard if he was to wrestle that pistol from him, so he must keep him talking and look for his chance.

'So you admit you took the diamonds?' he said, playing for time.

'I did, but I put them back.'

'Of course.' Wolf nodded. 'You did not need to sell them, did you, once you had Thriplow's money.'

'The young fool was ripe for the plucking. When I came back from Newmarket I hid the necklace in Florence's room, behind the loose brick where she used to keep the key to her jewel box. Didn't want the diamonds turning up again too soon. I wanted everyone to think you a thief as well as a murderer. Once you were hanged

I would make sure they were discovered and returned to the Sawstons. After all I shall inherit them, eventually.'

'Ingenious,' said Wolf. 'Tell me, Charles, were you and Florence lovers?'

Urmston's lip curled. 'Once she was with child she considered she had fulfilled her duty to you. We bribed Meesden to keep quiet, but although she disliked me she positively *hated* you for marrying her beloved mistress, and once she had begun taking money for her silence she was unable to say anything at all.'

Wolf had guessed as much and was surprised how little it mattered to him now.

He said, 'So the night she died, Florence quarrelled with me deliberately, to leave the way clear for you.'

'She did. That temper of yours made it surprisingly easy for us, Arrandale. Florence had given me a key to the servants' door. I went outside to enjoy a cigarillo, then up the backstairs to join her. If anyone missed me I could say I had been wandering in the gardens.'

'And you took the necklace.'

'It is mine by right,' snapped Urmston. 'I was Sawston's heir, not Florence. Why should I not have it? I needed the money. She laughed when I asked her for it, so I had to take it. She fought like a wildcat, followed me to the landing and tried to scratch out my eyes, so I—' He stopped, a look of anguish contorting his florid features. 'I pushed her away. She fell against the balcony rail and overbalanced. It was an accident. An accident. Then you came in, Arrandale. It was too good an opportunity to miss. I left the way I had come. By the time I was back in the drawing room everything was confusion. I rushed into the hall where you were kneeling over Florence. It was easy to suggest that you had killed her and to persuade your father to get you out of the country. He was glad to see the back of you.'

Wolf's jaw tightened. He could not deny it. He had reminded the old man too much of himself. He looked at the pistol pointed at his chest. Perhaps he deserved this ending. For one black moment he could think of nothing to say to prolong the conversation.

'And what of the necklace,' said Grace. 'Where was that?'

'Safe in my pocket. Meesden's shock when she discovered it was missing was quite genuine, but by that time Wolfgang was gone and everyone thought he had taken it.'

'Of course,' snarled Wolf. 'After all, if I would kill my wife I would hardly balk at stealing the diamonds.'

'Quite.'

Wolf's sharp ears had picked up a faint noise. Thunder, or horses galloping through the park. If Braddenfield and his men had arrived they would see the light in the chapel.

He said quickly, 'And having put the blame on me you went off to Newmarket.'

'Well, I did not wish to intrude upon the family's grief.'

'Generous of you,' drawled Wolf. 'So you took young Thriplow's fortune and left him to blow his brains out.'

Urmston shrugged. 'If it had not been me, someone else would have relieved him of his fortune.' He took another step closer. 'Now give me those diamonds.'

Wolf's hand closed over them and he held his fist across his chest. 'Surely you would not kill us before explaining how the diamonds came to be here and not where you left them?'

'Meesden,' said Urmston tersely. 'She caught me

hiding the necklace. I paid her to say nothing, gave her enough for her to buy her shop in London. But she must have realised that it was I and not you who was responsible for Florence's death and decided to have her revenge. When I heard you were back in England I posted here immediately, only to find the diamonds were gone.'

'And you had lost track of Meesden, too.' Wolf spoke quickly, trying to cover what was surely the sound of steps outside the chapel. 'And just how did you know I was back in England, Charles?'

'Your lawyer. I paid him to alert me if he should hear from you.'

'And was it Baylis who gave you Meesden's direction?' asked Wolf.

Urmston stepped closer.

'Yes. The fool thought I wanted her as a witness against you and was only too happy to help, no doubt thinking of the money he would make defending you.'

Wolf saw the merest flicker of light in the doorway and spoke his next words clearly, praying whoever was holding the light would hear Urmston's answer.

'So you forced brandy down Annie Meesden's throat and took her to Vauxhall, where you murdered her.'

'What else could I do? Oh, I tried to reason with her, I sat for an hour while she finished her mending, but she would not tell me what she had done with the diamonds. She even threatened to tell you. So I had no choice but to kill her. I thought the plan was pretty neat, dispose of Meesden and have her murder added to the list of your crimes. And this will be your final victim.' Urmston stared hard at Grace. 'I saw you at Horsemonger Lane. Wolfgang's lady of mercy. Hatcham thinks you helped him escape.'

'She is innocent, Charles. Let her go.'

'Oh, no. I have seen the way you look at her, Wolfgang. I think her death will hurt you more than the others.'

A boot scraped on the doorstep. Urmston's head came up. He swung the pistol towards Grace. He was so close, he could not miss, but even as he squeezed the trigger Wolf pounced.

He saw the flash from the pistol, felt the searing pain in his side but he kept going, landing against his opponent with such force that they both fell to the ground. Even as the blackness closed in on him he heard voices and the heavy tread of boots on the stone floor. Grace was safe.

Grace froze as the pistol turned towards her. In that same instant she saw Wolf drop the necklace and throw himself in the way. A shot reverberated around the little church and the two men fell, but although Sir Charles continued to struggle there was no sign of movement from Wolf, whose dead weight pinned his opponent to the ground.

The urgent shouts of the men running into the church broke the spell. Grace flew towards Wolf, helping the men to roll him away from Sir Charles. A red stain was slowly darkening Wolf's coat and Grace closed her eyes, praying harder than she had ever done in her life that he might be spared.

'Grace! Are you hurt?' Loftus was lifting her from her knees.

'He is innocent,' she said urgently. 'Wolfgang is innocent.'

He nodded, scooping up the necklace and the handkerchief that was wrapped around it and putting them in his pocket.

'I heard enough to know that, my dear. Come out of the way now.'

She sank down on one of the pews as everyone bustled about. Sir Charles was marched away, Wolf was carried to the house, but when Grace went to follow, Loftus stopped her.

'May I ask what you are doing here?' he asked. 'I received your father's note, saying you had but today returned to Arrandale.'

Grace exhaled. 'I have a lot to tell you, Loftus.'

Then, in the soft, flickering light of the church candles, Grace made her confession. She related everything, from the moment Wolf had first arrived at the vicarage to their night-time flight back to Arrandale. The only thing she kept to herself were the savage kisses they had shared. Those memories were too intimate, too precious to be divulged.

'I have been very careless of my reputation, Loftus,' she said at last. 'I helped him escape from prison and spent last night alone in the woods with him.' She raised her chin. 'I cannot regret it, I did it to save an innocent man. But I *do* regret the pain this must cause you. I beg your pardon for that.'

Silence fell in the chapel. Grace hung her head. Loftus really could not be expected to marry a woman who had behaved so badly. She would go home to Papa. If Wolf lived, if he decided to remain in England after all…

She would not think of that, not yet.

'I cannot deny that I am shocked by your confidences, Grace,' Sir Loftus began, with heavy deliberation. 'But I am also proud. You have integrity, the courage to act upon your convictions and I admire that. I am aware that the world would censure you most severely, if your actions should become known, but you shall not hear a word of reproach from *me*. And I shall not break our engagement. I have always considered it my duty as a magistrate to see that justice is administered and I am not such a hypocrite to turn away from you when you have followed your conscience. No, my dear, with your permission we shall instruct your father to call the banns next week and we will be married within the month. You shall have all the protection my name can give you.'

She felt his hand on her shoulder, a gesture of comfort and reassurance. To Grace it felt as heavy and confining as a yoke.

'He's stirring.'

Wolf was aware of the faint smell of lavender and a cool cloth wiping his brow. He opened his eyes.

'Grace.'

The frail whisper must have been his own voice, for she took his hand and squeezed it gently, smiling at him in a way that made him wonder if he was in heaven, being tended by an angel.

'You are safe now, Wolf.' She added softly, 'You saved my life.'

He glanced down at the bandaging around his chest.

'And who saved mine?'

'That was Raoul.' Lady Cassandra came closer, her husband at her side. 'You should be thankful that he brought his surgeon's case with him.'

Raoul grinned. 'I have learned that where there are Arrandales, there is trouble. However, on this occasion your life was not in danger. The bullet skimmed the ribs. A glancing blow merely.'

'Aye,' said Richard, coming up. 'Another inch to

the left and it would have killed you. How do you feel, Brother?'

'Damnable,' muttered Wolf. 'Where am I?'

'In the morning room at Arrandale,' Grace answered him. 'The day bed here was more convenient for everyone to look after you than trailing all the way up to your bedchamber.'

As she spoke Wolf glanced past the four persons gathered around him. Of course. The room was familiar, although in the bright light of day it looked much shabbier than he remembered. Neglected. Like the rest of the Arrandale estate. Ten years without a master was taking its toll. He frowned.

'How long have I been here?'

'The constables carried you in here last night,' said Richard, 'after Urmston shot you.'

As memory returned Wolf wanted more answers. He tried to sit up, but Grace's gentle hands pressed him back.

'No, no, you must stay there, at least for the present. There is no danger now. Loftus knows Urmston is the true villain. He arrested him immediately.'

'Aye.' Richard laughed. 'Braddenfield was as mad as fire when he found the fellow trying to kill his fiancée!'

Wolf's eyes flew to Grace. There was a faint flush on her cheeks, but she made no attempt to contradict Richard. Wolf caught her wrist as she went to move away.

'Grace, I must talk to you, alone. I need to know—'

The blush deepened. Gently she freed herself from his grip and moved out of reach.

'Hush now, sir. There will be time to talk when you are better.'

That was her answer, then. She loved him, wanted him, but she would not break her promise to marry Braddenfield. Wolf closed his eyes. It was best this way. Grace might love him now, but once the first joyful bliss had faded she would compare him to her first love. Let her marry her magistrate, she would go into that marriage with her eyes open, not blinded by starry infatuation. And as for himself, the sooner he was away from here the better. But first he must see his daughter.

He glared at Raoul Doulevant. 'How long must I stay in this cursed bed?'

'I would prefer you did not exert yourself today.' He put his hand on Wolf's brow. 'There is no fever and the wound is not deep, but it might start to bleed again. You have the luck most extraordinary, *mon ami,* but I beg you will stop putting yourself in the way of bullets. This is the second time I have, how do you say, *patched you up* and I may not be on hand if you should be shot again.' Raoul put his arm about Cassie's waist and pulled her close. 'You should settle down. I can recommend it.'

Wolf caught the adoring look that passed between Cassie and her Belgian husband and his spirits plummeted. The man was a hero, worthy of any woman's regard. What had he ever done, save spread mayhem and murder? The opening of the door caught his attention and his sister-in-law came in with Lady Hune.

Wolf's breath hissed out. 'Am I to have no peace?'

'Ungrateful brute,' Richard admonished him cheerfully. 'When the family have gathered here to support you! But we will be relieving you of our presence shortly. Now we know you are in no danger Phyllida is anxious to return home to little James.'

Ah, yes, Richard and Phyllida's son. And they were expecting another child, which might well be another heir. Wolf's black mood deepened. He did not begrudge

Richard his happiness, but it served to highlight his own bleak existence. Well, at least a nephew ensured the entail was safe and lessened the need to stay in England. As if to give an extra twist to the knife, Phyllida announced that the Davenports had arrived.

'Alex and Diana?' exclaimed Richard. 'Why the deuce are they here?'

'They have brought Florence,' said Phyllida.

'My daughter.' Wolf's hand clenched at the bedsheet. 'I must see her.'

'Not today, I think,' said Phyllida gently. 'It might frighten her to see you like this.'

He tried to sit up again. 'Then let me be dressed and I can sit in a chair.'

There was an immediate outcry. Phyllida and Cassie pushed him back against the pillows, talking over his protests until Lady Hune rapped her cane on the floor and called for quiet.

'This is a medical matter,' she declared. 'Let us ask the surgeon when Wolfgang may get up.'

All eyes turned to Raoul.

'Tomorrow,' he said. '*If* you rest today.'

'I will,' said Wolf. 'I will rest now and Grace can sit with me.'

'That is not possible.' Again that flush mantled her cheeks and she refused to meet his eyes. 'Kennet is here and he is anxious to attend you.'

Wolf was about to consign his valet to the devil, but Richard squeezed his bare shoulder.

'Miss Duncombe sat by your bed all night, Wolf. It is well past noon now; she must be exhausted.'

'Yes. Yes, of course,' said Wolf. 'Send Kennet to me,

then.' He glanced again at Raoul. 'I feel weak as a cat, but you say I should be able to get up tomorrow?'

'If you rest today, yes.'

'We'll leave you now,' said Richard. 'And it is not only little Florence who will visit you tomorrow. Sir Loftus wants to see you. We managed to put him off today, but he represents the law here, Brother, and will not be gainsaid.'

'No,' muttered Wolf, his eyes on Grace. 'Sir Loftus carries all before him.'

Grace went out with the others to the dining room, where a light meal had been laid out, but she had no appetite. Loftus had reluctantly allowed her to stay and nurse Wolf overnight, but only after she promised to leave as soon as he was out of danger. She had prayed so hard and vowed never to sin again if Wolf was spared and now she must keep those vows. She had behaved outrageously in London, but Loftus was willing to stand by her, to give her the protection of his name. His affection for her was deeper than she had realised and although she could not love him she must be a good and faithful wife. He deserved at least that.

Grace had already received an early morning visit from Papa and Aunt Eliza. She had been expecting it, because Loftus had promised he would call at the vicarage and assure them that she was safe. What *had* surprised her was their reluctance to remove her from the Hall. Papa said she could be of more use there than at the vicarage and as Wolf had not by that time regained consciousness, Grace had returned to his bedside. But now she wished Papa had taken her away. Then she would not have seen the warmth in Wolf's eyes when he awoke. It made leaving him so much harder, but it must be done. She was not free. She had pledged herself to Loftus and she could not withdraw. A line from an old poem went through her mind.

> *I could not love thee, dear, so much, Lov'd I not Honour more.*

A knot of unhappiness settled in Grace's stomach and she picked at her food, something that Cassandra, sitting opposite, was quick to notice.

'Oh, dear, are you too fatigued to eat nuncheon? Perhaps you would prefer to sleep first and we will order a tray to be sent up for you.'

'No, no—you are very kind and I *am* tired, but I was thinking that perhaps I should go home.'

Her suggestion brought a storm of protests, from Phyllida's insistence that she had had a shock and was not yet recovered, to a plea from the newly arrived Diana, Lady Davenport, that she stay to meet the children.

'I shall bring them downstairs later,' she said, smiling. 'And I am sure you would like to meet Wolfgang's daughter.'

Grace knew that would be a bittersweet moment, but in the face of everyone's kindness, she finally gave in.

'Very well, but only until Sir Loftus calls tomorrow.' She coloured faintly. 'I shall write a note, asking him to bring his carriage so that he can convey me to the vicarage. I am sure my fiancé will want to take me away with him, once he has spoken with…once he has finished his business here.'

Having won their agreement, Grace gave up any pretence of eating and went off to rest. She fell asleep almost immediately, waking only when a maid came in to inform her it was nearly dinnertime. Aunt Eliza had brought over her trunk, filled with the gowns she had purchased in town. Grace would have preferred something older and more demure, but in the end she settled for an evening gown of deep-rose silk with a snowy lace fichu filling the low neckline. She blinked when she found her aunt had also put in her jewel box. Heavens, what was she thinking? This was not some elegant house party. However, the company did include a dowager marchioness and a countess, so she decided it would be reasonable to wear her pearl ear drops.

Not that it matters, she thought as she made her way down to the drawing room. *I am not trying to impress anyone.*

And Wolf would not be there to see her.

When Grace walked in, the buzz of conversation halted abruptly. She hesitated, wondering if she was perhaps overdressed for the occasion, but a quick look around the room showed her that everyone had changed for dinner. Lady Phyllida came forward to draw her into the company, her manner so warm and welcoming that Grace was reassured. She saw two little girls, the Davenports' wards, and recognised Florence immediately. With her dark hair and serious grey eyes she reminded Grace so strongly of Wolfgang that her heart contracted painfully. She forced herself to smile and talk with the children, all the time telling herself that this unhappiness would pass. As soon as she was away from this house she would be able to forget Wolfgang Arrandale.

Lady Hune's French chef had risen nobly to the challenge of working in an outdated kitchen, and after her refreshing sleep Grace was able to enjoy the lobster and asparagus and even a flavoured rice pudding. Richard Arrandale, sitting beside Grace, kept her glass filled with wine and conversed so pleasantly that the meal was not the ordeal she had been expecting. He excused himself from the table when the dessert course was served and went off to see his brother, but he returned quickly, looking exasperated.

'Wolf has not yet dined,' he declared, going back to his seat.

'I gave instructions that he was not to be disturbed, if he was sleeping,' put in Raoul.

'Well, he is awake now and in the devil of a temper because Kennet has gone off to press his coat for the morning.' He swung round to look at Grace. 'I know it is presumptuous of me, but would *you* accompany Croft when he takes in my brother's dinner tray and remain while he eats it?'

'Me?' Grace recoiled. 'No, that cannot be necessary.'

Richard shook his head at her. 'It is very important that he eats well, to aid his recovery. Ain't that so, Doulevant?'

'Very important,' Raoul agreed solemnly.

Lady Cassandra leaned forward. 'We would take it as a very great favour if you would do this, Miss Duncombe. Wolf is far less likely to throw the dishes at you than at any of us.'

Something close to panic fluttered inside Grace. She had refused the syllabub, so she had no reason to stay. She glanced around the table, but everyone was either intent upon their dessert or looking at her hopefully. There was no escape.

The morning room was washed with the soft glow of candlelight. Wolf was on the daybed, propped up on a bank of pillows and with a white nightshirt covering his upper body. Grace thought how achingly handsome he looked, his lean cheeks freshly shaved and his dark, curling hair falling over his brow. He watched her, unsmiling, as she came in, but the look in his dark eyes was unreadable. Grace straightened her shoulders. She reminded herself that they would be bound to meet occasionally if he decided to stay at Arrandale, so she would have to get used to this. She summoned up her most cheerful manner.

'Croft has brought your dinner and I am here to keep you company while you dine.'

She stood aside while the butler placed the tray across Wolf's lap and a footman put a second, smaller tray with wine and glasses on a table at Wolf's elbow. When the servants withdrew she sat down upon a chair at a safe distance and folded her hands in her lap, watching Wolf pick at the succulent morsels the chef had served up to tempt his appetite. He looked pale, and a little tired, but he was calm enough. A suspicion began to grow that the Arrandales had planned this. They wanted her to be alone with Wolf. But to what end?

They want him to marry you and settle down at Arrandale.

Impossible! Had he not told her he was too restless to marry? That he could never be faithful to any one woman? Even if she was not promised to another man he did not *want* to marry her. He would certainly not want to be coerced into marriage by his well-meaning family.

'Will you join me in a glass of wine?' Wolf asked her politely.

Grace nodded, glad to be doing something, but as she poured the wine into two glasses her hand trembled and she spilled a little on the tray.

'Are you afraid of me, Grace?'

'Do not be ridiculous.'

'You are shaking.'

'I should not be here,' she said in a low voice. 'I should not be alone with you.'

'Then why are you here?'

Her shoulders lifted a fraction. 'Your family…'

'What?' He gave a mirthless laugh. 'Surely they know you are betrothed to Braddenfield?'

'Yes.' She handed him a glass. 'I told Loftus what had happened. I thought he would not wish to marry me once he knew everything.' She did not look at Wolf, knowing he was watching her intently. It was as much as she could do not to sigh. 'He admires my integrity.'

Wolf had finished eating so she moved his tray to the side table. She said, trying to sound cheerful, 'He is a truly noble man, I think.'

'Aye, damn him.'

'I do not know why you say that—'

'Don't you, Grace? Don't you know that I hate him because he will have you and I won't?

'No,' she whispered, her heart beating frantically. Wolf grabbed her wrist.

'Oh, I know it is fixed. There is no getting out of it now. You are promised to him, but that does not stop me wanting you.'

He was stroking the inside of her wrist with his thumb, setting her whole body on fire. From her toes to the crown of her head, she was aware of him. There was a lightness in her head and in her womb, her breasts tingled, they felt full, swollen and aching for his touch. She wanted to sink to her knees beside the daybed, to close her eyes and delight in the sensual feelings he aroused in her.

I could not love thee, dear, so much...

It took a supreme effort of will to pull away.

'I will not break my promise to Loftus,' she said, her voice catching on a sob. 'Neither will I allow you to behave dishonourably.'

His eyes held her prisoner. She felt the threads that bound them, strong as steel, tightening and pulling her towards him. One word and she would be lost. She would give herself to a man who would only love her for a short time, then he would move on. He would cease to love her and she would lose him, as she had lost so many other people she had loved. Grace crossed her arms, as if to hold herself back.

'Please, Wolf, help me. We must not do something we would both regret.'

His eyes blazed, but she dare not acknowledge what she read there, lest the final shreds of her control should snap and send her tumbling into his arms. Then, just as she thought she could hold out no longer, he looked away.

Wolf rubbed one hand wearily across his eyes. He had come pretty close to declaring himself, but what good would that do, she would not break her vows. It would only make her suffer even more. He had to keep to his original plan. Better she should think him unworthy.

'Go then.' He added harshly, 'You were never mistress material.'

'Wolf—'

'Go!' he snarled. 'Get out, damn you.'

Blinking away the tears, Grace turned to leave.

'And tell Croft to bring me the brandy,' he called, as she reached the door. 'I intend to get damnably drunk.'

* * *

Grace fled. In the empty hall she stopped, irresolute. Voices were coming from the drawing room, but she had no wish to join the family. They would know soon enough that their scheme had failed. If marriage had been their goal. Perhaps they were all as dissolute as one another and had wanted to see her disgraced. She ran to her bedchamber and locked the door, wishing with all her heart that she had never become mixed up with the infamous Arrandales.

Chapter Thirteen

The next morning Grace rose early and packed her trunk, instructing the maid to have it taken downstairs ready to be loaded into Sir Loftus's carriage. Then she sat in her room, determined to remain there until it was time to leave. She had kept her book and her tambour frame with her to while away the time, but both remained untouched as she stared out of the window.

You were never mistress material.

The words had haunted her throughout the night and she had soaked her pillow with hot, bitter tears. How dare he even suggest such a thing! But with the dawn had come resignation and it settled over her heart like ice. She could not change him. Wolf was a rake and a vagabond. He could not settle down with one woman, he had told her so himself. And he was right, she was not cut out to be a mistress.

There was a knock at the door and Phyllida appeared.

'Grace, my dear, Sir Loftus has arrived and asks that you join him in the morning room.'

'The morning room? Oh, no—I would prefer to wait for him here, or in the library, perhaps.'

'He needs to interview you and Wolfgang.' Phyllida put out her hand. 'Come.'

Bowing to the inevitable, Grace accompanied her down the stairs.

The daybed had been removed from the morning room and Wolf was dressed and sitting in a chair. Sir Loftus was standing in the centre of the room and when Grace went in he took her hand and kissed it. He was looking very serious.

'Is all well?' she asked him quickly. 'Sir Charles is safely locked up?'

'Yes, and on his way to Southwark for trial. With my testimony and that of the constables who also heard him confess to everything, there is no possibility of his escaping justice.' He took a turn about the room. 'I have been talking to Arrandale about the circumstances of his escape,' he said at last. 'We are agreed that no purpose would be served by mentioning your part in it.' He fixed his serious gaze upon her. 'We shall admit you visited the prisoner in Horsemonger Lane, but as far as the world is concerned you travelled to Arrandale with your aunt. As for what happened in the chapel, you brought a message for the family and became caught up in events. I think we might even avoid having you called as a witness.'

'Thank you,' she whispered, her eyes lowered. 'I am much obliged to you, Loftus.'

'Aye, well, it would serve no purpose to drag you further into this sordid business.'

'Quite.' Wolf eased himself out of his chair. 'Is that everything?'

'You will need to give evidence at the trial, Arrandale, but with Lady Hune to stand surety for you I do not see any need to lock you up again.'

'Much obliged to you,' drawled Wolf. 'Now if you will excuse me, I shall leave you.' He turned to Grace. 'We shall not need to meet again, Miss Duncombe, so let me thank you now for all you have done for me.'

A brief, polite nod and he was gone. The cold indifference of his parting cut Grace to the quick. She stared at the door, too numb even for tears. Behind her she heard the soft pad as Loftus paced back and forth across the carpet. He cleared his throat.

'Since we are alone, Grace, perhaps…there is something we must discuss.'

She was still looking at the closed door. She wanted to weep, but there was no time for that now. She turned, forcing her lips to smile. 'Yes, Loftus?'

He was frowning at the carpet. 'Sit down, my dear.'

Grace sat on a chair, wondering how much more she could bear. Loftus had been more understanding than she had any right to expect. Was he going to demand some penance from her?

He coughed again. 'I have been thinking, Grace. About us. The other night I promised I would stand by our engagement and give you the protection of my name.' He took another turn about the room and at last came to stand before her. 'I cannot do it, Grace.'

She hung her head. A confusion of emotions flooded her: shame and dismay that she had grieved this good man; relief that she would not be tied to a marriage she did not want. And regret. If she had not thought herself promised to Loftus, she would have given herself to Wolf last night.

And the eventual parting would have been even more painful.

She sighed. 'It was a very noble gesture, Loftus, but I quite understand.'

Impatiently he interrupted her. 'No, no, it is not that. I...my feelings have changed. I love another.'

So it was not her behaviour that had caused his change of heart, thought Grace. That was some small consolation.

'Claire Oswald,' he said. 'My mother's companion. She has always been such a comfort to Mama, but it was only these past weeks, when you were in town buying your bride clothes, that I realised she had become necessary to my comfort, too.' He coughed. 'If it was only my own inclinations then I would have fought against it, but I have reason to believe, to *hope*, that she returns my affections.'

'Of course she does, Loftus, how could she not?' She rose and gave him her hands. 'I am very happy for you.'

'Thank you. But I am aware this leaves you in a very difficult situation. I know better than anyone that your father's finances are very limited. The marriage settlement—he was looking to me to provide for you.'

'I shall explain it all to Papa. I hope...' Something was blocking her throat and she was obliged to swallow hard before continuing. 'I hope he will be pleased that I am not leaving him, after all.'

'And there will be speculation. With everything that has happened people will talk.'

She put up her chin. 'It will die down once it is seen that you still come to the vicarage.' She added, with an attempt at humour, 'I trust you do not intend to cut our acquaintance, Loftus?'

'No, indeed.' Some of the anxiety left his face. He picked up her hand and kissed it. 'Thank you, Grace. I had no reason to expect such understanding from you. I shall go home and speak to Claire immediately!'

Grace was so lost in her own thoughts that his last words did not register until he had quit the room.

'Loftus, wait!' She jumped up, but the soft thud of the front door told her he had left without her. No matter. She would ask Croft to arrange a carriage for her.

She sank down on the sofa. She should find Wolf and tell him she was no longer betrothed, but her heart quailed. It was one thing to succumb to him in the heat of the moment, quite another to offer herself so blatantly. And for what? A few months of happiness, until his restless spirit wanted to move on. Then he would leave her, or worse, he would stay and she would watch his love slowly dying. The unhappiness she had kept in check all morning now welled up and she dropped her head in her hands.

'Why are you weeping?'

The childish voice had Grace hunting for her handkerchief. She had not heard the door open, but now little Florence was standing before her, regarding her with her dark, serious eyes.

'I am being very foolish, I beg your pardon.' Grace wiped her eyes and smiled. 'Were you sent to fetch me?'

'No, I was looking for my father,' said Florence, climbing on to the sofa beside her. 'I wanted to see him. Diana said he was too ill yesterday and she would take Meggie and me to the drawing room this evening before dinner, but that is *such* a long time to wait.'

'It is indeed.'

'And he is *my* papa, not Meggie's, and I want to see him *first*,' declared Florence.

'Of course. I can quite understand that.'

'But I am a little bit frightened,' Florence confided. 'Will you come with me?'

'Me?' asked Grace, startled. 'No, no, I could not.'

'Why not? He likes you. I heard Aunt Diana and Lady Phyllida talking about it when they came upstairs last night. They said…' Florence screwed up her face as she tried to remember. 'They said he should marry you and settle down at Arrandale Hall, and I could come and live with you.'

'Oh.' Blushing, Grace slipped an arm around the little girl's shoulders. She said gently, 'I am not going to marry your father, Florence.'

'Why not? Is it because of me? Perhaps you would rather have babies of your own.'

Grace's blush deepened.

'No, it is not you, sweetheart. Your papa does not want to marry me.'

'But Lady Phyllida said she had never seen two people more in love.' Florence fixed her candid eyes upon Grace. 'Isn't it true?'

Looking into those innocent eyes, Grace was unable to tell a lie.

'Well, I love *him*,' she said sadly. 'With all my heart and soul, but he does not love me in the same way.'

Something made her look round. Wolf was in the doorway and suddenly Grace was on fire with mortification. How long had he been standing there?

She was aware of Florence shrinking closer and she put aside her own concerns. She forced herself to speak cheerfully.

'Ah, so there you are, sir. Florence came here in search of you.'

'And I was looking for *her*.'

'Then I shall leave you alone. If you will excuse me.'

As she rose, Florence jumped off the sofa and took her hand.

'*Please* do not leave me.'

Grace looked down at the little girl, but she addressed Wolf: 'Lady Davenport should be here.'

'She has taken Meggie riding,' offered Florence.

'Oh,' said Grace. 'Perhaps Lady Phyllida could—'

Florence shook her head and clung even harder to Grace's hand. 'She is lying down.'

'Well, we must fetch someone,' said Wolf. 'Miss Duncombe has to leave. Sir Loftus will be waiting for her.'

'Do you mean the man who came to see you earlier?' the little voice piped up again. 'He left a long time ago. That's why I came here, looking for you.'

Grace felt Wolf's eyes boring into her.

'He left *without* you?'

Wolf had entered the room, expecting to see Florence with her aunt and instead he had walked in upon a tête-à-tête between his daughter and the woman he thought he could not have. But if Braddenfield was gone and Grace was still here...

He must go carefully, she was looking as nervous as a hind and might bolt at any minute.

'Well then, if Miss Duncombe does not have to leave immediately, perhaps she would consent to bear us company while we become acquainted.'

'No!' cried Grace, distracted. 'Sir, we have nothing to say to one another.'

'But I have much to say to my daughter, Miss Duncombe. And she wants you here while we talk. Is that not so, Florence?' Wolf dropped to one knee before the child and smiled. 'There, my dear, I am far less threatening now I am not towering over you, am I?' He shot a quick glance up at Grace. 'I really do not wish to frighten anyone away.'

She was frowning, but he guessed she would not leave while Florence was still clinging to her hand. He turned back to his daughter.

'So, Florence, you were looking for me?'

The child nodded silently, apprehension in her eyes.

'Florence wanted to become acquainted with you before everyone meets in the drawing room this evening,' Grace explained.

Wolf marvelled at her kindness in speaking for his little daughter, even when she would clearly prefer to be anywhere else.

'An excellent idea,' he said. 'I wish I had thought of it.'

Florence looked at him warily. 'Do you?'

'Why, yes. One can never say everything one wants to say in a crowd. For instance, we must decide what we are going to call each other. I would like to call you Florence, if I may?'

'Of course, that is my name.' She looked at him shyly. 'And may I call you Papa?'

Wolf smiled. 'I should like that very much. And there is something else that I need to say. I must apologise for behaving like a brute.'

Florence giggled. 'But that's silly. We have only just met, so there is no need to apologise.'

'Oh, there is.' Wolf risked looking directly at Grace, hoping she would read the message in his eyes. She averted her gaze and he turned again to Florence. 'I am very sorry that we have not been able to meet until now, but you see, I only recently learned I had a daughter, and as soon as I could I came to England to see you.'

'You, you did? Uncle Alex said it was dangerous for you to come here. That you were very brave when the bad man shot you.'

'It was Miss Duncombe who was the brave one. Did you know she nursed me through the night? And I was so ungrateful that I said some very cruel things to her. Things I did not mean and for which I am deeply ashamed. But you see, I thought she was going to marry someone else and I could not bear it.'

'But why should she do that?' asked Florence, puzzled. 'She said she lo—'

'That is quite enough about me,' Grace interrupted her hastily. 'Perhaps your wound is paining you, sir, and you should leave this interview for another time.'

He ignored the hint.

'It does hurt a little,' he admitted, climbing to his feet. 'It would be easier if we could all sit on the sofa.' He held out his hand to Florence. 'You could sit between us, what do you say?'

'Very well,' she said, but she clung even closer to Grace.

He sat down at one end of the sofa with Grace perched nervously at the other. Florence was between them, leaning against Grace and holding her hand. Wolf smiled at Florence, but when he raised his eyes to Grace she put her chin in the air and looked stonily ahead.

'Do you know, Florence,' he remarked, 'since your mama died I have been wandering the world, quite lost.'

'Like a prince in a fairy tale?' said Florence. She was gazing at him much more openly now. 'Did you have lots of adventures?'

'Hundreds,' he replied promptly.

'Tell me!' Florence was no longer leaning against Grace.

'Well, there was the time I helped your cousin Lady Cassandra escape from the French...'

Most of his adventures were not suitable for a little girl, but this one kept Florence transfixed. Her eyes positively shone when he described how he had jumped on his horse and ridden away, chased by the French officers while Cassie and Raoul made their escape.

'They were taken on board a smuggling vessel and carried safely to England,' he ended.

'And did you escape from the soldiers unhurt?' breathed Florence, wide-eyed. He noticed that she had moved a little closer to him.

'Not quite. I was wounded and unfortunately my faithful horse was shot from under me.'

'Was that your black stallion?' asked Grace.

'Yes.'

Wolf was surprised she had remembered that. He was heartened, too, but she was already turning away and looking very stern, as if angry that she had been drawn into speaking to him. He turned back to his daughter. She had released Grace's hand and was now turned towards him.

He said, 'I have been thinking, Florence, that I should settle down and make a home for myself here at Arrandale. Do you think that would be a good idea?'

Florence considered this. 'Would I have to come and live with you?'

'You do not have to do anything,' he said quickly. 'I have discussed it with Alex and Diana, and they are happy for you to live with them for as long as you wish.'

The little girl nodded solemnly. 'I like living with them. And with Meggie. She is my *bestest* friend.'

'Then I would not take you away from her.'

Wolf smiled, but it was an effort. They were strangers still, he could not expect his daughter to throw her arms about him and beg to come and live with him.

'Perhaps you and Meggie could stay at Arrandale sometimes,' Grace suggested. 'It would be a holiday for you.'

Wolf threw her a grateful look, but she was still resolutely ignoring him.

'It would be a holiday for me, too,' he said. 'But I would need to learn how to go on. I have never had such young guests here before.' Wolf paused, then decided to risk all. 'It would help if I had a wife. What do you think, Miss Duncombe, do you know anyone suitable?' Grace was sitting very still. He added softly, 'Someone who loves me with all her heart and soul.'

Grace fought down a gasp of dismay. So he had heard that. It was embarrassing, but it made no difference. She would not give in.

She said icily, 'No, sir, I do not.'

He was not noticeably dashed and addressed his next remarks to Florence.

'It is important she loves me, because I must restore Arrandale. There are years of neglect to put right and I have to repay Richard too, so I cannot offer her a life of idle luxury. But then, the lady I have in mind would not want that.'

Grace maintained a dogged silence and after a moment he continued.

'And of course I must love *her*, too, with all my heart and soul, if we are to live happily ever after.'

'I do not believe in fairy tales, Mr Arrandale,' said Grace, goaded into a reply.

'Not even Beauty and the Beast?' he asked her. 'Where the hero is transformed by the love of a good woman?'

Florence giggled.

'That is what happened to Alex,' she confided to Wolf. 'He says he was *very* bad before he fell in love with Diana.'

Grace was surprised into a laugh which she quickly turned to a cough. It was too ridiculous for words! She tried very hard not to look at Wolf, but it was impossible. One shy, tentative glance showed her that he was smiling and her pulse leapt erratically when she saw the glow in his eyes. She tried to calm it, to keep her heart and her feelings wrapped in an icy numbness.

'There you are then,' he said softly. 'Miracles can happen.'

'No, they do not,' she retorted.

'That is not what you said when we found the necklace,' he reminded her.

She ignored that.

'I stopped believing in miracles five years ago when all my prayers and tears could not save Henry.'

'Who is Henry?' asked Florence.

'He was the best man who ever lived,' said Grace, chin up and eyes fixed firmly on Wolf. '*He* was no restless vagabond to capture a maiden's heart with false promises. His love was steady, constant.'

'And yet he left you,' said Wolf softly.

Grace winced.

'I must go,' she said. 'Pray be good enough to summon your carriage to take me home, Mr Arrandale.'

'Grace—'

He broke off as the door opened and Lady Davenport appeared.

'Oh. I beg your pardon; I was looking for Florence.'

Grace knew that Diana's keen eyes would assess the situation instantly: her own rigid posture, Wolf half-turned in his seat, gazing at her, and little Florence between them, blissfully unaware of the tensions swirling around.

Diana continued with barely a pause. 'I have been looking for you, my love.'

The little girl slipped off the sofa and went over to her.

'I have been talking to my papa.'

Florence said the words proudly, but Grace hardened her heart against feeling anything for Wolf's daughter.

'I am very glad to see it.' Diana smiled and held out her hand. 'But it is time to change your dress. No, no, do not get up, Miss Duncombe. I shall take Florence away and we will meet again at dinner.'

She whipped Florence out of the room and closed the door before Grace could force out one word. Even her limbs refused to move. She remained on the sofa, staring ahead, and all the time Wolf's gaze was on her face.

'I cannot stay,' she managed at last, although she still could not tear herself from her seat.

'Why did you not leave with Sir Loftus? Are you still betrothed to him?'

'He...he was going directly to Hindlesham.'

'Are you still betrothed?'

She bit her lip. 'I am not,' she admitted. 'But that

makes no difference. I will not stay. Please order a carriage to take me back to the vicarage.'

'Of course, but hear me out first.' When she put up her hand to stop him he said urgently, 'Let me have my say, then, if you still wish to leave, I will send you home and never trouble you again. You have my word on that.'

No, I must leave. I must go now, before his siren words break my heart.

But she remained on the sofa as he began to speak.

'Heaven knows mine has not been a good life, Grace. I was always in scrapes as a boy and I lived wildly in London, gambling, drinking, wenching. My marriage to Florence was arranged by our fathers, but even when I knew I could never love her I was determined to be faithful. A novel concept for an Arrandale, but I was determined to try.

'Then everything went wrong and I was exiled to France. I believed my family had abandoned me and I wanted nothing more to do with them. I struggled to survive, Grace, I admit that my life there was not blameless, but I *did* survive, I even prospered. I returned to England with a small fortune.' He slipped to his knees and took her hands. 'I want to stay in England, Grace, I want to restore Arrandale and make a home here for little Florence, but I cannot do it without you. I want you beside me. As my wife.'

She tried to free her hands. 'I will not marry you for the sake of your daughter!'

'No, for my sake,' he said, holding her even tighter. 'I love you, Grace, I cannot live here without you, knowing you are at the vicarage and as unhappy as I am.'

'Then *I* will go away!' She wrenched her hands from his grasp and ran to the door.

'So you would run away, even though you love me. I thought you had more courage than that.'

She stopped, her hands pressed against the wooden panels as his words cut deep.

'We love each other, Grace,' he said. 'Why does that frighten you? Is it because you think I might leave you?'

'No! Because you will stop loving me!' She gave a sob. 'I have dealt with loss before. My mother, my aunt, when she married, Henry...but I n-never doubted their love. I am afraid you would stop loving me.'

She felt his hands on her shoulders.

'I might indeed,' he said quietly. 'But not in this lifetime.'

Gently he pulled her around, but still she would not look up.

'I have never met anyone like you, Grace Duncombe. I have never felt a love like this before. It consumes me, but *your* happiness is paramount.' He put his fingers beneath her chin. 'If you cannot be happy with me then so be it, but do not expect me to remain at Arrandale, where there are so many memories of you. That would destroy me.'

She was obliged to look up, but his face swam as tears filled her eyes.

'I do not wish to destroy you, Wolf.'

'Then marry me, Grace. I will do my best to be worthy of you. I hope in time I can prove myself, even if I cannot change the past—'

Grace gave a little sob. 'Oh, Wolf.'

She put her hands up, cupping his face and pulling him closer until their lips met. He did not respond immediately, as if afraid to believe what her kiss was telling him. Then, suddenly, his arms swept around her and he returned her embrace with a passion that left her reeling. She clung to him.

'I do not care about your past, my darling,' she whispered. 'Only the present and the future.'

His arms tightened. 'I shall try not to disappoint you.'

She turned her head to kiss his cheek and when she tasted a salty tear, the final shreds of resistance melted. Her mouth sought his again and this time there was no hesitation. He plundered her and she retaliated, matching him kiss for kiss, allowing her instincts to guide her. She drove her fingers through his hair, pressing herself against him and feeling his body respond. She revelled in her power, threw back her head as his lips moved from her mouth and began to burn a trail down the column of her neck.

'I want to make you mine, here and now,' he muttered against her skin.

She shivered, her insides curling in delight. Wolf raised his head. She was pressed against the door, trapped by his body, and his eyes bored into her, so intensely that she thought they danced with blue-violet flames. 'Stop me now, Grace, or it will be too late for you.'

Impatiently she pulled his head down again.

'It was too late for me a long time ago, Wolf. I know that now.'

He swooped down for another kiss. She heard the click as he turned the key in the lock and the next moment she was being carried back to the sofa.

'Wolf, you are wounded!' she protested, half-laughing as she helped him out of his coat and waistcoat. 'You should not exert yourself.'

'I feel nothing,' he muttered, lowering her down on

to the cool silk. 'Nothing but an overwhelming desire to worship you!'

With a rapturous sigh she took him in her arms. At first she tried to avoid his bandaged ribs, but soon they were forgotten. Each kiss heated her blood and set her skin tingling. Every caress carried her away until she was almost fainting with the delight of it. She melted beneath his touch, revelling in the feel of his hands on her shoulders, her breasts, her thighs. She was softening, blossoming like a flower with his caresses, instinctively offering herself up to him. Gentle fingers readied her for the union to come. Gentle words eased her fears. She moved restlessly against him, feeling the pull of unfamiliar muscles deep within, the yearning ache to be one with this man. He enveloped her, her heightened senses breathed in the male scent of his skin, the smell of spices and leather and man.

She tore off his neckcloth and unbuttoned his shirt, desperate to explore him. The bandage around his ribs prevented her from running her hands over his chest, but she gripped his shoulders as her body began to slip out of control. She was kissing the line of his throat when she felt the cords of his neck tense. She cried out as he pushed into her and he grew still.

'Am I hurting you?'

'No.' It was an effort to speak. Something was building inside her, like the pleasurable swell of a giant wave. 'No. Go on, go on.'

Her body welcomed him. She was surprised to feel completed, not invaded, and bucked against him, forcing him deeper. They were moving together, skin on skin, slick and hot, his rhythm matching the pulsing waves in her core. He was carrying her higher, until she was flying, falling, and she cried out with the sheer joy of it as he gave one final thrust. She heard him calling her name as she tumbled from the heights into near oblivion and then they were lying together, panting and gasping in each other's arms.

A delightful lassitude had stolen over Grace. Wolf's body was pinning her down but she did not mind, she wanted to stay like this for ever. She cradled him until his breathing became more regular and all too soon he stirred, raising himself on one arm so he could look at her, seeing her contentment. His slow, teasing smile appeared.

'It is quite wanton, you know, to make love fully clothed.'

She smiled back. 'Then I must be very wanton, sir, for I found it quite delightful.'

He dropped a kiss on her brow, but when he raised his head again the smile had disappeared.

'Are you sorry we did not wait until we were married?'

'A little,' she admitted. When she saw his troubled look she added quickly, 'A *very* little. I have wanted you and imagined this moment for weeks now. This is the consummation of all my hopes and dreams.'

'It is merely the beginning, my love.' He kissed her again. 'Your father shall marry us, but it must be by special licence. I will not wait a day longer than I must to call you my wife.' His smile was tender, but a little rueful, too. 'I am afraid, my angel, you are no longer a virgin.'

She smiled up at him, tenderly brushing a dark curl from his brow.

'And you, *I hope*, are no longer a vagabond.'

'No.' He kissed her again. 'I have come home.'

* * * * *

MILLS & BOON

THE HEART OF ROMANCE

A ROMANCE FOR EVERY KIND OF READER

MODERN

Prepare to be swept off your feet by sophisticated, sexy and seductive heroes, in some of the world's most glamourous and romantic locations, where power and passion collide.
8 stories per month.

HISTORICAL

Escape with historical heroes from time gone by. Whether your passion is for wicked Regency Rakes, muscled Vikings or rugged Highlanders, awaken the romance of the past.
6 stories per month.

MEDICAL

Set your pulse racing with dedicated, delectable doctors in the high-pressure world of medicine, where emotions run high and passion, comfort and love are the best medicine.
6 stories per month.

True Love

Celebrate true love with tender stories of heartfelt romance, from the rush of falling in love to the joy a new baby can bring, and a focus on the emotional heart of a relationship.
8 stories per month.

Desire

Indulge in secrets and scandal, intense drama and plenty of sizzling hot action with powerful and passionate heroes who have it all: wealth, status, good looks…everything but the right woman.
6 stories per month.

HEROES

Experience all the excitement of a gripping thriller, with an intense romance at its heart. Resourceful, true-to-life women and strong, fearless men face danger and desire - a killer combination!
8 stories per month.

DARE

Sensual love stories featuring smart, sassy heroines you'd want as a best friend, and compelling intense heroes who are worthy of them.
4 stories per month.

To see which titles are coming soon, please visit

millsandboon.co.uk/nextmonth